# The Loss of Leon Meed

## JOSH EMMONS

SCRIBNER

*New York   London   Toronto   Sydney*

**SCRIBNER**
1230 Avenue of the Americas
New York, NY 10020

SCRIBNER and design are trademarks of
Macmillan Library Reference USA, Inc., used under license
by Simon & Schuster, the publisher of this work.

For information about special discounts for bulk purchases,
please contact Simon & Schuster Special Sales:
1-800-456-6798 or business@simonandschuster.com

*Designed by Kyoko Watanabe*

Text set in New Caledonia

Manufactured in the United States of America

1   3   5   7   9   10   8   6   4   2

Library of Congress Cataloging-in-Publication Data

Emmons, Josh.
The loss of Leon Meed / Josh Emmons.
p. cm.
1. Loss (Psychology)—Fiction. 2. Eureka (Calif.)—Fiction.
3. Missing persons—Fiction. 4. Older men—Fiction. I. Title.
PS3605.M574L67 2005
813'.6—dc22
2004057139

ISBN-13: 978-0-7432-6718-2
ISBN-10: 0-7432-6718-4

*For my parents*

*We have lingered in the chambers of the sea*
*By sea-girls wreathed with seaweed red and brown*
*Till human voices wake us, and we drown.*

—T. S. Eliot, from "The Love Song of J. Alfred Prufrock"

# Part I

# 1

Once, if you had driven north on Highway 101 from San Francisco past its outlying bedroom communities and vineyards and hippie enclaves, beyond blighted motels and one-pump gas station towns, over a road at times so winding and mountain-clinging that a moment's distraction could steer you off a cliff and into freefall, you would have reached Eureka, the coastal seat of Humboldt County in northern California. It was a city whose forty thousand inhabitants faced the Pacific Ocean on one side and all of America on the other. It sat between the deeps.

You might then have forgotten about it if you were continuing on to the cities of consequence, to Portland or Seattle. Or to the wind-swept streets and unspoiled air of Canada. Or to the North Pole. You might have been scaling the planet and in no mood for its way stations.

But if you had stayed in Eureka, you would have discovered a weathered city with an almost granular fog and a high cloud cover, with temperatures rarely dipping below forty-five or climbing above seventy-five degrees Fahrenheit, where tourists wondered how they'd slipped out of the California Dream. You would have wondered this, too, if you had compared the steely sky and faded architecture of Eureka with the sun and oceanfront villas of that dream. You would have thought that something was wrong.

The thing about dreams, though, is that they're products of the imagination, and the imagination, like all engines of terror and transcendence, can do anything.

On an afternoon in late November, the last of the school buses pulled away and fourth-grade teacher Elaine Perry realized that she hadn't asked any of her students to clean the chalkboard erasers. She stood by the tetherball pole and kicked a wood chip that sliced cleanly through the air and came to rest on the edge of the playing field where earlier that day a third grader had broken his leg. Children led dangerous, thrill-seeking lives. Spidering over jungle gyms, roof climbing, bike racing, contact sports. They chose the reckless and perilous, gravitated toward jeopardy and disaster. Adulthood is all about repressing that instinct, Elaine thought as she stared at Muir Elementary School's main building, and learning to desire the predictable and unthreatening. Principal Giaccone's office window was open. She hated cleaning the erasers and had been pleasantly surprised to learn when she began teaching in September that her students loved it. Giaccone had stopped by her classroom on the first day of school with a waxy red apple. "The forbidden fruit," he'd said, presenting it to her. "Only if it's from a certain tree in Eden," she'd said, holding it up and reading its small white sticker: "This one comes from Washington." Giaccone smiled and said he hoped her students appreciated what a clever teacher they were getting, that his own fourth-grade teacher, Miss Costigan, in addition to being the only centenarian in his hometown, had been a yearlong lesson in crotchetiness. Elaine caught the emphasis he gave to *crotch* and thought, These silly flirtations. I can't have an administrative fling. They go so badly. I could lose my job. He could lose his. Not to mention our respective families, my kids and hus— "Call me if you need anything," Giaccone said. "There should be a bullhorn in the supply closet."

Elaine, wife and mother of two, from the town of Red Bluff seventy miles away, graduate of Humboldt State University, hair straightener, *I Ching* dabbler, and mystery novel consumer, did her job very well. In addition to teaching twenty-three fourth graders, she supervised the chess club, directed the school production of *South Pacific*, and ran the Gifted & Talented program. Her husband, Greg, was having an affair with a nurse named Marlene who worked at the hospital where he was an orthopedist. Elaine sometimes left her car beside the grove of old-growth redwoods that bordered the Muir Elementary parking lot and walked home past ranch-style houses painted the primary colors—red, blue, yellow—in rigid, unbroken order. She sang "A Cock-Eyed Optimist" and tried to mean it. In July her father had been discovered to have a meningioma, a tumor growing out of the thin membrane covering his brain called the meninx, for which he underwent an unsuccessful surgery and was currently in radiation therapy and taking a battery of antiseizure medications that often made him forget what he was doing. When Muir experienced budgetary cutbacks—"those pricks in Sacramento," Giaccone had fumed in a moment of faculty meeting impropriety—Elaine learned that there might be layoffs of the last-hired-first-fired variety. Her husband grew lazy in his excuses for arriving home past midnight— "Honey, Steve might need me for an assist on a motorcycle wreck that just came in, some kid whose femur is sticking out of his kneecap. Don't wait up. Love you"—which gave her the opportunity to single-handedly feed, wash, encourage, and console their two children through their five- and nine-year-old growing pains. She ordered an awesome nine-inch dildo from a mail order company in San Francisco called Good Vibrations. *South Pacific* was a disaster. Two children, siblings who played the French murderer and Bloody Mary with amazing vivacity, were yanked out of school midway through rehearsals by their mother, then seeking a divorce from their father, and the rest of the cast seemed hopelessly far away from memorizing their lines—much less developing the wherewithal to sing in public—in time for the mid-December opening night. She found blood in her stool and was told by a gynecologist that she had an iron deficiency and needed to rest more during menstruation. But she never slept beyond four hours a night these days, reading macabre tales of murder and insurance fraud until her husband came home, at which time she'd feign sleep until his loathsome, sexually sated snore started up, and then she'd rise, fix herself a bologna sandwich, and resume reading in the TV den.

As she was clapping erasers outside, Principal Giaccone poked his head through the window and called down to her, "Elaine! Oh, Miss Perry! Could I see you for a minute?" And she entered the building and climbed the stairs to the first floor and knocked formally on his door and sat in front of him and listened to his spiel about financial constraints and the necessity of letting some top quality people go, and how he'd hate to have to do that to her, but how he might have to unless, well, unless they came to an agreement. Giaccone stared at a blank computer in front of him. Things have been building toward this, he said, concentrating on the empty screen and then turning to smile complicitly at her. His secretary had gone home and there was nobody else who could hear this stab at sexual coercion. This grossest form of blackmail.

"Are you saying," began Elaine, sliding her gaze from Giaccone to a picture of him in a lineup shaking the governor's hand, "that the only way I can keep my job is if I fuck you?"

Giaccone exhaled loudly—he'd been holding his breath—"God no," he lied. "What gave you that? It's just there are these extenuating circumstances, and certain difficult decisions have to be made—"

But Elaine was already standing up and straightening her skirt before reaching for the zipper along the side. "If that's all it takes," she said, pulling down her underwear.

Giaccone got up and stepped forward as though to intervene or help. "Don't be that way," he said. "I just thought you and I had this thing."

Elaine unbuttoned her blouse and untucked Giaccone's shirt. "We do. Lift up your arms."

"Look, you're doing this out of anger or something. There's nothing erotic about this."

"Of course there is. This is exactly how it works. Step out of your boxers. And take off your watch. Men should never wear a watch when they have sex. It's too tempting for women to look at." Elaine grabbed a tissue from the desk and used it to pull out her tampon, which she dropped in the wastebasket.

"Come on," said Giaccone, staring with embarrassment at the wastebasket. "I didn't know."

"Now you do. Is this how you normally respond to naked women?" Elaine had Giaccone's flaccid penis in her hand. Massaging it just below its head and then, as it grew and stiffened, stroking it up and down.

"Oh, yeah," said Giaccone, coughing the words.

"Yeah. This is what it's all about, isn't it?"

When Giaccone reached out to hold Elaine's waist she caught his hand and pushed him back onto the desk, and as he got bigger she climbed up and sat on him and enfolded him.

"Oh, Jesus!" Giaccone cried out, stretching his hands over his head, pushing documents and the phone off the desk, writhing like a merman caught in a fishing net.

"You can't bring him into it," Elaine murmured. "He's got nothing to do with it."

When it was over she dressed while he lay staring at the ceiling.

"That was—" he said. "You hate me, don't you?"

Elaine opened the door and said, "I don't hate anybody," closing it behind her. Down the hall she passed a wan twenty-something boy with thin blue hair wearing headphones and pushing a mop over scarred linoleum. He smiled at her and she smiled back, unable to gauge the innocence of the transaction, unable to gauge the innocence of anything. Outside, music was playing and she began to sing loudly, "I hear the human race/ Is falling on its face/ And hasn't very far to go,/ But ev'ry whippoorwill/ Is selling me a bill/ And telling me it just ain't so!"

"It just ain't so," she repeated to the trees and the cars and the houses and herself. "It could be awful and degrading and it could be a conspiracy of evil, but . . . but . . ." She let her voice fade to nothing and walked along as though carried by the wind, and when she remembered to look up through the breaks in the canopy of trees, the sky was a bright canary yellow.


Ten days later, at the corner of Broadway and Fifth Street, where Highway 101 hit the middle of its Eureka crawl, the night lights went off at the Pantry. It was seven thirty in the morning, and Silas Carlton had been drinking coffee and eating a Hungry Man Special for half an hour. He'd bought a *Eureka Times-Standard* on his way to the diner and read about the timber industry's response to recent environmental activism. Both the article and the response were badly constructed; key elements of each contained errors.

Silas raised his coffee cup in salute to Teri as she walked by with orange-and-black-lidded coffeepots. He forgot which color meant decaffeinated and which meant regular, a distinction he'd known all his life. Like the names of friends and relatives that now escaped his immediate recall. Once familiar objects that had become strange. Orange meant something.

"Silas," said Teri, pausing in her white sneakers and shadowy stockings, "I do declare I've never seen you ask for a third cup."

"So you've turned into Scarlett O'Hara?" he said.

Teri smiled and refilled his cup and returned to the kitchen. The *Times-Standard* weighed in at twenty-four pages—depressingly small for the county's largest newspaper. Silas read an article congratulating four county natives for running the Boston Marathon, although none had placed even in the top one thousand; an editorial explaining why the paper would discontinue its Public Safety Log, listing significant arrests (no longer had the space); and an Associated Press article about America's zany love of meatless hot dogs. He skimmed local sports stories that had larger headlines than bodies, wedding announcements and syndicated comic strips and a company-profile "Who's Who."

He read more carefully when he got to the obituaries. These he appreciated. These were a chance for Silas, age seventy-five, to see what others were dying of and how and when and where. The details of death were increasingly interesting to him, and not just because it was less "later when I'm old" and more "any day now," but because they seemed to come in two extreme varieties: the mundane and the horrific. Either "peacefully asleep in the arms of her husband of sixty years" or "shot in the head by a carjacker at the corner of H Street and Buhne," provoking a "she was a fine lady" or "what the hell is wrong with this world?" Silas wondered how frequently there was a correlation between one's death and one's life, whether the old woman's peaceful stroke ended a life of bone-deep righteousness or fantastic dissipation. And the carjack victim: choir boy or Hell's Angel? Did karma play any part in our end? Was poetic justice mere poetry?

Silas's life hadn't been exemplary by certain standards, yet neither had it been unforgivable. There were things of which he was proud: raising his former wife's diabetic son when she died and the boy's father looked to be a slipshod guardian; refusing Shell Oil's filthy lucre in exchange for his approval of their offshore oil drilling plan near Samoa; walking two miles in the middle of the night to a suicidal friend's house and convincing her that depression, like happiness, was only temporary. As there was behavior of which he was ashamed: sleeping with his best friends' wives (three best friends, five wives); knocking out a guy's front teeth over a disputed game of pool; lying (to everyone, all the time, with and without reason). Silas wondered how, if at all, these things would affect his death.

He was a retired bike shop owner and former city councilman and often lonely. His outspoken criticisms of Eureka's budgetary priorities and the state of America's forests, which for many years had identified him in the community as someone who thought about big issues, now made him a curmudgeon.

He was tall and skinny and had bad posture from years of hunching over desks and trying not to be conspicuous around shorter people.

Thick white hair shocked out of his head like a woodpecker's, giving his bony features an avian quality. He wore sturdy black-framed glasses and black turtleneck sweaters like some funky old beatnik Rip Van Winkling in the twenty-first century doing his best Samuel Beckett impression and staring down the combined forces of illness, fatigue, and moral collapse. Yet nobody noticed him these days as he walked around Old Town and sat in coffee shops and listened and tried to eke out a meaning to his days. He blended into the background as someone you'd seen a thousand times but could never place from where. The social life now open to him centered on his niece Rebecca's family—he'd once been close to his great-nieces Lillith and Maria—and chance encounters with people old enough to remember him. Very few occasions for him to forget names, altogether too few.

His death would make these people sad, and the other obituary readers out there would take note of it—perhaps like him they would speculate on its justice—and it would bring his family together for a day or two of discussing him fondly and resolving that life goes on. Silas's sound and fury would be like the other sounds and furies that had signified nothing. He would disappear.

He looked across the diner at two mustachioed truck drivers—noted the grossly obtruding bellies over scrawny legs and the padded nylon vests and the feet that knew how to maintain 65 mph for several uninterrupted weeks—who hit each other lightly on the shoulder with the backs of their hands to emphasize a point or command a laugh-along. Touching someone makes them your friend. Silas recognized one of the men and miraculously remembered his name, Shannon Koslowski, whose father, Pete, had led the move to price-fix dairy products in the area thirty years earlier. Pete died two weeks ago. Aneurysm. Making an omelet.

Glancing down at the paper, Silas noticed a small box beneath the obituaries that said "MISSING: Leon Meed, of 427 Neeland Dr. Last seen on December 1. Age 54, medium height, curly brown hair. Any information, please call 555/2471."

I'd rather go missing than die, Silas thought to himself. When you're missing you still have a chance.

Later that morning at McDonald's, Silas's great-niece Lillith Fielding stood in front of an enormous griddle range with her manager, Ron. Heightened-senses Ron who saw everything and forbade—he was honor-bound not to allow—sloppiness and unprofessionalism. She sniffled and he wordlessly, reproachfully gave her a tissue. Her starched uniform rubbed against her armpits—the blisters were a matter of time and patience—and her face was breaking out despite her abstinence from eating at work. As though mere proximity to grease could ruin one's complexion. She'd been on shift for five hours with only a single fifteen-minute break spent alone because no one else was on her schedule. In the women's bathroom she'd filed her nails and written a limerick about the weediness of Ron, brushed her shoulder-length brown hair and separated it into two pigtails, and translated the amount of her first paycheck into Wiccan supplies it would buy. Then the break was over.

"What's wrong with this picture?" Ron asked, not looking at her, having eyes only for the range, where three small beef patties curled up slightly around their edges. It was hot in the cooking area and the milkshake machine behind them ground its way through a hundred pounds of frozen soybean crystals and strawberry extract in a successful cold fusion. Everything was equally delicious and nauseating.

"I don't know," said Lillith.

"You don't."

"No."

"And you've had how many training days so far?"

"Four. But I wasn't hired as a cook. I'm supposed to take drive-thru orders and then start at the cash register. Ambrose said those were going to be my only two shifts."

"Ambrose is the assistant manager. I'm the general manager, and I thought I made it clear to you that we're a team. If Latifa, say, has a problem and needs to leave the range then it becomes everyone's responsibility to watch over her section while she's gone. If I ever see you ignoring a problem because it's not in your so-called section, I'll deal with the result and you won't like that deal."

Lillith looked at the little concave burgers, at the staid runnels of grease scraped to the range's corners, at the forearm-length spatula upside down beside three salt canisters. "Is the problem that the burgers are overcooked and should have been taken off sooner?"

"The problem," Ron said, reaching across Lillith to grab a roll of paper towels, "is that this paper product was only a foot from the range, posing a fire hazard. It could have burned the restaurant down. Then how would you have felt about not taking responsibility for it?"

Ron motioned for Latifa, who'd been standing back during this interrogation, to return to the range, and walked away before Lillith could answer, leaving her alone with the feeling that she was a professional failure, and that she'd been cruelly bullied, and that she wasn't observant enough, and that Ron was an idiot, and that she might lose her job, and that she hated her job and wanted to quit. But her feelings, she knew, were beside the point. This was about power and as in everything there were haves and have-nots.

Arriving home at the end of her shift, Lillith took off her colorful logoed baseball hat—one of the many things she hated about her job—crammed it into her bag, checked the mail, and unlocked the front door. Her one piece of mail was a flyer about an upcoming Wiccan festival in southern Oregon. Banana-grab and plop on the couch—ouch, who left a hairbrush here?—and TV-on and a few impromptu stomach crunches. It was important always to work on your abdominal muscles. She felt fat and the flesh folding over when she did a sit-up proved it. Maybe Sam had called. She rooted under the couch for the phone—where she preemptively hid it so that her little sister wouldn't be able to hide it from her—and listened to the voice messages. Her mom's gynecologist—dyke—and dad's "squash buddy" and a weird high-pitched voice addressing itself to the head of the household and her ancient uncle Silas and that was it. No Sam.

Fine. Maybe she didn't like Sam as much as she thought she did. He was short. Dwarfish. She'd have to buy flat-heeled shoes to go out with him and put up with his Napoleon complex and probably never get to be on top. Why bother?

The next day Silas Carlton carefully lowered himself down the foldout steps of Eureka Transit's number 9 bus at the South Jetty stop, where he stood between a peeling green bench and a former public bathroom in order to button up his barn jacket with cold, recalcitrant fingers. The bus groaned away and a bubbly blue car floated soundlessly into a parking spot to his left. He had particular difficulty with the top button.

Elaine Perry stepped out of the blue car and locked her door and a minute later was walking beside Silas, whom she didn't know, up the oversoft sand dune that led to the beach. They avoided eye contact and altered their speed in a vain effort to establish distance between them, like two pedestrians approaching each other on an empty sidewalk who feint right and left in unison, seeming destined to collide until the final second when, greatly relieved, they pass without incident.

Once in sight of the water and at last a few steps away from Silas, Elaine removed her shoes, rolled up her chinos, and went to the shore's edge. Silas stopped at the charred remains of an old bonfire and, responding to the strong easterly wind, hugged himself in a straitjacket pose and considered what a mistake it had been to make so many bus transfers (three!) just to reach this desolate stretch of ocean. Elaine stooped to pick up bits of shell and polished agates, looking for colors and shapes not already represented in her collection at home. Silas took out his bus timetable, which rattled angrily in the wind, and saw that there wouldn't be a pickup for forty-seven minutes. In the distance a dune buggy roared; if either of them had squinted in its direction they would have seen it spin around and around, the driver having the time of his life.

It had been years since Silas was last at the beach, back when he'd still had a driver's license and could chauffeur himself. It was a sorrowful thing to be dependent on public transportation in California. As it was to be old in America. He glanced around to find shelter from the insistent wind, but there was nothing other than the parking lot's restroom, an abandoned lean-to with survivalist weeds pushing through the cracks in its door, so he took refuge in a fantasy of being seated at home, with a bowl of microwaved walnuts and hot cider.

Elaine stuffed an arrowhead-shaped rock into her pocket. She had come home at lunchtime the day before and found her husband, Greg, performing cunnilingus on a big red-headed woman whom she at first assumed was his hospital affair, Marlene, but who turned out to be someone else entirely. Greg arched up his back and turned to her, his hands still gripping the woman's knees, an expression on his face like why-do-I-have-all-the-bad-luck? Elaine went to her desk and hunted around until she found their marriage certificate, lit it on fire, and dropped it onto the floor next to Greg's underwear. Just the week before, her friend Rebecca had discovered that her husband was a deviant Internet porn troll. Why were people so disappointing? Why did you get so enamored of them and then learn once it's too late to leave without serious psychological and emotional damage that they're selfish and hurtful and better at deceit than anything else? Greg sprang into action when the flame had eaten half the certificate by using his discarded undershirt to smother it. "Elaine," he said, his eyes smarting from the smoke, "it's not what you think." "Who's thinking?" she asked with a fairly insane serenity. "Who can think at a time like this?" Pivoting around, she left the bedroom and didn't come back until that evening, by which time Greg had cleared out an overnight bag of clothes and supplies and gone to stay at his friend Steve's, or so he claimed in a scrawled, self-abasing note.

The ocean was a puce green that produced violent eight-foot swirling white waves a hundred feet out from shore and small clear waves closer in that broke and spread like liquid glass over the hard-packed sand. Elaine kicked the water and sent up tiny sprays in front of her. Sand crabs burrowed into frothing holes. Seaweed eyelashes were splayed in midblink all around.

Silas, not gaining much traction in his daydream of warm nuts and hot drinks, opened his eyes when he heard the loud cries of either a man or sea lion coming from the water. He saw what appeared to be an arm rise out beyond the waves and then walked as quickly as his knees allowed toward Elaine, who stood by the shore surveying the horizon on tiptoes.

"Is that a person?" he asked.

"I think so," said Elaine, just as the cries ceased. They scanned the water where the arm had been, but where there was nothing now but the ocean's tumult.

Ten seconds went by.

"Where'd he go?" Elaine asked.

"I don't know."

"The undertow at this beach is—I'll call an ambulance."

"Wait, do you hear that?"

They listened and looked and there was the man again, calling out like he'd never stopped, "Hellllyelllp!"

"I'm going in," Elaine said, handing her phone to Silas. "Here, call 911."

Holding the tiny plastic device high and at arm's length to study its miniature number pad, Silas dialed and then spoke their imprecise location on the South Jetty as Elaine waded into the water and made slow, determined progress against the direction of the tide. The man crying for help was clearly visible now, a head and bit of shoulder being lifted up by the waves and ground into the egg-white surf. Elaine inched closer to him with effort. The man's voice sounded gargled and desperate; Elaine was practically swimming in place. And then, as suddenly as he'd stopped before, the man went silent and was no longer visible. Elaine kept valiantly swimming. A minute passed. Two. Three.

"I don't see him!" Silas called out hoarsely.

Elaine turned her head and was instantly pushed back toward the shore. "What?"

"He may have gone under!"

"Did you call the ambulance?"

"Yes!"

"Good!"

"What?"

"Good!"

"Yes!"

"It's freezing in here; I'm starting to go numb!"

"You should come back. It's dangerous out there!"

"His body could be floating around! I could drag him in!"

"That's too risky! You could get hypothermia!"

"I've had that before!"

"What?"

"I've had that before!"

"Come back!"

By the time Elaine reached the shore she was panting and coughing and purplish with cold. An ambulance dopplered into the parking lot beyond the dunes. Silas and Elaine went to meet it and explain that a man had drowned, that they hadn't seen him go out in the water, but that there he'd met his end. Elaine insisted that Silas sit with her in her car with the heat on full blast until the police arrived to take their statements. They didn't know who the victim was. A man. Impossible to speculate on his age, build, or ethnicity. Elaine, Silas, the police, and the ambulance workers all talked on the beach with one eye on the water to see if the body would wash up. Didn't. Nothing. Sleeping with the fishes. Elaine felt ill, as though she were still out among the waves, rising and falling, searching the water to see— what? What had she hoped to find that wouldn't frighten her beyond comprehension? Eventually nothing more could be said or done.

❧   ❧   ❧

It never snowed in Eureka. Too close to sea level—it *was* sea level—so when Eve Sieber woke up to see her car covered in snow she told herself she was still dreaming. Which wasn't true. When you're awake you know it, and you only say you're still dreaming in order to make a rhetorical point about the strangeness you're witnessing. Fine, so she was awake, but the snow was nevertheless unusual. Must have been the New Weather. The snows of Kilimanjaro were melting, the polar ice mass was decreasing, the average temperature of southern California had risen two degrees over the last twenty years. Why not snow in Eureka? Why not tempests and tsunamis and terrific tornadoes? This was a meteorological paradigm shift, and Eve was ready for it.

In the small aqua-tinted kitchen her caffetiere melded together tap water and coarsely ground Peruvian Blend coffee. A city-owned truck cruised slowly past her building as two men shoveled salt directly onto the snow-laden street. Shouldn't they have plowed the street first? Eve stared at the caffetiere and touched the side of its glass briefly—hot as a fire poker, not that she'd know from personal experience—and then stumbled into the bathroom. Diarrhea was a horrible feeling. She'd gained a pound by the time she was done on the toilet, mysteriously. *Is the scale broken?* She took a shower and stroked her sore nipples—Ryan had really gone infantile on her last night, nursing on her breasts with the suction vehemence of a cartoon baby One-Tooth, then insisting she tie knots in a handkerchief and stick it up his ass during sex with the instruction to pull it out when he came—and shaved her legs. She was as into experimentation as the next girl—hadn't the handkerchief been her suggestion?—but she had to worry now about them getting to a stage where normal sex—the old boy/girl in-out—would no longer appeal to her or Ryan. She loved him, or thought she did, which could be the same thing, but their tastes were doomed to become so extreme that eventually death would be their only unexplored sexual aide, and with mutual asphyxiation already behind them—last week, silk stockings, bed knobs and broomsticks—death might not be so far away. Think of what she'd leave behind: her shitty job at Bonanza 88 selling key rings and discount chocolate bars to large, prematurely aged women and their hordes of children. So many kids and such harried women and such sad interest in cheap imitation-brand clothing, not bought for durability or style but for sheer economy. The women didn't smile, and they were always alone with their kids. If a man was present, some errant father hauled in by the alimony police, he was so obviously just-released from a halfway house, detoxed and pathetically unable to focus on any object long enough to pick it up, that Eve had to think, Why do they take these losers back? This woman here at the register is grim and overworked and I'd hate to be her, but can it possibly be better when that brandied moron is around? Yet Eve knew that the only thing separating her from these women was ten years. Or five. She was twenty-three and still childless and not unattractive—with soft blue eyes and clean high cheekbones, she had, for Eureka, an almost otherworldly beauty—but she'd gotten to the point where she didn't lie to herself anymore and imagine a glorious future of fame and financial sanguinity. That wasn't in the cards. Her pair of deuces was the janitor at Muir Elementary School, whose junk habit was quickly getting beyond anyone's control, and whose celebrated love technique was turning into the kind of thing Houdini would have done if he were irreparably stoned and scatological. So much for the promise of youth. So, so much.

Eve put on a torn zip-up ski suit and a pair of moon boots—God, she looked weird—and kicked some clothes and magazines into a corner of the cramped living room. Then she left her two-story apartment building, a gray stucco edifice sandwiched on both sides by single-family homes, and walked to Sequoia Park, where the redwoods were impassively flecked with snow. The old stalwarts, never fazed, never in the least betraying anxiety, not even when the deafening chainsaw buzz finished and they were given a colossal nudge in one direction and fell, fell, were felled. She ripped off a piece of bark and brandished it like a sword, making Zorro curlicues in the air, stabbing at invisible enemies, sidestepping their retaliatory jabs. *Touché!* She won, for now, her imaginary battle.

Later that evening, in Old Town Eureka, at the Fricatash Club, Eve sat with an energy drink and a carton of cigarettes given to her by Ryan for safekeeping while he visited a self-taught chemist who was said to be doing exciting new things with crystal meth. Eve had come straight from work and so wore a pink short-sleeved shirt with her name stitched over her left breast in a luxurious cursive and the Bonanza 88 logo patched over her right breast. It was hot in the Fricatash and she worried that the black hair dye she'd accidentally gotten on her scalp earlier that morning would smudge down her forehead, half hidden by bangs, when she danced. And had she scrubbed the bathroom sink thoroughly enough that the dye wouldn't permanently stain it? The show tonight, consisting of four moon-faced bands, was to raise money for the skate park that the City of Eureka had just decided not to build. Eve loved one of the bands, Derivative, and got increasingly excited sitting there with her medicinally caffeinated drink and two hundred cigarettes. Would they be fined by their landlord for the sink's later cleaning or replacement? Did she even need to ask?

"Eve, you have all those cigarettes." Skeletor plopped down at her table like a kid late for dinner. He was lanky, he was all lank. Arms and legs like a stick figure's. Pure bone. Bony knees and elbows and shoulders. Big green eyes like they'd glow in the dark. A rictus for a mouth. You saw his jaw move independently of his skull. The guy was a walking X ray. "Since when can you afford a whole carton?"

"They're Ryan's."

"Since when can he afford?"

"Yeah," Eve said with mock curiosity, "I wonder how much he paid for them."

"You mean with or without tax." Skeletor gave a total-gum smile and you swore his skin was going to peel away. "I'd kill for a smoke right now."

"I can't break the packing seal. Wait'll Ryan gets here."

A concealed-disappointment: "Okay."

"When's Derivative playing?"

"Later."

"Could you be less specific, please?"

"Later or maybe earlier."

"And to think I used to tell people you weren't retarded."

"You're developing the potential to be a real bitch."

"I thought I was a cunt already. You said so last week."

"Whatever. Let's play dominoes."

"They put away the set."

"But it's not eight yet."

"Yeah, well, go tell it on the mountain."

Skeletor leaned back on the park bench that the Fricatash supplied instead of chairs at its tables and surveyed the crowd of sixty Crayola-headed Eureka cool kids of death. No music played and so they stumbled around on their own, borrowing money from each other. The ones not too stoned to converse conversed; the others made sounds in code, using the same low register "ahhhh" to mean I'm-hungry and isn't-she-hot and I've-gotta-sit-down-for-a-minute and when's-this-gonna-start and I-read-the-news-today-oh-boy. It was the one-note language of infants that some hidden recess of the brain could translate, a sound to represent everything and nothing.

The Fricatash bar was doing brisk coffee business, as this was a northern California establishment catering to minors. The management, a middle-aged Bengali man named Ravi, expected to be visited by the cops at least twice over the course of the evening and hassled and warned about slackening his vigilance against any on-site drinking by his patrons. Nobody was getting away with anything so don't get any ideas.

Through the crowd stumbled Ryan in his bomber jacket emblazoned on the back with a child's iron-on koala bear patch. He squeezed in on the bench between Eve and Skeletor and promptly started laughing, hardy har har at first and then the Crack-Up, body spasming around while he bent forward and muffled his screams in his arm, his long periwinkle-blue hair hanging over the edge of the table like a waterfall. Eve and Skeletor scooted away from him.

"Hey, man." Skeletor placed a hand on Ryan's shaking shoulder like a priest consoling a distraught parishioner. "Can I bum a pack of cigarettes?"

But Ryan could only give little tug boat toots and shudder. His brain was being tossed around on a trampoline, and when Eve looked at him she saw five hours into the future when he would be jerking through his nightly pantomime of sleep, in a constant cold sweat despite the seventy-degree room temperature. Eve would sleep fitfully for as long as possible, but eventually, at four or five in the morning, scared of the thought of having to get up and go to work at eleven, she'd take one of the prescription sleeping pills they bought from her aunt, and his twitching would get less noticeable, and she'd sink far from the material world until the alarm clock ripped her back into it.

"Tonight, ladies and germs, we have a very big shoe for you," said a young man with slicked-back hair doing a kind of Catskills Lodge emcee voice, an Ed Sullivan redux. He wore a pea-green thrift store suit that was too tight around the chest and high around the ankles, a Frankenstein fit that he exaggerated by holding his breath and pulling up on his belt. "I see lots of beautiful people and know you're going to have a beautiful time. So beautiful I can't stand it. So sunset beautiful I have a beehive in my belly." He dropped the microphone to his side. Someone from the audience told him he was beautiful. "Could we have a rilly big round of applause for . . ." he let the words hang in the air, "for . . ." his eyebrows went up searchingly, "you're all so beautiful," and now there was a hush and someone threw a water bottle at him that barely missed, "I love the nightlife baby," as the spotlight moved up and back, "people, come closer, I won't bite and neither will," to an assembled four-person band, "the Sloe Eyes!"

Pandemonium.

When the Sloe Eyes ended their set and left, Eve saw the guitarist for Derivative attach his guitar to an amp at the back of the Fricatash stage while the singer breaststroked in place. She got up from the table and pushed past Ryan, who had stopped laughing and now sat with his shoulders slumped forward on the bench like a boxer after losing a fight.

Eve squirmed through people and made a clearing for herself near the stage, where she waited patiently for the band to begin. Refused a swig from a bottle of soda that had been emptied and filled with gin. Just said no to drugs. Had a brief exchange with her coworker Vikram, there because he'd heard a woman he liked was coming, though she was nowhere to be seen and he was too tired to be bouncing around with kids half his age. Adjusted her bra strap that had somehow gotten flipped over.

Derivative began with its dolphin song, choruses of *eeek-yiiiik*, and Eve was put in a bad mood because how can anyone honestly like to listen to such annoying piercing shit? It was the band being perverse and frustrating their fans' expectations, which Eve admired in theory but hated in practice. She wanted them to frustrate the fans who expected something out of the ordinary like the dolphin song, not her expectation of their brilliant fifty-second threnodies.

The next song was a coy little number about a boy and a girl playing at being animals. And it got graphic real quick. "My birdie flies into your nest oh whoa oh." Eve loved this song and forgot all about Ryan's death on the installment plan. And the probability of Bonanza 88 going out of business. She was lost on a planet of sound and saw no reason to try to find her way back. "Try my acorn try my acorn I've hidden it just for you."

Eve stepped backward and forward in time to the music. She jostled bodies and felt around for floor openings in which to put her feet and soon realized that her shirt was clinging wet in back. Nobody should have had time to sweat that badly, so she turned around to see who was responsible for her wetness and saw an old guy, in his fifties at least, dripping in an open-collared shirt. Hair pasted to the side of his head. People had moved away from him, presumably because he'd also gotten them wet, so he was surrounded by a ring of clear space. Eve couldn't place where she'd seen him before, certainly not at the Fricatash. The man had no business being there. Not that

Eve was ageist. Far from. She just didn't think it was right for soaking wet old guys to thrust themselves into the middle of young people's fun.

The song ended and the bassist drank an iced coffee and the drummer buried his head in his hands. Eve glanced in Ryan's direction, saw Skeletor edge a pack of cigarettes out of the carton. A girl she recognized from McDonald's stepped into her line of sight. Facing forward she saw the old wet guy now directly in front of her, almost stepping on her toes.

"Excuse me," she said.

The man stepped aside and said, "Could you tell me where we are?" His voice was soft and respectful, not belligerent like the bums his age who'd given up on the niceties and now were just complete assholes. He even looked a little melancholy, appropriate for someone who'd been around a long time.

"The Fricatash. Why are you wet?"

"Is it still December fourth?"

"No," she laughed, "it's the tenth," although once she said it she was unsure. Something was—she'd seen this man before.

"What time is it?"

"I don't know, nine. Were you just swimming?"

"No. Did you see how I got here? Did someone bring me?"

"Oh hey!" she exclaimed. "You're the guy who's missing!"

"I'm Leon Meed," he said. "I've gone missing? You've heard this?"

"It was on the news and—"

Eve was pushed forward by a wave of people moving in to hear Derivative's next song, a gospel number, and in the resulting visual stutter she lost sight of Leon. People in the audience swayed and stomped and did little gyrations. They raised and lowered their hands like revivalists to these frail white boys, to the basso profundo "Our time it gets no righter/ Our load it gets no lighter/ Take me Lord to where the light shines brighter." And everyone humming the way you do when you can't contain the beck and call of whatever It is to you.

She looked everywhere and despite the density of people making escape impossible, Leon was gone. Her back was dry. There was nothing to say but amen.


At four thirty a.m., Silas Carlton stopped telling himself that he was asleep. His daily confession. He got out of bed and went to the bathroom and sponge-bathed his face and arms before padding into the living room, where he turned on the television with the hope of finding a local news story about the drowned man at the South Jetty. There was nothing on but a documentary about leukemia that spotlighted three American casualties of the war between good and bad white blood cells: a man, woman, and child whose stoicism never faltered on camera. Silas ate the remains of a ham sandwich he'd left on the coffee table the night before, fell asleep at a quarter past six, and, upon reawakening in an upright position on the recliner, patted his chest for his glasses that had slipped off. Failing to locate them, he muted the TV and stared at his fading reflection in the living-room window. Outside was a pallid gray dawn. He'd never before seen an accidental fatality such as had happened at the beach, someone overpowered by the forces of nature. Despite the frequency with which floods and earthquakes and erupting volcanoes and hurricanes took lives, he'd never—

Suddenly, in the window, instead of his dying reflection Silas saw another man's face. He rubbed his eyes with one hand and resumed searching for his glasses with the other. The man must have been a visitor—at last someone dropping by to check on him—but Silas couldn't see his features distinctly, could only generally make out curly hair and a brown shirt or coat. Pointing toward the front door, he said loudly, "It's open! Come in!" The man didn't move. "It's open!"

Silas found his glasses, wedged between the bottom pillow and armrest, and put them on, though because of the poor lighting outside he still couldn't recognize the man. Was it Beto the Argentinian stopping by to see if he'd like to fly his remote control airplane with him? Or one of his neighbors hoping to borrow a bicycle pump? Silas didn't understand why the man wasn't going to the front door, so he moved to get up and let him in, at which point the man disappeared. Silas was halfway out of his chair when he found himself looking through the window at nothing but a lava rock garden, mulberry bushes, mini lawn, street, parked cars, other houses, and wrought-iron sky. No man. He didn't rush to conclusions, for he was perhaps hypnagogic, his sleepy eyes playing tricks on him. He sat back down to consider things and adjust his glasses as though they were a radio dial that, properly modified, would clearly broadcast what had been garbled.

He waited and waited and sensed nothing but static.

## 2

In a beige house in the Cutten neighborhood of Eureka, an orthopedic surgeon named Steve Baker entered the music room, where a dark cherry wood piano stood as a four-legged accusation, a sixty-one key universe of potential sound whose silence was the loudest he had ever heard. He sat on the bench in front of it, on lavender varnished cedar dimpled over time by the hard fingernails of hundreds of frustrated eleven-year-olds sitting through thousands of mother-mandated lessons while thinking of millions of other things. He'd fought over this piano, defended his love of it in sotto voce with nothing-could-induce-me-to-give-it-up conviction.

And Anne, his wife, appealing to reason, had pointed out with growing impatience that he never played it, that he'd bought it for their never-conceived child, for the express purpose of her teaching this phantom progeny how to play, because *she* had studied it all her life, and *she* loved it and looked forward more than anything to twice-weekly sessions with Wendy, if it was a girl, or William, if it was a boy. She had oiled its strings, tuned it regularly, polished its fine wood grains and lacquered its ivory keys and fluttered around it during the move from Egret Road to Kroeber Lane like a paleontologist transporting a dinosaur egg.

It was absurd not to let her keep it, especially since she'd been so generous toward him with everything else—with the bread maker and the twelve-horsepower rototiller and the waist-high Klipsch speakers—although absurd was exactly what he felt their whole breakup was. Absurd because it was so rational and calculated. Their love? Plus one. His sterility? Minus two. And it was absurd because she insisted on living in a small town (*"Any* small town, I don't care. Can't you see how much choice that gives you? How many options?" she'd asked), and because he couldn't do little things like stay with her while she finished her breakfast on Sunday mornings—no, he had to retreat to his work study once he was done eating to work on his models, and he wouldn't acknowledge the symbolic importance of these abandonments—and because they had voted for different candidates in the last mayoral election ("The presidential election, sure, I grant you," he'd said, shaking the garlic press at her, "that would be enough for you to get angry and say that we're incompatible. But the Eureka mayor? Who cares?"). The pros and cons of their relationship were weighed, and a gross imbalance was found. Scales didn't lie. "But scales aren't the only thing to go by," he'd said. "Do you really want—because we could adopt and split our time between big and little towns and move toward political consensus in the future—do you really want to let it go just like that?"

Though it wasn't just like that. She pointed out that he'd conspicuously not mentioned the issue on which he was solely to blame and which most upset her, his inconsiderateness when she felt alone and needed his company, those times when he'd disappear and say he had to be by himself and that it was chemical and nothing to take personally. But how else could she take it than personally? She wasn't a machine, no matter how radically our language had upgraded from brain hemispheres to hard drives. And maybe this proved in a way that her love for him was insufficient and had always been insufficient, but that the possibility of raising children in a semirural community overseen by a wise, mutually agreed upon mayor had once been enough to supplement her feelings and make the relationship worth working on. Now, clearly, the situation had been exposed for what it was. She had accepted a job in the town of Willits, two hours south of Eureka—he hadn't even known she'd been looking—and packed up her things and moved out, leaving Steve with an untouched piano and the feeling that he would soon fade away. This was what he heard in the silence, the sound of his own diminuendo.

He closed the piano lid and pinched the tip of his long aquiline nose. His hair, an auburn brown rusting into gray, dug softly into his neck. His fellow doctor Greg Souza's suitcase lay open on the couch. Greg was staying with him while initiating divorce proceedings against his schoolteacher wife, Elaine, or maybe Elaine was initiating them against him—Steve didn't know the details of it and thought only that divorce was spreading like a virus.

He decided to go for a drive, which he did as an offensive against depression more frequently than he cared to admit, occasions on which he'd go anywhere, didn't matter, so long as he was moving and there was music and lots to look at and to distract him. His depression would be subdued temporarily, and he'd arrive home a few hours later, if not mentally restored then at least closer to being able to go to bed.

Today he drove to Table Bluff, a cliff and beach area five miles south of Eureka and near a recently built Wiyot community housing project, an evolutionary step forward in Indian reservations where the land was governed by the tribe but maintained by the State of California. With independent police and dependent roads. Steve passed it and thought, This is the sort of town where Anne and I could have ended up. Maybe not this particular town, because you have to be Native American to live in it, but somewhere this size where real estate is cheap. I could have made that concession.

He saw the ocean in the distance at intervals as the road wound up and down hills, with undulating fields of buffalo grass on the left and isolated homesteads and dilapidated barns on the right. Something was wrong. Steve pressed harder on the accelerator and found himself going slower. The fuel light had been shining empty for who knew how long. A gas can in the back? No, damn it. Embankment park and a leg stretch around the car and some self-reproach for not filling up the tank earlier. It wasn't more than two miles back to the Wiyot housing project, though he didn't remember seeing a gas station there. Noise up the road and Steve saw a truck round the bend at a dangerous clip and he stood helplessly—or with what he hoped was a posture of helplessness and entreaty—waving a hand for the truck to stop. It was maybe seventy yards from him when he saw, beggaring belief, a man clinging to the gun rack on the truck's roof. Lying facedown and spread-eagle, holding the edges of the rack for purchase, this man was head forward and Steve thought he heard—yes, without a doubt he caught—him shouting "Stop! Stop! Stop!" Steve hoped that his and the man's combined request would bring the truck to a halt, though this hope was dashed as the truck raced past him, its driver with the tensed and fearful expression of someone trying to escape the hounds of hell. Then the truck was gone and Steve stared after it. A haze of dust, nothing. He resigned himself to walking and the thought sank in that he'd just witnessed an act of recklessness for which he'd probably be called in to surgery later that day. And something else wasn't right. Something even less right than the obvious not-rightness of two men barreling down a country road in equal states of panic and unequal states of personal safety. Steve thought he recognized the face of the man on the roof. It was the fleetingest of glimpses, but still.

At the Wiyot housing project he received a lawn-mower gas canister in exchange for ten bucks and the promise to return it to a stern-countenanced, gloriously ponytailed man also named Steve.

The days passing meant nothing. At the office, the mental exhaustion that used to take ten hours to develop now happened in less than one. Another patient? X rays to examine? Deposing for a malpractice case filed three years ago? His constant torpor made it all seem so useless and unmanageable, like he didn't have the stamina and couldn't everyone see how much effort living cost? How it was a trek too far? He had difficulty listening to people. They wanted to tell him things—"my wife's cousin's daughter was a finalist for the Rhodes Scholarship, but was disqualified for lying about her LSAT scores, which everyone knows can be taken a million times before applying to law school and they average the scores, should that even be what she wants to do, and believe me my wife's cousin's daughter has some real reservations about that"—that he didn't want to hear. To foster the sense of self rapidly slipping away from him, he moved from his habitual stimulants (coffee, Coke, ginseng root extract) to borderline legal amphetamines that his friend and colleague and current house-guest, Greg Souza, prescribed for him.

This was unfortunate because as a surgeon he depended on his powers of concentration. It was his great gift as a doctor. He'd made a name for himself by being able to do a spine—seven hours of stand-ing in place with his latexed fingers sawing and threading and manip-ulating microscopic tools—without taking a bathroom break or pausing for a candy bar or sitting down to let his legs uncramp. In another life he'd have made an exemplary monk. Or mime. Or sentry in charge of protecting kings and emperors and other representatives of God on earth.

Before the divorce started he'd spent much of his nonworking time building fantastic miniature reproductions of medieval towns using balsa wood and soft chromium. His Salzburg could hold its own against any model out there. His Venice was the work of a maestro. But now he'd sit down at his worktable with a stack of three-eighth-inch wood squares and an X-acto knife and a tube of wood glue, unable to pick up anything without his hands shaking and a drifting—no, a *darting*—mind. In his current condition the only cities to which he could do justice were World War II–era Dresden or Hiroshima or Coventry. Maybe an earthquake San Francisco. And he'd reached a point in life where he hadn't any friends. Or: he had *friends*, but not friends whom he could call and tell about the he-said/she-said of the divorce, the Thursday afternoon meetings at Anne's lawyer's office, where he and his lawyer and she and her lawyer sat at a diplomatic table using diplomatic language better suited to the Treaty of Ver-sailles than to the breakup of two people who'd loved each other intensely once, who'd cried when the other got hurt and exulted when the other felt joy and said "forever" and "completely" and "unconditionally." The end of this marriage foretold everything. It said that he was incapable of sustaining a loving relationship and doomed, at best, to serial monogamy until he died. No growing old with someone. No twenty-year anniversaries and wistful recollections of their younger bodies and younger passions and younger worlds.

His colleague friend Greg Souza's divorce was because of rote infidelity and Greg had had nothing thoughtful to say on the occasion that he and Steve went through the verbal condolences with each other, the I-can't-believe-how-everything-changes. Although Greg was technically staying with him until he found an apartment, he'd been spending his nights at Marlene's and was never around.

So Steve was alone on Saturday, December 11, trembling knife in hand, when the doorbell rang. He'd managed to forget Anne for a minute and was remembering what Silas Carlton, an old patient, had told him about birds: they have extremely small lungs and so use their bones to circulate oxygen. "Very nice," he said, and opened the door.

Elaine Perry stood with one foot on the welcome mat, holding two plastic garbage sacks. Hints of the previous day's makeup were so subtle that he thought her lips were naturally the color of persimmons.

"Hi, Steve," she said.

They hadn't seen each other in maybe ten months. Anne had always praised Elaine as the best of his doctor friends' spouses, as a woman wisely unconcerned with extravagant houses and her children's orthodontic work.

"Hi," Steve said.

"I don't want to make this awkward, but Greg said he'd pick up these bags a couple of days ago and he never did. Do you mind if I drop them off? Is he here?"

"He's out, but I can take them." They were heavy and full of pointy, uncomfortable objects that dug into him as he held them against his chest. "I wanted to say—I should say I'm sorry about what's going on."

"Thanks. I'm sorry for you, too."

They smiled more by effort than by natural feeling. Like so many outward signs of health and normalcy.

"Would you like to come in?" Steve asked, unsure of what else to say. "For a cup of coffee?"

"No, thanks. I shouldn't be here when Greg comes back."

Steve was about to tell her that Greg never came back before noon, but then thought better of it. He shifted the bags in his arms and it didn't occur to him to set them down.

"I hope we can be normal with each other," she said.

"What?"

"I hope that you being Greg's friend doesn't mean we have to avoid each other at the supermarket or in Old Town or wherever."

"No, absolutely not." He'd never run into her at the supermarket or in Old Town before, but that didn't mean it couldn't happen in the future. Eureka was a small enough city that you sometimes saw your dentist or hair stylist or friends' ex-wives at restaurants. You perfected an ever-readiness to talk about your teeth or hair or neutral, non-friend-related gossip. You skated across the surface reality like a water beetle, and only when the surface broke and you fell in did you feel that drowning was inevitable, that staying afloat had been a fantasy.

Elaine said, "I just—maybe you feel the same I don't know—I don't want to feel like getting divorced means that a whole world of people will disappear. You know? All of Greg's friends and patients I've met. I'd hate to think that now we have to act like we've never known one another."

"I know what you mean," Steve said. "I agree."

Elaine held out her hand. Still holding the bags, Steve shook it awkwardly with his whole upper torso. Then she turned and walked to the street, massaging her left shoulder with her right hand. Steve watched her get in her car and drive away, someone else's former everything.

Several blocks away, Sadie Jorgenson's willpower deserted her in the wall-to-wall linoleum sparklage of her kitchen, with batter all over her hands, making one Swedish pancake after another, smothered in powdered sugar the weight and consistency of pixie dust. She was a therapist whose client list was longer than any of her colleagues', meaning that at the end of a grueling workweek she owed herself a little—or rather a lot—of pleasure. And so didn't she feel magical with each bite of pancake, a wild transport to zones of physical ecstasy she never experienced otherwise? Sadie, thirty-seven, hadn't gotten laid in years, which she knew was partly because of morning binges like this one, but what could she do since the cycle was already started and each production of one kind of happiness diminished her chances for the other? Undress another stick of butter. Fondle the pan handle. And the radio on and she with a lot of boogie left to her bottom that hadn't lost its attitude, so she let the pancake sizzle while she clapped her hands and danced around the island counter and nodded ("you know it, ah-*hahn*") and licked an ample finger.

And yet all this might soon change. Her sister Marlene had called the night before and known the perfect guy, an academic. An academic? *Yeah.* What's that mean? *Someone who traffics in ideas for a living.* That doesn't sound as lucrative as, say, trafficking in narcotics. *It isn't.* Is that why he's still unmarried? *He's new to town and hasn't met anyone. I think you two would hit it off.* Why? *Because he's interesting.* What's he look like? *He's tall and—* How tall? *I don't know, five ten.* You call that tall? *It's taller than you.* Don't be rude. How old is he? *Thirty-seven.* That's my age. *Yeah.* Guys don't go out with women the same age as them. It'd be better if he were older. He'd appreciate me more. *He seems above all that. And he's bald.* As long as he has the right head for it. Not too big or bumpy, like a smooth small skull that draws attention to his face. *Yeah, sort of. And there's one other thing. He's missing four fingers on his right hand from when he was young and worked with heavy machinery.* Oh. *Other than that he's normal and attractive.* Oh. *I didn't even notice until it came up in conversation.* Oh. *So what do you say?* I wish he hadn't lost those fingers. *I'm sure he does, too. Can I set something up, completely non-binding and informal, like the four of us have dinner at Folie à Deux this weekend?* What four of us? *Greg makes four.* How can you go out with Greg in public? *He and Elaine have a new understanding, an unspoken agreement not to pry into each other's personal lives.* Their personal lives? They're married. *You know what I mean.* So what has it become, an open arrangement? With their kids so young? *Not open, in that they haven't discussed it in those meaningful terms, but they're having problems and are basically separated for a while.* Marlene! Homewrecker! He's a doctor and you're a nurse and it's so predictable. How long do you think this can go on? *It's not about worrying about the future. So are you in for dinner? I'll arrange it and call you back.* I don't know. *What else do you have going on in your love life?* My love life. Spoken of as a thing in the world. *This guy is not an ogre.* I didn't say ogre. I just think after Stan. *Stan was three years ago.* Yes but the scar tissue. *You owe it to yourself to get out of the kitchen—I mean the house, get out of the house for a change and move forward.* I can't believe you said kitchen. What's this guy's name? *Roger Nuñez.* He's Latino? *He's many things.* Does he speak Spanish? *How should I know? Do I speak Spanish?* How'd you meet him if he's so new to the area? *At Dee Anderson's.* And I'm supposed to be reassured that you met him there? You know for certain he didn't lose those fingers because of syphilis? *It was in the middle of the afternoon, at a respectable artists' guild meeting. Roger is doing some work on Yurok blankets with someone else at Humboldt State University from the Native American Studies department, and he was at Dee's on a purely business-type level. It wasn't anything weird.* Hmmm. Okay, I'll meet him. *That's my girl.*

Sadie scraped the last runny spoonfuls of pancake dough from the mixing bowl and dropped them onto the frying pan. So many calories. One dinner with a six-fingered man wouldn't be the end of the world. And later that day she might go to CalCourts and do a bit of Stairmaster to counterbalance the morning. Patterns of behavior were only unbreakable if you didn't try to break them.

The next afternoon she fell asleep while watching a documentary about black lesbian poets, this being one of Roger Nuñez's academic specialties and so part of her homework before the blind date because with the possibility of love you've got to be prepared to meet the other person halfway, give-and-take, and when she woke up she remembered a few of the key phrases used—indigenous liminal subalternism, covert clitorogeny—and the pictures of close-cropped Afros and the loving women who sported them.

She was sweaty and had to take a shower. She was also starving and wanted to have some macaroni salad but thought it would spoil her appetite at dinner, which on second thought might be good. Dieticians recommended having six small meals a day instead of three big ones. Marlene's doctor boyfriend, Greg, had told her this wasn't true, although Greg was a philanderer who, if he was capable of cheating on his wife, was capable of cheating on Marlene and other lifestyle prevarications. Sadie worried about her sister and took off her blouse on her way to the kitchen and then felt an empowering self-denial and redirected herself to the bathroom.

There she fully stripped and untied her frosted hair, removed her penny-sized earrings. While waiting for the shower to heat up she faced the mirror and thought of how difficult it must be to be black and gay and a female poet all at once. An incredible quadruple whammy. Yet we were all born with certain disadvantages, handicapped in some way or ways from the get-go, condemned to spend our lives developing strengths to make up for our inherited disadvantages. Obesity, religious unorthodoxy, a big nose, eczema, hairiness, hairlessness, a poetic bent. When it came to gender, Sadie could empathize with black lesbian poets, she could say *right on* and there was that automatic sisterhood, though when it came to being black and lesbian she was just a honky breeder. Some important circles didn't overlap.

There was a rustle behind the shower curtain and a male voice said, "Oh, ahhh, what the hell!"

Sadie froze. Someone was in the bathroom with her and the door was closed. She felt a fear so heart-lurching of what was about to happen to her that she couldn't move. A man was lurking and scheming in her shower, hidden by the curtain but there. Surely there. She closed her eyes and the door was closed. There was the squeak of faucet knobs turning in both directions and the sound of water surging and slowing before shutting off completely. A man's retching and coughing water and throwing open the shower curtains, the screech of rings sliding along the metal bar, some psychotic onomatopoeia. Sadie knew she should try to defend herself but honestly hadn't the strength, and the man probably had a weapon. Intent on any number of penetrations, sexual and otherwise: vaginally, anally, orally, or perhaps knife stabs to her back, side, front, head. In her mind's eye she didn't so much see someone writhing on top of her as imagine him rubbing her face into the floor in an effort to erase who she was. Wasn't that what violent people did, tried to negate their victims? She saw herself being uncreated.

With her eyes closed the waiting for something to happen took an eternity. She heard the intruder clear his throat and she thought, *Soldered sang of ellllllll spot*. Waiting for the pain to begin. For it all to go blank. Maybe this would be a swift gunshot to the back of her head, and she was about to go to the Great Unknown. *Hamlet says relax*. She gripped the porcelain sink as though it were a walker, and her eyes were closed so tightly she saw breathtakingly beautiful kaleidoscope patterns on the backs of her eyelids, swirls of inchoate violets and reds and ambers, whorls of abstract space, splintering intimations of something, yes, strangely and unexpectedly, holy. For she was barricaded in her head now, come what may of this intruder. It got to be so that he didn't matter. When one door closes another opens. She was given over to a vision bigger and more numinous than her normal consciousness; she would survive the pain and emerge as from a chrysalis. Her body would fail, but that's what bodies did in the end, and the rest would be ascension. She'd shake off a mortal coil that had only ever been a sidelong glance at what's most true.

Fifteen minutes later Sadie was in a trance, a victory over the normal din of her thoughts. Fearlessly she opened her eyes and light flooded in and for a moment she didn't know where she was. Just for a moment. Then she was cognizant of looking in the mirror and seeing that there was no one else in her bathroom. The curtain was drawn and the water was off, but there was no man there. She hadn't heard him leave, though she'd been in a state where noise perhaps wouldn't have reached her. But why would he do it? What would be the point of sneaking into someone's bathroom and then leaving without further violence? Sadie was on terra firma again and didn't know what to make of it.

On Monday morning, in relentlessly white northern California, in a land of milk and no honey, Prentiss Johnson was a black man. As black as he could be. As black as any Eurekan could ever, in the wildest flights of their color imagination, hope to be or become. He worked at the public library in the stacks, was six foot three, weighed a hun dred and ninety-five pounds, and had a drinking problem. The night before, he'd said it again to eight of the fourteen people who attended his Mad River Alcoholics Anonymous meetings, "I have a problem with alcohol." Where were the missing six attendees? Probably on a bender through the saloons of Second Street, bottles of Old Crow evaporating before their very eyes, yelling *fuck that!* at the idea of rehabilitation and the childish amusements offered by sobriety. Prentiss had looked at the white people, each of them so very white, and said, "Every day is a struggle." What an understatement. What an outlandish reduction of the thirst, like an infant's, like the desert's, that he felt every waking second of his life. I am a drain, he thought, capable of swallowing everything. Eight heads of limp hair nodded up and down as he spoke. "I wish I could say it was getting better."

A week earlier, Prentiss had been at Safeway to pick up some eggs and a bag of potato chips and wound up patrolling the hard liquor aisle, his brain a crashing wave of foam and confusion, feeling an almost sexual longing for the amber beverages lined up in regulated rows. Whenever he got to the end of the aisle and told himself to turn left and leave, to just put that shit out of his sight, because he knew he couldn't go back to the way it had been, and the life he'd rebuilt after leaving the hospital could fold without so much as a huff or a puff, he turned around and made another pass at Johnnie Walker and Jim Beam and Lord Ron Calvert—all the old aiders and abettors— and thought *the magnet's not losing its pull.* A pretty girl with short black bangs whose Bonanza 88 shirt said her name was *Eve* grabbed a quart of rum and wandered off humming an unhummable song. It was brighter than day in aisle 11. It was baseball-stadium-at-night bright. And then some fourteen-year-old white kid in thrashed army fatigues and ballistic eyes sidled up to Prentiss trying to be cool, the studied subversion, with a "Hey man, what's up? Me and my friends outside are wondering if you'd be into buying us a bottle of Cuervo and we'd throw in something for yourself, like such as a few beers?" And the kid was so stoned and had such shitty teeth and stupidly cut hair and Prentiss knew it wasn't a play at entrapment. Though the point was—yes, the sad truth was—that the kid was angling for a way to jump into the very hole Prentiss was trying to crawl out of.

So tragic. Prentiss wanted to shake him real hard and say, It ain't like that. It ain't so easy you getting waylaid tonight and thinking it's no big thing and all bets are off, all the pain disappeared and you get to feel like some street-corner prince put on earth to fuck and run. Booze is the long-term proposition. Booze sets up residence in you and in return it gets rid of the pain but that's no fair trade, because the pain isn't gone it's just hiding, and while you're in that limbo and your nerve endings don't mean nothing, while nothing means nothing, your pain's developing immunities so that when it comes back it'll reintroduce itself and there ain't no movie this scary so that you're begging for mercy and it's you down on your knees penitent, and you didn't mean to let the pain get so big, honest, you were going to bring it back and work with it a little, treat it with respect and figure out what it's got to teach you. But by then it's too late. I'm saying, by then the clock's run out and you can't ever make a move on your own again. You're its slave forever on a plantation as big as your mind.

But Prentiss didn't say this. Instead he ran a black hand over his black face and turned to the kid and walked toward him and said, as gently as he could, "That's not a good idea for either one of us." The brightness of aisle 11 was practically blinding, and "I've Got You Under My Skin" wafted out of the ceiling speakers, all dulcet tones and why-not-pick-up-some-extra-gum. The kid backed into and over-turned a basket of limes and belligerently kicked one of the rolling green citruses and shuffled down the aisle and turned left and wasn't overcome with the shakes. Prentiss longed to follow him.

This Monday was another gray day, and a cement truck at the corner of Fourteenth and C Streets was grinding the devil's own bones. They should be handing out earplugs. Prentiss walked by it on his way back from A.J.'s Market, coughing the rising dust and wiggling his right big toe through a sock hole as he passed an old bird-looking dude he saw hanging around sometimes, not doing anything.

Prentiss was expected at the library in an hour and hadn't taken a shower or had breakfast or done his stepping. The stepping was hard. Pulling an apple pie out of its crinkle wrapping as he entered the two-bedroom apartment he shared with Carl Frost, he took a bite and stared at the fresh copy of *Daily Reflections: A Book of Reflections by A.A. Members for A.A. Members* sitting on the coffee table. He had no trouble with the first step: "We admit we are powerless over alcohol, that our lives have become unmanageable." Wasn't his totaled car, revoked driver's license, broken collarbone, and $61,000 worth of structural damage to the Fortuna Doll Emporium building proof enough? And the job firings and estranged girlfriends and chronic fatigue? Damn straight, his life had become unmanageable because of alcohol. As plain as an overhead B-52. But the second step was turning out to be a real barrier in his path toward recovery: "Come to believe that a Power greater than ourselves can restore us to sanity." Now, who in their right mind is going to hand over the steering wheel toward recovery to some Power that might not exist? That was just irresponsible. Prentiss had gotten himself into alcoholism, and Prentiss was going to get himself out. Simple as that. And it was this same "Power" that had allowed every tragedy he could think of to happen, from slavery to the World Trade. Prentiss was supposed to trust his recovery to that? What's the expression, you must be kidding.

"Prentiss, that you?" called out a voice from the bathroom.

"Me."

"Could you do me a favor and bring me some paper towels?"

"We out of toilet paper?"

"Looks that way."

"I wish I'd have known; I was just at A.J.'s."

Prentiss stuffed the rest of the apple pie in his mouth and took a roll of paper towels to his roommate in the bathroom. "That's a potent odor," he said. "Makes my fruit pie taste bad."

"Thank you."

"Seriously, you got a problem there."

"Mayday, mayday."

"You owe me money."

"I always owe you money."

"You got to put it up front now or they'll shut down the utilities."

"We have flashlights."

"The second due date is coming."

"We can make fires in the garbage can."

"Going to turn off the water and we won't be able to flush your evil shit away."

"I'll build an outhouse."

"Seventy-four dollars, Frost. Today. Seventy-four dollars."

"But I have to pay Sadie when I see her tomorrow."

"Who's Sadie?"

"My therapist."

"A man's got to have priorities. Don't make me look for a new roommate."

Prentiss went to his room and got out one of his work sweaters, a downy V neck decorated with rows of off-center maple leaves. Pulled on the boots. Patted his two-inch Afro into an approximate square. Started walking across town to the clean, well-lit Humboldt County

Library, where the books and movies kept piling up for his sorting pleasure. Pleasure. Yeah, right. About as much pleasure as having your balls licked by a cat. A frazzle-haired woman pushing a stroller with no baby in it breezed past him when he crossed the street to the courthouse. He was going to be late. But for seven bucks an hour, did he care? True, the county had given him the job as an alternative to living in a halfway house, and he had to be grateful for the little bit of freedom this allowed him, though it was a chafed freedom, a liberty restricted to fighting his impulse to sit down with a gallon of red wine and let the good times roll. Oh, but it was all sour grapes these days.

Prentiss had been living with Frost for two years and considered him his only close sober friend, though they didn't do much together besides watch TV and go to the flea market for the distinctive clothes Frost favored. Prentiss didn't pretend to understand Frost, who in high school had chastised him for not being black enough the irony of Frost's being white didn't seem to matter—but who lately had let slip a few race-is-irrelevant comments regarding affirmative action. Sometimes Prentiss stood in Frost's room, which had a map theme going on—every square inch of wall space was covered by maps of the world, of Uganda and Estonia and East Timor, of small towns and big towns and mountain ranges and highway grids and famous buildings (the Louvre, Buckingham Palace, the Carter House)—for an effect that was like staring at someone's brain circuitry. His own, maybe. There were stacks of *National Geographic* on the floor and piles of loud, colorful clothing on the bed and in the room's corners, as well as newspaper clippings about car accidents. Prentiss would wonder at this cartographic nerve center and then gratefully return to his own, normal room.

The next morning he got up early to go to the bathroom and couldn't fall back to sleep, so he poured himself a bowl of cereal in the kitchen and was examining the toy mouse that came in the cereal package, when a strange woman walked in and let out a half-second scream.

Prentiss threw down the mouse and tried to see straight. "You a friend of Frost's?"

"I'm sorry?" she said.

"Carl's. You a friend? My name's Prentiss. I was just settling down to some breakfast cereal and found this little Ziegfried the Marvelous Mouse toy come in the package." He looked from her to the table. Frost never had women stay the night. As far as he knew, Frost didn't know any women. "It isn't a regular thing me examining a plastic mouse this early."

"My name's Justine. I just met—I mean, yes, I'm a friend of Carl's. It's nice to meet you."

"Likewise." He looked at her and she stood there zipping her purse open and shut. "You want some toasted wheat biscuits?" he asked.

"No, thanks. Could you tell me where the bathroom is?"

"It's back there in the hallway on your left. But at the moment we're having a toilet paper shortage. I could offer you a paper towel."

"That's all right. I don't live far from here. I can wait."

"Suit yourself. But there's nothing so urgent to me as the first pee of the day."

"I don't suppose you," she said, staring nervously at the refrigerator and its magnetized poetry and clipped, careworn coupon. "I don't—"

Prentiss looked at her in the weak morning light and she seemed about to say something before stopping, removing her hand from the purse, and walking out the door.


That afternoon, Silas Carlton was in the Bead Emporium, staring at rows and columns of bead drawers. He felt the paralysis of choice that struck him sometimes at the grocery store when he'd face seventy-two different breakfast cereals (he'd counted them during one of his twenty-minute stupefactions). There were too many alternatives. Ah, he'd think, give me a Soviet food line any day where I have to take whatever they've got. Unburden me of these decisions. By that logic he should have grabbed the nearest cereal and not bothered deliberating over the bran o's and crispy muesli flakes and frosted chocolate nuggets, but he had preferences—he had tastes—and a bad selection would haunt him until he threw the cereal away and went back to the store, at which point the difficulty would begin again. Other people didn't have this trouble and were quickly filling up plastic baggies with beads. No hesitation. A silver-haired sales-woman with thin gold-framed glasses sat on a stool holding a closed book of crossword puzzles and staring at him. Silas didn't like people to pay attention to him while he shopped. Made him feel pressured, like he was being monitored and any deviation from standard browsing behavior—if he spent too long reading a label or talked to himself—would get him in trouble. As maybe it would.

He left the store without buying anything and felt a huge relief, like he'd resisted temptation, though all he'd done was fail to get a gift for his great-niece Lillith's seventeenth birthday. He walked down and up the dip in Buhne Street—exacerbating but not making unbearable the pain in his knees—and turned left on Harrison and stopped in for a fountain-style soda at Lou's Drugs.

Beto the Argentinian was at the counter with his long sideburns getting ever longer. He gently patted the stool next to him when Silas approached.

"Silas," said Beto.

"Beto," said Silas.

"It's good for you to join us."

Beto sat alone and no one was behind the fountain. The aisles of Lou's were empty. The cashier was gone. The ceiling corners of the store were without security cameras.

"Where's Lou and everybody?"

"I don't know."

"Did you just get here?"

"Since two hours ago."

"There hasn't been anyone here in two hours?"

"People were here. Lou was here. But they left."

"Why?"

"I don't know."

"Lou wouldn't just leave the store to be robbed by gangs."

"No gangs come in here."

"My point is that there are valuable items lying around."

"I'm not saying if it were my store I would go away, but Lou is different. He is a smart businessman."

"I've never heard anyone call him that."

They sat in silence for some time before Silas said, "You mind if I ask you something?"

"Okay."

"A few days ago, in the morning, early, did you come by my place and peek through the window for a minute and then run away?"

"Me?"

"I'm just curious."

"You think I spy on you?"

"That's not necessarily what I'm asking."

"I wouldn't do that."

"Okay."

Beto pulled three white gold rings from his left hand and laid them on top of one another on the smudged porcelain countertop. Silas reached around the soda dispenser for a glass that he filled with cola before adding a thick vanilla syrup. Beto stared at the carbonation running up the insides of the glass and whistled. Silas drank it all out of a bent straw.

"You were thirsty," said Beto appreciatively.

"Yes."

The front door jangled open and Lou walked in, a short man with a brush-bristle crew cut dyed jet black. His eyes were red from the conjunctivitis he claimed to have gotten from the redwood and marijuana pollen in Humboldt County's air. It clogged his tear ducts. Although he'd lived in Eureka for forty-seven years, his Georgia accent sounded thicker to Silas than any Southerner he'd ever heard. Lou talked about retiring in Georgia, but he hadn't been back to visit in over a decade and feared the changes time had wrought. Better the devil you know, he said.

"Lou," Silas said. "You left this place unattended. Beto and I could have broken into the pharmacy and taken everything."

"You'd have left fingerprints."

"True."

"I went to the police station."

"What for?"

"My employee Leon—part-time guy—is missing."

"I read that," said Silas.

"His mother's offering ten thousand dollars for his return."

"They think he's been kidnapped?" Beto asked.

"They didn't let on what they think."

"What'd you tell them?" asked Silas.

"That a couple months back he stopped coming in because of an illness."

"They think he's dead?" Beto asked.

"They didn't let on what they think."

"You going to hire new help?" Silas said.

"I am."

Silas left money for his soda on the counter and left. Walking down and up Buhne hurt his knees this time, and when he got home he took pills and lay in bed until his consciousness went blank.

## ⊣ 3 ⊢

In a small condominium in Old Town Eureka, Barry Klein dabbed water on the button-sized stain marring the front of his double-knit sweater and rubbed and rubbed it and then draped the sweater over the radiator. He went to the kitchen and placed two apples, a shearing knife, a corned beef sandwich, a pockmarked copy of *The God of Small Things*, and a thin folded blanket into a wicker basket, his Prairiewalker model Longaberger, and closed the top. It was four thirty and he wasn't gay. Sunlight dappled the checkerboard carpet on which he rested his huge feet in the living room. The hairs growing out of his two big toes were long and he was ashamed of their coarseness, of their pubic quality. He would never again wear sandals.

A cat meowed from the top of a bookshelf and he said to it, "You could easily be a dog. I could've gotten a dog and been happy. It's a cliché for gay men to have cats but that doesn't matter because maybe I'll meet a girl at Rainie's tonight."

He thought about eating half the corned beef sandwich, but then thought better of it. As a new guest, he was presenting at that evening's Longaberger party, meaning whatever he packed was what he'd show, and if that included a half-eaten sandwich, what impression would that make? That he couldn't control himself? That he was too poor to afford a whole one? That he kept an unkempt home? What a wrong impression that would be. Barry looked at the walls of his one-bedroom apartment and saw the Napa wine poster perfectly aligned with the street-facing window, a photo collage of his family and college friends, the theater masks of laughter and tears, a giant handwritten quote, "We are all in the gutter, but some of us are looking at the stars." Now hold on. Would he have an Oscar Wilde quote on his wall if he weren't gay?

"Don't be so literal," he said to the cat, which stared at him mercilessly. "Lots of straight people like Oscar Wilde. He has big crossover appeal."

He shaved again and applied antioxidant cream to the worry lines on his forehead and put on the sweater he'd cleaned, which was casual and said *I'm approachable*. He really hoped he would meet a girl at the party.

He looked in the mirror and raised his eyebrows and saw with a sinking feeling that the worry lines weren't fading despite the diligence with which he daily applied the cream. And the hairline at his temples was getting uneven. And that stain on his sweater hadn't gone away! What did he have to do, cut it out? Put on a patch? Bleach the whole sweater? He ran more water over it and said to the cat, who had followed him into the bathroom, "Last night didn't happen so I wish you'd stop thinking that." He'd been roaming around on the Internet and had paused to graze in a pasture that wasn't his *preferred* pasture, not his oriented field, and the stain was proving impossible. "I was just looking around," he said. "It doesn't mean anything." The cat sneezed. "Do you understand? Nothing." The image of loving a man and touching a man and intimate urgent kissing and reaching down to grab an erect cock and his grabbing yours . . . Tonight he would meet a girl and impress her with his observations about Rainie and the ridiculousness of Longaberger parties—twenty adults all swapping stories about how they use their Longabergers?— but that it was a good excuse to be social without getting drunk or sitting through a dumb movie. He would be supercharming. There was to be an eclectic group of Rainie's friends with names like Elaine Perry and Sadie Jorgenson and he didn't know how many of them would be single. But how long can you call it accidental grazing when in your heart of hearts it thrills and excites and fills you up with a longing so pure, so real, so intensely overpowering that you could turn your back forever on the prospect of a tepid marriage to someone you have to constantly tell yourself you're attracted to, and for what? Social approval? A military stint if he ever so chose? Freedom from fear of *Faggot! You like to suck dick, huh? How you like to swallow blood?* And bashed skull and helplessness and shame—oh God, the unutterable shame—and self-censure and the imprisonment in a life, a position, a love that dare not speak its name? Barry took off and folded up his sweater and placed it on the dry-cleaning pile. Then he put on another sweater and strategically ruffled his hair so that the thin parts weren't visible, making perfect his beauty. He felt good. He started crying. Tonight, maybe, he would meet someone.

A few hours later he was ready. The map to Rainie's house that came with the Longaberger party invitation unfolded on his couch like an origami flower bud, and Barry would have left it sitting there if he hadn't thought in the back of his mind that he might bring someone home later. Everything in that case should look neat and inviting, so he took the four-square-inch paper to the recycling bag. Then, with basket in hand, he met his neighbor Amphai in the hallway outside his apartment and gave her a light one-armed hug.

"You all set?" said Amphai.

"I feel like one of those Saint Bernard rescue dogs," said Barry, lifting his basket to his chin.

Within fifteen minutes they were at Rainie's, where a man neither of them knew welcomed them in. Barry shook his hand and—was he imagining it or did the man thumb-press his palm significantly?—walked into the living room, where he set down his Longaberger next to the fireplace and a cast-iron tool stand in which were slotted a mini-broom, fire poker, and extended-reach tongs.

"Amphai and Barry!" Rainie said, emerging from her bedroom in a knee-length yellow dress tied at the waist, her hair freshly released from curlers. "You're the first ones. Have you met Alvin? We used to work together at the Cutten Nursery. These things usually start on time, so the others should be here any minute."

"Hi, again," said Barry shyly, Amphai and Alvin nodding around the triangle.

"I had cucumber slices over my eyes for two hours today," Rainie said. "You want coffee? I'd peek a little and it was like I was actually inside the cucumber, you know you get cucumber juice deposits around the corners of your eyes. And what do you think of this dress? I got it and a hoop skirt at the Hop-Hop last weekend for only forty dollars, tax included. The guy who owns that store was in our year at Eureka High, Amphai. Jason with a Spanish last name. Who's got psoriasis or some really unfortunate skin predicament, but it turns out he went with Sandrine, remember that French exchange student our junior year who everyone thought was a lesbian, well according to Jason they were getting it on for three months."

"She left a used rag in the toilet once in the gym and I went in right after her," said Amphai, stirring her coffee. The spoon-on-porcelain *nrr-nrr-nrr* sound driving everyone a little crazy once they tuned in to it. "There it was like an aborted fetus."

"That continental charm," said Rainie. "The exchange students were always so gauche, to use one of their words. Except the German boys and oh God do you remember Claude?"

"With the big cock."

"Ladies, ladies," said Alvin, who had a thick, well-trimmed beard and curly black hair styled into a pompadour that Barry thought becoming. "Some of us haven't had our dinner yet."

"Sorry." Rainie poked him in the ribs. "Making you hungry?"

"I refuse to dignify."

"Then the three of you should sit down and the others will literally—oh, that's the door. Hold on."

By six fifteen, twenty people were standing or sitting in the living room, ranch-dipping celery sticks and saying, "the farmers' market in Arcata is a spent force" and "appalled by my mom's Tupperware parties and thought I'd have to be lobotomized before doing anything like it" and "broken condom is how she described it to me, not that they won't love it with all their hearts." Of the twenty people, eighteen were women.

"Welcome to those of you who it's your first time at a Longaberger gathering," said Rainie, pushing a cart stacked with baskets to the center of the room and smiling at everyone. She unpacked the baskets and arrayed them in crescent formation with their identifying name tags in front. The 2002 Ambrosia Combo. The Small Harvest Blessings Combo. The 2005 Founder's Market Basket Combo. "As most of you know I'm Rainie and I'm a Longaberger independent sales associate, which means that I'm licensed to sell Longaberger products by the Longaberger company itself." The first of the coughs and sneezes and body mutinies from the audience. "I'm going to give a little historical background and then show you some of the more fantastic models and give you a chance to buy the ones you want. I know that stocking up on holiday Longabergers is one of your main reasons for being here, but I think it's also important for you all to enjoy yourselves and get to know one another. I've made some of my best friends through attending Longaberger gatherings just like this one."

During the ensuing report on Longaberger history—the inspirational account of an epileptic and stutterer named Dave Longaberger whose learning disability prevented his finishing high school until he was twenty-one, a man who then founded and, against the advice of friends and creditors, sold two successful small businesses to finance his dream of creating the largest basket manufacturing company in the United States—Barry scanned the faces around him hoping to alight on an interesting and attractive person—*woman,* he meant— whom he might approach after the demonstration. His eyes kept hiccuping on Alvin's, who for some reason was looking at him, so that he had to yank his gaze elsewhere and settle on, say, Sadie Jorgenson, a generously built therapist with frosted hair and a thin silver necklace buried in the folds of her neck.

The history segued into an in-depth basket-by-basket examination of Rainie's wares, taking time for questions and for-examples and personal testimonials. Then there were three guest presentations, among them Barry's, about which he was nervous, though you'd never know it to watch him pull out his Prairiewalker's items, sandwich and book and blanket. In fact, to most observers his was the most accomplished basket packing, certainly the most comprehensive. With these items you could spend an entire day at Sequoia Park or the Willow Creek River or on a drive in some picturesque part of southern Humboldt. And *The God of Small Things* as his book choice; yes, this was a man worth getting to know, thought the curvy ladies in attendance.

When it was time for Rainie's closing remarks, before welcoming the chance to talk one-on-one with people and take their orders and write down their mailing information and email addresses to keep them in the Humboldt Longaberger loop, she thanked her guests and said, "You might wonder what's in it for me to provide this Longaberger service, and I don't mind telling you because that's fair and honest. If I sell $250 worth of merchandise tonight, I not only get my five percent commission but I also get the Inaugural Hostess Appreciation Basket and Protector, which is a beautiful basket, five and three-quarter inches by three and three-quarter inches by four inches, and it has a swinging handle and is woven of alternating red and natural quarter-inch weaving with a star-studded blue trim strip. It's only available to hostesses this month, so I really hope I make it."

The semicircle broke up and people turned to one another and asked which Longabergers, if any, they would buy. Barry told himself, *The woman with short dark hair who looks like Snow White,* and set off in her direction—*whatever you do don't look at him*—and passed by Alvin and his heart skipped a beat and—

He found himself staring at a man in his mid-fifties with curly chestnut hair graying at the sides, dressed in a brown open-collared cotton shirt, pleated wool slacks, and bubble-toed black boots. Lived-in clothes that looked tumble-dried and thrown on. Unconcerned clothes. The sort of ensemble you'd wear if you were taking a cross-country train trip and couldn't bring any luggage. Barry hadn't noticed him at the party before or seen him walk into his personal space and was frankly a little disturbed to be standing so close to him.

"What is this?" the man said, arching his shoulders. "Where am I?"

"Where are you?" said Barry.

"Wait a minute. This is my old apartment." The voice, a rock-rake gravelly sound, had panic stabbing through it. The man looked nervously at the trios and quartets of women—and Alvin—eating and making mouthful comments and nodding at the mention of others' children and husbands and termagant mothers-in-law. He took in and held a big breath.

Barry had heard of drug-addled bums—although drug-addled bums these days were usually younger than this fellow, some in their teens or even younger because the country's safety net had so many tears in its mesh—wandering into any house with an unlocked front door and having freak-out breakdown sessions in front of horrified, suspended-animation families or single mothers or amorous couples. Too much PCP and THC and LSD—not enough TLC. The bums, having worked toward this moment ever since taking their first cigarette drag or saying *bombs away* with a bottle of Everclear or tying off with a rubber tourniquet and nearby syringe, were generally unarmed and harmless if you could contain them somehow. The trick was to get them into a small empty room; otherwise they'd accost the furniture or wrestle with the leaf blower while screaming obscenities until the authorities arrived to take them away.

Barry's first impulse, therefore, was to try to keep the man calm while signaling for someone to call the cops. "You're at Rainie Chastain's house, where we're having a Longaberger party."

"Longaberger? Those woven baskets?"

"That's right."

"You're saying this is a Longaberger *party*? I'm afraid—what's your name?"

"Barry."

"I'm afraid, Barry, that I've lost my mind."

Barry reached up to scratch his head and made a check swish in the air hoping that Rainie or someone would see it. No one did. "That's possible. Is there a reason you think so?"

"Yes," said the man, nodding unhappily. "Yes, there is."

Barry looked down at the man's left hand and saw a hand grenade. He knew in a terrible instant that they all were going to die, that this guy was a holdout from the Symbionese Liberation Army, that they were going to explode into a hard rain of body parts and wicker and building rubble, and in that split second Barry experienced superre-gret at never having admitted to himself what he was just because of social opprobrium and other stupid intangibles. Barry, Barry, quite contrary, how does your garden grow? He *knew* how it grew and had always been too cowardly to openly acknowledge it and celebrate the strange and wonderful and natural things that grew there. Oh, he had lived life with one arm tied behind his back, he thought as his initial panic ebbed and with a surreal helicopter seed comedown he realized that the round stubbly object in the drug-addled bum's hand was not a grenade at all but a pinecone. He careened into awareness as the bum shook his head and walked heavily to the hallway leading to the front door.

"Friend of yours?"

Barry looked from the door to the person addressing him. Alvin. "No, I've never met him before."

"Rainie has the widest circle of acquaintances."

"Yeah."

They regarded the crowd around them and Alvin said, "Can you take a compliment?"

Barry didn't flicker with embarrassment when, after a moment of silence, he realized that he was staring hard at Alvin. Blood rushed to his groin and head at once and there seemed to be stability in this combination, a balance struck. He would neither rip Alvin's clothes off nor pass out. He stood calmly, coolly, and what would follow would follow.

Alvin said, "I really like your sweater."

"Thank you."

"Did you get it in Eureka?"

"No, I found it in a catalogue from a very small company in Healdsburg that manufactures their clothes by hand. Feel how much integrity the weave has?" And then he was saying that he had other sweaters like it, and perhaps Alvin wanted to see them—and Alvin did—whereupon the two of them gathered their things. As they filed out of the apartment Barry scanned the crowd and Rainie winked so subtly at him that maybe she didn't know. Maybe nobody would insert sex into his and Alvin's departure. And yet—what would it matter if they did? Would he make room in his head for their suspicions when at last he was full of certainty?

The next morning Joon-sup Kim called his friend Hyun-bae for their once-a-month California comparison, a Eureka versus San Diego debate. They had immigrated together to the Golden State from Pusan, South Korea, six years earlier when they were seventeen. Joon-sup, nicknamed Jack by his coworkers at the Better Bagel and only slightly shorter than the average American, with matted hair that hung like coils of moss down his back, lived in a Eureka tenement building occupied primarily by Laotians and Salvadorans who seemed all to have taken a vow of silence. He would step onto the lanai outside his second-story apartment and wave down at a freakishly over-groomed Latino family sitting in the courtyard around a murky half-drained swimming pool, eating *papusas*, Sunday best on a Tuesday afternoon. Not receiving a wave back, he'd follow up with a hale "Nice day for a picnic, know what I'm saying?" though it might be fifty-two degrees and overcast. One by one—man woman teenage boy little girl—they'd look up at him, never all together, and say nothing before pulling out more *papusas* from their Longaberger. "Weirdos," Joon-sup would mutter under his breath and then go back inside his dungeony bachelor pad.

He'd originally moved with Hyun-bae to southern California and then gone north after a vacation had convinced him that Eureka was where he was meant to be. There were trees and a temperate climate and the ease of mobility that only smaller cities offer. The smog was bearable. The people friendly. Plus, Joon-sup was something of a chef and would-be small businessman and had happily noted Eureka's dearth of Korean restaurants. Which, he discovered upon arriving there and getting a job as an assistant bagel maker and learning more about the area's cultural and ethnic components, was because there was a dearth of Koreans. Laotians, Vietnamese, and Cambodians, sure, plenty, enough not to render the phrase "northern California Asian population" completely nonsensical, but there was almost no one from his home country.

Hyun-bae liked to lord this over him—that Joon-sup was an island in a sea of round-eyes and boat people—but Joon-sup liked being unique, even if most whites eventually got around to asking him what he thought of Ho Chi Minh and My Lai, and he felt that this was a place where he would become American quicker than if there were a Korean community to fall back on. Here he had no choice but to go to all-night reggae jams and to bonfire parties at Moonstone Beach with the local university kids high on Native American herbs and the urgency of their environmental science major. Here he threw away the preppy stiff-collared shirts he'd bought in San Diego and adopted the local garb: alpaca tube hat, cotton-hemp hybrid long-sleeved pullovers, draw-string calico pants with neo-bell-bottom stylability, hefty mountain-climbing boots with graphite support system. Joon-sup went native.

His parents were disturbed by the pictures of himself he sent home, and by his increasingly foreign intonations when talking to them on the phone, for in his daily life the Korean language had become like a trophy sword kept over the mantel, an unused adornment. He had sex with American girls and seemed so at home in Humboldt that people from out of town pulled over while driving to ask him directions. Once when his van broke down he hitched a ride to a mechanic with a schoolteacher named Elaine who didn't know the first thing about efforts to strengthen the Environmental Protection

Agency's jurisdiction over the local logging industry, and when he informed her of them she was impressed and asked if he'd grown up in Eureka, which was a flattering question. He didn't plan ever to visit South Korea again. He was free.

At just after two in the afternoon Joon-sup finished reading thirty-four small-font pages of a loan application for the restaurant he wanted to open, the Joon-sup Experience. His head hurt and he had to go to a rally in Arcata for the Pacific black brant and other migratory waterfowl that annually made a stop in the shoals of Humboldt Bay, so he put down the hefty application and got in his turtle-green Volkswagen bus and put on a music collection of stoned hippie reggae standards about Marcus Garvey and sensimilla and the scandal of the Banana Republics. Lighting a sausage-sized joint, he backed out of his numbered parking space in front of his apartment, running bump over something that turned out to be a deflated football left out by one of the building kids. The joint smoldered as he came to a stop sign and his mother had called in the morning because she had met someone she wanted him to consider. Yes, she knew he was in America now and had adopted certain regrettable American customs and had once said, in a breach of filial respect so extreme it had left her speechless, that he would marry whomever he wanted, be she white, Asian, African, or transvestite, but she had met the most remarkable girl with a university degree and knew Joon-sup couldn't refuse to just look at this girl's picture and read her handwritten note about herself. He couldn't possibly be so insensitive. The package was on its way.

There was a trippy knocking sound in this dance-hall song, like an echoing submarine sonar noise, that was spacier for the subwoofer and thousand-dollar equalizer Joon-sup had recently installed in his van. He frowned at a red light on his dashboard that flickered on and off, thought he recognized the burrito maker standing outside Amigas Burrito, accelerated and worried about his lack of loan collateral, cursed his Asian hair for being so difficult to dreadlock, and figured that the picture of his "intended" would look nothing like she did in real life, that it would be doctored into the realm of fantasy. One of his old school friends worked in a photography studio in Pusan where ninety percent of the customers were women insisting that the studio airbrush to the extent of reconfiguring noses and lightening skin colors and trimming neck widths. Marriage was such a desperate business in South Korea, and what was Joon-sup supposed to do, see the picture and flip and—

Joon-sup snapped to attention. A man was standing in the middle of the road on the outskirts of Eureka, directly in front of Joon-sup's van traveling at 42 mph. The guy was maybe three seconds away, meaning that Joon-sup couldn't possibly stop in time, though he slammed on the brakes reflexively as a low scream got stuck in his throat. The man had appeared from out of nowhere, with his legs spread apart like he was about to draw in a shootout. Joon-sup thought, in a spasm of fear, *Holy fuck I am going to hit this guy* and braced himself for the impact, tensed and skidding and seeing everything in slow motion. His white knuckles on his enormous steering wheel, involuntarily closing his eyes and—

Nothing happened. No kerchunk and smashed metal and street-smeared pedestrian. Joon-sup was merely slowing to a stop just past Kinko's and a shoe store and a veterinary clinic, beyond the place in the road where the man had stood. Cars honked as they swerved around his parked van. Joon-sup craned his neck in every direction and then looked at the reefer in his hand. He'd had a hallucination. With his Gatling-gun heart going rat-a-tat-tat, Joon-sup shifted into gear and sped up onto the highway. He had to be cool, be cool. Cars continued to gust by and a highway patrol vehicle got a good look at him. Feeling the police stare, Joon-sup looked straight ahead and finally reached the speed limit and tried to seem unconcerned with the fact that he was holding a marijuana cigarette in plain view. It was only a cigar and Joon-sup was just a conscientious driver. But normal people looked around when they drove, so he made some natural-seeming head turns and saw the face of the highway patrolwoman, a Laotian in a flat-topped police hat. He smiled and made a little bow with his chin. She slitted her eyes and moved on.

When Joon-sup parked along the edge of the Arcata Plaza, still shaking, the Humans for the Pacific Black Brant rally was about forty people in clusters around an Earth Mother woman wearing a lavender sarong and standing on a large box with the word "soap" stenciled across every side. Two of Joon-sup's coworkers from the Better Bagel, Alleycat and Soulbrother, held hand-painted posters with colorful depictions of the black brant in flight. Majestic creatures, rare and fine with white bellies and noble dark wings, requiring large areas of undisturbed tundra in which to stop during their flights between the Arctic Coastal Plain and Baja California. Joon-sup had never seen one of these birds in the flesh, which was compelling evidence that something needed to be done to protect them. He had almost killed someone. Manslaughter. Plans to develop offshore oil drilling along the northern Humboldt seashore—and what a dangerous future the state faced without adequate electricity—were getting daily more serious, so a group of environmentalists and concerned local citizens had come to protest the quick fix of fossil fuel development. He had driven right through a man.

"Jack," said Alleycat in his feral purr, "what's the good word?" Alleycat was pot-bellied with a Vandyke goatee and Van Gogh red hair.

Joon-sup shrugged.

"The mayor was here a minute ago," said Soulbrother, "to bestow his blessing."

"It was a bestowal," agreed Alleycat.

"Said the city council has penned a letter to Congressman Sawyer demanding that the oil scouts be held in abeyance." Soulbrother wore a nest of Ugandan bead necklaces and held a jade-tipped staff in his left hand. Alleycat also had a staff, though his was a weathered piece of driftwood without ornamentation.

"Until it can be proven that the black brant doesn't nest in the sound."

"Except that everyone knows it does, so we'll get a permanent abeyance."

"It's crafty and it's just."

"The fate of the Pacific black brant is intricately tied to the fate of California itself," the woman with the microphone was saying. "If we allow its natural habitat to be torn up so Big Oil can come in and bleed the ocean for a few more years of gas dependency, what'll we have? We'll have a displaced black brant, which might just be an extinct black brant, and a wounded Humboldt Sound and further retardation of alternative energy research. Will the problem of California's energy needs be solved by however many millions of barrels of crude oil can be pumped out of our ocean? Of course not. There are far too many of us, and our needs are too great. All we'll have as a result is a permanently impaired ecosystem." She paused and looked searchingly at the crowd and someone made a low moaning noise. "Does anyone remember the Bligh Reef in the upper Prince William Sound, where Exxon spilled eleven million gallons of oil in 1989? While efforts to clean it up succeeded in some ways, there were still vestiges left over a decade later, in areas sheltered from weathering processes, such as in the subsurface under selected gravel shorelines, and in some soft substrates containing peat." A quick scan of the people around Joon-sup showed how unacceptable this was. Peat in the soft substrates? She might as well have been describing child pornography.

Joon-sup clasped his shaking hands behind his back and declined Alleycat and Soulbrother's suggestion that he get his own staff and join them for a walk through Arcata Park with some pot and a ukulele.


Earlier that day, Eve Sieber applied a darker shade of black lipstick than normal and wandered the aisles of Bonanza 88, noting how little effect the blue-light special on cutlery was having on the store's business. Despite the ad in the *Times-Standard*, potentially seen by over forty thousand people countywide, no one was thronging into the place to snatch up low-grade knives and forks and serving salad prongs. Was Eve surprised? No. The metal was cheap and flimsy. The spoons looked likely to bend under the strain of a bite of minute rice, and the forks were too small to provide the fulsome bites of steak and pasta that Eureka's bargain hunters demanded. Even with prices slashed below cost—and what a minor bloodbath it was—this sale barely competed with the deep-discount chain stores that, because of their size and intimacy with manufacturers, could afford to sell everything at the leanest rates.

Eve returned to the cash register and tried to figure out if she had a cavity in one of her upper left molars and organized the open box of chocolate eggs meant to be irresistible to women in the checkout line. Her manager, Vikram, was hanging a perforated-edged WARNING: GREAT SAVINGS HERE! sign over the cutlery display, a warning unheeded by the four customers listlessly examining paper cups and Limoges Nativity scenes. Vikram was a tall man with movie-star cheekbones and elephantine ears who'd moved to Eureka the previous year to work at a newly opened software development plant but was fired when the company's abysmal third-quarter earnings report led to layoffs of fifty percent of its employees. Vikram, by then in love with a shaggy-haired lesbian named Callie who worked at a travel store called Going Places, decided not to return to the Bay Area and instead to concentrate all of his psychological and romantic powers on winning Callie's affection. He described his life as an act of radical romanticism.

"Hey you!" Vikram said to Eve. "Could you do me the kindness to please bring two fishhooks here?"

Eve dug into the display supply box stashed under the checkout counter and brought them to Vikram. "We're never going to sell all these cutlery sets," she said, straightening a stack of boxes. "There's forty more in the back."

"Forty-four," he corrected her.

"So much the worse."

"That is the wrong attitude to have toward this fine Millennium Dreams Cutlery Set. In Gujurat we'd kill to get such inimitable craftsmanship, such loving attention to detail." Holding up a tarnished knife so flimsy that it almost wobbled, he whispered, "Such a bonanza of practical value."

The two of them laughed. Making fun of Bonanza 88's wares was among their favorite activities, though it usually led to an existential despondency—after all, they did nothing all day but sell these wares—from which they didn't fully recover until the end of the day.

"Do you know the bar Callie goes to, the Pleather Principle?" Vikram asked.

"I haven't been in it. Why?"

"The man who goes there might have an opportunity of knowing her in a more congenial setting than the Going Places."

"It's a lesbian bar."

"My point exactly."

"So men aren't welcome."

"What if the man looks like a woman?"

"You'd never get away with it and you'd end up humiliated. Maybe even beaten up by some hardcore bull dykes."

Vikram folded up the step ladder he'd used to hang the sign. "You're right. You see some things so clearly."

At lunch Eve went to the back office to use the phone. She had a responsibility as an adult to alert the police about the man she'd met at the Fricatash—not that the police were her or her friends' most trusted allies, but she acknowledged their authority in certain matters—and so called the sheriff's office. She was put on hold for twenty valuable lunch-break minutes, at which point she talked to an Officer Fuller, who took her statement and thanked her for the interesting information regarding the Leon Meed missing person case.

"What happens now?" Eve asked.

"With what?" Officer Fuller responded.

"Do I need to identify him or something?"

"He's not a criminal suspect."

"I know, but you don't need me to do anything else?"

"We'll be in contact if we do."

After this disappointing act of public service—she'd imagined being enlisted by the police as a consultant—Eve told Vikram she needed a longer lunch hour and then went to Amigas Burrito and talked to burrito maker Aaron Hormel, a primped skater she'd slept with when she was thirteen who now took occasional biology classes at College of the Redwoods and taught himself bass guitar and was someday going to move to Oakland and become either a veterinarian or a musician god. He'd been struck in the throat by a baseball bat in high school and suffered critical injuries to his vocal cords, so that he always sounded like he was breathing in while talking.

"Where's Ryan these days?" Aaron asked. "I haven't seen him at the Fricatash."

"Working at Muir as much as possible where—ooh, listen to this. So last week Principal Giaccone catches him doing junk in one of the bathroom stalls, he was passed out for just a moment, and Giaccone starts fulminating about—"

"Nice word."

"Thanks. So Giaccone was all, 'This is a school, godammit you little junkie! You can't be shooting up when kids are right outside playing basketball. What kind of place do you take this for? How long have you been working at Muir? I think it's time we reevaluated the desirability of your being here.'"

Aaron sprinkled cilantro onto a Veggie Behemoth burrito. "Did he get fired?"

"It turns out," Eve said, filling her cup with root beer, "that Ryan had walked by Giaccone's office the week before and heard him sexually blackmail a fourth-grade teacher, saying, 'You want to keep your job you're going to have to fuck me.'"

"No way."

"So Ryan mentioned what he'd heard and now his job is like lifetime guaranteed with a rosy little raise to boot. We're going to save up and move to Bel Air."

"That's so corrupt. Of Giaccone, I mean. Who was the teacher?"

"I don't know. Someone new."

"I used to want to fuck my fourth-grade teacher."

"Must be something about the job."

When Eve drove to Arcata after work she almost hit a van in front of her that braked in the middle of the road for no reason, and she was so flustered she didn't even think to honk and shout about what a stupid fucking reckless bastard its driver was. Saved her voice a workout. In Arcata she sat with Skeletor and Mike Mendoza on the Plaza and there was a political rally going on with some preachy woman and screechy loudspeakers so the three of them left to play billiards at a bar until Ryan joined them and they all did heroin in the basement storage room. All except Eve, who said to Ryan before they started, "After last night do you think you should be doing this?"

"Last night was what, was nothing." Ryan scanned his arm for usable veins, but they lurked below the surface with Loch Ness Monster furtiveness and he had to then strain his neck muscles to draw out an artery. It was horrible to look at. When he was done Skeletor tied off and shot up and Eve turned away.

"You went to the hospital," she said.

"I'm fine," said Ryan. "Don't be a worrywart."

Everyone smiled at the word "worrywart," including Eve, though for her it was a cover-up for feeling impotent and square and abandoned in the Old World by Ryan, who had crossed a chemical Bering Strait without her and was never coming back. And yet he, although gaunt and reluctant to look at her for any duration, knowing that their looks bespoke an intimacy out of place in the new scheme of things, was still the boy she'd once held on to for support and love and camaraderie, was still someone she had all this history with. All this immutable past. For in the beginning, before sex, when they used to meet in a rush before math class so he could copy her homework, his eyelashes impossibly long, the pencil eraser with which he poked her in play, the friends who couldn't distract him, his fingers grazing hers as they breathlessly reached for the classroom door, there had been a grander understanding than any she had thought possible. The kind found in storybooks. The kind found in pop songs. What was now but the lie of happily ever after, the emptiness of I'll always love you, and what could she do but act as though it weren't the saddest dissemblance imaginable?

"Worrywart, okay," she said, "but going to the hospital is serious."

Ryan was already melting with Skeletor and Mike into a bed of broken-down cardboard boxes as soft as fur, the three of them there in body but not in mind, placid and imperturbable expressions on their faces. Eve thought it was like a drink before the war, a decision by them to forget tomorrow's difficulties and instead to live in the moment by escaping it. Eve thought it was a way of disappearing and she would, if she could, give anything to keep Ryan from that fate.

That afternoon in Eureka, Lillith got on the bus after her McDonald's shift ended. She stared out the window until a man in a fishing vest sitting across from her asked for the time. The bus pulled up to a stop at Seventh and J. There was nothing behind the plastic bus shelter but a barren lot on which even crabgrass was having a hard go of it. A large black man climbed on board, scuffing the corrugated floor with his boots, and funneled change into the fare machine that made a satisfying burp when it tallied up a dollar. The black man sat behind Lillith and softly whistled "Greensleeves," which was odd to hear on a bus and very pleasing. Despite its lacking neopagan or even pagan connotations, it evoked for her a pastoral world in which there was a place for magic.

"You ride the bus a lot?" the fisherman asked her, for he was one of those guys who made conversation. Like it was his trade and he felt a professional obligation to talk to everyone about anything, though Lillith knew he did it not out of duty but because of a need to feel comfortable around strangers and because of a certain restlessness that drives people to reach out. She understood the impulse; she was often uncomfortable and wanted to be extroverted and would have said things like "You ride the bus a lot?" if she could.

"No," said Lillith, who was in her McDonald's clothes and aware of how alien they made her—uniformed people away from their jobs always seemed displaced and slightly suspicious, like escaped prisoners—"but today no one would give me a ride when my shift ended."

"The bus's not like it used to be. Doesn't give veteran discounts and doesn't go out on Cutten Road anymore."

"Yeah, it does," said the black man, who'd stopped whistling. "I'm going to Cutten right now."

The fisherman leaned to the left so that he could see past Lillith to the black man. "Don't you go to my AA meeting?" he asked.

"I haven't seen you there in a while," the black man replied.

The fisherman said, "I'm on a rickety wagon. Keeps throwing me off." The black man didn't smile. "But I'll get back on. Scout's honor."

Lillith gazed out the window at the passing Memorial Building with outdated MIA and Bring-Back-the-POWs posters and, at the end of Lincoln Street, Eureka High School, where she was in her junior year, though she could be a graduate student it felt like she'd been there so long. A beautiful man boarded the bus and sat in a window seat where Lillith saw him in profile, the slender eyebrows and golden skin and strawberry mouth. He had a thin white scar on his temple and messy brown hair. She coughed loudly and he didn't look her way. She knew she wasn't in his league, but still it would have been nice to see him head on. Life was a million desires unrequited. And Sam. Sam wasn't worth her obsession given how many options she had; really Sam was just a terrorist who'd taken her thoughts hostage and wouldn't let them go, had even stopped negotiating for them, had cut off all communication and gone underground and so where could she begin to track them down? It was a crisis, but crises passed.

"Take care now," said the fisherman when she got up to disembark.

At home her sister Maria was on the phone and she had to wait two hours before being able to check her messages: Tina and Franklin and still no Sam and this was the absolutely last day she would accept him so he was throwing away a chance at immense happiness. Whatthefuckever. Tina was waitressing at the Red Lion Inn lounge when Lillith called her house and got into the stupid nitpicking conversation with Tina's brother about when she was going to give him free stuff at McDonald's. Then she called Franklin, who told her that he and she and Tina needed to talk about the Wiccan convocation from the night before, that she wasn't going to believe what had happened. Twenty minutes later he picked her up and they drove to the Red Lion Inn with the car almost dying at every stoplight, Franklin putting his hand on the dashboard in a faith healing gesture.

They walked in and Tina waved at them from where she stood distributing beers to a table of six white-shirted guys near a television broadcasting the prize fight out of Las Vegas. The television was muted with closed-caption subtitles for the hearing impaired. The white-shirted guys studiously read the black-outlined words scrolling across the bottom of the screen, their faces like stock traders' in the Pit when the markets rumble, and then shouted their agreement or disagreement or bafflement at how the commentators could say something so stupid about such a clear punch, and then went back to reading and beer drinking.

"Who are those people?" asked Lillith when Tina came over on a two-minute break to sit with her and Franklin.

"The kitchen staff of Shanghai-Lo. They come for pay-per-view stuff."

"None of them are Chinese."

"Shanghai-Lo isn't so authentic. They get all their recipes from a 1960's edition of *The Joy of Oriental Cooking*. I'd never go again if I didn't love their fried wontons."

"Those are good," said Lillith.

"So what are you guys doing here?"

Franklin said, "I have to tell you about last night's convocation."

"He's being mysterious about it," said Lillith. "On the ride over he didn't say anything. And I begged."

"You didn't offer me a blow job."

"There'd have to be something for me to blow."

Franklin smirked and tapped his thumbs together and said, "So we start off at the convocation talking about the RenFair next month and this ayurvedic bookstore opening in Arcata and how there've been more attacks on neopagans in Kansas, and then Kathy stands up and she's in full effect with the sequin gown and the sapphire rings and the head wrap and she looks, you know, the complete sorceress, like she's ready to separate the hydrogen and oxygen atoms out of a glass of water, and she makes this speech about how a local guy named Leon Meed is on the Astral Plane right now, as in at this very second he's over there with the Goddess and the Horned Consort and all the spirits."

"What do you mean on the Astral Plane?" asked Tina. "A live person?"

"She says he's been there for a week."

"How would a live person get to the Astral Plane?"

"Kathy thinks the Horned Consort took him. The guy is a burl sculptor, and she says the Horned Consort fell in love with his statues and kidnapped him. She says she doesn't know for sure how it happened. But what's even more bogus is that Kathy thinks the guy is going back and forth between here and the Astral Plane. Then she challenges us to come up with a spell to bring him back. She gives it to us as an assignment, like we're her students or something."

"And then someone put her in a straitjacket?" asked Tina.

"You know how people never confront Kathy. And the thing is, a guy named Leon Meed really did go missing last week—there's a police investigation—and people have reported seeing him since then, which according to Kathy is proof positive."

"She gives witches a bad name."

"We just sat there when she was done explaining it. She wants to have a special meeting on Sunday to talk about our strategy for rescuing this guy."

Tina waved at her manager, who was pointing a finger at his watch from behind the bar, and mouthed "I *know* I *know*" and said, "I've got to get back to work. Maybe we should find a way to excommunicate her, if she's going to keep saying such dumb things."

"It's not dumb," said Lillith quietly.

"What?" said Tina.

"It's not dumb. I've seen him."

"Seen who?" said Franklin.

"The guy who disappeared, Leon Meed. At a show at the Fricatash last Friday. He was talking to that girl Eve you know she's going out with Ryan Burghese? and then he disappeared." As Lillith said this she looked at the table in front of her and saw an ampersand crack in the table's surface.

Tina waved her white dish towel at her manager like a peace offering and stood up. "Very funny. I'll see you later."

Lillith didn't indicate in any way that she was joking, and when Tina left Franklin said, "You're not serious."

"I am. You can not believe me but I saw him. And if other neopagans are saying that Leon's on the Astral Plane, then that makes sense to me."

"Why didn't you say anything before now?"

"I thought it was because I was drinking. I thought, I don't know what I thought. But the point is we've got to help bring him back if that's what Kathy's saying. We've got to cast the spell."

"You're becoming a Wicca fundamentalist."

"No, I'm not."

Franklin said, "Hmm."

Lillith said, "Hmm."

Then they smiled and they'd been best friends since they were five-year-olds and there were some things that they instantly forgave in each other.

# ⊣ 4 ⊢

"Jim!" said Shane. The third annual Boys in the Wood racquetball tournament was in midcontest at CalCourts, where Shane Larson and Jim Sturges stood next to each other in line to get shower towels from the front desk. Broad-bottomed women in stretch pants and sports bras strode purposefully to their aerobics workouts and weight-diminishing sauna sessions. Their thighs and hair were massive. Televisions tuned to different twenty-four-hour sports channels perched on all four walls like bird nests, a permanent squawk, competing for the attention of exercisers and exercise-hangers-on standing below, where the semifinals of the racquetball C division were about to begin on courts 3, 4, and 5, and the judges were being asked over the PA system to take their positions in the observation areas. "Man," said Shane, raising his voice a chirpy octave, "it's been forever. Where are you living these days? I'm married, did you know that?"

Shane was a changed man. He knew Jim would be expecting the old Shane: the Shane with skinhead leanings who sometimes beat up middle-aged men with families just because they were middle-aged men with families, the Shane who'd once dropped seven hits of acid and baseball-batted his way into a Rolls-Royce parked implausibly in downtown Eureka in order to defecate on its virgin-calf leather upholstery before being arrested. But eight transformational years had passed since they'd seen each other, during which Shane had embraced his family's Mormonism, the Larson faith for three generations already, and become an upstanding citizen.

"I didn't know that," said Jim, smiling mechanically. "Congratulations."

He has no idea how far I've come, thought Shane, who dispensed with the small talk by saying, "I've stopped drinking and smoking and extramarital sex." He stared penetratingly at his old friend. "Those were a fool's paradise."

"I see," Jim said.

But did Jim see? Could he comprehend the metamorphosis? He'd never been as ultraviolent and antisocial as Shane, and in fact he'd been something of a wet blanket about fighting and unprovoked cruelty back in high school, but that didn't mean he hadn't been a sinner. Because he had. Jim had fornicated with abandon. He'd drunk alcohol to the point of bodily harm. He'd had godless ways. And although time could also have changed him, Shane didn't think it had. No, Shane didn't see salvation in Jim's tired, distracted face.

Shane said, "I'm working now for Morland Memorial Services. It's customer relations, some floor sales. I'm selling caskets mainly, but recently I've been getting contracts to do land plots. It's a growth industry. The baby boomers are nearing their time. What'd you say you're doing?"

Jim got his towel from the putty-chinned receptionist and gave it a quick inspection. "I'm in Los Angeles. Just home visiting for a while."

Shane tried not to think about Jim's inability to appreciate how far he'd come since they'd known each other in high school—because it was a major failure of imagination—and instead he thought about the business opportunity presenting itself. Let the past be the past. His great insight was: friends and acquaintances could be customers, and vice versa. "I know what you're probably thinking in LA," he said. "You're probably worried because you have no idea where to be buried in such a huge city, right? I mean, down there where you don't know anybody and everything's so anonymous. It'd scare me to death if I was you."

Jim stared in the direction of the change room and said, "Honestly I haven't thought about it."

Shane tucked his towel under his arm. "That's what I'm saying. Why would you when the thought's so scary? Being buried in some big city all alone? Jim, you're going to want to come back to Eureka when you die, where your roots are. I think we should talk about this; I think it could be good for us. How long are you in town?"

Jim pivoted on one foot, his body aching toward the showers. "Not long," he said.

"Let me give you my card." Shane pulled out a buttermilk business card with blue embossed lettering: Shane Larson, Associate Sales Representative, Morland Memorial Services, 555 2432. "What's your number in town? I'll call you."

"Actually I'm busy for the rest of my visit, so I'll have to get ahold of you later."

Shane, knowing that Jim hadn't a clue how to conduct himself righteously in the eyes of God, that he was, spiritually speaking, a directionless person in need of guidance, said, "I have a better idea. We'll talk it over in the shower. I can get you a great price on a site right now. You like the Humboldt Overview Cemetery? Who doesn't, right? Imagine a place on the hill there, overlooking the bay, in a gorgeous casket made of beautifully contrasting white pine and mahogany, and with a crisp gold satin lining. Think solid mahogany swing-bar handles and sliding lid supports. Jim, I could take you down to the store after we shower and show you the displays and we could settle this today. Can you imagine how good you'd feel?"

Shane was really in the zone now, was in one of his total empathic mind melds, for despite his religious advantage over his erstwhile friend, he *was* Jim Sturges at that moment, seeing what he saw, anticipating the relief of putting the whole burial question to rest and maybe opening himself up to a higher power.

"Thanks," Jim said, "but I really don't have time."

"It isn't for me that I'm asking this. It's for you."

"I'm sure it is, but seriously. I'm not interested."

Shane closed the gap between them by six inches and spoke quietly, confidentially, importantly, as sports commentators droned in the background, "Jim, death isn't one of those things you can afford not to think about. You may want to, and you may get away with it in the short term, but it's there waiting for you. I don't know if you know this but I've become a Mormon, and that's because I had a big realization a few years ago that we're not here forever. I know what you're thinking, news flash, right?" Brief chuckle and then po-face. "But it had never really come home to me before I was in my car driving along and I heard on the radio about a guy down in Matole who ran out into the street to get his son's basketball and was hit by a car. Died on the spot. And I got to thinking, I don't know why, it was just pressing on my mind, but I began to think about what it meant to run into the street to get a basketball, a reflex motion, your mind on what's for dinner and how it's time to mow the lawn again and a new soreness in your left knee, when wham! you're dead. You don't see it coming even though you know it has to eventually. Death is an invisible speeding train and you're standing on the track somewhere, you don't know where exactly, could be far down by the river or could be two feet away. It comes back to we all have to go sometime. And where we go depends on what we choose to do while we're on this planet. You need to ask yourself. The soul and the body. Have you planned for them? You can either take out insurance—and we're talking a tiny premium, month by month you won't even feel it except as a feeling of comfort and security—so that you know you're covered, or you can be a miser and end up rotting in the ground in some anonymous city with your soul burning forever."

Shane had never expressed it so eloquently. He'd linked—pull the metal chain, feel its strength—his own personal epiphany with burial services and the afterlife. This matter of supreme importance—this primary undergirding—made him both vulnerable to scorn—people always sneered at the truth tellers, for guilty consciences are drowned out by nothing so well as jeers and ridicule—and strangely confident. After all, Shane was only human, he was an insignificant mortal, but the magnitude of God and of his duty to Him were commensurate. Shane was conjuring the infinite, evoking the ineffable. He felt measurable in joules. To decorate His crown.

Jim draped the towel around his neck and crossed his arms—what a tell! what a giveaway that he took this seriously and felt implicated!—and said, "I don't want to offend you, and I'm sure your death episode was the real thing, but monotheism doesn't resonate for me. When I die I'm going to donate all my organs and be cremated. But I appreciate what you've said and I'm going to leave now. Good to see you again."

Jim walked away and Shane stared after him. How can anyone be so tone deaf? Obstinacy is what it is. Denial. People's hearts get hard. They refuse to see anything but their own version of things. Sad, really. Sad.

So sad that the more Shane stood there thinking about it, as bruised racquetball players filed past him to get towels and chat with the counterwoman and buy a compensatory light beer, the angrier he got, like who the fuck do these people think they are? They're handed truth on a platter and do they accept it graciously, maybe even appreciatively because after all it is their immortal soul that's in question, I mean excuse me for trying to save you from the eternal fire, or do they refuse the platter and say, *No thanks, I'm not in the mood*? Not in the mood? *I don't want to offend you blah blah blah, but monotheism doesn't resonate for me.* Doesn't resonate? Like faith is some kind of bell that you ring and if it doesn't produce the right echo, you put cotton in your ears and head for the hills? *I'm going to leave now.* And did you see Jim's face when he said that, with that left-lip sneer that was part disrespect and part you're-a-nutcase-who-has-to-be-handled-delicately-or-you'll-detonate? It was so condescending, and who was Jim anyway but some nowhere man living in LA and thinking that he was cool enough to dismiss what was most fundamental as pure hokum? Like, *Save your fairy tale for the local rubes who don't know better.*

Shane's fingernails dug into the flesh of his palms and he felt heavy and congested. He hadn't had an alcoholic drink in four years. He turned to the counter and ordered a Budweiser. His wife, Lenora, was walking around Old Town in Eureka with her parents, who were visiting from Salt Lake City for a week, getting ice cream at Bon Boniere and trying on Celtic outfits at the Irish Shoppe that he would be angry if she bought. They pooled their finances now, which basically meant that Shane paid for everything since he was the only one with a job. He finished his beer and, an old habit rising from the murk of memory, squashed it into a thin disk on his right leg. *I appreciate what you've said and I'm going to leave now.* What a patronizing son of a bitch.

"Hey," he said, addressing the counterwoman, "I need another one, on my tab."

"You know we send an itemized bill, don't you?"

"You think my wife pays the bills?"

"Just thought I'd mention it."

It was like he'd never been away. After four more beers Shane was feeling the old body carbonation, like there were air pockets in him rising, making him a light and humming creature, clearing his brain and his vision and the space between him and any challengers out there. *I'm sure your death episode was the real thing, but monotheism doesn't resonate for me.* Shane laughed and ran a hand through his short black hair, exposing its advanced widow's peak. He rubbed his beak-shaped nose. Did Jim think he could treat Shane like a fool and then no hard feelings? *Whoops, didn't mean to shit all over your most sacredly held beliefs, see you around.* Shane stacked the five aluminum disks on the counter and walked toward the showers. Pushed through the swing doors and into the steam of the locker room. A bunch of bald fat fucks sitting astride padded benches talking about you should have heard what counsel for the defense wanted to plea bargain with, and I was netting sixty a year on property speculation in

Tahoe until the county increased regulations on undeveloped land that was more than thirty percent forested. Shane passed them by and stepped on the bare foot of a lobster-faced man resting his elbows on his knees, and when the man yelped in pain Shane told him to shut the fuck up. He was six foot four and his muscles were so toned and there was so much strength in his every sinew every atom and he was so light he could just fly up to some obstacle and overpower it yes because he was energy he was forward momentum and woe unto him who denies the truth and that's what that fucker Jim was he was a truth denier and it was people like him who kept the whole world from achieving peace and brotherly love and the fruits promised the human race by a benevolent God. One bad apple. Past the sinks and the weigh scales and the towel closet, through more swinging doors and Shane was unswervingly determined, like a Tomahawk missile, to find his target. But Jim wasn't in the showers or the saunas or the hot tub and Shane checked everywhere twice and he was forward momentum.

"Hey," he said, pausing in the hot tub room, to the tub's only occupant, a bearded man leaning front-forward into a white water jet, "you see a guy in here a minute ago who's got brown hair, in his mid-twenties, looks like a real yahoo?"

The man turned his head to face Shane. "Nope."

"You sure?"

"Yeah."

"I've seen you in here before. What's your name?"

"Alvin."

Shane was floating there, surveying the scene, the mist rising from the tumultuous water and Alvin Driscoll facing the back wall of the hot tub with his pelvis positioned where water was surging out and wasn't that weird. "What are you doing?" Shane asked. "Are you sticking your dick in the jet?"

Alvin slid away from the jet and was visible only from the neck up, his curly black hair thick with water droplets. "No, I was just— Nothing."

"Yes, you were. You had your dick in the jet." Shane's eyes gleamed with rheumy mirthlessness and he was light light light. "What are you going to do, cum into this public hot tub and anyone who gets in it later will be taking a bath in your sperm? Do you know how disgusting that is?"

"I don't know you. You'd better leave me alone."

"And what are you going to do about it, huh? You fucking queer. I bet you sit in here and stare at everybody's dick while your own dick's in the jets. Oh, man, that's—"

"Leave me alone."

"'Leave me alone,' yeah all right." Shane turned to go and put his hand on the door and then stopped. "Just one thing first. Stand up. I want to see if you've been sticking your dick in the jets of this public hot tub. Just stand up. If you don't have a hard-on, then fine, I'm wrong."

"Go away."

"I'll kick your ass, you little faggot, if you don't stand up right now."

Alvin didn't move, and within a second Shane flew into the water—he was all energy—and pulled him up by the armpit and saw that Alvin indeed had a flagging erection, all varicose veined and darkly pink, whereupon Shane began hitting him, first on the side of the head and soon Alvin's ear and cheekbone were bleeding in a diluted smear of sweat and mist and blood, then in the chest and the groin and back to the face—great thumps and Shane's knuckles were aglow with pain and light—and the smacking sound on the wet skin was like a horse whip and a few blows glanced off though most of them connected and with one well-aimed swing Shane heard and felt Alvin's nose snap which precipitated almost immediately Alvin lowering his guard and slumping into the water on the verge of losing consciousness. Shane was lifting him up again for more comeuppance when he felt two huge men—weight trainers on the CalCourts staff— on either side of him in the hot tub, grabbing his arms and yanking them sharply behind his back, so that Shane screamed with pain as he was dragged out and into the locker room for ground restraint.

Pinioned on the floor, his eyes thrashing about in their sockets, he saw Jim Sturges at the edge of a group of onlookers staring down at him, and he thought, There's Jim Sturges. I hope he gives me a call soon, because I could set him up with a nice spot at Humboldt Overview Cemetery. The soul and the body. Doesn't he know that they're one and the same?

Lying there with heavy breathing all around—the big guys were really in a lather now—he relaxed and gave himself over to what came next. He ceded control to Him, ready once more to do necessary work.

That morning, Elaine Perry had woken up forty minutes before school was to start with a tingly dread that she hadn't done something she was supposed to do the day before. Oh God, what was it? Call her mother on her birthday, pick up her friend Beth's mail so that it didn't look like she was out of town, pay the rent to her irascible and threat-happy landlord? Or was it something closer to home, a kind word unsaid to her son Abraham whose failure to make the intramural basketball team wasn't because he was too short but because he wasn't any good? Despite the effort. Despite his putting on shoes whose price per square inch was higher than a Pacific Heights mansion's, and his grabbing the two-tone ball, and his walking seven blocks every day after school to practice at the recreation center near the marina, where she knew from his clipped "all right" when he got home that it hadn't gone all right, that he'd flailed about while his sure-footed peers grabbed and dribbled and shot and rebounded and left him increasingly untrusted on the Outside. But did she press it? Did she tell him what he already knew, that nobody gets good at anything unless they pick themselves up again and again after falling down? Or did she suggest that he shouldn't knock himself out on a sport that may not be his thing, that maybe he'd be better at soccer or lacrosse or even ballet? Or, what was desirable given the attraction and repulsion of both of these approaches, did she instead say nothing and hope that he learned from this while she explored job opportunities in southern California and instructed her once-a-week yoga class and went to neighborhood parties for a night of how-are-you, the most disingenuous question in the world? While her marriage to Greg was so very ended.

She went on to have a strange day at school. During lunch she was alone for five minutes in the faculty lounge with Principal Giaccone, where to avoid intimacy she'd complained about the insoluble clumping of powdered nondairy coffee creamer to the point where she was sincerely angry—she read aloud the creamer's ingredient list as though filibustering—and Giaccone's smile faded and he stopped voicing his agreement and started regarding her like she was a park bench bag lady. Then others came in and she slipped away and felt it all unraveling. Ten minutes in a bathroom stall, hugging herself and staring at the dented toilet paper dispenser. Just three weeks before, she'd pulled off a sexual derring-do with Giaccone, and where had that strength come from? Why didn't she have it now? The graffiti on the bathroom wall was alternately innocent and enraged. *Joseph is cute. Brenda is a bitch needs her ass kicked.* Elaine felt alternately innocent and enraged. Oh to be unwavering in the face of what threatened you.

After she left the bathroom she went to the *South Pacific* dress rehearsal from four to six o'clock in the gym, where the disturbance happened.

"I just," said Petey, the only student not wearing his costume, "if I go to Bali Ha'i and spend all this time with Bloody Mary's daughter, then it'll look like I'm in love with her."

"You *are* in love with her," Elaine said, pleased that the boy cared about the plot of *South Pacific* but dismayed that he grasped so little of it. "The point of 'Happy Talk' is that you and she fall in love. And when you sing 'Younger Than Springtime' to her, it's a love song about how lucky you are to have found her. In fact the play is about your love affair as much as it is about Nellie and Emile's."

Petey nodded and then shook his head. "Yeah, but my girlfriend's going to see it and I don't want to kiss Alice in front of her. It would be, she'd be mad, plus Alice is kind of I don't know, I don't want to kiss her."

"This is a play. People do things in plays that they wouldn't do in real life. The audience will know this. Your girlfriend will know this. Besides, you won't actually kiss Alice. You're going to be behind a tree so that it only *looks* like you're kissing."

Elaine hoped she didn't sound too impatient, because if Petey dropped out—and the cast's collective morale was hitting lower and lower nadirs—the show would not go on. It would be the end of her directing venture, which might prompt the school board to try to override Giaccone's decision to keep her on, and it would be impossible to find another job midyear, and Greg was going to fight whatever alimony figure she and her lawyer suggested—he'd come right out and told her to expect a Crimean War divorce—so she had to keep these kids happy.

Elaine called everyone to their places and Petey, whom she imagined was a popular eighth grader given his relatively clear skin and height and regular features, did the scene admirably and with a certain enthusiasm she hadn't seen before, and she thought another disaster had been averted. Every now and then the other shoe doesn't drop.

"All right," Elaine said in the midrange shouting voice she used to direct, "that was great, Petey. Take a break. Now could I have everyone who's in the 'I'm Gonna Wash That Man Right Outa My Hair' scene come to the front of the beach, please?" From different conversational circles five girls gathered before an eight-foot-high construction-paper backdrop with a custard-yellow sun and palm trees and gold sand beach; three of the girls looked bored and one nervous and one eagerly attentive. "This time remember to keep your elbows up when you're pretending to wash your hair. It'll make it look authentic since we can't actually get your hair wet."

"Do I really have to do that lame two-handed wave during the 'wave that man right outa my arms' part?" one of the bored girls asked.

"Yes."

"It's so lame."

"I'm sorry you feel that way."

"I don't feel it. I know it."

"This is a *musical*. It's about larger-than-life gestures. Think *West Side Story*—wait, no, don't think that. Think *Moulin Rouge* or *Chicago* and how animated everybody is in those. We want to be full of energy, full of life. The thing about musicals is that they're an answer to boredom. People in them get excited doing even small things as a way to show that life can be fully lived and not just tolerated. You girls are at an age where you still get worked up over boys and clothes and music, but as you get older those passions dry up and living becomes a chore instead of a chance to love and be connected with others and do something worthwhile. Age drains that from you. Musicals are replenishing."

God, she sounded morbid and unbalanced and old and proselytizing for a genre she didn't much care about. The attentive girl nodded and the nervous one looked worried and the bored ones made weak efforts to stifle their laughter. Elaine felt like an idiot in front of the almost-laughing girls. She wished she could concentrate on the girl who was sympathetic to her instead of on the haughty girls' ennui and disdain, on a contempt that shrank her like an Alice in Wonderland pill. She told herself to snap out of it. There was no need to fixate on the negative when the positive was just as real. Shift your thoughts a little. And then suddenly an older man was there onstage doing a backward dance with his arms windmilling between the girls and Elaine, and he fell to the ground on his elbows. Elaine forgot about her humiliation. The man was unshaven and looked rabid and desperate, like a mistreated animal recently uncaged.

"Excuse me?" Elaine said, walking over to him and gesturing for everyone to stand back. "Excuse me but this is a closed rehearsal. What are you doing here?"

The man looked up at her and got hesitantly to his feet and took erratic steps as though playing Pin the Tail on the Donkey. "I'm sorry to bother you."

"Well, it's not okay. Now get out, please. I don't recognize you. You don't work here, do you?" She was responsible for the safety of eighteen children and each was so vulnerable against the world's deranged. The man looked like a prisoner of war. In theory Elaine felt goodwill toward crazy people, she empathized with their state of permanent conundrum—and which of us doesn't feel that our own semi-permanent conundrum could upgrade to permanent at a moment's notice?—though in practice she felt uncomfortable around them. They smelled bad and said insensible things and were depressing to look at. And although they usually didn't mean any harm and suffered from a serious disability, which meant that Elaine had a moral imperative to help or at least to understand them, facing this scruffy man made her mad.

"Where is here?" he asked.

"This isn't twenty questions. Out. Now. Let's go." Without thinking, Elaine clapped her hands three times and then pointed to the exit. "There are children present. Can you summon the decency to leave before you scare them to death? I have nothing against you personally, but—but how did you get in here, anyway?"

The man slapped the dust off his pants and didn't make any threatening movements. "Something strange is happening to me. Is this a school?"

"Muir Elementary."

"Yes, you're right. And you are?"

"Elaine Perry. Now I really—"

"My name is Leon Meed."

"Could you please leave?"

"Yes, I'm sorry."

She stared at him crossly and with a slight body tremor he moved in the direction of the exit, sidestepping two of the boys who played sailors. They regarded him like an enemy stowaway they'd let escape—what was their captain thinking?—and Elaine's heart beat so quickly she might have had tachycardia. In large enough doses fear was a stimulant; instead of passivity and restraint it inspired conviction and courage. The man carefully closed the door behind him after failing at first to do it when his coat got in the way. This minor difficulty of his reminded Elaine of her father, of a similar disorientation. Minds and bodies gave way. Strength was humbled. The proudest were brought low. A King Lear growing inside of every adult. And as she balanced the relief she felt from surviving the confrontation with her sympathy for its protagonist, she felt that sometimes we get exactly what we need from situations that promise nothing.

At the Eureka Public Library, Prentiss Johnson picked up and loaded onto his rolling cart two oversized children's books, a guide to crocheting, a biography of the apostle Paul, and a style magazine telling middle-aged white women how to dress, decorate, and entertain other white women who bought the same magazine. He was in the reading lounge, where people perused books and periodicals until they fell asleep and then groggily woke up and did little self-alerting head shakes and walked away in a greater or lesser hurry, leaving whatever they'd been reading in unordered heaps on the coffee tables placed there for this purpose. Prentiss's job was to clean up the mess left behind. His was a rage for order.

"Hi, Prentiss," said Mary Ellen, his supervisor and the woman who met with his parole officer to talk about Prentiss's work habits almost as regularly as he did. She was in her early forties, full-figured for her petite frame, wore her hair in a bun, had big horn-rimmed glasses. You didn't look at her without thinking that she was playing up the librarian stereotype, someone who looks so exactly as you'd expect that it has to be an act.

"What's the forecast?" he asked.

Mary Ellen looked at the recumbent kids and adults and shelves upon shelves of books with little gaps needing to be filled where things had been taken out. "Heavy travel guides early in the morning with some scattered magazines around noon. By midafternoon there will be clear stacks in the history, life science, and advanced mathematics sections."

"It's incredible how you do this."

Mary Ellen sifted through the books on Prentiss's cart. "We still haven't gotten back any of our witchcraft or magic books. I checked and a patron named Franklin Strosser has had all of them for eight months. Some of the kids are getting upset. I don't know how many overdue reminders we've sent him."

She clucked her tongue and left. Prentiss pushed his cart to the children's section and began inserting books into their call number slots. He had to meet this dude Alvin after work on account of Alvin was going to be his new AA sponsor. Since his drunk driving trial ended two months earlier, his second such arrest that year, Prentiss had been attending meetings five nights a week, two hours a session. Every spare second he had outside of work he was in a meeting. He took to calling himself Mr. Meeting and would say, rubbing a little lotion onto the ashy patches of his skin, finding a knot in his neck and massaging it out, "Mr. Meeting, what shall we discuss with the people this evening? Our love affair with Chivas Regal? Those one-night stands with Cutty Sark? The tenderness of a twelve-pack of Coors?" At his second-ever meeting, when he had to choose a sponsor to be his moral support and on-call advisor, he chose Jamal because Jamal was black and had a born-again commitment to sobriety, a real fire in his eyes when he discussed the evils of the sauce. Man wouldn't touch root beer. Took Prentiss aside and said, "The others here, forget them. Some are giving it the old college try, but let me tell you they possess weaknesses that're going to topple them; they carry thirst in their souls they ain't never going to quench. You stick with me and I'm a help you put a stopper in the bottle for good." But then Jamal sustained a workplace injury that may or may not have happened because he'd been drinking, and the AA leaders suggested that Prentiss select Alvin as an interim sponsor. This fruit-at-the-bottom dude who never said anything at meetings except to thank everybody for speaking—"Thanks, Sherice," Alvin would say, "I know just how you feel, I think we all do"—and he'd smile sometimes at Prentiss in a way that was probably just friendly but that could be read in other ways, too. *The Little Engine That Could,* now that was a classic. Bona fide. As a kid, Prentiss would stare at the anthropomorphized hero of the book, a train with a round face and big shiny cheeks and bug eyes, as the train struggled up the steep hill, and Prentiss's fists would clench in solidarity and hope. It was a powerful story, the underdog triumphing over adversity in the end. Prentiss was an underdog, and just like the Little Engine That Could he'd planned as a kid to fight his way to the top against crazy odds, maybe become president of a business or an anesthesiologist someday. His aunt Edwina was an anesthesiologist. But then life interfered. Life introduced him to the world of spirits, and now he was struggling to get out.

From the children's section Prentiss rolled his cart to the fiction and nonfiction territories, and then back to the drop-off bins, where more books awaited him. The hours passed. He took a break on the library's roof and had a grilled turkey sandwich and called his mother to see if she wanted to see a movie that evening but she was wracked with the arthritis pretty bad and didn't feel like going anywhere. His shift ended and he said good-bye to Mary Ellen and the people at Information who were always debating the merits of this movie versus that movie, never books. On his way out he stopped at the computer station to check his email.

"Excuse me, but I'm signed up for this computer," said a woman behind him.

"I don't see your name," Prentiss said, not looking back but instead pointing to a clipboard with a blank signup sheet on which people wanting to use the computers put their name and the time.

The woman picked up the clipboard and then set it down. "This sheet is empty. There was one on top with my name that someone must have stolen."

"I work here and there's lots of so-called thefts and what have you, but nobody ever runs off with the signup sheet."

He turned around and gave her a shame-on-you look.

She folded her arms. "I was here for twenty minutes and just went to the bathroom for a second. There was a woman at this computer and I was in line behind her." The library lights flickered for a few seconds and stabilized. "I just have to check if I got a certain email. Can I do that very quickly, please?"

"If you'd've asked nicely from the beginning instead of pulling some imaginary jurisdiction, I might have said yes. As is, I'm inclined to sit here till closing."

"I didn't lie to you. Someone really did steal that sheet."

"You only making it worse for yourself."

Prentiss had started to feel playful but stopped when he saw the woman's eyes water. She didn't say anything, just opened her mouth a little so she could take deep breaths without making any noise and then turned around and walked away. Some people get all in a huff, take things so personally and it's on account of their being so sensitive. Overemotional. Too human for their own good. Prentiss felt a twisting inside and got up to follow her.

"Hey, I'm sorry," he said when he caught up with her at the exit door. "You go on ahead with the computer. I was just playing."

"No," she said. She was crying formless tears, smiling politely. "This isn't because of the computer. I've been— It's personal. Thanks, though."

Prentiss wanted to give this woman a cup of hot chocolate. Why, he didn't know. Lots of people out there had their sadnesses and inexplicable pains and he didn't go out of his way to help them along. But there was something about this situation, and then also—

"Don't I know you?" he said.

The woman's complexion had red patches at her temples and the tops of her cheeks. She was pretty in the way you thought old Dust Bowl women were pretty, the ones Prentiss had seen in the Walker Evans photographs that led off *Let Us Now Praise Famous Men*, an interesting book that some codger had left out one afternoon. With a tan, flat, freckled face, she was maybe thirty-two and had big searching blue eyes that were as light and dark as dusk. Chin-length straw-colored hair that curled up at the end like musical notation. She wore a navy blazer and black slacks.

"I don't think so," she said, rubbing away her teary mascara and leaving grainy erasures across her red temples. War paint.

"That's not a line I'm giving you," he said. "I really do think . . . I think we— Oh yeah, I remember."

She frowned and stepped out of the way of an older gentleman with a walker and examined Prentiss's face closely. "You do? When was it?"

But Prentiss was shaking his head now and smiling. "That's cool, we don't need to get into it."

"Oh God, was it at the Jambalaya last month? I was drinking and my friends said I did some stuff on the dance floor. Embarrassing stuff."

"No, wasn't there. If you can't remember, that's all right. Nothing illegal."

The woman made a face like she'd swallowed a bug. "Oh God. I remember. We met at that guy's house, didn't we? Yes, we did and you were in the kitchen with the toy mouse. Oh God."

"My house, too. Me and Frost are roommates."

"Oh God."

"Nothing to be ashamed of."

"Are you kidding? I didn't know him and we met at the Rathskel-lar and neither of us has called the other and it was such a sleazy encounter all around."

"If it'd make you feel better Frost doesn't usually bring women home."

"What if you don't tell him you saw me?"

"I could do that. But first you got to do me a favor."

The woman squinted as a patch of sunlight hit her eyes. "Oh yeah?"

From the wariness of her voice Prentiss could tell she thought he was trying to hit on her, and he felt bad. Not because he really was hitting on her—the thought hadn't crossed his mind—but because now that it *had* crossed his mind he knew what her reaction would be. He said, "I want you to go in there and use that computer. I was just fooling around on it, nothing dramatic. You go back inside and check on the email. Grows like the national debt you don't watch out."

The woman deliberated for a minute and then smiled and held out her hand. "I'm Justine," she said.

"Nice to meet you again. I'm Prentiss."

"You work here?"

"For a little while now."

"And you get to be around books all day."

"I do all variety of fun things like put back the same *How to Get Rich Without Trying* book every other afternoon. I figure by now this town must be about a hundred percent lazy rich people."

"I'm not one of them."

"When a copy of the book comes back I can put it aside for you."

"Sounds too good to be true."

"It is."

After another handshake they went in opposite directions, Justine to learn that she hadn't gotten a job she applied for, and Prentiss to discover that some sponsors are better than others.


That night Sadie Jorgenson got a call from her sister Marlene right before leaving the house telling her that Roger Nuñez had to postpone their date because he'd come down with pneumonia—it had been, he thought, a harmless chest cold until his doctor called and gave him the test results and ordered him to rest in bed for a week—and she'd said that was fine and agreed to reschedule for Christmas Eve.

"It'll be more cozy this way," said Marlene, "and we'll have lots of eggnog."

"I'm holding my breath," Sadie said.

"He wants you to know how sorry he is—he held off until the last minute because he thought it was just a minor little thing, but now that he knows it's pneumonia he obviously can't risk putting you at risk."

"Nope. Can't risk risk."

"I'm glad you're taking it this way."

Sadie changed back into her bathrobe and lay on the couch with a candle burning beside her on the floor. Why hadn't she told her sister about what happened with the intruder in the bathroom? Because she'd been delusional, that's why. She was obviously under a lot of stress and susceptible to little aberrations in her sanity, so that the mountain of sugar she'd ingested that day had nudged her over the edge. In a court of law she'd use the Twinkie Defense. No biggie. She'd soon be right as rain. And yet she couldn't help thinking that those fifteen minutes—or however long she'd held the sink and zoned out—had brought her near to a Higher Power, she wouldn't presume to guess which one, but some Thing against which death and the physical misfortunes that await mortals are meaningless— that those fifteen minutes were a sliver of experience capable of teaching her all that she needed to know. She thought of yogis and inspirational speakers and church leaders and drug dealers and everyone else who claimed to bring people to more elevated states of mind. She understood their appeal for the first time in her life. They claimed to see further and promised that there was sufficient space for you and everyone you knew to join them. They said, *the more the merrier.* Sadhu Indians hanging from flesh hooks, delighted. Sri Chinmoy Kumar Ghose stopping his heartbeat and opening his eyes. People swept up in the Rapture. And pharmaceutical ecstasy giving you access to benevolent dopamine impulses you've starved and neglected in the unmapped parts of your mind. Will you just look at that row of unmolested charity over beyond the fence of your neuroses? And that orchard of tenderness just above the field of affection growing without care or manipulation, waiting for you to discover it?

She woke up from a semidream and the late-afternoon light in her bedroom was a gentle transition from the idiotic abstractions she'd just thought of. She made and ate a pot of lentil soup, followed by a tomato and half a carrot and twenty-two frozen ice-cream bonbons that she thought she'd thrown away. *You thought you'd thrown away dessert. That's funny.* She got on the Internet and chatted with people who believed that these were the Last Days, millenarianists who'd been abducted by God and told exactly what to expect of the Earth's next phase. Despite her professional contact with people suffering from various emotional problems, she had never met anyone as overtly loony as these people with names like Shepherd 45677777, and whose faith in something Out There that was about to reassert itself on our desolate planet made her smile.

Sadie stared at the computer. "He touched me," wrote one nameless person, "and my body exploded into mist, and I rose into Him." This was exceptionally weird and sexual and Sadie loved it. It continued, "He told me that we will not have to wait much longer, for how can anyone look at mankind's sins such as the depleted ozone layer, the proliferation of bar codes, and state-funded abortion, and not recognize that we've come to the End?" To this list someone added talking dolls, ethanol-enhanced gasoline, full frontal nudity on cable, captive animals at aquatic theme-parks, nuclear testing, and the Church of Scientology. Shepherd 45677777 responded, "The Book of Revelation lays out John's vision very clearly, and it is encouraging. We may expect a thousand-year reign of peace once our age of vice and wickedness ends. We may expect to be compensated for our suffering. Be grateful that He touched you, and know that very soon He will touch all who are in preparation."

Sadie went to the freezer and there were no more bonbons and she quietly withdrew from the Internet chatroom. She had to find something to do that evening and forget she'd ever had that embarrassing hallucination in the bathroom. It was, now that she thought seriously about it, simply the latest manifestation of the low-level anxiety that had compelled her toward psychotherapy in college. Ironically, given that she wrote prescriptions for and received samples of every selective serotonin reuptake inhibitor on the market, and had tried a large percentage of them, she hadn't found a chemical solution to the problem yet. She told herself to give it time.


After dinner Lillith Fielding ensconced herself in the bathroom, where both of the pregnancy tests she took came up positive. She was sixteen and had had sex with precisely one boy, Eric, a month and a half earlier. In a brief, spastic experience of which each later gave opposite accounts, they kissed and groped in the sunken TV den of Eric's house while his parents slept two rooms away. Eric's erection was unpredictable and kept failing at the attempted moments of intercourse, which he blamed on the pressure he'd been feeling from the wrestling team in light of the upcoming state championship. Lillith was understanding and cooed into his ear that whatever happened or didn't happen was all right, and then she tried a few stimulation methods recommended by *Cosmopolitan* that didn't work. Only after she gave him an exhausting blow job and tickled his anus was he able to work his way into her for a minute of unsatisfactory jiggling before his inspiration failed again and he shrank out, cursing the tyrannical coaching style of Mr. Fitzpatrick. Practically in tears, he gathered his clothes and hurried from the den, leaving Lillith to get home on her own. They hadn't spoken since, though Eric the next day had bragged to everyone that he'd "maxed Lillith out." She had corroborated nothing and now regarded him as a stupid and sad little person. In fact, she'd only decided to sleep with him in order to make that other stupid and sad little person, Sam, jealous.

But her pregnancy was real. In the middle of her Wiccan preparations, of her crusade, of her youth, an evening's botched sex had made her a potential mother. She lay on her bed staring at her McDonald's uniform and feeling stomach cramps. Probably psychosomatic, though pain was pain. She dialed Eric's number and hung up when his mother answered. Abortion. She located Planned Parenthood in the phone book. Or would she keep it, or give it up for adoption, or drown it in a brook after giving birth alone in some isolated woods? How could she have been so dumb as to get pregnant? What a way to fuck up her life. What a way to fuck up.

"Lill?" called her mom from the hall.

"What?" answered Lillith.

"Could you come out here, please?"

"What is it?"

"Could you just come out here?"

"Could you just tell me what you want?"

"Don't make me ask again."

Lillith got up and put a hand on her belly and winced and opened the door and saw her makeup-less mother. Things that go bump in the night. "Presto."

"Could you please tell me what this is?" Her mother held up a purse.

"Dead cow hide," Lillith said.

"It's my empty purse."

"Oh."

"Do you know why it's empty?"

"Because you bought me a really expensive present? Oh, Mom, you shouldn't have!"

"Guess again."

"Because you think I stole your money."

"That's not what I'm saying, I'm only asking. Maria says she hasn't touched it."

"That girl and you believe her? After the alleged B she got in biology?"

"I'm posing the question in a civilized way. Did you take forty dollars from my wallet or not?"

"Not."

"Okay. That's all you need to say."

"To go from being innocent until proven guilty in this country."

"Let's not start."

"Fine with me."

Back in her room Lillith called Tina, who stressed that the time and place to have a baby was not here and now, that Lillith had to get an abortion because otherwise she'd be an unwed teenage mother and the scourge of society and unable to fulfill her responsibilities as a witch. There was so much to do and see in the world, and they were still so young, and a baby would spoil everything.

"That's really clinical and selfish-sounding," Lillith said. "This is a human being we're talking about."

"Not yet, it isn't."

"Yes, it is."

"Don't be dumb."

"I was dumb before, now I'm just pregnant."

"So don't be dumb again."


At five thirty the next morning, Joon-sup and sixteen others marched in single file along a fire lane through a predawn grove of old-growth redwoods four miles west of the Avenue of the Giants. They were bent forward under the weight of their sleeping bags and freeze-dried foods and tools of protest, an encampment on its way to camp. The inspiration for the march was Pacific Lumber's recently announced decision to log twenty thousand acres of land far enough away from Highway 101 that no one would hear or see it. It was to be an out-of-sight-out-of-mind operation. And to show that it was acting in good faith and interested in viewpoints other than its own, Pacific Lumber had listened to the concerns of environmentalists and tourist boards and then passed these concerns on to unbiased and rigorously non-partisan scientists whose impact assessment in the end favored the proposal.

A stray cicada sang an uncopyrighted tune. The ground beneath the quiet marchers crunched and crackled with twigs. The walkers' silence was measurably pitched not because they didn't have anything to say to one another—they could have talked for days about spontaneous cilantro, for example, or the neurohypophysial effects of meditation—but because they weren't going to turn this protest into another episode of drunkenness and fevered coupling. They'd decided to keep their behavior on a Beefeater level of seriousness, unlike protests in the past that had devolved into everybody getting overly friendly and forgetting the reason they'd gotten together. People having too good a time had compromised those protests' effectiveness, in the aftermath of which critics had said, "That didn't accomplish anything. You can't serve both God and man." Therefore there had been a call for a return to gravity. After all, Gandhi hadn't handed out tabs of acid to everyone who showed up for the Salt March, and Martin Luther King Jr. hadn't arranged for kegs of beer to be at the March on Washington. This outing was going to be as solemn and sober as the crisis and solution called for; no one was going to enjoy themselves while saving these twenty thousand acres of pristine forest.

Joon-sup was grateful for the strictures placed on this social activism because it meant there wouldn't be any drugs to make him possibly trip out so hard that strange, older, open-collared men would show up from out of nowhere and scare the shit out of him.

That night, after a flavorless dinner, Joon-sup sat about a campfire with the other protesters. There was no discussion of sex or honey-glaze body rubs. No juggling, hacky sacks, victimless jokes, games of hide-and-seek, ghost stories, lines of blow, or shared television memories. In the spirit of their protest they confined themselves to talking about fluctuating yearly rates of deforestation and the successful tactics of past tree-sitters. People were in bed by eight thirty. No one coupled up and conjoined sleeping bags. Everyone used roll-up air mattresses, but there were so many rocks and serpentine tree roots rippling over the ground that it was hard not to think of the Princess and the Pea while shifting in vain for the perfect position.

The night passed wretchedly, and eventually the gray dawn light was bright enough for Joon-sup to see most of the surrounding forest clearly. A few people were zipping up their bags and munching on trail mix and smoking cigarettes and performing their ablutions with little cups of water they'd filled in a nearby stream. Joon-sup got up and stretched and scratched his stubble and felt an accordion note of soreness in his legs and back. Luckily, coffee had passed the fun censors, and a guy in army fatigues brewed it over a small fire. Something slithered in the bushes; something squawked in the sky.

"Hey, Jack," said a woman in what looked like a potato sack, stirring yellow mush in a mixing bowl by the fire, "how'd you sleep?" Her name was Barbara and she sounded like she was recovering from laryngitis, though she wasn't. In addition to being one of this group's few lifelines to sixties radicalism, one of the great former menaces to Berkeley traffic, she was the mother of Soulbrother's girlfriend, who had backed out of coming when her dog began coughing the weekend before. Barbara had remarked sadly that her daughter demonstrated the relaxed commitment of today's political activists, that progressivism wasn't making progress.

"Barb," Joon-sup said, tapping the tin coffee cup he'd taken from his bag with a strong forefinger, "beautiful morning."

"Isn't it?" The mush was grainy with black flecks of (one hoped) pepper and clung thickly to the sides of the bowl. "The dew makes everything look like it's in the produce section of the Co-Op, you know those little mist sprays that cover all the spinach?"

Joon-sup knew but made only a tiny nod.

"I heard we might get arrested today," Barbara said.

More bodies stretched into sitting positions around them, resisting the temptation to sleep all morning. They had to get up and organized.

"Really? I didn't think the cops would come until tomorrow morning at the earliest; that's what John said." Joon-sup had to urinate and thought of almost hitting old men in his van and ignoring his mother's desire that he get married and taking a nap and the stories of past protesters who'd been pepper-sprayed by the police. They were thoughts made painful from tiredness.

"John said that?"

"Yeah." Joon-sup looked around for a trail that would take him to a secluded pissing place. "He said that the South Fork Police Department called him before we left and said it'll happen as soon as they can requisition the vans to take us away."

Barbara tasted the mush and made a smacking sound.

Joon-sup set down his cup and left the camp. Once beyond sight of the others he stopped at the crux of a pair of trees and was about to relieve himself, but then decided to keep walking farther into the forest. The invigoration of morning, the hunt for pure quiet, the reward of walking for no other reason than that it felt good to move among these stately trees so early when the air had an organic stillness and cleanliness and cloister calm. He stepped over a well-regulated flow of ants. He examined a patch of clover and didn't find any with four leaves. He saw deer shit and banana slugs and miniature stands of running bamboo. He heard the morning dove, ruff, and sparrow. It was a place without noisy conflict, like the Japanese rock gardens scattered around Pusan. Coming to a gathering of moss-covered redwood stumps, where to the right a single two-hundred-foot giant redwood roared up to the sky, he sat down to tie his shoes. He was starting to get hungry and hoped that the yellow mush would be eaten when he got back so that he could dig into the prepackaged snacks. He was starting to think that he'd like not to return to camp, but instead to keep walking until he came to an exit.

"Hey!" came a voice from above.

Joon-sup looked around and then up in the direction of the call. "Oh, hey!" he said, standing and stepping away from the tree to get a better view of the man addressing him. "You're already up there? Did you come with another tree-sit crew?"

"My name is Leon Meed," the man said. "I'm starving. Do you have any food?"

"They sent you up without anything?" Joon-sup didn't see any provisions slung over the branches or tucked away in a woodpecker hole. It was just this person Leon up there. Usually tree-sitters were outfitted with enough to eat, drink, stay warm, and read for a week at least, even if they were only expecting to stay up for a couple of days. The idea was that the ground crew—people who volunteered to bring the tree-sitter supplies—might get arrested or detained by security guards hired to starve the tree-sitter down, and so there should be extra everything in case they couldn't come back for a while.

"It's hard to explain," said Leon, "but I wasn't sent by anybody. I should say, nobody I know. The fact is that I was sent here, but the sender is unknown to me."

Joon-sup would have said something like "You speak in riddles, old man," except that this Leon might be crazy. Wrecked by too much outdoor living or too much booze or too much intellectual lassitude. Joon-sup considered heading back to camp to tell the others about this guy who was possibly a danger to himself. "Why don't you know who's responsible for you being up there?" he asked.

"Because I've disappeared," said Leon.

Joon-sup nodded as though he agreed, but then said, "You look visible to me."

"No, I mean before. Until a little while ago I lived in Eureka and then suddenly I was being deposited in different places all over Humboldt County. I'm being transported but I don't know why or by whom."

Joon-sup nodded again. "I can get help for you but you've got to promise not to do anything dangerous like jump. Do you promise not to jump?" He moved slowly, as though Leon were a bird and any sudden action might make him fly away.

"I'm not insane," Leon said, "and I'm not suicidal. I am literally disappearing and appearing randomly, and I'm very hungry. I need food. So far I haven't been left in a grocery store or restaurant; it's either been out in the ocean, where I froze and almost drowned, or in the middle of the street in Eureka where I almost got run over by a van. Or—"

But this was impossible and Joon-sup didn't want to hear any more and a sick feeling collected in his stomach, like a sack of sludge had been emptied into it. He'd heard enough. *Middle of the street in Eureka where I almost got run over by a van.* He pressed his palms flat against his ears and created a suction that he built up and dissipated several times, humming as he did so. He rubbed his eyes and his forehead and the base of his spine. He stood up and hopped in a circle with his eyes closed. This was not happening. He was fine. He was all right. He was not out of his mind. He shouted, "I am alone!"

Then he opened his eyes and stopped hopping and breathed deeply in and out and listened. Silence. He was indeed alone. He had only to look up at the tree to see that no man sat there asking for food and describing having been almost hit by a van. He had only to look. But he didn't. It was the marijuana, clearly, that had done this to him. And the magic mushrooms. There was nothing wrong with the man in the tree, because there *was* no man in the tree. Against his better judgment then he slowly looked up with the most fervent of hopes and saw, dishearteningly, Leon staring down at him.

"Of course you don't believe me," said Leon. "I nearly don't believe it myself. But I believe my stomach, and I believe the feel of this branch underneath me; I'm not about to slide off to test whether or not I'll hit the ground. Many things could be happening. I could be asleep and you're just a part of my dream, or you could be asleep and I'm a part of your dream, or something even more extraordinary is afoot."

Joon-sup said, with a twinge of sadness, "I thought I was going to hit a guy in Eureka when I was driving my van a couple of days ago. He looked like you, and he disappeared. I hope somebody is dreaming; I hope it's me."

"Aha! So you've seen me out there? Somewhere besides here?"

"I think so."

"You think! Yes." He scurried along the branch to the tree's trunk. "Maybe you could help me."

Joon-sup said nothing.

"I've been reported missing. I know that. My name, again, is

Leon Meed. First of all if you could get me some food that would be ideal."

Joon-sup stared up morosely at Leon and didn't think, because thinking led to such unacceptable conclusions—that was the word, *unacceptable*—and then he headed back in the direction of the camp, to get food or crawl back into his sleeping bag to cry, he wasn't yet sure.

# 5

Silas and Eve lay on adjacent reclining beds in the Humboldt Plasma Center, hooked up to IVs that extracted their plasma at the rate of one pint per two hours. They were the only donors on a dark and wet Wednesday afternoon lit up by occasional lightning over Humboldt Bay, God flash-photographing His creation. They nibbled on cookies from a plate of frosted gingerbread men and gingerbread men crumbs on the table between them, though generally they were motionless in front of a low-volumed television. The guy who'd checked them in and set up the equipment was either distracted or simply bad at sticking veins with needles, for he'd missed Eve's major arm artery twice, producing a massive bruise at her elbow joint, before finding it. He'd left the room quickly thereafter.

"I get so lightheaded sometimes giving plasma that it feels like I'm in an antigravity chamber," said Silas during a commercial break from the drama they were watching about twin children orphaned in Newfoundland.

Eve looked at Silas out of the corner of her eye, the way you'd surreptitiously look at someone who talked to himself in public. Her arm throbbed in pulse time. "Yeah," she said.

"It lifts my spirits even," he continued, while on TV a truck the size of a small cloud climbed a steep, rocky mountainside as its sticker price flashed in solar yellow. "Imagine having a truck that powerful,"

Silas said softly. Blood drained from him into a plastic sack shaped like an ice pack, trickling cells. For providing necessary plasma to patients all over the county and country, he and Eve were being paid twenty dollars. The money meant little to Silas—he had adequate savings from his bike shop business and the dividends of wise stock investments—it was more the feeling of *This is a way to fill up my hours that doesn't make me think about me.* Because he was tired of the endless ego that confronted him in his retirement; yes, he'd been around himself for so long and knew his thoughts so well, could anticipate what he'd think before he thought it—and what a horrible skill this was—that he relished any chance to do something not for his own benefit. A refuge from the self. After this he would go to Ramone's and order a small coffee and play chess with an albino man who lived on government assistance with his mother. An opponent with natural chess inclinations who wore sunglasses that made his thoughts on the game impossible for Silas to read, a man who feared the sun with vampiric intensity. But before those chess games, as in right now, lying in this building just off Harris Street, where buses passed by at fifteen-minute intervals taking the day wanderers like himself wherever they needed or aimlessly decided to go, Silas was feeling a buzz. Now as at other times he was caught in a mind-body frisson that wiped clear the layers of accreted dust and sediment on his brain and made him see things anew. It wasn't just the blood donation making him lightheaded and euphoric: no, ever since the morning he'd sat on his recliner and watched a man disappear he'd felt like a tabula rasa capable of psychospiritually recording more than he'd ever known. It didn't matter where he was or what he was doing—he could be walking through the public library or sitting on his haunches at the Arcata Sanitation Marsh, staring at egrets and rubbing dirt between his fingers—the feeling was the same. Like being in an anechoic space without parameters, without confines. He breathed in and it was the oxygen of eternity.

"I watched a documentary on leukemia recently," he said to Eve, "that discussed how few people give blood these days. After the World

Trade Center attack, people came out in droves, but now we're back to the way it was."

"If you don't mind," said Eve, "I'm pretty involved in this show."

Silas shifted on his bed and scratched his stomach. He focused on the television for a few minutes. "Why would someone who hates children so much run an orphanage?"

At this Eve smiled and looked at him. "I don't know. I was wondering about that."

"Then you're a threat to television. They don't want you to wonder about that, or about how realistic is it that your average person who buys a truck is going to go off-roading up a mountain. My name's Silas. What's yours?"

"Eve."

"How old are you?"

"Twenty-three."

"Are you from Eureka?"

"Third generation, thoroughbred Humboldt County. My pedigree weighs a ton."

"This is a good place to be."

Eve tilted her head. "Not really. My parents moved to Oregon nine years ago and I went with them, but I came back after a month because I had this idea that I loved it here."

"When you were fourteen?"

"They put up a fight, but I won because I could yell louder than my mom, and my dad can't handle confrontations very good. I lived with my friend Miranda until I finished high school."

"Eureka's a magnetic place. You wouldn't have wanted to leave your school friends."

"Eureka's hell and my friends are in arrested development. I wish I'd stayed in Oregon or gone anywhere but here."

"That's a desperate thing to say."

"This is a desperate place. And now it's too late to leave. Eureka's put a spell on me."

Silas said, readjusting a leg that threatened to go to sleep, "You sound like someone staying in a bad marriage for no good reason."

"I don't know about that."

Silas raised his left hand. "Falling out of love is the same whether it's with a person or a place or an object. With a person, at first you're madly in love with them and then a year later—or twenty years later—you look at them and wonder how you ever found them attractive. Romeo and Juliet were lucky to die when they were so young and in love. They never got on each other's nerves and turned into Montague versus Montague, case number 4387, Honorable Judge Vanzini presiding."

"I guess so. You're a weird guy."

"You're not the first to say that."

"I mean it."

"So do I."

They nodded at each other like neither could agree more, like they felt exactly the same. On TV dolorous Canadian children planned to escape from the captivity of their orphanage. The plasma attendant entered the room to check on the progress of Silas's and Eve's contributions, which he found satisfactory before saying nothing and leaving.

"Is this your first time donating?" Silas asked Eve.

"Yeah. I would've done it sooner, but my boyfriend isn't clean—he doesn't have AIDS, but he's used needles before, let's put it that way—so for a while I thought, Who knows? I should get a blood test first. So I did, and I'm okay."

"That's good."

"Yeah, it's a big relief. I get to get old."

"Old isn't the end of the world," Silas said.

"It seems like the worst fate there is, no offense."

"You'll get over that feeling. The only difficulty is the little recessions, the bifocals and the forgetting of things you used to know. You adjust, though."

Eve twisted her body toward Silas without disturbing the IV. "But aren't you sick of adjusting? I adjust to jobs I hate and my boyfriend losing it and my favorite bands breaking up and my rent increasing. Circumstances change and I get disappointed and so I adjust and make do with less. I don't know if I can handle fifty more years of it. I can't afford to lose that much more."

Silas looked at this girl. At her glossy skin—oily would be the unkind word—that she rubbed with her palm to remove its sheen. And the tiny blackheads surrounding her nose ring. And her lips slightly ajar and without lipstick, the upper full and the lower drawn in as though to protect her teeth from scrutiny. He took into account the room's unflattering lighting, which meant that her youth and comeliness were probably better evidenced at other times of the day, in other settings, though seated here he could see an approximation of what she'd look like at his age.

"Don't think of it as a lump sum," he said, "as fifty years of compromise. At a certain point your responsibilities become a kind of pleasure, when you raise children and discover what you're good at. It's not all about lowering your expectations. And what I've found is that you get back some of the power you had when you were young. Certain abilities you didn't know you'd lost return to you."

Eve frowned. She'd begun noticing halos around lights at night and so would have to save up for an eye exam and glasses. Breast cancer had been diagnosed in women as young as her. She occasionally thought there was a gap in her hand-eye coordination. "Like what?"

"Do you remember as a child your senses were more alive? Food was sweeter and music clearer and occasionally you saw things that other people couldn't? Certain phenomena were revealed only to you, and you kept it to yourself like the whereabouts of a secret treasure. It was as if you could slip in and out of a state of grace. But then as you got older you repressed that receptivity. You lost out on the world of the imagination and believed in whatever was agreed upon as the real world. I'm saying that that receptivity comes back."

Eve was a little uncomfortable being alone with this man, whose rapt expression was too rapt, whose eyes were too beady. "So your senses are more alive now?" She thought of Derivative's dolphin song and *eeek-yiiik* screeched in her brain. She thought of Leon Meed, as though he'd swum up from Atlantis, asking her what day it was.

"Have you ever experienced something that can't be explained rationally, heard music that wasn't playing or seen an object that wasn't there or felt a presence in more than just your body, the way that amputees feel heat and cold in their lost limbs?"

"No."

Silas looked at the lying girl and said, "There's wonder still in store for you. Life isn't all a downward slope."

Eve said quietly, "Have you considered that maybe you're insane?"

Silas's smile was bittersweet as he turned what was left of his attention to the jubilant escape of two orphans from captivity. Eve saw it too but comprehended nothing.


Because it was the Yuletide season, and the last day of school, a Thursday, Elaine Perry, whose consumer sympathies lay with the locally owned and operated shops of Old Town, guiltily toured the mall's discount clothing stores for the presents she knew her sons, Trevor and Abraham, didn't want—they wanted toys, and lots of them and *no clothes* this year—as well as a marked-down pair of shoes and a black dress for herself for the *South Pacific* opening night. She ran into her student Troy's mother outside the electronics store and avoided giving a specific answer about his behavior in class. Troy was a classic attention deficit disorder child, and although Elaine hated the thought of medicating children for anything nonfatal, she was going to approach his parents at the beginning of the spring semester with the school nurse's recommendation that he go on Ritalin. The mother seized on the ambiguity of Elaine's answer and interpreted it, with obvious relief, as news that her son had improved.

At the grocery store on the way home Elaine couldn't find a single unbruised apple, and her credit card was declined twice at the checkout counter. A humpbacked, slightly retarded man in a green apron was called over to return to the store's shelves the $73.19 worth of food and household cleaning items that Elaine couldn't pay for. Outside, someone had keyed her car along the passenger side. Seeing the white sine wave running across the two doors and tail almost made her cry.

At home in the living room, Trevor was playing with a boy she'd never seen before while Abraham sat seven inches from the television screen. Her credit card bill had been due two weeks earlier. A check her father had promised to send was not in the day's mail. A cursory glance at the kitchen cupboards decided their dinner: chicken soup and boxed mashed potatoes. Greg had not called.

"Mom?" said Trevor, padding into the kitchen with a plastic gun whose trigger had broken off. He wore a red cape that Elaine had made for him out of an old pillowcase. "Can Brian stay for dinner?"

"Who's Brian?" asked Elaine.

"My friend from school."

"We've talked about this, Trev. You know the rules about inviting friends over."

"But his parents already said yes."

"You asked them without permission from me?"

Trevor said, "I just wanted him to stay for dinner."

"I know that you just wanted that. But you can't go ahead and assume that it's okay without asking. What if we were all going somewhere as a family? Or what if I'd had to work late and get a sitter?"

"Why can't Dad be here to watch us?"

"We've already talked about this."

"When's he coming back?"

"Remember how I said things are going to be different? How you'll get to see Daddy in a new house sometimes?"

"But I don't want to see him in a new house. I want to see him at home."

"You're going to have another home, an extra home."

"I don't want an extra one." Trevor's eyes and cheeks reddened.

He grabbed hold of a drawer handle and opened and closed it rapidly. "I want Dad here!" A tear was blinked from each eye and he rocked back and forth on his toes. Elaine reached out to hold him and he pulled away violently, earning a small gash on his elbow from the metal drawer handle and issuing a redoubled cry of anguish. He was lost to consolation now, and Elaine with fixed worry hooding her eyes and darkening her mien, thought I can't believe that son of a bitch Greg hasn't called to talk to his children and what am I supposed to do about this friend staying for dinner when I need to make the point that in times of chaos and catastrophe—like now—we have to follow the rules and do things in an orderly fashion, because otherwise, if we let chaos get the upper hand, we'll collapse and our whole tenuous enterprise of being a family and supporting one another will break apart. Worse than it has already. She dearly wanted to allay her son's fears and ease his pain and make it all better. Her instinct demanded that she produce Daddy and happily set Brian's place at the dinner table. Her instinct was to restore peace at any cost.

"I'm sorry," she said, wetting a rag to attend to Trevor's wound. "I know you're upset—we're all upset—but you're not allowed to have friends stay for dinner unless you ask at least a day beforehand. So I'll be glad to give him permission to eat with us tomorrow, but tonight it's not okay. In fact, I should probably take him home now, it's getting late."

And Trevor, out of his mind with rage, crying with rhythmic abandon, turned around and went to his room, where he barricaded the door and didn't emerge until the next morning.

Across town, alone in his apartment, Barry Klein said, "I don't know why I'm telling you this. It probably has nothing to do with it and I'm just wasting our time."

He pushed play on the tape recorder: *"Go on, please. We're off to a good start."*

He pushed stop and continued, "So I met this man at the county courthouse named Shane Larson. He was tall and well-built and even though his face had acne scars it was beautiful—I shouldn't notice these things now that Alvin and me are, but, well, I do—the point is that he had this firm handshake and he was asking me a lot of questions like was I from around here and did I have family in the area and what sort of insurance did I have. I figured he was either really interested in me or he was a salesman. As it happens he's a salesman of burial plots."

He pushed play. *"That's interesting. Please continue."*

He pushed stop. "I didn't want a burial plot but I did want to keep talking to him—now that me and Alvin are a couple I feel so free to talk to people and it's nice because before I'd be afraid—so I took his card and asked about the available plots. Was that wrong?"

He pushed play. *"This is going well."*

He pushed stop and rewound the tape a little. "The line we were in was a joke; we weren't moving forward at all. But Shane had such delicate eyes, dewy and green and exactly how a sensitive man looks, and I could have stared at them forever. I came close to asking if he wanted to go to the bathroom with me. Right there in line to see the sheriff's secretary at the county courthouse. Can you believe it? I wanted him so badly that I was on the verge of nothing mattering. Naturally I didn't say it because just because I've come out of the closet doesn't mean I'm suddenly Mr. Libertine who can act on all of his impulses. Do you think I'm being too timid or shy, or am I wrong to even have these thoughts about someone I've just met especially since I have Alvin?"

He pushed play. *"—ease continue. This is going well. You're hitting on something here."*

He pushed stop. "It's hard for me to keep up the illusion that you're helping when you only ever say the same dumb generic encouraging things!"

Play. *"I'd like to hear more if you don't mind continuing."*

Stop. "I rode the lily-livered pink hippo over the top of Old Smoky."

Play. *"That's very interesting. Can you elaborate a little?"*

Stop. "The pink hippo flies by candlelight into the rosy-fingered dawn and deposits me on a mound of poo."

Play. *"I see. What do you think this means in regards to our earlier discussion?"*

Stop. "It means I can't afford therapy!" Barry leaned back on his pillows propped at a forty-five degree angle between the bed and the wall. He gripped his handheld tape recorder in despair. "But you're all I've got. So where was I? Right, so I act interested in the burial plots and ask Shane what he's doing at the courthouse, and he tells me that he had been arrested the day before for assault and he's there to set up a court date. He'd spent the night in jail. I was pretty interested in the jail part because it's one of my rape fantasies. I maybe shouldn't be admitting this, either, but since we're here in the spirit of total frankness and honesty I'll go ahead and say that I've thought about being put in jail and kind of forced to have sex with a man. That's not as bad as it sounds, is it? Oh God, it is, it is. But anyway, so Shane's dismissive of the whole jail thing and says, 'Yeah, lockdown for a night. If it's your first offense as an adult they don't throw you in with the psychopaths. I saw worse guys in juvey when I was a kid.' Then he asks me what I'm doing there, so I tell him about how I'm going to report the man I saw at the Longaberger party, the one who's missing, Leon Meed. Shane isn't all that informed about local news, so I explain it to him and he gets curious about why someone would go missing and then show up at a Longaberger party and then disappear again. He asks about the reward for finding him, and I mention the ten thousand dollars his mother's put up. Then he really grills me about what Leon and I said to each other, and what he looked like, and all of my impressions. I would've told him anything. But eventually it was his turn to talk to the secretary, and when he was leaving and I was going up to the window I said how it was great meeting him and I hoped we ran into each other again someday, but he just nodded and didn't answer."

❖   ❖   ❖

As far as Shane Larson was concerned, the day had been a waste until he sat down at the bar of Folie à Deux next to a man who reeked of mortality. Who was old and full of days. Shane wept inner tears of joy at being delivered a guy such as this right before Christmas. He'd be able to make a sale and shut that bitch Lenora up about money and *I can't believe you got in a fight, that you instigated it even and now we have to spend all our savings on lawyer fees.* All our savings. Funny, he didn't remember her contributing anything to all of "our" savings, but that was beside the point. The point was that he'd already had to put up with the police and the courts and being contrite enough for that faggot. He'd had to jump through hoops the size of bracelets to keep the cops and all the lawyers happy, and when he came home did he get love and support and, most of all, quiet? Did he get a little sympathy for the mountain range of bullshit he'd had to traverse? Or did he have to listen to her hissy fit and recriminations and name-calling: *Are you some kind of savage? Is that it? Did I marry a beast of the wild when I thought I was marrying a sweet and dependable guy?* She'd married him, Shane Larson, so whatever he was should be good enough for her.

"Really packed tonight, isn't it?" said Shane to the ancient man. Shane was there to meet a friend of a friend who wasn't happy with her dead husband's grave in McKinleyville and might want his body moved to Humboldt Overview. The commission was practically burning a hole in his pocket *are you some kind of savage.* It was six forty and he had twenty minutes and this geezer here was just waiting to be hooked and reeled in.

"Like a moving truck instead of a restaurant," the man said with a small laugh.

Shane guffawed although the joke, if it was one, was obscure. A moving truck? Laugh anyway; laughter was always appropriate. "My name's Shane. Good to meet you." He hadn't been closing much lately but tonight he was going to. He was going to close twice. Two on base. He was that kind of confident because you had to be, confidence being the most attractive of scents, and you caught more flies with honey (not that flies were what any right-thinking person wanted).

"Silas," said the man. Who must have been seventy-five and looked it oh yes he was old. *You are old, Father William*. They shook hands. "Usually I come here on Thursdays and the place is half empty. Must be the holiday cheer."

Shane raised his bushy black eyebrows ingratiatingly. "You come here a lot? This is my first time. I've heard the chef, what's his name Michael Frontiay or is that it, he's supposed to be top of the line. The foie gras they say is dynamite."

"You won't be disappointed."

"I'll bet." A little acid jazz music dripped out of the ceiling speakers. The bartender quietly and efficiently went about her business of measuring and pouring and wiping. Shane looked at the seventy-five-year-old next to him whose face was all bisecting wrinkles, and tingled. The average American male lived to be seventy-eight. He took a sip of his martini and thought, You're going to close this guy tonight. Before you even get to the mourning widow you are going to have a sale. Things are turning around. "What line of work you in, Silas?"

"I'm retired. Used to own a bike shop."

"Retired." Shane smiled in contemplation. "That's coming in loud and clear. The golden years, right? You've put in a lot of hard work and now you get to coast. Take it easy."

"You could put it that way."

Shane leaned over and rested a hand on Silas's shoulder, not too heavy but with a certain trustworthiness, squeezed, and let go. "What I envy about you—and as you can see I've got a lot of years ahead of me to bust my hump—but what I see as the beauty of your position is that you can concentrate on enjoyment, your hobbies and family and the rest of it. The only business you have to worry about now is life insurance and your burial arrangements. But you've probably already taken care of those things, right?"

Silas sipped his red wine and puckered his mouth. It was a bitter vintage. "No, I don't plan on passing away just yet."

"Of course not, and that's where I can see you're a wise man. You're not obsessed with dying. But you know what? There are some who say it doesn't hurt to be prepared, just in case. It even occurs to me that I might be able to help you out, because I work for Morland Memorial Services, and I'd be privileged to talk to you about what we can offer a man like you. It doesn't take much time, and it's important to do."

"If you'll excuse me for a minute," Silas said and then moved toward the men's room.

Shane, staring longingly after him, suddenly saw an entirely new man sitting on Silas's bar stool. Where the hell did he come from? Shane drew back. What? "Hey! Hey, buddy, not to be rude, but my friend is sitting here."

The guy looked flummoxed and had tree sap and green stains on his brown pants. What an untouchable and how did he sit down there so quickly? Silas was on his way back and Shane, seeing that the freak wasn't moving, reached over to lift him from the stool. The guy tried to fend Shane off for a second but was quickly overpowered and forcefully propped against a support column a few feet away. "He was in your seat," Shane whispered when Silas sat down. The stranger stared at them. He wasn't going anywhere. Shane wanted to resume his pitch but felt the kind of performance anxiety you got from trying to pee at a public urinal when someone was waiting in line behind you. Shy pee-pee, his brother used to call it. No matter how intense the pressure to go, a muscle freeze prevented anything from coming out, thus making worse the physical discomfort and the panic of being judged somehow by the other guy. Shane couldn't say anything to Silas so long as this son of a bitch was there, and he was so close to closing the deal that it was indeed like the pain of not being able to urinate—this stranger was a kidney stone—and he winced. "Excuse me, if you don't mind," he turned to the stranger and spoke in an unnaturally high and sharp voice, "but you're too close for comfort. Maybe you could back off because it's not working you standing so close like this."

"That was unnecessary roughness," said the stranger. "What's going on?"

"You're really pissing me off."

Silas opened his mouth and was just agog at this stranger.

"Is this Folie à Deux?"

"Bingo," said Shane. "Shove off."

The stranger's face—pug nose and burnished cheeks with a faint magenta tint—contracted. "This is a restaurant. I have as much right to be here as you."

Shane stood up and stepped into the stranger's personal space. "If we were outside do you know where you'd be? On the ground. So don't make me follow you out. Leave."

"Listen," said Silas, "I think something extraordinary is happening. We need to calm down and talk to one another. This is something we want to take slowly."

Shane swallowed the last of his gin and tonic and chewed on ice. "Oh, yeah," he said, breathing sharply as though they were at a high altitude, "let's just do that." A waiter passed by carrying a tray of steaming dishes. "You, Pierre," Shane grabbed the waiter's arm, "I know you're busy, but my friend Silas and I are ready to sit down. It's just about seven, so maybe you could talk to the hostess for us and find out when our tables are going to be ready so we don't have to keep sitting here dealing with pricks like this guy." The waiter said he'd see what he could do and walked away, his tray-supporting arm tilting slightly. Shane tipped the rest of the ice from his glass into his mouth and swallowed it whole.

"Shane? Is that you?" A young man approached the bar with fey stride and poise, catching little glimpses of himself in the mirror behind the bar. "It's me, Barry. Remember we met at the county courthouse?"

"Who?" Shane said, confused by the sensory data overload.

"In line at the courthouse, remember? I was reporting a missing person, and you were there for sentencing."

The stranger was gone—lucky for him—and Shane looked at Silas apologetically like this-kid's-unstable and said, "I was there making an appointment. Not sentencing." Silas didn't appear to believe or disbelieve him, his expression puzzled as he walked around the column next to which the stranger had just been standing, and Shane realized that he wasn't going to close the deal. A fucking stranger had come between them and now here was a flaming queerbait ruining his chances for a sale. Which meant a real, appreciable loss of income and a bitter wife and further struggling to manage and defaulting on the car payments and the student loans from Brigham Young. Shane saw: a smaller one-bedroom apartment in a worse part of town, one bath instead of two; no eating out; postponing the first child; imitation clothes; another bank loan at Shylock rates. Shane thought: I'm trying as hard as I can and there are these obstacles, Lord. I'm strong for You, but You don't want me to suffer so much, do you? You know that in these times we have to fight for righteousness and see the good prevail. You're on my side.

"Isn't it funny how we're both here?" Barry asked.

"It's a laugh riot," Shane said.

Silas excused himself and moved to the entrance, where he greeted a South American man with very long sideburns. Shane watched the meeting for a moment and then saw his potential client, the mourning widow he'd been waiting for this entire time, enter, and he tasted bile in the back of his throat and looked angrily at his glass with no more ice in it, and the man who'd come between him and Silas, the guy who'd ruined his commission, was gone and Shane couldn't punish him.

"I'm a disc jockey at KHSU," said Barry in his mellifluous voice that was almost a croon, "over at the university. Can I buy you a beer?"

Shane waved at the widow and rose to meet her. "Not thirsty."


That evening Prentiss Johnson went to the Lost Coast Brewery on Fourth Street, near the old Bistrins building and the Downtowner Inn. He thought, Now what kind of shit is this? A couple of major alcoholics meeting at a bar. Like two wolves on a diet going to a hen house. But it was Alvin's idea, and as Prentiss's new sponsor Alvin had explained that there was a reason for it so not to worry. Prentiss sat at the bar drinking a Shirley Temple while the beers on tap were poured one after another for the happy-houring working folks. All these guys wearing business casual who in the middle of ordering would turn backs to their tables and shout "Rog, what did you want again?" and then tap their twenty-dollar bills on the countertop in semidrunk impatience, doing shave-and-a-haircut, and then say "Cheers" when their pint glasses were placed before them and collect their change and flick off a dollar tip. The functioning alcoholics. There was a distinction you learned at AA meetings between functioning and nonfunctioning alcoholics. The former were characterized by their ability to hold and sustain the basics of adult life: a job and a relationship. They tended not to need a drink upon opening their eyes in the morning, and they went entire days completely sober. But they were still alcoholics: they drank to oblivion and drank regularly and drank even when another drink could do nothing for them but concrete, head-punishing damage. And they spent a disproportionate amount of their mental energy and money on alcohol, and they formed friendships based on a mutual love of alcohol, and they did many things they later regretted under alcohol's influence. But functioning alcoholics lacked the insatiability that defined the standard nonfunctioning alcoholic, the Prentiss kind. For that one little difference they were allowed to live on their own and rarely, if ever, admit that they had a problem.

"Prentiss, hey!" said Alvin, sliding onto a stool next to him. He had that ridiculous hairstyle going, a sort of wavy pompadour that advertised homosexuality as blatantly as a rainbow decal arcing across your forehead. And some kind of overcrafted beard. More disturbingly, however, his face had swollen shiny bruises and his discolored nose slanted to the left. "These peanuts look tasty." After a handful, "Mmm! And they are. Gobble gobble." He grinned at Prentiss.

"Alvin, something happened to you."

"Yes, I was attacked."

"What was it, some kind of gang activity?"

"No, it was a psycho at CalCourts. I was minding my own business when he jumped me."

"Your nose is broken."

"Yes."

"I'm sorry."

"Thanks. It's only my face, though, right? He could have done something vicious like throw my towel in the shower." He said this as a joke and it was funnier than Prentiss expected. Some people could lose their legs and start talking right away about the money they'd save not having to buy shoes. Alvin signaled for the bartender's attention. "Two whiskeys and a couple of beer backs, please. For me and my friend." He nodded in Prentiss's direction.

"What the?" Prentiss said, straightening his back and looking over his shoulder. Every internal alarm he had sounded off in doomsday peals. Jesus Christ, a whiskey and a beer back! Might as well rape the first fine woman he saw and rob a couple banks while he was at it. Why not? If law and order were to be flushed down the toilet. A whiskey and a beer back, that was a cyanide tablet in your hand when they were coming to lynch you. "You got to understand me. I'm not going out like that."

"All in good time. A wonderful thing has happened to me, and I want us to make some real progress tonight. I know how you must feel about Jamal relapsing. We all do. It's like losing a dear friend to AIDS."

This was turning out to be a disaster, this new sponsor deal with Alvin. Tomorrow Prentiss would ask the AA leaders to suggest someone else. Say that it was bad chemistry between him and Alvin and he wanted someone he could relate to and who else might they know looking to extend a helping hand. "I can't say about the AIDS, but it's true I'm not happy about Jamal. That didn't need to come to pass. Still, the man could be innocent. There's nobody said yet he was sipping."

Alvin nodded. "True." The drinks were placed before them and Alvin picked up his whiskey. "Prentiss? Will you join me?"

Prentiss, who as he looked at the drinks felt his mouth fill up with saliva, got off his stool, rubbed his lower lip, and said, "I'm serious. This is where I split. I'm not going to say anything to anybody about this, about the drinks, but nor am I going to fall off. I been sober five months, I'm doing it and I'm not going to quit."

A sort of gay white man's bemusement stole across Alvin's face, what in another time and place, and without the bruises, would have been called debonair. "Hold on a minute, you determined man. I want you to pick up the whiskey and hold it in your hand and lift it up to toast with me. We're not going to drink it, we're just going to toast and then set it back down."

Prentiss looked at him with consternation. "You out of your mind?"

"If you bear with me for a few minutes this will all make sense."

"Listen, I'm admit it if that's what you want to hear: I'm a weak man. I don't have what it takes to be walking the tightrope if there's no safety net underneath."

Alvin stood up, placed the whiskey in Prentiss's hand, and, holding Prentiss's drink hand in his own free hand, clinked the two glasses together and raised them up to Prentiss's and his lips. Prentiss's heartbeat was so fast he thought it would run out of power and just stop. He was sick and stared at the whiskey poised three inches from his mouth, with all of its malts in a beautiful swirl, those currents of correction, and thought of how maybe jail would have been the better option after all, that yea though he walk through the valley of the shadow of death and neither hear nor see evil, he could feel it deep in the molten core of his self. The magic books were all checked out. White women afraid of you because you're black, they're the beauty and you're the beast, and sure in the fairy tale they might see through their fear and recognize your humanity but in the real world no one had the time or inclination to see through shit. Our first impressions were all we cared to have. And there was damnation at his fingertips.

"To rejuvenation!" Alvin said. And then, in a diffusion of tension so great that later Prentiss could only think of those spy movies in which a ticking bomb, seconds away from detonating, is disconnected by a sweating-bullets hero, he lowered Prentiss's hand as well as his own. Whiskeys returned to the table. Pain, pain, go away, and don't come back another day. Alvin looked like they'd scaled Everest. Prentiss had a splitting headache. Alvin smiled from ear to ear and with the graciousness of a maitre d' guided Prentiss onto his stool and returned to his own. "You've got to be cruel to be kind sometimes. I'm sorry. It's what my sponsor did with me, and it's what I believe works. You can't say you're building up your resistance to alcohol if you shut yourself up in meetings and never confront the problem. Oscar Wilde said he could resist everything but temptation. I'm here to make sure you can resist everything *including* temptation."

Prentiss took a deep breath and said, still a little wobbly in his thoughts and with an ice pick in his brain, "I hear what you're saying."

"I know you do. It's what I sensed from the beginning."


For weeks the signs had been all over Eureka. On lampposts, in store windows, suspended banner high between stoplights on Fourth and Fifth Streets. *"Come to 'South Pacific,' where true love waits on some enchanted evening!!!"* The enchanted evenings in question began with the show's debut on Friday, December 20, a date printed on the signs just above its location, the Muir Elementary Gymnasium. Gymnasium was spelled "Gimnasium" on all of the signs except for the Fifth Street banner, a mistake that made Elaine cringe and want to sail away to the real South Pacific, but that endeared Eurekans to the show. The mistake got people thinking I-haven't-been-to-a-student-play-since-I-was-a-student-myself, and they kept the opening date in the backs of their minds, and then they found themselves buying tickets at the door. Elaine couldn't believe the number of cars parked there on opening night when she peeked around the corner from the gym's back door, which she then entered for a last-minute pep talk to the cast.

"You all did perfectly at yesterday's rehearsal and you're going to do it even better tonight!" she said.

One of the sailors asked how it could be done better than perfectly, and she smiled as though he weren't being sarcastic. Many children had to pee. Elaine did, too, but she was nervous about leaving the remaining congregation of actors, so she held it in and snapped her fingers briskly and looked through the curtains and saw the seats filling up with parents as well as a number of unfamiliar faces. Some became recognizable upon prolonged inspection. Steve Baker was there, as was a twenty-ish girl named Eve who lived in the apartment building next to Elaine's house, and various others. She closed the curtains and noticed that a million things were wrong with the set at the same time that a million things were right.

In the audience, Prentiss sat with his mother and searched her handbag for the arthritis ointment she swore was in there but, if it was, must have been invisible. His mother had a tendency to be short with him, and he really wasn't in the mood for it presently, as he'd been lambasted at work by Mary Ellen for misfiling three science-fiction book series that had appeared to be one, all the books having nearly identical covers and titles. Bring on the damned enchantment, he thought, shaking his head at his grimacing mother. Behind him Lillith sat with her friend Tina because her younger sister Marie had a small role in the play, and this was a family obligation that she didn't relish—a *three-hour* musical—but had to perform lest certain privileges be taken away from her, such as the Christmas vacation freedom she'd need to perform the spell at Moonstone Beach in a few days. She and Tina chewed spicy cinnamon gum. Not far from them Sadie shook a bag of popcorn she'd bought from the concession stand in the gym's foyer, bringing to prominence the largest popped kernels. She ate the salty snack and grew thirsty and felt conspicuous being alone, imagining that everyone around her considered attending a Rodgers and Hammerstein production by oneself unspeakably pathetic. But she was an adult, so she put on a face like I'm-fine. It was almost defiant but not quite. In fact, she so successfully looked fine and almost defiant that Silas, sitting a row and seven columns over, stared at her for a few minutes before concluding that she was something of a Mona Lisa, one of those women whose secrets buoy her over the turbulent waters of every day. Silas crossed and recrossed his legs, unable to stand the accumulating pain in his knees for more than thirty seconds before repositioning them. He was with his albino friend, who pointed out that the music being played quietly over the gym's loudspeakers as they waited was "Everything's Up to Date in Kansas City," from the *Oklahoma!* soundtrack. The albino said, "Kansas City until recently was the greatest cow town our country has ever known." Silas agreed. He'd driven through it in 1963 with his first wife and been impressed by the livestock smell extending out twenty miles from the city limits. The young man sitting behind him was Barry, there because his boyfriend, Alvin, loved musicals. Loved them. "Musicals are God's gift to cock lovers everywhere," Alvin said, which Barry thought was a crude formulation. Besides which, musicals were stupid. He preferred a good Chekhov play. Something contemplative. Something that questioned our roles in the world. Alvin stealthily held Barry's hand and Barry hoped no one noticed not because he was afraid of being outed, but because he didn't want other queer men there to know he was taken. He didn't like feeling so annoyed and told himself to relax; it was okay; he'd made his choice. But it was like his body was crawling with lice and he'd never been so uncomfortable, so that Steve, slouching into a seat by the fire exit, was grateful to notice someone in the audience apparently suffering as much as he was. Steve had come to the performance because he'd spent the afternoon at his office gripping the phone, not calling his soon-to-be ex-wife Anne. He'd canceled patient after patient and thought seriously that he was going out of his mind, and so decided at seven p.m., when the office staff had cleared out and the building hummed with sleeping computers and medical equipment, that he would distract himself by going to the student production of *South Pacific* he'd seen advertised on a billboard recently. Three seats down from him Eve was biting the last bitable shred of fingernail she had left, feeling the frigidity of the empty seat next to her as though it were a wind tunnel, for Ryan was supposed to have been sitting in it. Which made her mad, because it was *he* who worked at Muir, and *he* who'd told his new friend Principal Giaccone that he would come to the show, because when two men possess incriminating evidence against each other, they are prone to act like the best of friends and go out of their way to express interest in the other's well being and so in this way persuade their girlfriends to do things like come to see an elementary school musical as an act of shrewd politicking. Eve stared at the smudges of blood at the tips of her left ring and right pointer fingers until the lights went down, at which point Joon-sup, sitting nearby, woke up. He was sober and this play was going to be a deeply normalizing experience for him. Surrounded by the burghers of Eureka society and entirely drug-free, he was going to sink into a classic of American pop culture he'd never seen but knew to be absolutely without weirdness or psychotropic undertones. A Leon-free environment. For added comfort, he would have liked to hold the hand of the old lady sitting next to him, but he knew this to be impossible and so refrained.

The *Oklahoma!* soundtrack was abruptly cut off.

A kind of prerecorded quality crackled in the air then, with a hundred and thirty people shifting in their chairs at once in blackened synchronicity, and throats were cleared and keys fell out of pockets to land, in metallic accident, on the floor, with arms stretched down at once to swoop them up, to restore a silence that had never been.

"Hello and welcome!" Elaine said when a burst of light found her onstage, standing before closed curtains and holding a clip-on microphone. "We're pleased that so many of you could make it tonight for what I know you will enjoy tremendously." She was nervous and began to feel a touch of displacement, as though she didn't know precisely where she was or what she was supposed to say. *This is only a brief introduction. This is only a brief introduction, and everyone is naked.* "We had a little trouble with the printer today, and that's why our program guides aren't quite ready for you, which means I should just say that *South Pacific* takes place in 1944, in the South Pacific—but that's obvious I guess," her breath began to back up in her throat and she couldn't exhale, "and it centers on the American military," so that she needed air desperately and didn't know what to say and her nervousness was erupting into a full-blown panic attack, "and so here it is!" She hurried offstage and there were thirty seconds of silence as the sound engineer, a sixth-grader with goggle-sized glasses who'd expected her introduction to take much longer, scrambled to attention and pressed all the right buttons. Elaine leaned against the fold-up stadium-style aluminum benches in the dark and slowly came back in control of her breathing.

The girl in charge of cueing actors' lines asked if she was all right. "Fine, thanks," Elaine said, and didn't know when someone had last asked her that question. Couldn't place her most recent brush with compassion. She smiled and followed the cue girl back to the wings to watch the show.

For a while everything went well—the kids' voices were strong and their blocking correct—but then Elaine saw in profile what everyone in the audience saw head-on. Midway through "There Is Nothin' Like a Dame," as little boys in sailor suits marched around one another and an agile child did a back flip, a ceiling light crashed down onto a pile of sand. It made a thunderous whump. No one was injured, and enough cries went up both from the actors and the audience that when a second light dropped from the ceiling rafters, the space below it was clear. People made an orderly stampede for the exits. Only a single light remained in its perch, and those who stopped to look up saw what appeared to be a human figure shimmying along the rafters. Its face was hidden in shadows, though some of those present thought they knew who it was.

Elaine was relieved that none of the children were hurt and, when the regular lights were turned on and she appraised the damage, was grateful and amazed to see the show lights basically intact. The sand had cushioned their fall so that they wouldn't need to be replaced. There was by this time no trace of a man or woman crawling along the

ceiling rafters, and Elaine, not having seen him or her, was as per-
plexed as the children about what could have dislodged the lights.
Chalking it up to a mysterious disaster that could have been far worse,
they cleaned up and went home and the next day put on a trouble-
free show, honoring all tickets from the night before, glad to see most
everyone return for the enchantment that was delivered as promised.

## 6

*December 24*
**7:23 a.m.**

The milk was bad. Lillith regarded the Cheerios floating among tiny coagulated curds in her bowl. She felt a gagging reflex and didn't have to get ready for work. Tonight was the spell with Tina and Franklin and she felt such affirmation that they trusted her and she'd be the mistress of ceremony. Inside of her was a zygote and she thought about the potential baby that she was going to have removed. Choose life. Papa don't preach. Unwed teenage mother. Me and you against the world. Feeding time. A cry in the dark. Teething. It was one thing to be biologically able to have children and quite another to be psychologically ready. Women die in childbirth. More die of heartbreak. And it was clear that having a child now would in no way liberate her, which was the argument some girls made about how it was *your* baby and *you* made the decisions on how to raise it and what an entrée into the adult world with its tax credits and school vouchers and what're your thoughts on breast-feeding versus formula—that it would be the ultimate form of bondage for a girl who was mature and blessed with common sense and involved in a spiritual crusade bigger than herself. Bigger than everyone. She poured her cereal down the drain and a few o's got stuck in the scratched sink basin. She saw a game of tic-tac-toe and thought it unwinnable.

**7:55 a.m.**

Silas in a black turtleneck walked along I Street, drinking from a discreet thermos the espresso blend he'd brewed at home, his hair like so many pins in a cushion. Mornings were the best time to see and understand Eureka. When the Laotian women trudged home from the Asian market and the shopkeepers crisscrossed the paths of graveyard shifters and the children began to play, immune from the working world's difficulties, more than occupied by difficulties of their own. He'd been conscious of his knees since beginning his walk a half hour earlier, and although this consciousness usually segued into sharp pain after a few minutes, right then they felt fine, like the joints of a man who'd never groaned going downhill. He raised a fist in the air to celebrate them. He could see to where the street ended seven blocks away at a rotting wharf on the bay. Thirty years ago, when the city's fortunes were brighter and that part of town had had hotels and seafood restaurants and penny arcades, he'd spent Saturday afternoons talking with county developers about increasing Eureka's population without turning it into a factory town. Thirty years ago it had seemed possible to make Eureka a desirable place to be.

What had happened in the interim—the failure of any industry to take root after logging and salmon fishing began their steady decline—was no longer as depressing to Silas as it once had been. Communities, like empires and life and perhaps time itself, began and ended over and over. The city of Troy in Asia Minor had been built and destroyed on ten occasions and enjoyed fame only for its seventh incarnation, Troy VIIa; the other nine Troys were unknown because they lacked a defining tragedy. They hadn't burned to the ground. Their demise was of the prosaic, Eureka variety, a slow fade to black. Silas the Reincarnable was three years shy of seventy-eight, when the average American male died, and he hadn't drawn up a will or bought a burial plot—as if anyone without a morbid attachment to their corpse would do such a thing! That man at Folie à Deux was an imbecile! Death might be the beginning of the beginning, and the here and now merely a preamble. And after Eureka would come another Eureka that perhaps would be called something else, and would precipitate still other Eurekas or non-Eurekas. Silas looked at the latticed veins and spreading skin cancers on his hands. He experienced pain-free knees. Beside him waiting for the stoplight to turn green at I and Seventh Streets was a young boy with a *Times-Standard* satchel over his shoulder. His hands were white and undefined, and he said, wearing a stiff baseball cap, "Paper?" Silas looked at him for a moment and then counted the bills in his wallet: "I've only got ten dollars." The boy considered this and said, "It costs forty cents." Silas handed him all his money: "I want you to spend this on someone you care about. Doesn't matter what you get, so long as it comes from you." Then he accepted and uncreased his copy of the *Times-Standard* and crossed the street while searching for the birth announcements page. There were seven.

**8:01 a.m.**

Shane stared at Lenora's ass. Usually he didn't think twice about it. It was always there, there it always was, and what he wouldn't give to have a little variety and this was another of the great Mormon traditions, polygamy, and why wasn't he in one of the millions of small Utah towns that condoned it? His cock was on standby. He could lube it up in the bathroom and take care of himself, but why be married if you have to resort to that? Lenora's ass was within his jurisdiction. He had proprietary rights. He put his hand on it and she swatted him away. He rubbed his dick against it and when she began to swat it she felt what it was and made a low groan and put her head under the pillow. Shane peeled back her underwear slowly so that the crack of her ass was visible, then more visible, then in one swift motion he pulled her panties all the way down. Lenora's head jerked out from under the pillow, "Stop it. What time it is? I had an awful night's sleep." But Shane's pajama bottoms were already bunched at his knees as he forcefully lifted her ass in the air, rubbed saliva onto his cock, and directed it into her with tight, economical thrusts. Lenora tried to scoot away but was stopped by Shane's firm two-handed grip on her waist. "Stop it!" Lenora shouted, "Stop it right now!" Shane closed his eyes and sped up his rhythm. Lenora cried, "You're hurting me!" Shane flinched and mumbled "yeah" with gathered energy and face-scowl, as though he were rowing crew and the finish line was just ahead, and then with a loud "ahhh!" he came and thumped his left foot on the bed and then pulled out of his wife, who was silent and glazed over, stunned staring at the bedpost in front of her.

**8:02 a.m.**

Prentiss stood in the shower soaping up his underarms and elbows and thinking that for all the bad he could say about the library—and this was a lot of bad—he appreciated its time-off schedule. Every other week, it seemed, there was a holiday for this president or that murdered humanitarian. It was as nice as working at the post office. Prentiss felt so good and proud of not having drunk anything in five months. Like he'd made it up the steepest mountain, like he really was the Little Engine That Could. His longest dry spell ever. He had, maybe, let's just consider the possibility for a minute, overcome his addiction, and to celebrate maybe that night if someone offered him a beer he would accept it like it was no big thing, and there'd be no awkward explaining to this girl Justine about him being an addict, and who was to say that the once-an-addict-always-an-addict line you got from AA was true for everybody? Look at how he'd resisted that whiskey with a beer back that Alvin had shoved in his hand. And the resolve with which he now walked past the liquor aisle in the super-market and didn't look at more than his reflection in the windows of the bars he passed going to and from work. These were the charac-teristics of a man in control. He felt real good. It was possible that he was cured. No it's not no it's not no it's not you're sick forever. Sick sick sick. One sip of beer and you'll wake up in the hospital, recovery aborted. Jail time. No Justine. No job. Just justice. "It ain't necessarily like that," Prentiss said to the showerhead. *Yes it is*, it hissed back.

**8:37 a.m.**

Sadie lifted the band of her underwear and saw the skin beneath it flush from white to pink. She'd have to wear her slimming pants to the night's dinner with Roger Nuñez and her sister and Greg. Her sister, probably with the aid of a hospital's worth of amphetamines, had kept her high school figure, or at least her junior college figure, and was five years younger to boot, which would invite comparison between her and Sadie's bodies at the restaurant, which was so unfair. Sadie had once had a very nice body. In tight jeans and an undersized T-shirt she'd made everyone wince, girls from envy and guys from desire. Did our past glories count for nothing? (Nothing.)

**8:51 a.m.**

Steve and Greg stood over an elderly lady's open upper thigh. She'd fallen the night before while reaching for a dish towel and sustained an acute fracture to her left femur bone. The surgery was routine and without complication. The assisting nurse was unusually quiet. Greg had told Steve in the changing room earlier that he'd invented some new sexual positions with the assisting nurse recently, porn-grade stuff, and that he had to be careful which hospital corridors he walked down with her, because Marlene's job now sent her all over the third and fourth floors. Steve had called his future ex-wife Anne before going in to surgery to ask what she was doing, to see if that night he might drive down to Willits and take her to dinner or a movie, and a man had answered the phone at her apartment. "What do you expect, Steve?" Anne said when she took the phone. "You thought you'd drive two hours to go to dinner? You and I aren't even on speaking terms." What kind of thing was that to say? Well, it was weary and unsympathetic, for starters. It was zero patience and unromantic and

unnostalgic. It dismissed out of hand the possibility of their friendship, much less their reconciliation, and he should have expected it.
Steve mechanically washed his hands when the surgery was done and
Greg asked what he had planned for that night. "Nothing," he said.
Greg rubbed his head and his face and all the itches he'd had to suppress during surgery, and said, "It's Christmas Eve. Meet up with us
for drinks. I'm going to dinner with Marlene and her sister and some
guy, but afterward we're going to the Jambalaya. Around ten. You
should come. I'm worried about you, buddy." Steve forced a smile
and said, "I'm all right. But maybe. Maybe I'll come."

**9:08 a.m.**

Elaine's father in Red Bluff wasn't answering his phone and he didn't
have an answering machine. Said it took away the spontaneity. He
liked sitting around with a good action movie on the tube and hearing the phone ring and having no idea who it might be. There was so
much suspense when he answered. Elaine made her kids French
toast and afterward they, superamped on sugar, fled the scene of
sticky table and half-empty glasses of milk and a misshapen butter
stick to jump on their bicycles and speed away for adventure's sake,
the younger trailing after the elder, their shouts dying in the fullness
of morning. She listened to a message left on her machine by Principal Giaccone the day before, a rambling apology for his collaboration
with the private investigator that Greg had hired—he'd told the
detective about his and Elaine's afternoon tryst, and Elaine had
received a note from Greg saying that if she thought she'd lay the infidelity charge on him with impunity, she was sorely mistaken, because
he had ammunition—and the hope that they might see each other
later in the week. A possum had strewn her garbage all over the front
lawn. There was no more spray cleaner for the table. *No more a smart
little girl with no heart, I have found me a wonderful guy. I am in a
conventional dither, with a conventional star in my eye. South Pacific*
was on permaloop in her mind.

**10 a.m.**

"Lill?" Lillith's mother came into the living room with the top of her blouse unbuttoned. Her foundation and blush were applied thickly, giving her a marionette effect. "What are you doing watching TV? We have to leave in ten minutes and you're not dressed."

"I'm not going."

"Let's not have this conversation. We know it by heart."

"But you don't listen because I told you that I'm a nonbeliever. A *nonbeliever,* Mom. I don't think Jesus died for our sins and I don't think he walked on water and I don't think God spoke to Moses out of a burning bush and I don't think Abraham lived to be a hundred and seventy-five years old and I don't think it rained for forty days and forty nights and I don't—"

"Lightning's going to strike any minute and I can't afford the repairs. So I'd appreciate it if you'd get dressed. We now have eight minutes."

Lillith went to her room and put on slacks and a rib-knit pullover and boots. She checked her email and had been spammed by eight adult sites offering her good money if she'd agree to go to some chat rooms and talk explicitly about her sexual fantasies of older married men. How gross! And her email server was so slow in deleting all of it even though its spam-blocking feature was supposedly so sophisticated.

"Honey?" her mother tapped on her door. "Could you please help the twins? Two minutes."

"I'm busy."

"So am I. Please do this for me and I'll take us to lunch at the Red Lion after church."

"Yippee."

In the hallway her youngest siblings, fraternal twins Mordecai and Bethany, were spit-shined in untied shoes. Lillith sang the laces song to them while demonstrating again how a pretty bow was made as their other sister Marie stomped by on the rag and was such a bitch. Oh, Jesus. *Ella es la puta del diablo,* the whore of satan. Lillith's baby could end up like Marie; they shared genes. Someone pass the coat hanger. She took the twins' hands and led them through the open front door and into the back of the car. There she waited in the quiet that overcame the twins whenever they donned their church clothes, a Pavlovian silence. She was skinnier than Sam's last girlfriend and Sam would never like her. Her mother suspected her of lying and stealing and occultism. Her father called her Pooh-Bear and bought her inappropriate underwear. Her McDonald's manager, Ron, stood next to her for five minutes at a time even after she'd been fully trained at the register, and he made a production every day of counting out her cash tray with her cent by cent. Teenage girls felt powerless. Lillith was a Wiccan. Girls aged twelve to nineteen went through tumultuous physical and emotional changes, and experienced for the first time sex and drugs and familial estrangement, and inherited a set of women's values some of which were deeply self-destructive. Lillith that evening was going to preside over a spell to save a man's life. The rate of depression among girls her age was twice that of boys. Cast the corners and light the joss sticks and time her incantation to the low tide, with Tina and Frederick acting as her auxiliary magi. Anorexia was about control over one's body more than being beautiful in the way that rape was about power more than sex. She was going to plunge her ensorcelled hands through the Astral Wall, grab Leon Meed, and bring him home. Emotional violence among girls equaled physical violence among boys, and Lillith would climb up the rope ladder she'd spent so much time weaving, look around at the new world, and embrace it.

**10:11 a.m.**

If anything it reminded Joon-sup of when he first came to the U.S. and misinterpreted conversations. He'd think people were talking about prenuptial agreements when really they'd be discussing cross-country skiing, and he'd make the apology with crimson face and go numb with embarrassment at having said something about the caution that defines weak love. His was a feeling of *I-don't-have-a-toe-hold*. And yet he'd thought clearly then and he could think clearly now. He could get to where he needed to go and feed and clothe himself. In many ways he was still okay; he was fine. Fundamentally, however, he was not okay or fine. He was out of sync, misaligned with reality, and he shouldn't postpone seeking a remedy.

Driving to the Better Bagel he didn't call himself crazy because that was too broad a term and included mass murderers and people who thought they were Caesar Augustus. He knew he was Joon-sup, of Pusan, South Korea, and he preferred thinking of himself as "touched." There were no voices in his head. He was not violent. He understood the value of stoplights and birthday cards and having a good credit rating. He was just a little off. But the sad part about being just a little off—of being touched and not crazy—was his constant mindfulness of this offness, his appreciation of how much help he needed. Joon-sup had to check himself into an asylum. He had to insist that they lock him up and not release him until he was sure never, ever to see Leon Meed again. He had to demand that they keep him under surveillance and in regimented therapy, and he'd not open his own restaurant or meet a girl he liked or play a part in local environmentalism. He would be gone a long time and return with mental scars, a veteran of his internal civil war.

Sitting in the Better Bagel when Joon-sup arrived was Barry, spreading hummus over an onion bagel and tearing open a paper packet of salt. Blood pressure be damned. Barry had changed quickly in the last couple of weeks. He was twenty-four and had thought everything settled, having lived by himself for years, slightly shy, a sexual teetotaler, convinced that Eros held nothing in store for him. Long nights of refusing to acknowledge the emergency in his lap. Whereas now he was a SWAT team attending to the emergency all the time. With and without Alvin. It was as if he had to make up for all his past neglect of sex by fixating on it with Olympic intensity. Everywhere he looked was a doable guy, a possible tango, and it was so exciting. Unreasonable, yes, but exciting and such a relief, like he'd been the sickly boy kept indoors all the time who was now cured and got to play outside, this great new lease on life that had previously seemed unattainable.

Barry bought a bagel to go and lingeringly placed money in Joon-sup's hand. He sighed oh well when Joon-sup didn't respond in kind, and left.

**10:17 a.m.**

Eve sat in Skeletor's house with Skeletor's mom and Aaron and the Odd Wala, watching a televangelist's hair. They all were. They were transfixed by this hair that shone like a wet otter on the head of the thick-necked preacher grafting God's word onto the everyday problems facing Americans. A man making scripture relevant to people. He was talking about how Joshua's six-day march around the walls of Jericho, with his seven priests carrying the ark aloft, may appear to us an inadequate method of overcoming our enemies, of conquering their resistance, but that against faith in God Jericho's forty-foot-high walls were like bedsheets in a windstorm. Faith was harder than titanium, faster than light, more mercurial than water. Armed with faith you were equal to any challenge.

"I'll bet he uses brilliantine," said the Odd Wala, a downy-headed twenty-year-old with enormous baseball-mitt-sized hands, a guy who looked both ten years younger and older than he was, like one of those broad-forehead kids who seem simultaneously middle-aged and preadolescent, "and beeswax."

Aaron riffled through Skeletor's music collection and said, "Mousse and blow dry, then hair-spray."

Eve thought that a faith harder than titanium might hurt to land on if you were falling, but she liked the idea of it also being mercurial, able to flow over and around any obstacle. A marijuana cigarette was handed to her that she passed along without smoking. This was a big contradiction, this hardness and mercurialness. Maybe faith changed in different situations, a protean energy adaptable to your needs. When you required strength it was titanium, for speed it was light, and for flexibility it was water. It endowed you with every conceivable survival skill.

"Do you think he's had his chin worked on?" asked Aaron.

"Look at that cleft," said the Odd Wala. "It's a golf tee."

"Marcus!" cried Skeletor's mom. "What are you doing in there?"

From his bathroom Skeletor yelled, "Nothing!"

Eve's parents were Christians, but of a purely circumstantial variety given that they were brought up in America; they no more questioned their faith than they did their support for the local football team. They never mentioned it when she talked to them on the phone.

**10:21 a.m.**

Elaine's father sounded hoarse on the phone, like he'd been ringside all night, shouting for his contender to quit losing. But it was nothing. A little winter cold that she shouldn't worry about.

"Do you have plans for your birthday?" she asked.

"I'm going to fix my shortwave that broke a couple weeks ago, when I was listening to—" He got quiet.

"Dad?"

"Yes."

"I miss you and so do the boys. They're always asking when we can come visit."

"That'd be fine."

"Are you doing better at concentrating? Have you been practicing on the crossword puzzles and brain teasers, the focus exercises your doctor recommended?"

"Could do that."

"I should tell you that Greg and I are splitting up. It's a long, complicated story, but that's the gist of it, and now there will be more room in the house for you if you decide to come live with us."

"I don't know when that is."

"What I'm saying is that I want to repeat my offer for you to live with us. Greg has moved out."

"Where has he gone?"

"To a friend's house. The point is that you could move in."

"I see."

"Are you feeling the head clouds again?" The head clouds were how Elaine's father described the confusion that overtook him sometimes, the fog obscuring his thoughts.

"The what?"

"Dad, it sounds like you're not following me. I'll call you later. I just want to wish you happy birthday."

"That's nice. Thank you."

"I love you."

"Thank you."

"I'm going to come visit in the next few days. I'm on Christmas vacation."

"Thank you."

She hung up and began washing dishes.

**10:30 a.m.**

Eve walked along Tenth Street and passed the Congregationalist church with its small assembled-letter sign listing the day's service times and pastor and topic. Eve had nowhere particular to be that morning, except maybe "around," whatever that meant, when Ryan woke up, and she thought it might be interesting to sit in on a religious service for once in her life. As a look at how the other half lived. As an experiment. She climbed the steps and entered a crowded reception lobby and stared across to two sets of open French doors that led into the worship hall. There was organ music and the scent of an electric radiator underlying seventy brands of floral perfume and aftershave cologne. Eve was the only person wearing black lipstick. Families and the individually faithful talked and read the program and generated a quiet hum of high-stakes gossip. Someone's brother had prostate cancer. Someone's daughter had broken off her engagement. Someone's nephew had joined the ministry. Eve turned to leave with the sinking and petty thought that the people of God were dull and tried too hard to smell like flowers.

**12:24 p.m.**

"It was rape," Lenora said.

Shane glanced at the odometer. "We're married."

"I didn't marry you. I don't know who I married, but it wasn't you. To go and beat up someone you don't know at CalCourts and be drunk. When you made a vow! You made a vow, Shane! You'd had this crazy childhood but when we met you said you'd reformed. I mean, and you did and it wasn't a lie until— You've been completely normal until— And then this morning I can't even tell you what I felt like when you raped me. Like a whore. Like—"

"We're not going to have this talk. We've had this talk." Shane smoothed a crease in his trousers and signaled left at Emery Lane. A logging truck roared past them trailing diesel exhaust. They were going home to change and then meet friends at the Pantry for lunch.

"We have not had this talk. This is the first time for this talk. The CalCourts thing—"

"There's nothing more to say about CalCourts except that that guy pissed me off and he deserved it. He was beating off in the hot tub and I should have put him in the hospital."

"What kind of talk is this? You sound like a TV character with the put-him-in-the-hospital. He *did* go to the hospital, but anyway that's only one episode. This morning what you did was unacceptable. Just because we're married doesn't give you the right to—"

"It gives me the right to do what husbands do. I swear sometimes you must be listening to the feminazis with all this about marriage isn't a holy union and you have these individual rights. What do individual rights have to do with us? We are going to be together for an eternity. Even after we die. You know this. This is scripture."

"Drinking alcohol and beating up someone you don't know and raping your wife is not scripture."

"Say it one more time. Say 'rape' one more time and there's going to be consequences." He waved at a neighbor walking her poodle. "It's like you don't want the marriage to work anymore so you're putting this crazy spin on everything."

"Tell me how you justify beating up that guy and drinking alcohol. The Book of Mormon forbids those things. These are the most basic tenets of our church."

"Do you drink Diet Coke?"

"I can't believe you'd compare that to what you did."

"Do you? Tell me, is having caffeine not a violation of church doctrine?"

They were in the driveway and a light rain fell and the windshield wipers noisily and smearily cleared away the water. Their bull terrier, a three-year-old named Cassie, pressed her nose through the wire mesh of her kennel and howled.

"It is," said Lenora. "It's a violation and I admit it but there's a sizable difference between that sin and beating up—"

"So you admit it and I admit that in some respects I shouldn't have got in that fight, except that he was a dirty faggot which is worse than anything I did. He was jacking off in the hot tub, and that means he was the one sinning against God and I was just an agent of his punishment."

Lenora shook her head and watched Cassie pace back and forth. "Are you calling yourself an agent of God?"

"I'm just saying. There's maybe more than meets the eye here, but you'd never consider that because suddenly you're defending every faggot and women's lib fanatic out there. How can I communicate with you when you've gone off the deep end? I don't even know you when you're like this."

"I don't know you, period." She got out of the car and walked briskly inside, not waiting for Shane to come up behind her before slamming the door and going to her room to cry, lunch abandoned.

**1:38 p.m.**

Eve placed her hand on Ryan's forehead. He was cold. You heard about how quickly body heat dissipated after death, that within two hours the body's blood seemed always to have run cold, but you weren't prepared for the actual feel of it. Like skin-textured silicone, lifeless and pliant and cool. Their apartment was a cold December, and perhaps he'd been dead a long time already. His eyes were almost closed and he wore a ripped cartoon T-shirt; his blue hair lay stagnant around his neck.

Eve sat down on the British flag they used as a throw rug and stared dumbly at the body. Nausea welled up in her stomach and she vomited into a flowerpot that once had held a house fern but now was full of pennies and garbage bag twisties. The stereo speakers emitted a low-fi buzz from the amplifier that was left on and an open CD case implied that the last thing he'd heard was the hopped-up world beat of Anglo-Zimbabweans.

A fly landed on Eve's knee and she thought of how ironic it was for the fly to mistake her body for the corpse. *He is dead.* She began to scream, to wail, to give egress to a force of absolute terror and loss and disbelief. She was momentarily insane and she screamed and her ears rang. It was such a force, a juggernaut charging through the space between her and Ryan and the place to which Ryan had gone, if he'd gone anywhere. Nevermore.

She screamed and screamed and screamed and then shut her mouth and got to her feet, but her ankles were made of putty and she crumpled to the floor, where she lay hugging the ground and knew not to move.

Which was how Elaine found her ten minutes later when, responding to the noise that reached her outside, she let herself into the apartment. At first Elaine thought that both prone bodies were dead, but then she saw that at least the girl was breathing. The boy, he looked familiar and yes upon closer inspection he was the janitor at Muir. She'd passed him in the halls a hundred times and had remarked on his hair, how much she liked it, and he'd smiled and said he liked *her* hair, which was plainly a joke but a good-natured one. The boy was dead. She remembered how, leaving Principal Giaccone's office on That Day, she'd worried that he knew what had happened and would think less of her. That they wouldn't be able to imagine the best about each other anymore.

"I'm Elaine Perry," she said, stepping away from the body and looking down at Eve. "I live in the house next door."

"He's dead." Eve gazed hypnotized at her unlaced tennis shoe.

"Did you just find him?"

"Mmm."

"Have you called the police?"

"No."

Elaine located a cord coming out of the wall jack and followed it to a clear plastic phone buried under socks and underwear. She called the emergency number and then sat down on the floor next to Eve.

"I think you need to get up and explain how this happened, because the police will be here soon."

Eve didn't stir but was intent on that shoe. "He did smack."

"It was a drug overdose?"

"And so say all of us," Eve sang quietly, brokenly, mesmerically, "and so say all of us."

"I heard you screaming."

"That nobody can deny, that nobody can deny. For he's a jolly good fe-he-llo, that nobody can deny."

Elaine pushed a strand of hair behind her left ear and hugged her knees to her chest. She'd never seen someone in shock before. She reached out to stroke the girl's back and Eve shot up straight and her face was excited and long and alabaster white.

"I was fifteen," Eve said. "Ryan he was seventeen but he was in my math class in high school because he never studied and I did so I'd give him my homework to copy. We'd meet on the Row and he'd scribble it down with his beautiful hands; I'd sit across from him on a bench and supposedly study but really I'd watch the muscles of his hands working, they were so graceful. Sometimes he'd frown and you

could tell he was trying to understand the math, and I'd point out
when he miscopied a number and he'd look up at me and say, 'I'm trying to make it look like trial and error.' Then he'd press the eraser side
of his pencil into my knee and wink and one time I felt this explosion
travel from my knee to my head and it was love. I don't know where it
came from, like when you shiver and suddenly realize you've been
cold a long time. We weren't going out and he'd never said anything,
but he was so beautiful and we had this daily ritual and it had become
overpowering. I mean Juliet couldn't touch the hem of what I felt. So
that I wanted to dissolve into him, on the bench on the Row in front
of God and everybody, just collapse into this love. To disappear. After
a while I couldn't keep it in any longer, but I couldn't say anything out-
right, so one day I wrote on my homework in the middle of the math
problems *I have something to tell you but you have to guess*. I gave the
homework to him in the morning and he started to copy and I sat
there pretending to read for English. After every word that might as
well have been Latin I had such an impossible time understanding
them, I'd look up and see where he was in the copying, as he worked
his way toward what I'd written, and he had short hair then and it
spiked out and I looked at it and couldn't think what to do if he started
laughing or got mad when he read my note. I tried to prepare myself
for whatever happened. Then he was on the problem right before the
note and I closed my book I couldn't even pretend to read. Then he
was copying the note and I waited almost hyperventilating for him to
look at me, but instead he just moved right on to the next problem,
and I figured that he must have been thinking about something else,
otherwise how could he not have acknowledged it? Then it occurred
to me that every morning his mind was probably a million miles away
from me. All I thought about was him, but he was thinking of food or
getting high or his skateboard or whatever. I sat there thinking that
Ryan only smiled at me and poked my knee with his pencil because I
let him copy my homework. It was so obvious and I'd been a fool. I
mean, what did I think? That he could have done the work on his own
but was copying mine as an excuse to be with me? I was so upset that

I started crying and that was even worse, oh God that was horrible because I couldn't control it. And Ryan didn't notice, he just kept copying away, and I'd never felt so alone and humiliated and awful. I tried to be quiet but my chest made these little moans. Then he was done and he looked up and I hated him then, I hated his eyes and upturned nose and spiky hair and girly lips and he ignored that I was a wreck, that my face was red and I couldn't breathe. Then he said, all blasé, 'Could you check this over for me? I got a C on my last assignment because you didn't catch a few mistakes I made.' I was so mad and hurt I couldn't say anything, so I took his paper and looked at it but couldn't read it, my eyes were flooded with tears. Then I gave it back. 'Looks fine,' I said. He was like, 'I don't think so. I see something right here that I need your help on.' And he gave it to me again and pointed to my note that he'd copied on his paper, so I read it as well as I could and it wasn't the same thing I'd written. It said, *I have one guess and one thing to tell you. My guess is that you want me to quit being so stupid and ask you out. My thing to tell you is that I was about to do it anyway. Us math idiots have a hard time making the first move.* I must have read it a hundred times before I looked at him, and he was anxious, like *he* was the one who wasn't sure how *I'd* respond. We sat for a minute like that and I had a headache from all my crying and my nose was congested. Then it was like I'd woken up from a nightmare and the world was so clear. Every crack in the school walls, every warped piece of wood in the benches, every beautiful shade of brown in Ryan's eyes. I handed back the paper and my mouth was frozen in this huge grin, I just couldn't stop smiling, it was like trying to keep your hair down in the wind, and he put his hand on mine and leaned forward and we kissed. People applauded and catcalled and I was in another world where things work out in the end."

**3:30 p.m.**

Sadie wore a diamond broach and lavender silk blouse because she wouldn't have time to go home and change before meeting her sister,

Roger, and Greg for dinner. She was volunteering at the Free Clinic until six thirty. She held a diet cola in one hand and wrote a patient evaluation with the other. The two-week period beginning December 20 and ending January 3 was the busiest at the clinic, when it worked in closer tandem with the Suicide Prevention Hotline and treated a swollen number of walk-ins, and when it relied on trained counselors and therapists like Sadie to absorb the spillover from the permanent staff's caseload. Sadie sat in an examination room by herself and pretended to turn down the volume of the piped-in "O Tannenbaum," which was playing for possibly the fourth time that afternoon. She heard a knock at the door and a receptionist opened it to usher in a young Korean man.

"Dr. Jorgenson, this is June Soup Kim," said the receptionist, who smiled at Joon-sup and at Sadie and then retreated, closing the door behind her.

"Hi," said Sadie. "Please, have a seat." She patted the armrest of a foam-cushioned chair and put aside the evaluation and kept her cola. She noticed a small tear in the sleeve of her new blouse that hadn't yet given her the months of confidence she'd anticipated when buying it. Beauty was so fragile. "We could start by talking about why you're here, if you feel comfortable with that."

Joon-sup nodded and folded his hands on his lap. "I need you to write a recommendation to put me into a mental hospital."

"What's the matter?"

"I'm schizophrenic."

"Have you been diagnosed by a professional?"

"No."

"What makes you think you're schizophrenic?"

"I've read the literature. I have both the positive and negative symptoms."

"I see. Could you explain what those are?"

"My positive symptoms are delusions and hallucinations. My negative symptoms include blunted affect, apathy, and social withdrawal. I'm very far gone."

Sadie finished her cola and placed it on a table behind her chair. The tear was in the shape of an L. "You've had hallucinations?"

"Yes." Joon-sup sat rigidly still with an intense yet immobile expression, as though awaiting the results of an election in which he was running. He cleared his throat. "I require hospitalization and antipsychotics. I'm aware that I'll be giving up my right to move about freely. And I'm aware that I won't be released unless a board of doctors thinks I can make it on my own with the help of the antipsychotics."

"You're prepared to give up a lot."

"I want to get better."

"That's good. Did you make the decision to seek help on your own, or have your friends or family been involved?"

"On my own."

"Do you have SSI?"

"What's that?"

"Social Security Insurance. It covers most treatment expenses and provides some compensation for missed work. I only ask because hospitalization is expensive, and you may want to think about how to pay for it if it comes to that."

"I have health insurance."

"I should tell you right off that schizophrenia is hard to diagnose accurately. It's often confused with manic depression. How long have you experienced its symptoms?"

"Two weeks."

"That's not very long."

"It's felt long to me."

"Could you describe your symptoms in detail?"

"The main one is that I'm seeing someone who doesn't exist. I mean, he exists, but he doesn't exist in the places I see him."

"Could you explain that a little more?"

Joon-sup leaned forward with his elbows on his knees, hands still folded, and said, "I see a man named Leon Meed appear and disappear. Really, though, I'm seeing the product of my imagination. An example is when I was driving in Eureka recently and he appeared in front of my van too close for me to not hit him, and then he disappeared. I was just going along and suddenly there he was and there he wasn't. I slammed on the brakes and nearly had a heart attack."

"That sounds traumatic."

"It was."

"Do you see this man a lot?"

"I see him enough."

"What about the other symptoms? The apathy and social withdrawal."

"I went with a bunch of people to southern Humboldt last week to protest a Pacific Lumber clear-cutting project, and after I saw Leon there I didn't want to have anything to do with the protest. I thought it was pointless, so I came home early and haven't talked to my friends. I've been sullen and antagonistic. I feel anxiety and self-doubt."

"You're good at recognizing what's wrong. Most people with schizophrenia aren't aware of their illness and so they resist treatment. Your desire to get well is going to be one of your best weapons in doing it."

Joon-sup stared at the floor.

"I wonder," said Sadie, "if you take any drugs now, prescription or otherwise?"

He shook his head. "Not since I began hallucinating."

"Were you taking drugs before then, that first time?"

"I may have been smoking marijuana."

"You may have?"

"Okay, I was. I was stoned, and so for a while that was how I explained it to myself. But then after the protest I knew that it wasn't the drugs. There's something wrong with my brain."

"Is there a history of mental illness in your family?"

"My aunt was involved with Aum Shinrikyo, the cult that pumped sarin gas into the Tokyo subway in the 1990s."

"Does your hallucination tell you to do certain things?"

"Leon? He wants me to bring him food."

"Your hallucination is hungry?"

"He can't get to any restaurants or supermarkets."

Sadie didn't notice her blouse's tear when she adjusted her glasses on her nose. "What's your diet like? And your physical regimen. Do you exercise?"

"I play Ultimate Frisbee. And I eat, you know, everything. Lots of vegetables. Lots of barbecue. I'm hoping to open my own restaurant, which is one of the reasons I'm so upset about my schizophrenia. It could hurt my chances to get a loan. Once I have a record of being mentally unstable, my life is going to be harder."

"I wouldn't assume that you're going to get that record."

"Why not?"

"Because I'm not convinced that you have schizophrenia."

"Yes, I do."

"Seeing someone who isn't there could be stress related. Or it could be a side effect of recreational drugs. In many significant ways you seem to me sound and in full possession of your mental faculties. I wouldn't want to recommend hospitalization unless you felt like you were a threat to yourself or to others."

"No, but—"

"I'm willing to prescribe a neuroleptic—an antipsychotic—and see how you respond. That's the best way to proceed from here. Think of it like there's no need to give you anesthesia for a headache if a couple of aspirins will do the trick."

Joon-sup said, unfolding his hands, "I hear what you're saying, but I don't think you hear what I'm saying. I'm a sick man."

"I'm going to start you on chlorpromazine and fluphenazine. And I'm going to give you my card and suggest we set up a meeting for a month from now. It takes a couple of weeks for the medication to take effect. I have my own practice in Henderson Center, so call there after Christmas and my secretary will arrange a time that works for you."

With that Sadie took out a pad of paper, scribbled in small, illegible cursive, and handed the prescription to Joon-sup, who stood and left without saying anything.

**5 p.m.**

At home Elaine found that her children had what it took to be mob-sters in charge of ransacking operations. They'd mastered search and destroy. Witness the inside-out clothes blanketing the floor, the video game cartridges launched two rooms away from their storage box, the bowls of slushy cereal and coloring books and board game pieces and (her) jewelry and (their) marbles and coins and sports equipment and dirty napkins and spilled juices and bric-a-brac everywhere. All in just two hours. It was amazing the thoroughness of the chaos. A butterfly flaps its wings in Mozambique and there's a tornado in a Eureka home. Elaine was overwhelmed before she even started cleaning—look at it, where to start?—but then she willed herself into collecting the clothes under one arm and the dishes in one hand. Every thousand-mile journey begins with a single step. Her older son was nine, fifteen years younger than the boy who'd overdosed next door. Fifteen years between an immune system destroyed by pleasure and one that had never known anything impure, save the junk food Abe quaffed at every allowance. Why did people turn from innocence to experience, knowing as they did the final outcome? So many reenactments of the Fall. So like moths to a flame.

Fifteen years ago she'd been set to enter a PhD program in English, had written an acceptance letter to Duke University and prepared to take out massive loans to fund seven years of rigorous and mind-building study, had convinced Greg that Durham, North Carolina, was a beautiful town in which to practice medicine and raise children when he finished medical school. She arranged for everything. But then, overnight, she decided not to go. Told Duke she couldn't come for personal reasons. Greg was relieved and so was she. Her career, whatever it would be, could wait. So she sub-stitute taught and then had Abraham and then Trevor. She got a master's degree in teaching at Humboldt State University. And soon after that she had a permanent job and a broken marriage and an ail-ing father and two unhappy children and a blackmailing principal and a craven addiction to bologna sandwiches. The house looked better.

Putting off the rest of the cleaning until later—the boys were outside playing and could tidy up a little when they got in—she grabbed a six-hundred-page mystery novel and lay on the couch and sank gratefully into the story of a homicidal maniac being hunted by Philadelphia's premier celibate police inspector. Fifteen years ago she'd lived on a steady diet of George Eliot and Leo Tolstoy and Charlotte Brontë; now it was mass quantities of mass market paperbacks. Her standards had fallen off a cliff. She felt like a one-time vegetarian eating cheeseburgers three times a day. This tectonic shift away from virtue and self-discipline. Was it just a variation on that boy-next-door's slide from a chemical-free life to a heroin habit? Were we all deteriorating, and only some of us showed it? She closed her book.

**6:33 p.m.**

"What are you doing?" asked Carl Frost as he knocked and then opened the door to Prentiss's bedroom and leaned against a grandfather-clock-sized chest of drawers.

"I'll give you three guesses." Ties were laid out on Prentiss's bed like a salesman's samples beside a pair of black trousers and light-glinting shoes, and he was buttoning up a stiff white shirt he'd bought earlier that afternoon. It still had section creases from the cardboard square around which it had been wrapped in plastic sealing; it was hopeful and stiff and nervous.

"It looks like you're putting on a suit."

Prentiss picked up an amoeba-patterned tie and examined it for stains. "You must be taking the ginkgo and the vitamin B complexes."

"My question is why?"

"Got a date."

"Slow down. This is the first I'm hearing about it."

"And it'll be the last."

"Why's that? Is it a man?"

"Fuck you."

"Then tell me who it is. I tell you about all my women."

"Don't know what women that'd be."

"How about Justine? The one I scored at the Rathskellar where an hour after I meet her she's calling me Daddy. I told you about that. My pimp ratings soared through the roof and you know it."

Prentiss buttoned his collar—tight—and tried not to think about what Frost was saying, because the past was history and this Justine-Frost thing happened and that's that and there ain't no point getting all worked up about it. We all of us got pasts, and none of us is a saint and we're not pure and we're animals that do animal things but that doesn't make up the whole picture. Prentiss himself had done things that he'd rather not have Justine know about because we're all on a journey that's bound to have a few wrong turns and her peccadillo before she met him was, so what.

Frost said, grooming his mustache with his thumb and middle finger, "You're the one who hasn't gotten any since you moved in."

"We're not going to talk about this."

"You've been dry for months. It worries me."

"That's a waste of compassion. I'm all right so you can go back to whatever you were doing before you stopped by for this friendly chat."

"No, seriously. I'm glad you have a date. Everyone deserves someone, especially you since you're such a good guy. You know, when I was grinding on Justine I thought about sending her into your room when I was done, just to give you a little."

"You're a generous man."

"You can thank me later."

"Okay, then."

"And don't think of it like affirmative action," Frost said. "Don't be like, 'mercy fuck,' because it's not like that."

Prentiss's chest tightened and he was going to ignore the implications of this because they were ambiguous and could be read in dozens of different ways but no wait hold everything. Hold the pots and pans. Still the racket. There was a veiled significance to Frost's words. Prentiss bent over and pulled a ferocious knot in his shoelaces. Standing up with tucked-in white shirt and black slacks. He looked at Frost and he had a real fucked-up sensation of being hollowed out at this particular moment. Because he was doing some serious deduction. What now, why did he have to think this? Like maybe Justine was going out with him on account of Frost told her to. Prentiss felt sick. It made sense from a certain angle, because he was just a drunk nigger working the stacks of the public library—thirty-two years old and taking baby steps toward sobriety and had a queen for a sponsor and he was never going to be a white lawyer—and she was this beautiful white girl who Frost could have put up to it. Prentiss was a charity case, was how she would see it. And here Frost was toying with him trying to get him to brag about Justine so Frost could laugh and say that he'd masterminded the whole thing, that he had so much control over this pussy that he could give it away.

"You'd do that for me, wouldn't you?" said Prentiss. Despite himself his voice broke.

Frost straightened up and turned in the doorway. "If you get tired of her in the morning, send her back my way. I'll be asleep but that don't matter."

*Send her back my way.* As good as admitted it. Prentiss couldn't remember feeling so sick without having gotten drunk first. Except maybe once when he was a kid and had been friends with a boy named Phil and they'd ridden bikes together through Old Town and gone looking for sea anemones at Centerville Beach and they'd been blood brothers until one day when Prentiss was crouched behind a hedge at recess, just playing by himself, he heard Phil tell Travis Jacobson that Prentiss was a stupid nigger, and that he only played with him because his parents made him "be nice to the black boy." Prentiss remembered that moment so well he could still feel the hedge digging into his skin with its leaves and thousands of gnarled branches. He could hear Travis's laugh in Frost's, and disappointment and shame blended together in him like a double malt scotch. One rough liquid. His eyes stung. People are nice to you because they feel sorry for you.

"I got to take a piss," Prentiss said, brushing past Frost. And inside the bathroom he shut and locked the door and punched the wall tiles in the shower, kicked at the tub, and beat the porcelain, and converted his tears to rage—such a small alchemy—and kept doing it until he couldn't anymore and had to sit down on the rim of the tub, like a bird dazed from flying into glass.

**7 p.m.**

"The very thought of water in a public place makes me queasy," Alvin said, watching Barry pack his towel and swimsuit into a deflated nylon duffel bag.

"I won't tell you about it later," Barry said. He couldn't find his goggles. Or his flip-flops. He stepped over Alvin's legs dangling from the bed and ran his hand behind the laundry basket, where so much dust had collected he was tempted to forgo swimming and sweep the floor instead. Except that he'd made a new resolution—to be super-toned, super quickly—and shouldn't set the wrong precedent. Who knew when he'd next need to impress someone (Shane) with his shirt off, when the mystery of his body would be revealed (to Shane) and a soft belly might make everything else soft (God forbid)?

"Want to meet at the Ritz later, around eight thirty?" Alvin asked.

"I'm not sure I'll be done by then. How about nine thirty?" Barry said this casually, yet it seemed to elicit a look of suspicion from Alvin. Was his motivation for swimming obvious? Or that he was worrying more than normal about his appearance? Barry had to relax. They'd only known each other for two weeks. He thought of the parable about the dog on a bridge with a bone in its mouth that sees its own reflection in the river below and barks for the reflected dog's bone. Its bone falls into the water and the dog is left with nothing. Alvin was stable and a known quantity and Shane might want nothing to do with him and to pursue him he'd be throwing away a sure thing for this chance in a thousand. Though perhaps it wasn't like the dog parable at all, because wasn't that impossible chance, that minuscule possibility, if its success offered a great enough reward, the one Pascal insisted we take in order not to lead lives of tragic inconsequence? His wager that we had everything to gain? Of course Pascal was talking about faith in God, but love was love was love.

**7:22 p.m.**

At A.J.'s Market, Steve picked up a package of Hob-Nobs—its waxy orange paper read *One nibble and you're nobbled*—and walked down the aisle past the disposable toiletries, his thoughts an auctioneer's soliloquy about the plastic razors and cotton swabs that would end up in California City, a town of hundreds of empty desert square miles that was slowly turning into a full-time landfill in the Mojave Desert. What would the state do when California City ran out of space? Where would it look? Steve momentarily forgot why he'd come to A.J.'s. Orange juice. He set down the Hob-Nobs next to the nasal decongestants and went to the partially frosted glass refrigerator doors to select a gallon of juice and a small tub of cream cheese. At the cash register the clerk rang him up and Steve pulled out money and then said to wait a minute. A Korean guy behind him in line made no sign of impatience. Steve ran to the nasal decongestants, snatched the Hob-Nobs, and ran back to add them to his purchases. "Could I get a receipt?" he asked.

He ripped off the top of the orange juice container at the door on his way out and took a long, deep drink. His craving for the juice was intense. Why had he gone back for the Hob-Nobs? He only liked the chocolate-covered kind and these were plain. He wasn't even hungry. The Methedrine he'd taken an hour ago. A.J.'s had the dirtiest parking lot in the world. Vivid potato-chip wrappers like sloughed-off shells, as if the chips had molted and crawled away as so many chip bodies, and the soda cups and beer cans and shattered glass and cesspuddles of oily urine with incoming rivulets of spit and blood. It was horrible. Steve drank more orange juice and this was an apocalyptic scene. The door opened behind him and the Korean guy crossed the lot—the landscape of riotous decay—to a faded green van. Steve felt like he understood California City then and looked up at the A.J.'s door, atop which was a silver video camera, a raptor cold and bloodthirsty, panning from left to right to left. Steve no longer craved the orange juice. He wanted to throw it away or dump it into the cesspuddles. Crumble the Hob-Nobs into dust and scatter them to the wind, for all is vanity.

His heart beat like a hummingbird's and the still air whistled.

The Korean guy came back across the lot toward him and said, "My van's not starting and I think it's the battery. Do you have jumper cables? I took mine out last weekend for some reason."

"Jumper cables?" Steve didn't want to go home with the orange juice and sit there all night staring at photo albums of Anne; perhaps he'd meet up with Greg later. He went to his car and opening the trunk left tracers on his eyes as though the world were made of taffy, and he gave a thumbs-up sign to the Korean guy. He stood up straight and the cables writhed in his hand like red and black snakes. He drove to the van and parked facing it, the front bumpers four inches apart.

Hovering over the exposed engines, the two men began arranging the cables positive to positive and negative to negative.

"Thanks a lot for this. My name's Jack, by the way."

"I'm Steve."

"Yeah, this is a corroded battery; I may have to get a new one but I'm—"

"Would you excuse me?" Steve left one of the cables unclamped and grabbed the Hob-Nobs from his front seat and jogged back to A.J.'s.

Joon-sup watched him go and couldn't do anything more by himself, so he leaned against the side of the van and felt head-sore. He'd had a hard day since learning that he wouldn't be hospitalized. He'd spent hours doubting Dr. Jorgenson's professional competence and resolved to get a second opinion. His interview had been so superficial that only the most careless of doctors could have concluded anything on its basis.

As he stood there a knock on the window came from inside his van. He turned around and his worst fear was confirmed: Leon sitting behind the wheel, waving at him.

"I'm having trouble with the door!" came Leon's muted voice as he knocked on the window again and pointed down. Joon-sup looked at him and could not tell a hawk from a handsaw. He wanted to get Steve but knew that Steve would see nothing there, for Leon was only a hallucination in his mind—he felt like a lucid dreamer recognizing the irreality of his environment—so he ignored it. Hallucinations were like royalty or paper money, worthless if you didn't believe in their value. "I'm sorry about being here," Leon said, rolling down the window. "Is there a trick to the door or something?"

Joon-sup fought the urge to answer, like suppressing a cough, and when Steve returned without the Hob-Nobs, Joon-sup didn't point to Leon because Leon was gone.

**7:58 p.m.**

It was a surprise for Silas to learn that his waitress at the Red Lion Inn lounge was a friend of his great-niece Lillith's, who ran into the bar and grabbed Tina by the hand and was pulling her out the door when Tina broke free and said she had to tip out and to fill in her time card, during which activities Lillith noticed her uncle and the two of them hugged awkwardly and established that she would give him a ride home.

"You're sure it's not too much trouble?" Silas asked. "And why aren't you at home tonight? It's Christmas Eve. Your mother must be disappointed."

"She'll get over it," Lillith said. "Plus I'm a Wiccan. Christmas doesn't mean anything to me, in a religious sense, that is."

"It's the ritual that's important." Silas had never believed this more than at that moment. "And what do you mean, you're a Wiccan? What's that?"

"It's a type of neopagan. We're witches, technically, and we're like the fifth- or sixth-biggest religion in the country now."

"I had no idea."

"We keep pretty underground because there's so much persecution of witches. Christians freak out about it and think we're the devil. They attack us sometimes."

"You've been attacked?"

"Not me personally. But other Wiccans have been beaten up and killed. It's a pretty regular thing."

Tina joined them and yelled good-bye to the bartender and they left, Silas following the girls to the car in the Red Lion Inn parking lot, where he was introduced to Franklin and got in the back next to his waitress, Tina, who was, like Lillith and Franklin, a junior in high school. Tina began talking. She'd only been working at the Red Lion Inn for two months, though it seemed longer given how little business the restaurant/bar/lounge got and how slowly time passed for Tina and her coworkers, who had to look industrious even when no customers were there to appreciate their industry. The manager thought that idle hands were the devil's business, and he said so, often and with feeling. He had a nervous habit of asking the workers to tell him what they were doing all the time, even when it was obvious that they were prepping for the late-dinner crowd, folding napkins, or getting a customer a side of ranch dressing, and this habit annoyed the workers and made them in turn nervous and resentful of the manager and desirous of fucking him up one night in an anonymous alleyway ambush.

"So yeah, I kind of hate it," she said to Silas, chewing gum and looking straight ahead. "Except sometimes I love it. The dishwashers are these crazy kids from Zoe Barnum, you know the alternative high school, and when the manager isn't there we get stoned and play with the buffet table, which is the funnest thing in the world to do."

"I'll remember that," said Silas.

Tina smiled and said, "You were my favorite customer tonight."

"Thank you," Silas said, blushing a little. He'd been in a peculiar mood all day and didn't know exactly what he'd do when he got home. He had eaten a quarter pound of peanuts at least and memorized the beer mirror triptychs and exhausted the novelty of sitting among travel lodgers, and now perhaps he'd go to sleep. He thought of the conversation he'd had with Eve, the girl at the plasma donation bank, and felt that he'd spoken truly, that life did reintroduce wonder at its close. If not another childhood, old age was at least another occasion for discovery, like waking up from an afternoon nap to better appreciate the crepuscular light show. In the front Lillith and Franklin were talking too quietly for him to make out their conversation, so he leaned back in his seat and rested his eyes for a moment that became a long moment so that when he opened them he saw a sign for the turnoff to Arcata coming up. "Excuse me?" he said to Franklin, scooting forward and tapping the driver's shoulder. "Aren't you taking me home? I live in Eureka."

"He does?" Franklin asked Lillith. "You do?" he said to Silas's reflection in the rearview mirror.

"I told you he lives on E Street," Lillith said.

"I thought you meant in Arcata."

"Why would you think that?"

"I don't know. You should've said something before now. We've been going north for ten minutes already."

"Goddamn it," said Lillith. "Uncle Silas?" She turned around in her seat. "I'm sorry but we're kind of late for an important event up at Moonstone Beach and we don't have time to take you back to Eureka. Do you mind getting a cab back if we drop you off in Arcata?"

"A cab?" Silas said. "But I was just in Eureka. I would've walked if I'd known you couldn't take me. I don't have money for a cab."

"We can give it to you."

"I'm broke," said Franklin.

"Me, too," said Tina.

Lillith did an exaggerated double take. "What about your tip money?" she asked Tina.

"It was a shitty night and I only made ten bucks, and plus I owe five of it to my mom when I get home."

"I can't believe it," said Lillith.

"He's *your* uncle. You should give him the money."

"I spent all my last paycheck on presents already." Lillith slouched in her seat and twisted her hair around her left forefinger and brooded and said, "Uncle Silas, what if you come with us to the beach for just a little while, and then we can take you back later?"

Silas felt a gnawing in his stomach and burped painfully and although he'd been ambivalent about going home earlier, now he wanted nothing more than to be sitting in his recliner with a glass of buttermilk. "It's forty degrees out. The beach is a terrible place to be. I want to go home." Just then the highway rose in elevation and to the right he looked down on a valley where an aqua-green luminescence glowed from the treetops. Everything sylvan. Silas stared and felt a descending roller-coaster sensation.

"You can't," said Lillith.

Silas tried to suppress his elation in order to sound indignant. "Then you're kidnapping me. I demand that you take me home now."

Franklin looked at Lillith, who rolled her eyes and pointed forward. "He'll get over it," she said.

"I will not get over it!" Silas yelled from the backseat, getting into his role and delighted to be making a scene. "This is an attack on my dignity. Your mother's going to hear about this."

"It's an emergency," said Lillith. "We have to rescue someone from the Astral Plane. I don't expect you to understand, but we have a limited amount of time to perform the spell, and so we can't take you home right away. Sorry."

The green exit sign for Moonstone Beach briefly flashed to life and then went black as they turned off the highway and into a parking area.

"We're here," said Lillith. "Uncle Silas, it'll only take an hour or so. You can stay in the car and listen to the radio."

"No, I'll go with you."

"You can't. What we're doing is for Wiccans only. It's private."

"I don't want to sit in the car."

"We don't have time to argue. Please just stay here."

"No."

Through the window Silas could see outlines of the offshore rock islands. Lillith sighed and opened her door. Silas took off his seat belt and stepped out into the settled, wet cold of an evening beach at low tide.

"Let's go to the fire log," said Lillith, starting off down the beach. They trudged along the sand's waterline until they came to a boomerang-shaped log the size of a family couch, where they stopped and rubbed their arms and their eyes adjusted to the dark. "Uncle Silas, could you at least stand over there while we talk about some things?" Lillith pointed to one end of the log. "Maybe you could look at the water or . . . or the sky. Or something."

Silas moved to where he'd been directed and glanced noncommittally at the starry sky, a vast scroll of black taffeta with light pinpricks and it was a universe festooned. The ocean waves broke invisibly nearby, and it occurred to him that he'd grown complacent toward the beach, what at one time he had most prized about living in Humboldt County. He'd taken beauty for granted and imagined that it had nothing new to offer him. And just then the sky seemed deeper than normal, both impenetrable and welcoming, a space to swim into and be, at last and forever, submerged. Let these kids have their rites and rituals and fairy tales; he'd be their prisoner if this was what it entailed.

"All right," said Lillith, "Uncle Silas, since you're here I may as well tell you what we're doing, which is there's a guy from Eureka who's stuck in a place called the Astral Plane, where spirits and magical creatures live. The ancient Celts called it *Búi*, and they discovered that the wall separating it from us thins and thickens on a seasonal basis, and that sometimes a hole forms in the wall. That's how gods and harpies and things get over here."

"The hole is for them to come to us," said Franklin, "not for us to go to them."

"But somehow this local guy found a way to get over there, and he's doing damage to the wall," said Lillith, "and probably hurting himself at the same time, so we're going to cast a spell that keeps him here permanently. According to our calculations, the wall is going to be at its thinnest in about ten minutes."

"When it gets thin enough we should be able to override whatever magic is keeping him there and bring him back," Tina said. "His name is Leon Meed. He's from Eureka. He's a burl sculptor."

Silas hugged his arms to his chest. "I've heard something about him."

While Silas had been off to the side, the girls and Franklin had inscribed a circle in the sand and built a small pile of stones in each of the four directions. Driven into the sand in the middle of the circle was an altar made of bundled twigs with a dinner plate affixed to the top.

"We're going to begin by invoking the Lords of the Watchtower," said Lillith, "which means we face the cardinal points and salute the god or goddess of that direction, in north-east-south-west order because that's the order of increase as opposed to, um, decrease."

Silas watched as they removed their shoes, entered the circle, held their hands out, palms up, and invited the direction gods to look favorably upon their request. Tina approached the altar and placed a small figure with a newspaper photo wrapped around its head onto the plate and said, "Poppet, I name you Leon Meed," before stepping back into the circle.

Franklin sneezed and then placed three candles, a handful of dirt, a cup of water, and three lemon wedges around the poppet. He lit the candles and said, "By dark and by light, we beseech thee as we might, for all to be done and all to be right, return the captive to this site." The plate wobbled dangerously.

"It's going to tip over!" said Lillith anxiously.

"No, it won't," said Franklin. A gust of wind blew out the candles and Franklin steadied the plate and lit them again.

"I knew candles were a bad idea," Tina said.

"Shut up," said Franklin, "they're more important than that Barbie doll you're using for a poppet."

Tina glowered at Franklin and Lillith said, "Quit ruining the atmosphere!" Then Lillith stepped forward and removed three joss sticks from her jacket pocket. Lighting them with the one candle that hadn't gone out, she said, "We three pay honor and succor to the beings of the Astral Plane and conjoin our spirit to theirs therein. Hear our call. Feel our incantation. The mortal among you is a refugee and we humbly request his return to this world, so that he and we may gain through our contributions, to the greater glory of the Goddess and all in her dominion."

Then Tina and Franklin joined her, and the three again placed their hands out, palms up, and with their eyes closed chanted together, "To the greater glory of the Goddess and all in her dominion . . . to the greater glory of the Goddess and all in her dominion."

They turned their palms down and Lillith said, "The word goes forth and comes into being, so mote it be."

Opening their eyes, the three looked at the altar for five full minutes and then walked backward out of the circle, at which point they put on their shoes and sat on the log.

"Are you through?" Silas asked them.

"Yes," said Lillith. "Leon will be here any minute, and then we can go."

"You think so?" Flickers of credulity had passed through Silas's mind during the spell, when he had to acknowledge that pagan magic was as likely an explanation for Leon's disappearance as anything else.

"We used a bunch of superpowerful aids to make sure that he comes back right away."

Silas felt a certain excitement that maybe these kids' fancy wasn't fancy, and he would be lucky enough late in life to learn the truth about the universe and the gods and how life operated. Maybe he'd come full circle and wound up in a second childhood that was better and more illuminating than his first. He sat next to Lillith on the log and stared with them at the altar. And stared and stared. After two hours nothing had happened besides a loud argument. Tina accused Franklin of overloading the altar and not taking it seriously enough, and Franklin said that Tina's crude Barbie poppet had been a mockery to the gods and it was no wonder Leon hadn't come back, because if he had his body would have been that of a six-foot anorexic blond airhead. Silas sighed a slightly-but-not-too-disappointed sigh. And Lillith cried by herself in the car, where the conviction seized her that everything wrong was beyond her power to fix, that instead of coming away from the night a more powerful woman of goodness and change, she was to slink away an enfeebled and spirit-crushed little girl.

**9:11 p.m.**

Lenora was locked in the bedroom. Shane pounded on the door and told her she was being unreasonable, but she made no sound in response, not even to defend herself, because she was being selfish and ill-tempered and carrying this grudge like a baby to term. She was giving form and focus and substance to their marriage's problems. She was showing that a certain harmony was now impossible and that maybe there would be less love and respect in their future together. Pouring their difficulties into a gelatin mold.

But Shane wasn't going to let it get to him. He could adjust to the new state of affairs. If she was going to fall out of love with him he'd retaliate by falling out of love with her. Tit for tat. So he pocketed his wallet and left the house; while she festered and felt miserable he'd be at the Ritz, making acquaintances. Outside the dog whined, wanting food and affection. Like every animal in the world. Food and affection. On the afternoon he and Lenora had bought the dog, early in their marriage, Lenora had rested her hand on his thigh and said that she'd always believed that women were equal to men and should find self-validation and know their own desires, but that she needed a counterpart to complete her—not because she was female but because *everyone* needed a counterpart to complete them—and now she'd found Shane, and it was a wonderful feeling. She'd looked at him like he was a prophecy come to pass. Shane had said nothing and so implicitly agreed that he also felt fulfilled, though in fact he didn't, in fact his marriage was a rote part of his move toward a respectable life and Lenora could have been anyone, it didn't matter so long as she made him appear upstanding. Their love was a fiction, and fictions, like blue jeans, became more comfortable the longer you lived in them. Then like blue jeans they wore thin and tore apart.

The ripped black vinyl stool at the Ritz seemed to have been kept warm just for Shane as he slid onto it. He hadn't been in a bar—not a bar bar—in so long that he'd forgotten how intimate they felt with their dark lighting and mood music and aromatic people. The opportunity for confession and seduction. The cloistered bacchanalia. He had a few drinks and they were like muscle relaxants and he learned the bartender's name and looked around and saw a few prospects in the corner, talking among themselves, one brunette in particular looking cumhither fuckable. "You know them?" he asked the bartender, pointing to the corner ladies.

"They been here a few times."

"Good to go, or what?"

"A few guys made their moves."

"Yeah? Any of them do okay?"

"They all did."

"Those are my kind of odds," Shane said too loudly, and tapped his glass to signal a refill. He had the idea that the bartender was bored and would welcome a discussion of Morland Memorial Services. He thought he might send complimentary drinks to the prospects. So he'd gotten in a fight and had lawful sex with his wife. So fucking what? There was something perverse about the way these days you could be demonized for doing what people had always done, what was part of human nature. Shane was no reactionary, he was fine with people asserting their rights, but the way you could be punished for exhibiting a little passion, now that showed a world out of whack.

"Yo," he said to the bartender, "you have family in the area?" At that moment he felt a tap on the shoulder and turned around.

"Shane?" It was the faggot from the courthouse and Folie à Deux. "It's me, Barry. I don't know if you're following me around, but I'm going to think it's fate if we keep meeting like this." He flashed the warmest, creepiest smile and there was so much neediness in his expression, so much enthusiasm that Shane felt ill.

Shane told himself to remain calm. Ignore the queer. Keep your nose clean. The prospects in the corner were doing tequila shots and the bartender went to the other end of the bar to grab some empty bottles for recycling. Shane put on his buck private mien and folded his thick arms. "Yeah, fate, that's a good one."

"What are you having?" Barry asked.

"A drink."

"Oh, I *love* those!"

The door opened and a black man and white woman came in and sat at a table next to the prospects. Shane regarded them for a moment, the chess set couple. Why? Why did the woman do it? There were more than enough single white men out there for her. Why'd she have to be with a spearchucker? Some things Shane couldn't explain just made him mad, like this beautiful blonde out with a black guy, and here was this fairy making eyes at him and acting for all the world like this was a pickup.

This was a moment of deep confirmation for Barry, who saw this as fate directly intervening in his life. To go from never having seen Shane before to meeting him randomly three times in the space of a week was uncanny. All great love stories featured coincidences leading the two protagonists to be together: *A Room with a View,* Shakespeare's comedies, *When Harry Met Sally.* Barry felt this was preordained.

"Is your wife in the bathroom?" he asked.

"She's at home," Shane said and took a big sip of his drink and looked at the black man/white woman couple.

Barry wasn't thrilled to hear that Shane was married, but this didn't necessarily mean anything. There were sissynecks everywhere. "You couldn't get a sitter, or . . . ?"

"She wanted to stay home; I wanted to go out."

"It makes sense you want to do your own thing. We all have to do our own thing sometimes or we go crazy, right?"

Barry could feel the twelve inches of empty space separating his left elbow from Shane's right. He loved the doo-wop song playing and would have liked to sing along to it if Shane would only give him some encouragement, some signal that this was more than just two guys sitting at a bar, drinking swill. They could have looked into each other's eyes and dueted. What a dream come true that would have been. A smile or a joke or even the neutral I-like-you-but-I'm-not-a-fag voice men used to disguise the possibility that they might be attracted to you, a voice that suggested a need to be defensive, a voice that implicated itself if you thought about it. Barry used to use the voice around his straight friends. If Shane used it, it would say so much.

The white woman stood up then and shouted at the black man to go to hell and she was crying and her shawl hung tenuously over the crook of her arm, the confrontational right shoulder thrust forward. The women at the adjacent table glanced over so inconspicuously that it was conspicuous and the break in their conversation spoke volumes and the white woman had to be oblivious not to feel their chigger eyes burrowing in. But Justine only looked at Prentiss.

"You'd like me to go to hell and every other witness I bet," said Prentiss from his armless chair, his back to the wall, frowning at Justine's rockslide fury, and the whole room could hear them, and he and she just didn't give a fuck. "On account of you're a cold woman with a battery-operated heart. So go on, now. Skedaddle. You probably got a ten o'clock waiting somewhere."

A few seconds passed and Justine lifted her shawl up to her neck and, in a half-voice that everyone strained to catch, said, "Why are you saying this?"

"Just making conversation." Prentiss said the words like they burned his throat. His features were set in clay.

"No, something happened but I'm not a mind reader and if you won't tell me then I'll go."

"You're trying to give us a last chance when we never had a first one."

"That's what you think?"

"I'm not stupid. You may think so but I'm not stupid. Get the fuck out."

Putting her fingers to her cheek as though to check for a hand-print, Justine left. The women stared at Prentiss and he stared back and they got uncomfortable and so turned away and quietly discussed what had happened like sportscasters analyzing the final round of a boxing match. Prentiss gulped down his water and pushed away the glass, folded his arms, and shook his head like he'd been in a bad car accident and was staring and marveling at the wreckage. Was that his severed leg on the hood of the car? And his eyes were tearing up and you would have said it was from the smoke in the bar, except that there was none. Rising he tipped over his chair, which he righted before walking to the counter.

"What can I do for you?" asked the bartender, rag in hand, bow tie on crooked.

Prentiss wagged his chin side to side and examined the halogen-lit bottles lined up in front of the wall mirror. "Double whiskey," he said, and now tears turned to dewdrops in his eyelashes and he wiped them away; no one would see them fall. His hand shook a little—could be from the cold—laying a five-dollar bill on the counter. He regarded the whiskey before him like an offering. To hell or heaven, it didn't matter. What mattered was that he was here and he'd just had a disastrous experience with someone he could have fallen in love with, and all this unnecessary pain had defeated his puny defenses, had led the armies of alcohol to stand poised at the gate, preparing their charge. Prentiss braced himself.

Shane was sitting two stools down from the nigger, who was a big son of a bitch and looked vulnerable and Shane knew that big black vulnerable men were to be avoided like angry mother bears. Now was a good time to send those drinks over to those ladies and then join them, and get away from the faggot at the same time. Lenora would give birth to and raise his children, and for this reason he would put up with a lot, but he wouldn't put up with pattern behavior like hers today. If she pulled another stunt like this in the future, he'd bash down the bedroom door and shake her until sense dribbled back into her head, because he couldn't afford—mentally or spiritually—the aggravation of her little rebellions.

"Hey," Shane said to the bartender. "How about lining up a tray of tequila poppers for the ladies over there?"

"Yep."

"You're buying them all drinks?" asked Barry, whose voice was sticky and sweet and nauseating.

The door opened and Shane hoped it might be yet more women, but instead it was the faggot he'd had the run-in with at CalCourts—Jesus Christ what were the odds?—and now the jukebox was hopping with some crazy funk hip-hop "urban syrup" bullshit and the lights kicked down a few watts and the ladies in the corner talked louder. Things were really swinging now at the Ritz. Be-bop-a-lu-wah.

The glass was cold in Prentiss's hand. He took a sip that his tongue absorbed like a dry sponge. Earlier that night he'd knocked on Justine's door and she'd been ready to go, purse in hand, shawl pulled evenly over her shoulders, a dazzling smile that made Prentiss feel patronized and pitied. On the ride to dinner she did all of the talking while he grunted affirmation or made questioning "ohs?" and it became obvious that he was not paying attention to her words. But she kept talking and gesticulating and laughing at everything as they sat down at Mazotti's and ordered water and fried mozzarella sticks. Then all at once she shut her mouth and looked at him questioningly and Prentiss felt her silence like an executioner's hood pulled over his head. She asked if something was wrong and he paused for a minute and then said, as coldly as if he were in a Tennessee Williams play, "Wrong? What gave you that idea?" "You're being very quiet, and I'm wondering if something's bothering you." "No," he said, "everything's spiffy. Tip-top. Maybe you're taking your role too seriously." "What do you mean?" "I shouldn't say anything about that. An actor doesn't break character till the curtains come down, right?" "I don't know what you're talking about." "That's better," he said, staring fixedly at her, his spine straight, summoning the will to cliff-dive.

Barry couldn't have been less pleased to see Alvin just then, though he knew that it had to happen. They were supposed to meet at nine thirty, and here it was only nine twenty-two; Barry by rights should have had more time to talk to Shane, maybe to get his phone number through a pretext like could he borrow his power tools.

"Barry," said Alvin, looking so happy to see him as he took off his windbreaker and squeezed Barry's arm in lieu of the lip-to-lip slavering kiss that in a big-city boys' town would elicit whistling approval but here would lead to a riot. "How was the swim?"

"Fine," Barry said, and he felt caught, this relationship pinning him like a butterfly against life's corkboard, when all he wanted was to flap his wings. "Alvin, this is Shane."

"Oh my God," Alvin said. In a loud whisper, "Barry, this is *him*, the guy who attacked me."

"You're joking," said Barry.

"He's not joking," Shane said. This was one of the unluckiest nights of his life. This was the kind of night to make you believe that evil forces controlled the universe.

"Let's go someplace else," said Alvin, who then noticed Prentiss and rushed over to him. "Prentiss! What are you doing? Jesus, what am I dreaming?"

"Alvin, my friend," answered Prentiss. "Sit."

"Prentiss, you can't do this. This is someone else. This isn't you."

The glass of whiskey was empty. None had spilled onto the counter. Prentiss leaned forward steadily. His lips were moist and his eyes glassy. His thumb kept music time. With a delirious castaway grin he said, "I am many things."

"What about last week when you stared down that whiskey?" Alvin looked like he'd found Romeo just as the vial dropped. "What about the last five months? That's the Prentiss you want to be. You don't want to give it all up for this. Oh, shit, Prentiss. Fucking hell."

Prentiss's face turned from clay to stone. "Leave me alone." A clenched fist next to his glass.

Barry came over. "What's going on?"

"This is Prentiss; he goes to my meetings. I'm his sponsor, remember I told you about him? And here he is."

"Here I am," said Prentiss. He swiveled around on his stool and looked at the three women in the corner who were talking about whether Pluto was a planet or, as some scientists claimed, simply a large icy rock. Except that he knew they were really talking about him, about how obvious it was that he was sick and alcoholic and black and doomed never to mend. Oh, people took such pleasure in seeing you fail to get better. They loved it when you fell back down. Because it would be too disheartening, wouldn't it, if everyone recovered from their illnesses? Over whom would we then have an advantage? Others' misfortunes were our private delight. We were so greedy for them; we were so covetous; we were so estranged from empathy that satisfactions we should have abhorred we instead relished. Prentiss felt a great welling up of disgust and rejection—yes, he'd tried to get along in the real world and forge friendships and do right by others and now he saw that it wasn't working, it simply wasn't panning out—and he thought that it was an insensitive God—it was a callous and frigid Power—that let him try so hard only to see all that effort, all that hope and aspiration, amount to nothing.

The three women in the corner got up and were leaving when the bartender brought them Shane's prepaid tray of tequila shots. They refused the offer, saying they were late for a dinner party, but thanked Shane at the bar before leaving. The bartender set down the tray and went to clear their glasses. Shane stared after the women as if they were the last taxi out of a dangerous neighborhood. Prentiss demanded to know whose the untouched drinks were. Alvin tried to block them from Prentiss's sight with his body.

"Hey," said Prentiss to Shane. "You buy those?"

"Yeah," said Shane.

"Let me have one I'll give you top dollar."

"Don't," said Alvin to Shane. "He's in AA with me, and I don't want him drinking any more. He's having a bad night."

"You stay out of it." Prentiss slid off his stool and placed a menacing hand on the back of Alvin's neck. "I can do what I want and if you try to get in my way . . ."

"What about your parole? If something happened and you got busted."

"If what happened? This a threat, you threatening me?"

"No. Just take a minute to calm down."

"Move now."

Barry returned to his seat next to Shane and said, as casually as he could while whispering, "You didn't attack Alvin because he's gay. There was another reason, right? Because I have a feeling about you. Maybe I'm wrong. Tell me I am, but I don't think so."

Shane turned from the Prentiss/Alvin confrontation. The music was a leg-vibrating presence. Shane flexed his right arm and on his hand the veins rose like a relief map. And then for a moment his arm relaxed and his veins subsided and a more credulous cast came over his features and his face was soft like a weathered coin's, his acne scars invisible. And there was plenitude and possibility. And Barry felt a wondrous complicity.

An old guy sitting next to Barry said, "I met you at the Longaberger party," and Shane stood up swiftly and grabbed the back of Barry's head and slammed it down onto the bar counter. Prentiss pushed Alvin away, drank a tequila shot, and moved to restrain Shane, who as soon as he was touched let go of Barry and said, "No problem here. It's nothing. Nothing happened. Drinks are on me." And Barry, shocked by how abruptly it all had gone down, rubbed his forehead, where a red band flushed into being just as the old guy sitting next to him disappeared.

**10:10 p.m.**

Around the table at the Jambalaya sat Steve, Sadie, Roger, Marlene, and Greg. Everyone was dressed in shades of black except Sadie, who in addition to her lavender blouse wore a buttercup sash like a ray of light streaking across their collective darkness. Steve looked

at his colleague Greg and swirled a martini and thought sympathet-
ically about Marlene, who loved Greg and mistakenly thought that
she was the only woman in Greg's life now that he was divorcing
Elaine. Steve had always disapproved of his friend's promiscuity and
felt bad that Marlene would suffer for it. Steve was thinking that he
shouldn't let this deception go on, that he should say something,
especially seeing Marlene so happy with Greg, seeing her territorial
hand on his, the overlaid fingers, the comfortable slouch into his arm
around her. Steve had never thought of other women when he was
with Anne; he'd been constancy itself. Now he was alone and where
was the justice? It was important that he end the charade of Greg's
tenderness, reveal the disgusting and specious nature of his relationship to Marlene. Steve's body ached to do it. The Methedrine
he'd taken had spread to a beautiful consistency in his bloodstream
so that he felt possessed of great and important truths, with a manic
street preacher's need to proclaim them. Only someone with vision
as clear as his could manage it. It occurred to him then that he should
take Equanil to calm down a little, that maybe he was too wired.

Greg said something.

"What was that?" Steve asked.

"I asked what was going on with the case of your missing patient,
Leon Meed," Greg said. And then, for the benefit of the rest of the
table: "A guy Steve treated last year for—what was it, torn menis-
cus?—went missing a couple weeks ago. It's been on the news."

"Eight hundred and fifty thousand people a year go missing," said
Roger. "You know how many of those cases the police and FBI solve?"

"Nothing new as far as I know," Steve said, "but a couple people
have reported that they've seen him. Or someone they think is him, so
maybe he's hiding out around here." He couldn't condone Greg's
faithlessness any longer. He had to take Marlene aside and tell her
that Greg would never be the kind of man she needed, that Greg used
people and didn't understand the fragility of the human heart, didn't
know that it was made of glass rather than plastic.

"Why would he do that?" asked Marlene.

Sadie took a sip of wine and then with her thumb rubbed a lipstick smudge from the rim of her glass. Leon Meed was the name of her patient's hallucination. What had happened in her bathroom had to be ignored because she was a rational person, committed to the real world and all of its certainties. She said, "I've heard that most missing people show up within a few months, and the others aren't found because they don't want to be found. They're all tax dodgers and petty criminals."

"One percent," said Roger, with a television talking head's earnestness. "All of one percent of missing-persons cases get solved."

"The FBI is a government agency," said Greg. "What do you expect? Except with the amount of money we pay in taxes you'd think they would try to earn at least some of their salary."

Steve got a leg cramp and realized he'd been flexing his calf muscles. Why was he doing this? The people and tables and dance floor and performance stage of the Jambalaya appeared slightly jittery, shaking ever so much, like he could see their kinetic natures. Movies were projected at the speed of twenty-four frames per second, which meant that you saw 1,440 still shots a minute. There was so much going on at a given instant. So much action and emotional nuance and subtext and overt movement. He might want to consider Equanil immediately. Roger's right hand had only one finger, and he wore a leather holster over his fist that covered the finger socket scars. Steve noticed that it was a model from the early nineties. Two-tone leather. Tarnished brass snaps. And Marlene, a warm and generous and gracious person, shouldn't be dragged deeper and deeper down by Greg to the point where, when she discovered what a duplicitous weasel Greg was, she'd drown. Steve started to say something and his mouth was so dry.

"What was that?" asked Greg.

Four expectant faces turned to him and they all were flat backdrops with bumpy noses and eyebrows and mouths.

"Nothing," said Steve. He really needed to calm down, take an Equanil, have a bath and relax because he was feeling too aware for

his own good. Nothing positive ever came from this much raw consciousness. It was as though he had been reduced to an alien brain of
the omniscient variety from old science-fiction movies, blobs of cere-
brum that scared you because they were the intellect of God but without God's beauty. Or compassion. Just pure analytical matter. No, you
didn't want the brain of God divided from His handsome white beard
and endless love. Oh, qua qua qua, no. Steve repeated, "Nothing."

"Thought you said something," Greg said, giving Marlene's ear a
playful twist that amused her.

Sadie looked at Roger and felt nothing in her heart or groin. It had
been so long since she had been on a date, much less a blind one, that
she had forgotten how they dragged on if you didn't like the person.
And how difficult it was not to show that you were having a bad time,
so that an inverse relationship developed between your appearance
and your feelings: the more bored you were, the more you tried to
look contented. Adults pretended just as much as children did.
Played just as many games. They even pretended they weren't pretending and that their games weren't about winning. Adults were
weirdos. And what was going on with this Steve guy? Such a bouncy-
bouncy. Looking around all wide-eyed and nervous. He had nothing
to be nervous about. He didn't face a ride home in Roger's car and an
awkward good-bye that needed to strike a balance between warmth
and explicit indifference, a good-bye that communicated how it was
nice to meet you but don't call me again.

"Sadie," said Marlene, obviously divining her sister's feelings about
Roger, "did you know that Roger spent six months living in Lisbon?"

Sadie had always wanted to visit Portugal. "No."

"It's true," said Roger. "I was working on my dissertation and had
friends with a condo in Lisbon they weren't using. It's a beautiful
city."

"I've heard that."

"I have a photo album full of pictures from that year if you'd ever
like to see them."

"I'm sure they're interesting."

Lisbon didn't provoke further discussion—it was an easily exhaustible subject—so Sadie took more frequent sips of her drink and looked around at people sitting at other tables, all of whom were laughing and hooting and yelling out punch lines and tickling one another and in general having a blast. Everyone else's lives seemed at their best when yours was at its worst. Being single when others were a couple. Not having anyone when people you knew had the comforts of intimacy and love and confidence and sex and companionship and relief from the idea that we are solitary creatures. For much of her life—her single life, anyway, which was largely the same thing—Sadie had viewed her friends in relationships as a negative commentary on her. They stated implicitly that two were better than one, that safety lay in numbers. And wasn't this reinforced by every movie, book, and television show in existence? Wasn't it understood that no more horrible fate existed for women than becoming old maids? Yet at this moment, sitting beside Roger and considering her options—to set aside her preferences and settle for him and thence be coupled, or to follow her inclinations and reject him and remain alone—she felt that this global old-maid understanding was superannuated and untrue. For security and comfort came in many guises, and she could be single without being inadequate. She could, even, be envied for it. For living the life she wanted. Defining herself according to who she was rather than in relation to someone else. She wouldn't buy into the tyranny of couples and chain herself to someone just for the sake of being chained. If love came, wonderful. If not, she would resist eulogies for all the might-have-beens.

"Roger." Steve leaned forward in his chair, his left eye twitching like he had tic douloureux. "Do you think that honesty is the most important thing in making a relationship work?"

"Why bother with more small talk, huh?" Roger said with a chuckle.

"It was getting old," seconded Greg, looking at Steve warily.

"Seriously, I'm curious," said Steve.

"That depends," Roger said, upending his drink and tonguing an ice cube the way Sadie imagined a salamander would, "on the level and degree of honesty you're talking about. Honesty should play a minor role in the minor issues—such as how your partner looks in a certain outfit, or how much you like an anniversary gift—and a major role in the major issues—such as whether or not you love each other, and the degree of your discontentment in life, and of course sexual fidelity."

"Aha!" said Steve. "So you think a relationship where there's sexual deceit is a bad relationship."

"I don't think it's healthy, no."

"Herr Doctor," said Greg, and you could detect the ridicule with which he said the word "doctor," "don't you think that people's hang-ups about fidelity are too exaggerated? I mean, if you were to stray—and everyone's human—and *if* it didn't interfere with your love for the person you're with, then wouldn't it be better not to say anything about it?"

Roger folded his hands into a chin rest. "That's the adulterer's million-dollar excuse. And it's unfounded for three reasons. One, it establishes an arbitrary system of disclosure and honesty that, if continued, will lead people to lie at random for the sake of their own convenience and to avoid responsibility for their actions. Two, lying about infidelity signifies a contempt for the person being lied to, an unwillingness to let them decide whether to continue the relationship with all the facts at hand. Three, it's selfish and greedy."

"I agree," said Steve, looking positively deranged.

"That's, I don't know, a hard line to take," said Greg, moving his empty wineglass to the middle of the table. "Oh, look, the band's about to start up again."

And so it was. Music and dancing and drinking. Greg took Marlene to the dance floor followed by Roger and Sadie. Steve stayed at the table contemplating an Equanil and an exit-door confession to Marlene. Roger cut in with Marlene and Greg obligingly switched over to Sadie. Steve rearranged the drink glasses on the table and thought about writing Marlene a note. Sadie returned to the table and sat down. Greg cut back in with Marlene. Roger sat next to Sadie. Steve got up and tapped Greg on the shoulder and danced with Marlene, where after a minute of frenetic box stepping they switched to a slow-dance stationary basic.

"I have to tell you something," Steve said, trembling like a greyhound.

"What's that?" Marlene asked.

"It's about Greg. He's sleeping with a nurse from ER, and with other women, too. He's not capable of monogamy. I think you should know this."

"Oh."

"It's for your own safety that I say it."

"My safety?"

"I mean your own good."

"I'm going to sit down now. Thanks for the dance."

Steve was left on the dance floor, where couples glided past him and a few loners swayed in time. His head felt like a microwave, so many atom thoughts were pinging and ponging around inside. Perhaps he was radioactive. Perhaps he shouldn't have said anything to Marlene. His future ex-wife, Anne, was probably now in bed with the guy who had answered the phone at her place the night before. The music felt like water and he had a hard time moving through it to a table, to any table but his own, because he needed to sit down.

"Here," said a man in an open-collared shirt and wool pants, with a poet's head of short curls, next to whom Steve found himself, "have a seat."

"Thanks." Steve sat at a table just to the side of the stage and looked at the man and played with a drink coaster and craved an Equanil and wondered if honesty weren't really a kind of poison disguising itself as nectar. Maybe it *was* unnecessary. He looked harder at the man, whose face had Pop Art coloring. "A lot of people are looking for you, Leon."

"I know."

"How's your knee?"

"Never been better."

"I'm a good doctor."

"Yes, you are."

"You're one of 850,000 missing people a year," Steve said. "Just one." The room began to throb with color then, and the music was the sound of a great factory, a caterwaul of churning and churning and production. Steve rubbed his eyes and said, "It's not right. You can't just disappear. We're all connected and there's a ripple effect. You create a void and other people fall into it. You've got to come back. You've got to keep living your life."

"Doctor Baker, are you okay?"

"I've said too much." There was a silence. "What do you think?" Leon was gone. Steve looked under the table and his head was spinning.

"Hey, get up," Greg said, standing over Steve and taking off his jacket. "I said get up."

"What is it?"

Greg folded his arms and his expression was an angry football coach. "Now's not the time to play dumb. Get up."

"I'm sitting here. I just saw Leon Meed."

"You're going to tell me what you said to Marlene and why, and you're going to do it now."

Steve looked at the empty chair where Leon Meed had just been. "Because people don't exist to be used," he said.

"I'd like to know what people exist for but I'm too pissed off right now to ask. So get up." And with that Greg lifted Steve up and they were face-to-face and Steve felt disembodied.

"Greg," said Marlene, squeezing in between the two men, "come on. You've done enough damage for one night."

"I haven't started."

"Yes, you have. And you've finished. Let's go."

Greg stared at Steve and shook his head slowly, then questioningly, then dismissively. "Yeah, let's go."

The fireworks in Steve's head stopped and he lay down to rest.

**11:57 p.m.**

Elaine's children were asleep. She prayed that visions of sugarplums were dancing in their heads. The stocking stuffers were wrapped— the candies, action-figure toys, putties, and coloring utensils—and the presents laid out and the tree lit. Greg hadn't called, which was fine with her although the kids were devastated. Had he always been capable of such lapses? Had she been out of her mind when she married him and bore his children and believed his declarations of love? No. Everything had been in its right place. There'd been a kernel of truth in every "I love you," and she shouldn't chalk up his current promiscuity and divorce wranglings and child neglect to pure evil, but instead to a drift in his affections and interests that caused awful collateral damage. He wasn't malicious; he just orbited in a sad galaxy of solipsism. She went through the house clearing away his books and music and folders and favorite decorations. One box, two boxes, three boxes full. Santa could do more than give; he could take away.

At the end of which she was tired and went outside, where a nickel-sized moon shone upon a row of bicycles and a broken-tongued rake next to the garage. Elaine accidentally knocked the bicycles over and then got in her car. The motion-detector porch light came on. She put *South Pacific* in the stereo and reclined her seat. After the overture, a medley of the soundtrack's most epic melodies, came the opening keen of "Bali Ha'i": "Most people live on a lonely island/ Lost in the middle of a foggy sea/ Most people long for another island/ One where they know they would like to be." She'd outlast her divorce and the sexual intrigues of Muir Elementary School and the suspicion that she'd failed her children and father. She'd outlast her regret. And although perhaps she should have gotten a PhD and married Daniel Fitzribbon and lived in rural Pennsylvania—her once-upon-a-time dream state—the alternative she'd chosen had led her to this precise moment, and it was better to think of it as an opportunity than as a repercussion. Life was the words we dressed it up in, and if we thought sometimes that we were acted upon rather than actors, it was a temporary misunderstanding. Elaine thought of everything she could do. "Bali Ha'i may call you/ Any night, any day/ In your heart, you'll hear it call you/ Come away . . . come away."

Yet she wouldn't come away. She would stay where she was and continue to make mistakes and err and be human and forgive and be divine, and if she got fired she got fired. She loved her children. She liked her job. She even liked Eureka, and stranger things had happened than a single mother divorcee with a sick father and uncertain professional future finding a shard of happiness and caring for it and, however long afterward, discovering that this was enough. Stranger things happened all the time.

**11:59 p.m.**

Eve was in the gully in Sequoia Park where she and Ryan had once done acid and sat with perfect stillness for three hours as a test of their willpower. The drug tried to make them fidget and beat the ground and scream and get up and rub their faces in the ferns and run along trails and leap spasmodically into the air, but they triumphed over it. And when the test was over they got swervily to their feet and grinned at each other and their bodies felt like they'd been cryogenically frozen, though their minds had been afire, so they lightly scratched each other's arms and were amazed at the sight sound touch as they Adam and Eve'd (and she *was* Eve, this wasn't role-playing) through the park, naming the plants and animals they saw and laughing for no reason, the most innocent phenomenon. And when they came down from the acid and were cast out of the park— leaving because they had to meet people downtown—they saw each other for the first time, despite their knowing every inch of the other's curvilinear bodies and faces, despite the blindness that familiarity breeds. Love remade all.

But after that day their love was beaten down by three hard years of living together and Ryan's degeneration and Eve's awareness that life was not a banquet of opportunities to which she could return again and again until she was ready to lie down forever. Life was a life sentence: *You shall not rise above your station.* And now Ryan was dead although it didn't seem possible, a tragedy the size of all disappointment. Faith was harder than titanium, faster than light, more mercurial than water. Somebody had once told her that Christ was wonderful and Christians terrible. She wouldn't go that far—the people at church that morning were too bland to be terrible, not even a case of the banality of evil—and anyway what interested her was less Christ than God. Maybe she was Jewish. Though it wasn't God as He was known popularly, the Ancient of Days with a wizened face and carefully drafted covenant; it was God as the ultimate investor of meaning. An entity that laid out morality and gave life a knowable purpose. A God who didn't so much promote our humility as rescue us from triviality. From childhood she'd suspected that every action had a consequence that did more than mandate behavioral caution or karma—if I do something bad, something bad will happen to me— that pointed to a larger ethical structure in the universe for us to explore and affirm. Eve had been given hints of God's existence— while Derivative sang its spirituals she'd found and lost Leon Meed— and didn't know why she'd failed to draw the proper conclusion.

Faith before then had had the connotations of a prison cell.

Faith she now saw was an undying Yes.

From somewhere nearby in the forest she heard a rustling of rocks and branches.

"Is someone there?" she asked, her voice surprisingly steady. It occurred to her that one of the dozens of homeless people who camped in the forest could come by and casually murder her.

"Yeah," said a man invisible in the night.

"Do you live in the park?" Eve asked, not afraid though fear seemed like the right response. She felt calm. "Do you know Hortense? I'm friends with him. He knows I'm here."

"I don't know Hortense. And I don't live here. I'm just walking around. Don't mean to scare you. My name's Joon-sup, but you can call me Jack."

"Do you have a jacket I could wear just for a minute? I'm freezing."

"Yeah. I'm pretty warm from walking." Joon-sup wended his way through nettles and mosses and ferns to Eve's clearing, where a patch of moonlight struck her hair and arms and feet, though her face and hands were in shadow.

"Thanks," Eve said. "I'm almost too cold to get up and walk home. I mean, that's an exaggeration, but still. What are you doing here?"

Joon-sup shuffled off his coat and handed it to her and stumbled a little. "I had nowhere to go tonight and it's Christmas Eve so here seemed like a good place to think."

Eve put on the thick down jacket, which smelled of sandalwood. "What do you need to think about?"

"A lot of stuff. What are you doing here?"

"Trying *not* to think. My boyfriend died today. I'm trying not to think about that."

"I'm sorry. That's horrible. That's . . . how did it happen?"

"Drug overdose."

"When was . . . how old was he?"

"Twenty-four."

"I'm very sorry."

"Thank you."

"Did you . . . I mean, did you find him?"

"Yeah. But let's not talk about it. I talked about it all day. I'll probably talk about it for all the days to come. I'm feeling peaceful right now."

"I could tell you what I'm thinking about if you want. To take your mind off it for a minute."

"Okay."

"You'll think I'm crazy."

"Probably not. I know crazy people and you don't seem like them."

"But even I think I'm crazy. Not in a dangerous way, just in a crazy way." Joon-sup lit a cigarette. "Do you mind if I smoke?"

"We're in the great outdoors."

"That's true."

"And besides I smoke, too."

"Oh, then, do you want one?"

"No, thanks."

"Okay. So where was I?"

"You're crazy."

"Yes. It started with my mother."

"Come on, I thought you were serious."

"On the phone—she lives in Pusan, where I'm from—we talk about her wanting me to be married and me not wanting to be married, and we fight over it a lot. So it got to the point where I ignored everything she said, and then I started to feel guilty, and then one day I was driving along and I saw a man disappear right in front of me."

Eve smiled and felt like the Cheshire Cat, like only her smile existed.

"I was driving down Fifth Street when this guy appeared in the middle of the road and then he was gone just as I was about to hit him," Joon-sup continued. "I could describe him perfectly; that's how real the hallucination was. Last week I met him in the forest, and we had a conversation and he told me how he disappears."

Eve stood up and held out her hand. "That's crazy, all right."

"Yes."

"You know what's even crazier?"

"What?"

"I've seen him, too."

# Part II

*January 15*

I'm badly injured. I'm writing this because I'll be dead soon and I want to leave a record of my last days. My name is Leon Meed. I don't know how much longer I have so I'll write until I finish or until I can't go on anymore. The bruises on my arms and face are healing, but the ones on my lower torso have spread into each other. These are the ones that concern me. A solid six-inch black band encircles my waist and probably accounts for my constant abdominal cramps. A *Merck Medical Guide* is sitting on my desk, but I won't look at it. I want to be one of the few Americans who can't name what's killing him.

My death won't be the major act. That's done already. The major act began a month ago and led more or less directly to my injuries. I would be in perfect health if it weren't for that. Some would argue that I died symbolically a long time ago, but that's not true.

There's nothing left in my kitchen but canned beets and tuna. This is okay because I hardly move and don't need much food. The beets alone could last me a week. I've spent most of today lying on the couch. Generally it's quiet, but sometimes the neighbors' dog barks at deer and rabbits like a town crier who thinks every passing traveler is an enemy spy. From birth the dog has been paranoid and violent, and many times I took an axe outside when it wandered into my back-yard. I considered all the animals I'd save by killing it, though in the end I let it be.

I think of this note as an SOS to the future, except that I don't expect to be rescued. I don't think you'll read it and come back to make everything right. But maybe you will. Maybe when you read this time travel will be easy, and you'll have already prevented the world wars and famines of the past, and you'll be on the lookout for smaller former problems to solve. I doubt it, though. I doubt there will ever be a cure for what happened to me.

Before last month I was a normal person. Nobody looking at my life from the outside would have thought twice about it. They might have been struck by its tragic elements, but only for a minute. They wouldn't have wanted to linger over them. They would just have said that I was unfortunate to lose my wife and daughter in a boating acci-dent, and then they would have moved on. If I were them that's what I'd have done.

But I'm not them, and at the time of the accident—ten years ago on December 1—I was teaching at Winship Elementary School. The county sheriff called to give me the news. After hanging up I sat down in the school office. It was a busy place and no one noticed me for a long time. I didn't believe it. My wife and I had had problems the way couples do, and my daughter had been in some ways a moody teenager, but in general I'd felt happy and blessed. I'd thought my friends were wrong to say, "The day you wake up and don't feel any pain is the day you know you're dead." So I sat in the school office and figured there had been a mistake. I stared hard at the telephone expecting it to ring at any minute. The sheriff would apologize and say there'd been some confusion over whose boat had been found wrecked on the beach, and that it turned out not to be my wife and daughter at all who were presumed dead.

The phone rang many times that afternoon, but it was always par-ents and other people. Then when it was finally the sheriff again wanting to talk to me, he didn't say anything about a mistake. He only told me that they still hadn't recovered the bodies, but that he would call if and when they did.

That evening I contacted my wife's family, coworkers, and friends, and then my daughter's friends and teachers. Everyone was devastated. They wept and when they stopped they offered condolences. They said it was impossible. My wife and daughter were wonderful women. They couldn't imagine what I was going through.

I couldn't imagine it, either. It was like I'd suddenly been relocated to a foreign country where everything was unintelligible. People talked and it sounded like gibberish. I knew they were trying to make the transition easy for me. They were trying to teach me how to survive in this new country, but I had no intention of staying. I didn't want to survive there; I didn't want to understand the language. Winship gave me a mourning leave of absence, so I sat at home waiting for my wife and daughter to return. I took up wood carving and watched television. I left the front door ajar. I made small cedar statuettes of them, knowing they couldn't be gone permanently. I knew that if I waited patiently, they would eventually push open the door and explain where they'd been. I rehearsed how I would take them both in my arms and shush their explanations. "It's okay," I practiced whispering, "it's all right."

But they didn't come and their bodies were never found. After several months I ran low on money and sold my house. I asked Winship if I could work part-time. They put me on their substitute teacher roster. I also got a job at Lou's Drugs manning the soda fountain. I appeared to be getting on with my life and learning the language of survival.

The reality was that with other people I used the new language of acceptance and resignation, whereas with myself I used the old one of contentment and happiness. With myself I spoke as though nothing had changed. There was no grief, no fear, no solitude, no death in that language. Those words didn't exist.

Using the money I made from selling my house I bought a small cabin on Neeland Hill in Eureka, where I've lived ever since. The

nearest house is a quarter mile away and belongs to a family of four—
a man, a woman, and their two grown sons. They own the angry dog.
I built a one-room addition to my cabin to use as a woodworking studio. In it I taught myself to sculpt life-sized statues using burl, the
large, workable outgrowths of redwoods, oaks, and Douglas firs.

To date I have made a hundred and thirty, which I keep in the
cabin and outside. They are all of my wife and daughter.

When I went back to work and moved to Neeland Hill, my friends
thought I had come out of my solitary phase and was ready to share
my pain with them. They said I should expect to feel sorrow for up to
a year or longer. It was okay to cry and wonder what was the point of
carrying on. My friends brought comfort food and sat with me in my
cabin, where I cried and wondered at the point of carrying on. They
sympathized and left satisfied. When they came back they made small
talk by asking what I had been up to in my studio. I showed them. My
efforts then were crude compared with my later work, but they
clearly showed my wife and daughter as they'd been before the accident. They were done with love and care. My friends had little to say
about them at first.

As the months passed and I made more burl likenesses of my
family in various poses, they began complimenting me. They openly
admired my technique—I spent a great deal of time and energy on
burnishing the statues, so that the wood was perfectly smooth,
glasslike, its shades of dark brown rich and lustrous—and said it was
wonderful the way I was processing my pain by doing something
creative. They were also impressed that I'd chosen burl sculpture,
because it is considered a low-class art form by most Humboldt
County residents. Here I was using a tourist gimmick to memorialize
two beautiful people. I was showing, with the deftness of my cuts and
the proportionality I achieved, so that one friend correctly noted the
influence of Leonardo da Vinci's *Vitruvian Man* on my approach, that
it had greater possibilities than were generally recognized.

After a year, when I'd completed about twenty statues, my friends
stopped praising me and suggested I try another subject. They said

I'd find it fun and interesting to challenge myself with something different. It would also be therapeutic. They recommended I take classes where I'd meet others interested in art, and where there would be live human models to sculpt. They said variety was important, and some even offered to sit for me themselves. Grieving was one thing, and obsessing was another.

They didn't understand my plan to expand the space around me in which to use the old language. With the statues of my wife and daughter I could be happy again and shut out the voices of the new language that I found alien and disturbing. I could re-create the country I'd been exiled from. To this end I made statues of my family eating, running, sleeping, crouching, yawning, walking, writing, juggling, planting. I had them holding hands and hugging. I had them watching television. I had them telling their stories and listening to mine.

There was only one activity I didn't have them doing. I was afraid of that thing for many years and so put it off, even though I wanted to sculpt it more than all the others combined.

My friends were upset when I didn't take their advice. Our relations grew strained. They said I should go to therapy and I told them there was nothing wrong with me and that they had taken an unhealthy interest in my affairs. They accused me of being stubborn and self-destructive. One called me morbid and then apologized, saying he didn't mean it although I knew he did. They staged an intervention where they all came together and told me that I was in trouble and needed help. I thanked them for caring but said it would be better if we stopped being friends. I no longer had anything to say to them. Most gave up then and agreed to the break, though some continued to call and send me letters that I ignored until they too stopped.

My mother—the only person I've kept in contact with—told me I was wrong to cut people off in this way. She said I'd made Ahab's mistake of blaming God for my life's tragedy. It's not right, she said. Think about Job and the trials he suffered, and how he felt as persecuted as you do without rejecting his creator. She said my turning away from the world of men was as much a crime against myself as it was against the people I turned away from. This was typical of the new language, and I explained to her that I would have nothing more to do with it. My mother meant well but was mistaken.

Over the last ten years I've lived modestly. My combined salary from substitute teaching and working at Lou's has been enough to pay bills and keep me in woodworking supplies. Even before I became injured I didn't eat much. I split my own firewood. For clothes I went to the Salvation Army and found nice, inexpensive items. You can spend very little in America if you try.

I am fifty-four now and had planned to retire at sixty. With my pension and savings account, and with Social Security beginning in my sixties, I worked it out several years ago and saw that I would be okay. I have almost finished paying off my mortgage and car loan. Even with a healthy allowance for burl slabs and for tools, my money would hold if I lived long enough to need it.

I wrote before that the major act began in December, but that's not true. It really started in September, when, because the ten-year anniversary of my wife and daughter's accident was approaching, I thought it was time to make the statue I'd been avoiding: a model of them swimming. My idea for the statue was of them fully clothed, side by side, in a synchronous brush stroke, with their faces turned up for air. I envisioned them shooting across the surface of the water.

I bought a large burl slab from a man who lives down the road from me and gets excellent specimens from his job at Burl World Supply Store. I also replaced the blades on two of my carving knives and the grade sheet on my electric sander. In every way I readied my workplace and myself.

It was a quiet morning when I sat at my studio desk to draw a preliminary sketch of the statue. Light filtering past the trees came in through the window and I thought it was a promising sign. I felt warm and strong. My old fears about making the statue seemed foolish. I expected to finish the sketch in an hour or two.

But when I started drawing, my vision grew blurry, as if I'd put on someone else's prescription glasses. I blinked and rubbed my eyes, but the paper in front of me stayed fuzzy and indistinct. I kept working and soon faint geometric shapes appeared floating in the air. It didn't matter where I looked, there they were. I thought that my excitement had mixed badly with the caffeine from my morning coffee and that they would soon go away.

Instead, the shapes grew sharper the longer I drew, and I developed a headache of such fierce power that I had to quit and lie down in my bedroom with a cold compress on my forehead. Faint light hurt my eyes; quiet breezes sounded like air raids. I figured I was coming down with an illness and took it easy for the rest of the day.

The next morning I felt better and went back to the sketch. I made a good beginning and improved on my original idea, but by noon the geometric shapes returned, followed by another headache. I was scheduled to work at Lou's that afternoon but called in sick. Then I lay in my room again with the shades drawn, wanting to detach my head.

Over the next few days this pattern continued. I'd start working and pretty soon my vision would worsen and I'd see floating geometric shapes that led to headaches of incredible pressure and volume. On some afternoons I threw up; on others I couldn't do anything but lie still and try not to move my arms and legs.

On the seventh day I went to a neurologist, who gave me a series of tests and interviewed me about my diet and lifestyle. He wrote down what I said and nodded. My headaches were classic migraines, he explained, the primary symptom being the visual distortion that preceded the pain. He called it the aura period. My case was unusual because migraines happened more to women than men, showed up before the age of twenty, and subsided as one grew older. Also unusually, I got them in the morning, did not suffer fatigue, and had had no exposure to bright light, loud noises, powerful odors, or changes in weather. I didn't drink alcohol or eat strong cheeses.

Something to consider, the doctor said, was research suggesting that migraines came from abnormalities in one's neurotransmitters. If you got too much or too little dopamine, serotonin, or norepineph-rine, you were at risk. There were two treatment options. You could either prevent the migraine by eliminating what triggered it, or you could cut it short by taking nonsteroidal anti-inflammatory drugs and lying in a quiet, dark room.

I'd already tried the quiet dark room, so I decided on prevention. This meant figuring out what triggered the migraine, which I knew to be my work on the statue. There was no rational way the two were related, but all the evidence pointed to it. So as an experiment, on the following morning instead of sculpting I mowed the lawn and ran errands in town. None of my symptoms returned. The next day I weeded the garden, wrote a letter to my mother, and failed at three games of solitaire. I felt good, if bored. At night I slept peacefully, and in the morning I went to work at Lou's, where I put in overtime. I ate dinner at an Italian restaurant called Mazotti's and stopped at the Ritz for a lemon cola. Again that night I slept as though comatose.

When I woke up I decided that my headaches were a spell of bad luck that had ended. It was a coincidence that they had shown up when I was sculpting, nothing more. I felt alive and eager to go back to work on the swimming statue. But I didn't rush to it. I had a slow breakfast and listened to the news. I took a long shower. Then, late in the morning, I got out the sketch I'd managed to complete during my week of migraines. I knew exactly how to execute it and guessed I could be done in a month.

I started early the next morning. The burl I'd bought was an oblong Douglas fir slab without many knots or too much moisture. I drew grid lines and shaved off a few edges. I could see the finished sculpture in my head. My wife and daughter were swimming. Side by side they were kicking with their legs and pushing the water away with their arms. They were breathing powerfully. I shaved off more edges and thought about where I would put the completed statue in my bedroom in order to watch them swim forever.

Almost immediately the blurriness and geometric shapes returned. By one o'clock I was back in bed with my worst headache yet. I was disappointed, but I was also determined not to let my pain stop me. From that point forward I worked on the statue in small morning increments before giving in to a torture that stretched into the night. I made progress. I took my name off the substitute teaching roster and told Lou that I had to stay home for a couple of months. My mother was concerned and called every day, afraid that I had a brain tumor. She insisted that I get a CAT scan and MRI. I nailed blankets over my bedroom windows to better shut out the light, and removed the clocks that made noise. I learned to soften even my heartbeat and breathe in time to the shooting pains in my skull.

On December 1, ten years to the day after the accident, I finished the statue. My headache erupted as I set down the electric sander and took an appreciative step back. I felt triumph and pain in equal measure, as though I'd run a marathon. My wife and daughter as they should have been, the correction of a horrible mistake. I thought that I'd been foolish not to make this statue long before.

At that moment came the major act: at that moment, without warning, I found myself floating in the Pacific Ocean, about a hundred feet from shore, in the middle of light gales. One second I was standing in my woodworking studio, the next I was in water so cold it felt like liquid electricity. My headache was gone and I knew I was dead. Given my recent pains, I figured I'd died from an aneurysm. There had been many warning signs in the weeks leading up to it, and I wasn't surprised. There was even a timeliness to the event: I'd just finished the most vital statue of my wife and daughter on the anniversary of their death. I'd perfected the old country and there was nothing left for me to sculpt.

I waited, and after a few minutes I noticed that I was dog-paddling in the water. This was strange. If I were already dead, I reasoned, I shouldn't have been afraid of drowning. I tried unsuccessfully to still my hands and feet but couldn't. Water came into my mouth and I spat it out.

This was hard to understand and I struggled with the contradiction until it occurred to me that I was about to see my wife and daughter.

Obviously I'd been sent to the ocean because that's where they lived, and they would come up from below to greet me. They would help me past my fear of drowning and take me down with them, and we would live together in a watery afterlife.

But then, as suddenly as I'd left, I was back in my studio. My clothes and body were damp, and I was very cold. There was a draft in the room. I sneezed and dried myself with one of the rags I kept to wipe away sawdust. Although I knew myself to be dead, I felt very alive. The water had invigorated me, and I felt none of the calm and tranquility I expected of death.

Then I saw that the statue of my wife and daughter swimming was no longer a statue. It had reverted to the raw burl slab I'd bought from the man down the road. From every angle it was as rough and unformed as it had been. There wasn't a sanded or sculpted inch on it. I checked the blades on my carving knives and the grade sheet on my electric sander, and they were new. If I were dead, I'd been sent back three months in time.

I removed my soggy shoes and socks and went to the living room. The calendar said December 1. I turned on the television. Its programming was normal. I called my mother and asked if anything unusual had happened. She said what sort of anything. I said anything anything. She asked what was going on with my headache. I said it had gone away. She was overjoyed. I asked if I were still alive. This upset her, and she cried into the phone that I had to be on fearsome medication indeed if I'd lost sight of my own aliveness.

I hung up and got into bed. My mother phoned back many times but I didn't answer. I was frightened and didn't know what to expect. Had I lost my mind? Was I dead? Would I meet God? The devil? Would my life force fuse into nature?

I stayed in bed until the middle of the night, at which time I got hungry and ate two large turkey sandwiches. By early morning I decided that I hadn't died or gone crazy. I'd had a little spell. I would get up and find my wife and daughter swimming. Everything would be okay. I slept until after noon.

As I expected, nothing was different in the living room when I woke up. The photo albums were where I'd left them. As were my books, food, clothes, cleaning supplies, and furniture. I watched television—news about a cataclysmic earthquake in India that had taken twenty-eight thousand lives—and then went to my studio.

There I was horrified. The burl was still a slab, not a statue. I looked for my sketch and it was gone. This made me frantic. Grabbing a carving knife, I prepared to make the opening shavings from memory, when I again found myself in the ocean. The water was calmer than it had been the day before, and I had an easier time keeping afloat. I recognized where I was. A hundred feet away the beach curved up to a buffer of sand brush above which the Louisiana Pacific Pulp Mill pumped black smoke into the air, indicating that this was the South Jetty in Eureka.

I dog-paddled for a minute and then was transported back to my studio. I ran to my bedroom and stayed in bed for two days, getting out only to eat and go to the bathroom. I don't want to describe the scenarios that went through my mind. I ate, slept, and had panic attacks. The phone rang often during those two days, and I ignored it. My mother left messages threatening to come up to Eureka from her home near San Francisco if I didn't call her back.

When the doorbell rang late one afternoon, I got up. My mother had arrived. I planned to make a clean breast of everything and welcome her suggestion that I check into a sanitarium. On the way to the door I stopped in the studio to look again at the burl slab, on the remote chance that it had reverted to my wife and daughter swimming. But the burl was the same raw object, the only difference being that now it seemed to mock me. It seemed hateful in its shapelessness and I was overcome with rage. I cannot explain even now how angry I became at that piece of inanimate wood.

The doorbell rang insistently, followed by loud knocking. My mother yelled from the front porch. The neighbor's dog howled viciously. I decided to destroy the burl slab by chopping it into pieces. I decided to teach it a lesson and I was full of righteous fury.

From the fireplace, I grabbed an axe and returned to the studio and lifted it above my head to bring cleanly down upon the burl. I anticipated splinters flying and gnarled pieces falling to the ground. I saw the end of a confused and agonizing period in which the little solace I had left in this world had been replaced by a blank lump of featureless evil. At this point, however, on the verge of destructive satisfaction, I found myself in the ocean for a third time. The waves were rough, and the water felt colder than before. I was still in such a state about the burl slab that my heart beat wildly. I began to lose strength in my arms and felt the pull of the water on my legs. I yelled for help to two people I saw standing on the beach. I anticipated drowning and thought that maybe that's what I should have done before. Maybe my fear of drowning had been a test, and if I passed it I'd sink to be with my wife and daughter. The real them and not their wooden counterparts. I expelled the air from my lungs. One of the figures on the beach had entered the water and seemed to be coming for me.

Instead of drowning, I found myself in the middle of a group of young people at a rock concert. I spoke with a raven-haired woman who told me I'd gone missing. This seemed incredible, for I had only been gone a few minutes, and when I asked the date and time she said it was nine in the evening on December 10. Days had somehow passed. The next thing I knew it was early morning and I stood in front of a living-room window, and then I was on top of a truck turning onto a road near Table Bluff. After that I was in a shower in someone's bathroom. Then at some kind of basket celebration party. From then on I understood that time moved forward for me in fits and starts. Sometimes I lost mere hours going from one place to another, sometimes entire days.

I didn't try to go home. Changing my clothes and showering would have been nice, but my regular visits to the middle of the ocean cleaned me off. On occasion I was presentable, although generally I wasn't. I found myself going to the same places and meeting the same people, some of whom I talked to about what was happening. One man, Joon-sup Kim, told me at our last encounter a week ago that I was a collective hallucination he and Eve Sieber were having. He hadn't pinpointed the cause yet, but he suspected lead in the water, radioactivity in the ground from nuclear waste buried nearby, or airborne fallout from weapons testing in Nevada. I stood in the dining area of the Better Bagel, where he worked, late one night after it had closed, while he swept up dust and bagel crumbs and said that I could be the result of years of chemical pollution along the Klamath River. Eve later told me she disagreed with Joon-sup and thought that I was a sign from God, a kind of unwitting prophet, sent to Earth to spark mass conversions to one of the Abrahamic faiths. She described herself as one of the masses. Although only a tool, I had led her to the one true God and shown that human tragedy—her boyfriend had just died—was inevitable but tolerable so long as people lived for Him. A teenage girl named Lillith Fielding, after seeing me show up in her room one evening as she sat with a boy and girl her age, excitedly explained that I'd been kidnapped by a pagan spirit and held captive in a hidden world called the Astral Plane, and that she and her neopagan friends had released me by casting a beach spell. Against my protestations that I had never heard of the Astral Plane, much less been there, she said that my "amnesia" was a favorite tactic of my kidnapper, the Horned Consort, when he'd failed at something in the human world and wanted to cover his tracks. An older man whom I recognized as a customer from Lou's Drugs, Silas Carlton, compared me to visions children have, to a prelapsarian nodule of human consciousness accessible to people new or old to the life phenomenon. He said that only he and others who were beginning or finishing Consciousness could appreciate what I meant for the life of the mind.

It doesn't matter to me anymore why this happened. My transports recently turned dangerous, and I don't have much longer to consider the question. It was a sudden change. Whereas for over a month I bounced around Humboldt without incurring any harm to myself, a week ago I landed in trouble. I was sitting at the bar of the Ritz one night drinking a lemon cola when a man named Shane Larson introduced himself. We'd had an unpleasant encounter before, and I didn't want to talk to him, but he ordered me another drink and acted very chummy. Much of what he said didn't make sense—about weight lifting and the sales instinct and marriage—until he laid a hand on my shoulder and said that he was angry at me. With a smile so thin that a toothpick could hide it, he explained that I had deprived him of a sales commission at Folie à Deux. Because of me, he said, his wife would not get a surgery she needed. He had a ruddy complexion and a pitch-black receding hairline that came to a sharp point in the middle of his forehead. I didn't touch the fresh lemon cola set in front of me. He said I could make up for my actions by allowing him to hand me over to the police so that he could collect the ten-thousand-dollar reward money my mother had posted. I owed him this, he claimed, and in return he would promise not to tell anyone that I'd been fooling them, letting them think I was missing. We could invent a story that I'd been lost in the woods and he'd rescued me, or that I'd been sick and he'd found me. I could make up the fiction, he said.

I turned down his offer. He told me to think about it. I said no. He said I wasn't listening to my best instincts, and that my conscience would punish me. He said he could spare me that pain. I put down money on the bar and left. When I looked back on my way out Shane was staring at his drink. Two minutes later, when I'd put the incident out of my mind, he caught up with me at the corner of Third and F Streets, twisted my arm behind my back, and marched me into an alley. He ran my head into a garbage can and said that he was going to take me to the police whether I liked it or not. Then he kicked me for a while and said he'd tell them that I attacked him and that he'd had to defend himself. He would collect the reward. To provide evidence for his story, he bit his left forearm so hard that blood poured down his chin, and then he shoved me into the back of his car.

As we drove through the night streets of Eureka, past liquor stores with partially burned-out neon signs and bail bondsmen's offices, I examined the people on the streets, the bands of women and interlocked couples and single men, all with their pockets full and their thoughts tossing back and forth like shuttlecocks over their day jobs and night proclivities and presumptions of the past and future. I felt intensely connected to them—to a state of humanity I'd avoided for ten years. There were so many people, so happy and sad, high and low, with hands wishing for something to hold and heads wishing for something to hope. Despite my discomfort and Shane's profane mutterings and reckless driving, the ride was invigorating, and I wanted it to last forever. I felt like I'd arrived at something.

Then, as we pulled into the police station parking lot, I was transported to the house of my old doctor, Steve Baker. It was morning and the place was empty. In the bathroom I found a mini pharmacy of Demerol, OxyContin, Benzedrine, Dexedrine, Methedrine, Equanil, meperidine, morphine, and paregoric: uppers, downers, routers, and loopers: an astonishing quantity of pills for every occasion. Concerned for Steve's welfare—the last time I'd seen him he'd been reeling from the effects of one or more of these drugs—I loaded the bottles into a paper bag and left him an anonymous note saying, "Dr. Baker, if you continue to abuse drugs, I will respond appropriately."

I walked several blocks and placed the bag in a trash can outside of a blue ranch-style house. Its door opened and Elaine Perry came out and stood on the stoop. She recognized me from her play rehearsal and wanted to know what I was doing in her garbage. I said I was throwing something away. She asked why I'd chosen her trash can specifically, and when I said it was a random choice, she shook her head and accused me of working for her husband, of helping him gather incriminating information to use against her in their divorce trial. She called me a muckraker and hoped I suffered for the part I'd played in this perversion of justice, because she hadn't been the first one to treat her marriage vows like they were some youthful indiscretion she could ignore now that she was old enough to understand that the only purpose in life was to gratify one's own desires. And she hadn't abdicated her responsibilities as a parent and left their two sons to concoct wild fantasies about where she had gone. And she didn't want Greg's money. I was to tell him this for her, so he and I could end the smear campaign right away. She may have been a public school teacher, but she could provide for her two sons without his help, if that was what he wanted. She went back inside her house crying.

This was a painful experience, and although I didn't know Elaine or her husband, I felt implicated. From the sidewalk in front of Elaine's house, I blinked and found myself in a familiar shower stall. It was pitch black for a few seconds before a light went on and someone entered. I said hello and began to apologize for being there, leaving the shower curtain drawn so as not to scare the person. Almost immediately I was ablaze with pain as a very hard object—my guess is a crowbar—pummeled me from the other side of the shower curtain. I held up my hands and arms to protect my face as blows rained down upon my hips, shoulders, stomach, legs, arms, and then, because there must have been an exposed area, on my head.

I passed out and awoke in a kitchen, where I lay with my hands tied up in packing rope. I vomited from the pain and listened to a woman explain that she'd called the cops and would shoot me if I ever again broke into her house. Her name was Sadie, she owned a gun, and she was not kidding. I asked her to take me to the emergency room, and she said the police would decide about that. I told her what a mistake it was for me to be there, and that I meant her no harm, but again she deferred to the police, who very shortly knocked on the door.

When she went to answer it, I was transported to a leather couch in Steve's living room. He came in as I was getting my bearings, and, after recovering from the shock of seeing me, he asked if I had written the note stuck to his bathroom mirror. I said I had, and he read me a riot act about the sanctity of a man's medicine cabinet, and how I'd committed a serious crime, and how he was going to get the law involved. Then he asked what had happened to me at the Jambalaya a few nights before.

I opened my mouth to answer and found myself sitting at a table at Mazotti's across from a black man pouring himself a glass of wine. He introduced himself as Prentiss Johnson and asked my name. I told him. Leon Meed was a good, solid name that I could be proud of, he said. He hadn't gone to work that day and as a result had gotten a call from his manager, Mary Ellen, who was a gentle spirit, and he let his machine pick it up because his roommate Frost was gone already, and Mary Ellen said it was discouraging that he hadn't called in to say he was sick or give an excuse. She had a great deal invested in Prentiss's good working track record, and she hated to see him squander it on account of his feeling lazy that day.

He then asked if I would help him finish the half-empty carafe of wine in front of us. I told him I had to get to the hospital and he nodded in agreement. He could see I was suffering, just like him, except that my pain was physical while his was emotional. Prentiss put a large hand on my neck. He would buy me one drink at a nearby bar called the Shanty to make me feel better before I checked into the hospital. The doctors would likely make me wait a long time in the waiting room without any kind of painkillers, and I would wish I had had a single drink before coming, just to take the edge off. Plus he could use the company at the moment. I wasn't to get him wrong—the folks at the Shanty were top quality—but you couldn't take it to the next level with them. Did I know what he was saying? You'd be talking to one of them and it'd be well and good, and you'd be digging, but you'd never reach the next level. I was different, he could tell.

My few drinks at the Shanty were the first I'd had since my wife and daughter died—I was never a drinker although I had occasionally had wine at parties—and they numbed my aching bones and reduced the terror I felt at being me. Prentiss and I toasted the balmy weather and jointly selected tunes from the jukebox. After these drinks things seemed better. I told Prentiss about what was happening to me, and although he joked that I was taking it much deeper than the next level he'd been talking about, he believed me. He suggested that there were people who'd give anything to have my condition, to be able to travel across space without foreknowledge or explanation. Prentiss said I should relish the opportunity I'd been given instead of seeing it as an affliction. The fact that two people could lead identical lives and one would say it was heaven while the other said it was hell demonstrated the importance of perspective. Wasn't happiness, like beauty, in the eye of the beholder, and wasn't it my duty, if I couldn't change the world, to change myself?

Then the exuberant stage of drunkenness passed and I became morose and self-pitying. Nobody had ever had it as badly as I did, I said. I was condemned to a long state of existential whiplash, unable to settle anywhere. I was the unluckiest person alive and when a man with osteoporosis stumbled into the Shanty and ordered a drink and was refused service and told to get out and fell over a chair and lacked the reflexes to break his fall with his hands, and thus smashed his forehead on the ground and everyone in the bar looked away, I thought that even he was better off than I was.

Prentiss wiped his lips and looked at the jukebox as the last song we'd programmed ended. Sometimes, he said, he thought the blues was the most honest type of music; at other times he thought only fools felt sorry for themselves. It was impossible to know which feeling was right.

Shane entered the bar then and, seeing me, stopped in the middle of the room. He wore black and his hair was wet. He approached me and said he was sorry. His wife had almost left him. The night I'd escaped he'd gone home and she'd cleared out all her things. He was humbled. And he deserved it. He'd let greed and rage get the best of him. There was no excuse for it. He'd been bad before and then improved and then lapsed again into even worse behavior. He held out his hand and I shook it.

At that instant I found myself at home, where I've been since this morning. I don't know why I've come back any more than I know why I left. Possibly I'm not grasping something elemental, the thought of which seizes me as I get up and wander the house, reexamining objects bought in a happier time, when I was married and a father and never conceived of being alone. I've visited the burl slab in my studio, unchanging as a monolith, and in that piece of wood, I've thought, is an answer. I wouldn't know where to begin finding it, though. I wouldn't know what to do. I've walked around the slab and felt its fibrous skin and not threatened it with an axe, and I've watched it in the different morning and afternoon lights and almost picked up my pencil to draw a sketch of what it could be, that great unknown, almost seeing through its roughness to a shape within.

# Part III

# 1

Once, if you had stayed longer than you'd intended in Eureka, postponing your northern trip for whatever reason, you would have heard the story of how the city got its name. A short but revealing tale, it began with *The word "Eureka"* and ended on *the town never recovered*. The polite thing would have been to listen and nod along, just as the prudent thing would have been to remember that stories, like all copies of a lost original, leave out more than they include, that they are the shorthand with which wisdom overlays fact and fiction—where conclusions lurking in a distant penumbra can, with patience, be formed. Stories, you would have kept in mind, reward concentration.

The word "Eureka," Greek for "I have found it," was shouted by Archimedes of Syracuse when he discovered how to verify that the king's new crown was pure gold by immersing it in water, measuring the volume displaced, and dividing the crown's weight by that figure to establish its density. He was so excited, according to legend, that he jumped naked from his bath and ran screaming down the street *Eureka! Eureka! Eureka!* He'd sat down in a tub of water intending only to get clean, and instead alighted on a way for all future generations to distinguish real gold from its fakes and forgeries, its fool's counterfeits. He had shown that you could find what you needed when looking for something else.

The town of Eureka in California came more than two thousand years later, in 1850, when a motley group of seasoned and amateur prospectors traveled upstate from the Sierra Nevada Mountains hoping to locate a new outpost of the Gold Rush. When they reached a strip of foul-weathered coastland buffered by mountains to the east and the ocean to the west, they christened a town Eureka with the thought that by doing so they would ensure an underground store of vast, easily tapped gold reserves. They were wrong. There was nothing to extract from Eureka but dirt. The women were bewildered and the men heartbroken as they set down their tools and felt the infinity of worthless soil beneath them. So many dreams lost and no one to blame but their mistaken expectations.

Lacking money to return to the homes they'd been eager to leave just months before, they stayed and became fishermen and lumberjacks, exiles from their imaginary Eden, yoked to heavy labor. And although they eventually made peace with misfortune, accepting their lot as a kind of divine judgment, some later said that discovering no gold was a disappointment from which the town never recovered.

Nearly ten years after Leon Meed stopped writing in his journal, at the end of November, his dead body and a collection of nine burl statues were found in a cabin on Neeland Hill by a teenage boy who'd gotten lost while hiking. According to the story that ran in the *Times-Standard,* Leon had long been considered permanently missing by the police, though his body was in a fresh stage of decomposition suggesting that he'd died only recently. It was unknown whether he had lived incognito in the woods the whole time or just returned from someplace else, although a lawyer, Mr. Rasmussen, said he'd drawn up a will for Leon two weeks before. The newspaper story, despite a number of lurid quotes about the "corpse" from the boy who'd discovered it, was buried on page eight.

Of the people to whom Leon's death would be important, only one had no earthly access to the story. Silas Carlton had suffered a heart attack four years earlier and passed away in his sleep. A loving half-page obituary written by his great-niece Lillith Fielding followed in the paper, after which three hundred people attended his funeral, a record for the hosting church.

Shane Larson didn't read the article about Leon's death because he was at that time living in Provo, Utah. On the morning it appeared he woke up with a walleyed hangover in a two-bedroom condominium beside his wife, Lenora, whom he had once begged not to leave him and promised that his lapses from Mormon propriety would stop. Meaning he had plunged a knife into his own back. And given himself an ever fresh cause for regret that drove him to new heights of deceit and fraud and theft and betrayal with no other reward than distraction from his home life. He lay in bed then, unalterably flaccid, and wished Lenora would run away with a church elder or fall off the red cliffs of Mt. Zion. Release him. Quit being a deadweight in every way save the literal one. Shane had had enough.

In Eureka, Eve Sieber didn't see the story about Leon because she didn't read the paper. She was thirty-three years old and lived alone in a single-bedroom efficiency apartment on F Street decorated with Byzantine prints, wall rugs, and garlands of dried peppers and flowers given to her by the customers of Going Places, the travel supply shop where she'd been assistant manager since Bonanza 88 went bankrupt seven years earlier. As part of her professional skill set, she could tell you where to dance the *tambu* in Curaçao and which monasteries were most impressive in Moldova. Set down in Riga on a cloudy day, she could find the closest hospital and the cheapest hostel. Burundi was her briar patch. Oman was no scarier to her than Omaha. Yet if these places weren't altogether foreign, neither were they immediately familiar. She'd never gone anywhere and so knew the world only by hearsay and report. No worse than Emily Dickinson. On Tuesday afternoons she volunteered as a big sister at the YWCA. On Wednesday nights and Sundays she went to the Sacred Heart Church on H Street. On other days she worked and gardened and ran and did collage art and saw friends. Although she lacked for nothing, sometimes in the middle of this or that activity her thoughts ran over the men who expressed romantic interest in her and whom she always turned down. Despite knowing that God's love was the only kind she could count on, her imagination occasionally sprang ahead of her like a dog forgetting its leash, and she pictured dates and hand holding and babies and what it meant to be a woman three years shy of her sexual peak.

It was slow at the shop on the morning the Leon story ran, so Eve inventoried the travel guides, which that year were selling like books about male-female communication. Some winters everyone stayed at home to shop and watch movies; others they all went to Tutuila or Tierra del Fuego or the Guandong Province. Sometimes people threw themselves into the farthest-flung places of the earth and it was a widely felt need for growth. When she finished with the books she moved with her neatly maintained pad of paper to the wall of cards.

The phone rang. "Going Places," she said, rapidly counting cards with Indian photographs on the front, epic shots of flat-bellied children grabbing each other's wrists in the Ganges as a nation in liquid floated by. Her nails were short and unpainted.

"Eve?" said Joon-sup, a friend she'd met while under the spell of Ryan's death ten years ago. There were two more cards than there were envelopes. Customers were careless.

"Hi there," answered Eve, fanning herself with the extra cards, wondering how to restore balance.

A loud tinkle sounded at the door. She glanced at a rough-hewn man who entered, wearing an oversized, badly patched army jacket with tarnished medals and peeling decorations. He had a minor bronchial fit—all catarrh and scorched larynx—and then ran his hands over the travel shaving kits, picked up an expensive titanium compass, and looked for the in-store camera. It was a failed lesson in the art of cunning.

"Is this an okay time to talk? Are you busy?"

Eve saw outside that it was drizzling and a fire truck screamed past. The compass was gone from its display shelf when the man moved to another part of the store. "Actually," she lowered her voice, "now's not so good."

"Did you see the paper today?"

"The *Chronicle*?" She felt a twinge at the base of her back. Several months before, she had abandoned a calisthenics regimen because the pain around her upper sacrum was persisting. Perhaps she'd given up on the treatment too soon.

"In the *Times-Standard* there's a story that I think—"

The army jacket now bulged with a satellite tracking device. "I'll call you back," she said, hanging up and then going to lock the door and phone the police. Shoplifters, as a stark black-and-white sign next to the fire capacity warning on the back wall read, would be prosecuted to the fullest extent of the law.

After the thief's complicated denials and her handing over the in-store video footage to the police, who led him away with some situational embarrassment, the store was again empty. Her back was a sharp message center. Her boss, Callie, wasn't coming to relieve her for another two and a half hours, and she felt the want of an ice pack in the store.

Eve picked up the phone and dialed Joon-sup's number. Then, while reaching down to pick up the trash behind the display counter, her lower back went into spasm for the second time in a year. Helplessly she fell to her knees, banged her head against the counter door, and then sat propped against the display-counter slide door, breathing heavily and feeling for blood on her scalp. The pain made her want to curl into a ball, but she didn't budge other than to click off the phone while it was ringing. Next she called Callie to explain what had happened and then slowly, carefully escorted herself to the emergency room—her mind was a young lady and her body an elderly charge—where they gave her Valium and repeated what they'd told her the last time: lumbar muscle strains like hers took a week to heal. Her head was fine. The black male nurse named Prentiss who walked her to the exit and made sure she could drive home was especially nice, and he joked that she shouldn't go bungee jumping or play tug-of-war anytime soon. "Cartwheels," he said, assuming a grave expression, "now don't even think about them."

Five minutes after Eve promised not to think about cartwheels, Elaine Perry arrived home and picked up three letters from her mailbox. The first informed her that she'd been nominated for Humboldt County's Teacher of the Year Award, which surprised her not out of false modesty but because Muir teachers were never nominated due to an anti-Muir bias among local educators. It was an enormous honor and made her head tingle so hard she massaged it with both hands.

The second letter was a note from her son Abraham with a health insurance form that needed her signature. *Dear Mom,* the note said, *The semester is almost done and there are a million things I have to remember for finals. If only I hadn't smoked so much pot in high school! Are we old enough to joke about that yet? I'm already choosing classes for next semester and am thinking marine biology, because it's a good program here, and because I don't know what I want to take. How's Trevor and the canines? Is Mr. Lockjaw still being a prick about your creeping ivies "strangling" his junipers? Tell him he better watch out when I come home to visit. I'm taking judo lessons. Love, Abe.*

She separated the insurance form from the letters, the third of which was in an unfamiliar hand and so got stuffed into her briefcase, and went inside the house, where an avalanche of unfolded clothes sat on the dryer, waiting to be set in motion. She peeked into Trevor's room—empty—and went to her bedroom and lay down on Steve Baker's running shorts and ankle weights. The cats had been at the bedspread again, pulling out loose threads that now resembled so many strands of angel hair pasta.

Were they old enough to joke about Abe's obsession with marijuana? About it subsuming every interest Abe had ever had, so that if he wasn't talking to his friends about gravity bongs or soil pH levels or the auxiliary benefits of being permanently stoned, he was in a stupor in front of the television? That hadn't been anything to joke about; that had been a source of deep-welled worry, in which she'd explained to Abe the dangers of so much dreamtime, had read to him the section in *The Odyssey* about the Island of the Lotus-Eaters and how its inhabitants were too tranquilized to realize they were drowning when it sank into the sea. She'd initiated a battle for his soul, in which he'd been a reluctant ally and frequent turncoat, and for a time all had appeared to be lost. But then it got better. Abe grew out of it. Lost his drug paraphernalia and didn't replace it. Sold the last of the dope he'd grown himself. Read a book. Elaine thought that some problems solved themselves, and a reflected patch of sunlight on the ceiling grew suddenly bright.

Steve would be home soon, her husband of seven years and the former colleague of her former husband, Greg. She thought about a stir-fry vegetable medley for dinner. Checked the couscous level and the time, four fourteen, and tossed vegetables into a colander in the kitchen sink. She put on folk-tinged music in which there was a love habit that couldn't be broken—a denim voice crooned, "Don't know why I relate to every gap-toothed man named Nate"—and went into the living room to water the plants. Then the front door slammed and Steve entered the house wearing a stethoscope on his temples like alien tentacles because, surprise, he was home early, got a couple of afternoon cancellations, and he was taking her to dinner at the Smile of Siam—*and the vegetables I've already started washing?* A little bath never hurt a legume, they could go back in the fridge—and voilà he was dragging her half-protestingly to the car. *I need to change!* No, you look great. *But it's only four twenty-five!* So we'll have time to walk around Old Town. They squealed out of the driveway and onto the road. He smiled at her and it was amazing to know that love needn't die, that after years it was still capable of surprise and passion. Not always, she knew, but sometimes. And often sometimes was enough.

They parked on Second Street and walked along a boardwalk made of concrete-reinforced wood pulp with their arms around each other's waists, and Elaine tried to match her stride with Steve's. She always tried and never managed this—they remained a half-step off—which was slightly uncomfortable, like walking with a limp. Steve never noticed; he was too busy commenting on the Pacific black brants flying overhead or whistling Dvořák or recounting some droll surgery story. Elaine, rather than saying anything, thought, The more I hear Dvořák, the more I like him.

At five o'clock they turned around to limp toward the Smile of Siam. The cold sun set to the west, casting a row of four-story Victorian buildings as fairy-tale silhouettes. There was a feeling of abrupt evening; streetlights came on and sounds broke with their sources. Cars slowed down, their drivers strained to see crossing pedestrians blending into the shades of dusk. Elaine and Steve walked past their parked car and around a small crowd of people examining the sandwich board menu of the Fricatash, which had been converted under new ownership into an ice-cream parlor. An untethered French poodle stood several feet away on three legs, and Elaine stopped to pet it. Steve drifted over to a nearby sidewalk bench and flipped through a copy of the *Times-Standard* stuffed between its boards, where he came upon and closely read a story of immediate significance to him.

Turning from the dog back to her husband, Elaine tried to remember the name of the Dvořák piece and would have asked Steve if he hadn't begun making the throat-clearing noise he made when anxious. She approached him and motioned for them to continue walking to the restaurant.

"Is something the matter?" she asked.

"It's nothing."

"What's nothing?"

"Nothing's nothing. I just saw in the newspaper that they're going to tear down the old Bistrins building."

"Good, it's been empty forever. Will anything replace it?"

"Don't know. I only read the headline."

Elaine placed her arm around Steve's waist and expected him to drop the dark prophet act and return to the semiromantic mood he'd been in before. His arms stayed unresponsively at his sides. "I have something to tell you," she said.

"What is it?"

"I can't say until dinner. It's a surprise." She waited for him to press the question, and when he didn't she said, "You're not going to have the curry, are you?"

"Maybe."

"But what about the diarrhea—you told me last time to make sure you never got it again."

Steve didn't answer but kept clearing his throat. When they reached the restaurant Elaine opened the door and he entered wordlessly. After they sat down she batted her eyelashes at him as the mock southern belle she did sometimes to amuse him, but he didn't notice, and then she ordered the pad thai and he the chicken curry. She broke apart her chopsticks and laughed when instead of dividing evenly down the middle, one snapped in half. Steve drank his water quickly and asked to have hers.

"Why are you being so solemn?" she asked.

"I'm not. What are you going to tell me?"

"It's not bad so don't make that face. In fact, it's good. I've been nominated for Humboldt County's Teacher of the Year Award. Only three people are in the running, so I have a thirty-three-and-a-third chance of winning."

"What does that mean?"

"If I win I'll be up for the state award, meaning I'd go to Sacramento for a year to work with the state superintendent of schools office. I'd have a hand in crafting statewide curricula and see how the administration operates from the inside."

"You'd live in Sacramento?"

"Just for a year."

"Oh." Steve settled back in his chair. It had been forever since he'd gone overboard with prescription speed, since that afternoon ten years earlier when he came home, as pale and thin as an Edward

Gorey butler, and found his medicine cabinet cleaned out with an ominous note telling him never to use drugs again, and then discovered a battered Leon Meed reposing in the living room like he'd been invited on a social call, and then watched as Leon ceased to be there. "Sacramento—that's seven hours away."

"Which isn't too far," Elaine said. "I'd come back some weekends, and you could go there."

"You're going to be really busy."

"I'm not going to get it. I've only been nominated. Even if I won here I'd have an impossible chance of winning the whole state."

Their waiter, a teenage boy wearing enormous triangular glasses and a gold medallion depicting an entwined eagle and cobra, refilled their water and set down a pot of tea. The kitchen was temporarily out of the glass noodles used in pad thai, but could he recommend pan-fried soba noodles instead?

"Sure," said Elaine. Then to Steve, "Why aren't you happy for me? Why don't you congratulate me?"

"Congratulations."

"Thank you. That was extremely heartfelt."

"I don't feel well."

"What's wrong?"

"Nothing."

"Steve, I'm not going anywhere. I probably won't win. It's just nice to be nominated, you know? It's nice to be acknowledged for what I do."

"I'm happy for you."

Steve poured tea into their cups. Finding his pills gone ten years ago he'd sat on the toilet seat with his head in his hands; his wife had already left him and he'd had nothing to prop him up. There hadn't even been enough aspirins in the house to end it all. He'd stood up in the bathroom and felt for his car keys and on his way to the door run smack into Leon. "Anything else happen today?" he said.

"I got a letter from Abe. He said he's having a hard time memorizing for his finals and asked if we could joke about his pot habit yet.

As if it's been years since the crisis time and he's completely out of the woods."

"It's been a while."

"It's not even been five months."

"I don't think he'll backslide."

"Remember the parents' meetings we went to that were all about how easy it is to relapse? That addicts are always at risk? I never would have thought he had an addictive personality when he was a boy, but—"

"Not everyone who quits using drugs is susceptible to relapse."

"But we can't assume that Abe is one of the unsusceptible ones."

"He's not the type to have a problem with drugs all his life. He's got too much going on in his head."

"Smart people are destroyed by drugs all the time."

"Abe's like me. He'll be able to walk away and not look back."

"What do you know about walking away from drugs?"

"I know."

"How?"

"I used to take uppers when Anne and I split up."

"Uppers?"

"Speed."

"You were on speed!" She lowered her voice too late.

"Yes."

"Are you serious?" She looked around to see what kind of impact her voice had had on the room's other occupants. "I didn't know that. Why haven't you ever told me?"

"There wasn't a right time. When we first got together you'd just seen that kid die of an overdose, and then my own problem began to seem unimportant. It became a phase I'd gone through." He stared at her levelly and drank everything on the table.

"I don't know how to respond," she said. "During all the worry and confusion about Abe you never said a word."

"Are you angry?"

"I don't know about angry. I can't say I'm angry exactly; it's more like I'm shocked. This is a huge thing to keep from me all these years."

"I wasn't doing well then. The divorce was so painful I can't explain it."

"We've had a million conversations about your divorce."

"It was just one detail I left out."

"What made you quit?"

He looked at her and rubbed his chin.

"*Did* you quit?"

"Yes. I just told you it was easy to stop."

"Why?"

"I don't want to talk about it."

"You brought it up."

"I've said all there is to say."

"You haven't said anything except that your divorce was hard—which I already knew—and that you were addicted to amphetamines. Why won't you tell me why you quit?"

"Thank you," said Steve to the waiter, who placed a full water pitcher and their plates in front of them. The waiter went to the door and returned to seat an old woman at the table next to them.

"I don't see what difference it makes," Steve said.

"Yes, you do, or I wouldn't have to keep asking."

Steve stirred the small pieces of chicken on his plate, sure that Elaine would move to Sacramento. He'd once known that the permanence of happiness was illusory; why had he forgotten it? Anne remarried around the time he did—seven years ago—which meant she'd been with her current husband for four years longer than she'd been with him. He was incapable of sustaining love. He looked at Elaine; she already appeared far away, as if he were remembering her face instead of seeing it directly.

"Is your food okay?" asked the waiter, standing near the cash register wiping down menus.

"Fine," said Steve. Then to Elaine, "It's going to be immediately clear why I don't want to tell you."

"Okay."

"I wish you'd let it go."

"And I wish you'd come out with it. I thought we told each other everything. You've always said that you prized our openness more than anything, and now I'm hearing this."

"I quit because I saw a former patient of mine disappear."

She frowned and made a face like she was trying to locate a hair in her mouth with her tongue. "What are you talking about?" she said.

"I saw a man named Leon Meed go from being in the room with me to not being in the room with me in the space of a second."

"Leon Meed?"

"Yes."

"He was the man I thought was helping Greg blackmail me."

"Yes."

"But it turned out he'd gone missing and the police were looking for him."

"Yes. There's an article in today's paper saying he just died."

"And you saw him do what?"

"You won't believe it so let's not discuss it anymore, but what happened was he visited me a couple of times and threw away my pills and warned me not to do them anymore. Then he magically vanished into thin air."

She shook her head quizzically. "You mean you thought he vanished because you were on drugs."

"No, I saw him disappear."

"Steve, you didn't."

"I told you you wouldn't believe me."

"Why are you lying about this?"

"I'm not."

"I don't understand. You come home in the best mood I've ever seen you in, and then suddenly you used to be a drug addict and you saw a man disappear ten years ago."

"It doesn't matter. None of it matters." Steve grabbed the bill and went to the counter, followed by the waiter trying to tell him that he'd take care of it and Steve didn't need to get up.

What's going on? Elaine thought, reaching for her water glass without realizing it was empty. What is going on?

The next morning, Sadie Jorgenson woke up and forced herself to walk the plank of showering, dressing, and going to work, where there were twenty-nine messages on her phone service that she didn't have the energy to listen to. In her office she smeared peanut butter on vegetable crackers and ate methodically, great mouthfuls of instant paste. She wore a loose polyester blouse and a cotton skirt and freshly resoled clogs, the cork on the bottom of which she dug at with a penknife while waiting for the day to begin.

Her first patient was a teenage boy named Peter whose parents sent him to her because at night he went around the house breaking appliances—clocks, televisions, computers, microwaves, refrigerators—as would, in their words, "a sinister elf." During his opening sessions with Sadie he'd said that his family was too materialistic, and that he was showing them the error of their ways. When she suggested that boredom was the real cause of his vandalism, and that he might want to take up a hobby, something physical that would tire him out by the time he went to bed so he could go right to sleep, he said she was a terrible therapist. Sadie took the insult well—she agreed with him in her heart—and got through the session on autopilot. Her next patient that morning was a first-timer who claimed that everyone disliked her, even strangers. Even Sadie. When Sadie said that this wasn't true, that most people didn't like or dislike someone without knowing them first, the woman responded by saying that Sadie was just trying to make her feel better. Sadie couldn't deny it, and when the hour was up she flipped through a gardening magazine and was herself bored.

At twelve thirty she knocked on her colleague Bob's door and suggested they go to Amigas Burrito. She had to get out of the office right away. Bob was reading dictation into his computer and paused in mid-sentence, his shoulders hunched over the keyboard like a cresting wave. "Don't you have a one o'clock?" he asked.

"I canceled them, Bob."

"Why?"

"I'm too hungry to listen."

"I thought the problem is that they don't talk."

"Have I discussed them with you? Am I that unprofessional?"

"We discuss them every week."

"Get your coat, Bob. It's raining."

They took Sadie's station wagon, which was long and wide and had wainscoted doors. They had an asexual relationship, but not for lack of trying—they'd dated nine years earlier until Bob admitted, unsolicited, that his antidepressant made him impotent, at which point they downshifted to friends—and now ate together regularly, dueting on love songs to and from restaurants.

"You know," said Bob, "I'm not sure I'm in the mood for Mexican."

"Yes, you are." Sadie honked at an old woman in the crosswalk in front of them who'd dropped her purse and was kicking it slowly to the curb. "Can you believe this lady? If you ever see me doing that, run over me."

Bob removed his glasses and wiped them with his undershirt. "If I said you cancel patient appointments a lot these days, would you get defensive?"

"I don't do it a lot."

"So that's your answer."

"Today's couple is doomed, and the three of us know it. She wants kids, he doesn't, and nothing anyone says will change that. By canceling our session I'm saving them money, which they need because when they break up one of them will have to find a new place to live and that's a lot of outlay to set up electricity, water, etcetera."

"I'd rather hear about their sexual foibles than their money troubles."

"That's because you're a pervert, Bob."

"Didn't you tell me this guy was on the fence about kids, that he might want to have them someday?"

"He only says that as a stall. He's not going to want kids. At least not with her."

"Why do you think that?"

"There's no love in the room during their sessions. I arrange the chairs beforehand so that their arms are touching each other, and when he comes in he moves them apart. Without even thinking. And not just a little so that he'll have more leg space; he actually lifts up his chair and sets it down two feet away."

"Does she notice?"

"No. She's getting out her tissue to tear into a million pieces so that I have to vacuum up after they leave." There was nothing good on the radio. Sadie switched it off. "Sometimes I think it'd be better to work in a hospital with the truly ill, like you did before you went into private practice."

"You don't want to do that; it's demoralizing. In the three years I worked at Kimbote Psychiatric, I never helped anyone into release. Not once. Take the feeling you have now of not making a difference and multiply that by a hundred if you want to know what it's like."

At Amigas Burrito they went inside and ordered numbered specials with colored rice and refried beans. The walls were painted a three-dimensional San Cristóbal *zócalo*. Sadie was substantially heavier than she'd been ten years earlier. She loved carbohydrates purely and unconditionally. Bob looked slight and effeminate next to her. There were free drink refills; his was diet and hers was vanilla flavored.

Sadie said, "I'm burned out. I see seven people a day, and most of them have been coming for years. Do you know what I think, Bob?"

"No. And I'd like to point out again how much you say my name."

"People don't want to overcome their neuroses; they just want someone to listen to them. They don't want health; they want an audience."

"You don't believe that."

"Couples only come to me when they've been sleeping in separate beds for months, and then all I can do is ease them into divorce or splitting up. I'm tired of being the emcee of broken relationships. There is no hope for anyone."

Bob placed a small hand on Sadie's. "Maybe you should take a sabbatical for a while, until you feel like yourself again."

"I feel like myself. That's the problem."

"Everyone gets tired of their job. They forget why they went into their profession. You've got to remember the story of the two men on the beach."

"With the starfish?"

"Yes."

"I hate that story."

"Two men are walking on a beach. The first picks up a starfish to throw into the ocean. The second says, 'What difference does that make when there are hundreds of starfish on the beach?' The first man answers, 'It makes a difference to this one.'"

"I still hate that story. Besides, I throw a starfish toward the water and it ends up in the dunes behind me."

"That's not always true."

"Nothing's always true."

Bob chewed and swallowed and said, "True."

Sadie appreciated Bob's wanting to help but marveled at his ineffectiveness. She was living proof of her point that no one could be helped, that we would live with our problems until death do us part. More certain than any marriage. And when she pushed back her chair to stand she knocked off a stack of newspaper sections from another table. She looked at the mess on the ground, and facing up was a picture and article about a man who had gone missing ten years before and recently been found dead in the woods. Sadie read it all in a ten-second gulp.

"Bob," she said.

"Yeah?"

"Bob, I need you to drive on the way back."

✿   ✿   ✿

Across town where she worked as a secretary at Steve's office, the Coastal Orthopedic Medical Group, Lillith Fielding prepared to leave early. She raced through two short stacks of filing, sorted out a confused box of sample painkillers, and searched for a misplaced invoice. Then she told her coworkers that she was on her way to Humboldt State University for her radio appearance. They wished her luck and said they'd tune in, which made her nervous even though she'd known them forever and didn't need to impress them, and they all respected her neopaganism for what it was, or at least they didn't say anything critical to her about it. The trick to being on the radio was not to think about the people listening, the way you weren't supposed to look down while climbing a ladder.

The man who was going to interview her, Barry Klein, had warned her that the KHSU station control room would give a worm claustrophobia, and it was easy to take the joke seriously when she arrived to be a guest on his show, *Live from Somewhere,* sitting thigh to thigh beside him and talking into the small microphone that grew out of a busy gray console like an iron thistle. She was there to discuss the North Coast's rapidly expanding neopagan community and had met Barry a year earlier at Club Triangle, the gay-themed night at downtown Eureka's East & West Club, where she'd accompanied her friend Franklin, whom Barry later went home with. Barry had called her a month ago saying he'd found her name on the Internet as a neopagan spokesperson and wanted her to be on his show.

The on-air light turned green after a few service announcements and sponsor acknowledgments, and Barry said, leaning back in his chair to make Lillith feel more comfortable, because she was evidently nervous, quaffing breath mints, "Now I'd like to welcome listeners to *Live from Somewhere.* This week we have as our guest Lillith Fielding, a local organizer of Wiccan and other neopagan events, to discuss her faith and its increasing importance in this area. Thanks for being here, Lillith."

"It's my pleasure."

"First of all, you're a witch."

"Yes."

"Is there a reason you call yourself that, considering the word's negative connotations? Are you reclaiming it the way gays did with queer? Or blacks did with nigger?" Barry didn't even try to cross his legs in this small space; he knew what a tangle of wires and cords that would create in addition to inconveniencing his guest.

"No, it's what we Wiccans have always called ourselves." Lillith articulated every word like a speech coach and sweat gathered on her forehead. Her throat was dry. She fished about in her purse for a half-liter bottle of water and took a silent sip.

"How long are we talking here? That is, how long have Wiccans been around?"

"We trace our tradition back thirty-five thousand years, to the first nature-worshipping peoples of central Europe."

Barry nodded and folded his hands, pure encouragement. "This brings up an interesting point. Some people claim that Wicca really dates back only to 1950, when Gerald Gardner wrote *Witchcraft Today,* an alleged history and explanation of underground pagan sects in England that's been proven to be made up. Practices that Gardner claimed had been in place for millennia are no more legitimate than the Mormon Book of Abraham. How do you answer these charges?"

Lillith's eyes flickered for a moment. "Every religion has detractors who deny it tenet by tenet. Christians and Jews have atheists telling them they're living a lie. Buddhists and Hindus have Christians and Jews telling them the same thing. It comes down to a question of faith. Either you believe in the spiritual validity of Wicca or you don't. It does a lot of people good and that alone is reason to support it even if you're not Wiccan. It's empowering for young women, for example—actually, for women of all ages—because it says that the grand creative force in the universe is feminine, the Goddess."

"You're talking about belief and how you either believe or you don't. Most Christians and Jews would say they believe because of the

Bible, or because they have a relationship with God. Why do you believe in Wicca?"

Lillith sat up straight in her chair. "Because it speaks to me. And because I believe in the sanctity of nature, which according to Wicca is the seat of all goodness in the universe. Nature provides for us while we're alive in every way—it gives us food and medicine and beauty—and then welcomes us into its hidden world when we die."

"Its hidden world? What's that?"

"A place called the Astral Plane, where spirits and magical creatures live."

Barry said, a nasty tone rising in his voice that he didn't try to suppress, "A phrase like 'magical creatures' is likely to make people laugh. How do you get anyone to take Wicca seriously?"

"I don't know why magical creatures are funnier than angels or the devil."

"Do you believe in magic?"

"Yes."

"Have you ever worked magic yourself?"

"Yes."

"What did you do?"

"Lots of things. I've cured friends who were sick. I've helped to bring about rain when forests were dying."

"That happens even without magic."

Lillith was frustrated for a moment and the silence frightened her, all those listeners out there stopping to hear how or if she'd answer. She said, "I've brought someone back from the Astral Plane."

"You've what?"

"There once was a man named Leon Meed stuck on the Astral Plane, and I brought him back to our world."

"Why, so you could kill him?"

Lillith opened her mouth to answer but lost the words before she could pronounce them.

Barry continued, "The paper didn't say how he died, so if this is a confession I'll have to detain you until the police arrive."

"I don't know what you're talking about." Lillith had been told this would be a friendly chat about Wiccan events and resources in northern California. A chance to enlighten and educate. She was organizing a three-day retreat at Wolf Creek in two weeks and this was to be an opportunity to promote it. "It'll be like an infomercial," Barry had told her over the phone. Instead it had taken an inquisitorial, sadistic turn. She didn't know where the hostility was coming from.

"My guest today on *Live from Somewhere* is Lillith Fielding, a local neopagan activist and organizer. We'll be right back after a word from our underwriters and the community announcements that matter." Barry flipped a switch and the on-air sign turned red. Rubbed his temples with his forefingers. "This is going well. I like the Leon Meed angle. You're doing an improv thing now, a free association. It's working."

"You know who Leon Meed is?"

"Weren't you here when I read my news summary?"

"Yeah."

"Then you heard me read the article about him from the paper."

"What article?"

"Don't play dumb when we go back on the air." He lifted and moved stacks of folders and miscellaneous papers. "Here." He handed her the *Times-Standard* from the day before. "Let's keep going with it. I think we've exhausted the Wicca stuff."

Lillith, touching her forehead with her left hand as though feeling for an abrasion, stood up, collected her purse and sweater, and opened the door.

"What are you doing?"

"Leaving."

"But you're doing great. There's no need to be nervous."

"I'm not nervous. I'm upset that you're acting like a shock jock out to attack everything I say. This whole thing is biased and cynical, and I don't have time to be publicly mauled like this. It's not worth it. I thought this show was going to be different."

Barry followed her into the hallway of the Van Duzen Building,

where students passed by in herds and there were bulletin boards listing tai chi classes and emergency environmental interventions and
guru appearances. "I'm only trying to make it interesting!"

Lillith walked out the double doors, which closed behind her and
were immediately opened by another wave of entering and exiting
students. Barry then returned to the broadcast room, where he had to
go back on the air too quickly to think of a good excuse why his guest
was gone. Therefore he used a bad excuse; he said that Lillith had
gotten sick and was throwing up and couldn't return to the show.

He played music and read everything in the read box, and when
his time slot finally ended he handed the microphone over to Trey
Pallance, a tragically straight undergraduate who always camped it up
around Barry, in solidarity perhaps, and went outside to begin hating
himself. Passing through the games of Frisbee and hacky sack and
drum circles and solitary readers and hoarse evangelists, he went over
in his head what had happened. He unlocked his mud-splattered
Honda and drove to a fast-food place and got a hamburger, remembering the betrayed look on Lillith's face during the interview, as if
she were a lamb led to slaughter. Barry asked himself, So am I the
butcher? He came to a stoplight. He took a shark bite of burger. In
the car to his right was a nancy boy to whom he could have given the
Signal—pointed to his watch and flashed five fingers signifying *I can
get you off in five minutes,* an admittedly simple signal because after
all gay men weren't the Masons—and been a quick top or bottom in
the nearest public bathroom. He could have amused himself the way
he did whenever he felt bad about being a bitch: by cruising or watching television or opening a bottle of this or that. It was like, once upon
a time he'd been a sweet boy, a painfully shy child effeminate enough
to make a hundred male poets grateful that the world was minting
their successors, and he'd blushed whenever he was the center of
attention, so that in seventh grade one of his classmates had said,
"Hey, everyone look at Barry," and he'd gone bright red on command
as twenty-three twelve-year-olds laughed like wind chimes in a hurri-
cane. He'd been *homo sensitivus*. He'd had a porcelain heart. But

now Barry was unfazed as the center of attention, sexual or otherwise, and perhaps this brazenness was merely a by-product of growing up and developing the calluses necessary to survive. Staying as tender-skinned as he'd been as a child would have killed him. But was his adult personality an improvement? Built on confrontations and an acerbic wit that could eat through steel? That waited like a tyger tyger burning bright for somebody, anybody to express genuine sentiment? The man in the car to his right pointed to his watch and held up five fingers. Barry floored it as the light went green.

That evening Steve was called in to surgery and didn't finish until three thirty a.m., at which time he and nursing assistant Prentiss Johnson were hungry and deliberating in front of a vending machine on the fourth floor. Steve held his money like a racetrack betting slip and watched the machine as though it were a closed-circuit broadcast of the race. Prentiss looked expectantly at him, waiting for his turn to slide in money. Both wore scrubs and hair caps and form-fitting slippers.

"What, you getting a cream pie?" Prentiss asked, balancing on one leg as he pulled the other foot up to scratch his calf. "At this hour?"

"Especially at this hour," Steve answered, feeding dollar bills into the slot. "Cream pies are manna from heaven."

"Those things'll kill you. It's not doctors who eat healthy. It's us nurses. We're the ones who're going to live forever. Med school was wasted on you all. Step aside." Prentiss got a nonfat yogurt, a bag of raisins, and a guava juice, and then they went to sit on the overstuffed houndstooth couch in the doctors' lounge, a pan flute rendition of "Acrid Avid Jam Shred" playing in the background.

Soon after he'd been hospitalized for alcohol poisoning the third and final time, ten years ago, Prentiss enrolled at the local junior college and then got his nursing degree at UC Riverside. Three years later he returned to Humboldt County and was sober except for two largely uneventful occasions (a night of utter loneliness and a chance encounter with his old AA sponsor Alvin, who had just broken up with Barry Klein again and was feeling low). He now lived two blocks from the hospital on Evergreen Street and kept a house pig named Ferdinand—pigs were his favorite animal—and he'd made a set of friends for whom alcohol was a minor concern. In Riverside he had gone out with a woman and it had gotten serious, but then she moved to Georgia for her job and that was the end of that. He hadn't dated anyone in years and had recently placed an ad in the personals section of the *Times-Standard*.

"What do you think the vote's going to be on the highway rerouting?" Prentiss asked, pointing to the front page of the paper announcing the March county referendum.

"It'll pass," said Steve. "People hate that the 101 goes through Eureka. They've always hated it and this is one of the last towns that doesn't have a bypass."

"But Eureka needs the highway to survive. Look at Cloverdale and what a noplace it's been since they built the bypass. We've got to force people to drive through town. It's self-preservation says that, and anyone who votes against it is against Eureka. Might as well declare this place a ghost town and get put on the historical interest map, make the tourist dollars that way."

"Eureka will survive. It has a lot going for it."

"Name five things it's got going for it."

"Five—that's unfair."

"We cut Eureka loose from the highway and there's no reason to stop here for your average traveler. The 101 passing through it is an incentive to see the city. I'm telling you, it's all a web with everything connected to everything. Without the highway there's less jobs, means people move away, less sick people, less funding for the hospital, you're out of a job, I'm out of a job. It's already bad enough I can't meet a single woman over the age of twenty around here."

"The real reason you're upset."

"No, it's the interconnectedness I'm talking about. The preservation."

They waved good night to a doctor who saluted as he passed by the open door. They fixed themselves cups of complimentary coffee. Prentiss was nonplussed that his favorite sweetener was gone and vainly rooted around in the supply cabinets, overturning stacks of plastic lids and boxes of figure-eight straws. "Why're you still here, anyway? What's your wife think about you not rushing home to her after a hard night's work?"

"She's asleep. Tomorrow's a school day, so I might as well stay till she wakes up."

They sat back down and were stirring their coffee and taking unpleasurable sips and letting their minds and bodies unwind, when Prentiss said, rubbing his lamb's wool beard, "Your hands ever rash up from surgical gloves? I'm thinking I have an allergy to the petro-chemicals."

"Hmm. I'd love another cream pie."

"I can't believe they even sell those fatty things in a hospital. You see they took out the cigarette machines years ago and then the healthy improvements just stopped. Like it's okay to have the blood pressure of a sumo wrestler so long as you don't get lung cancer."

Steve meditated on the steam belly-dancing out of his coffee cup, and his lips moved silently. He swiped off his cap and placed it on his knee. "You lived in Eureka before you got your nursing degree, right?"

"Yeah."

"Do you remember a missing person story from ten years ago, guy named Leon Meed?"

Prentiss squinted and stared into space and from fatigue his eyes were red and watery. "Yes."

"It was in the papers for a while."

"Then it popped up in yesterday's, about him dying. Why you asking?"

Steve tightened the corners of his mouth and studied his friend. Hospitals hummed, and if you were silent long enough, the humming sounded like screaming. "No reason."

"As if I'd believe that." Another meditative silence rose into an uproar and Prentiss said, "You know how I've never asked if Elaine had any single women friends?"

"Yeah."

"What if I asked now if maybe she knows a teacher or some other type of unattached woman from the education field. I could—"

A distant yet clear voice paged Dr. Baker over the loudspeakers. Would he please come to ER right away? Steve stood up and threw away his quarter-full cup of coffee and said, "She might. Right now isn't the best time for me to find out—we're having issues—but I'll ask as soon as I can."

"No pressure," said Prentiss. "Just if she happened to know someone who wanted to be set up on a date, I'd be interested. That kind of thing."

"You got it."

"And don't stay here too late. I want you home when your wife wakes up."

Steve shrugged and left the room.

## ⊣ 2 ⊢

What Shane Larson liked most about Eureka was its lack of bullshit. You walked into a store there, a grocery store, say, and nobody told you about the day's specials or asked if you were finding everything okay. There wasn't the automatic assumption that you were a fucking retard. Similarly, when someone bought a funeral plot in Eureka, they listened to your pitch and then said yes or no. *Sans* bullshit. Elsewhere—such as in Provo—they tried to lowball you or sneak around you to talk to the manager and insist that they get prime placement—a Lily of the Valley spot, or one in Ivy Grove—for standard placement price, thus robbing you of a commission and getting you in trouble for being inflexible. It was wrong and it was bullshit. So that after a while you reached a point where Provo could shove its lowballing so-called Mormons up its ass, a threshold where you were ready to leave, no questions asked, no answers given, just hop on the bus and get yourself free.

Having crossed this threshold the week before, Shane found himself back in Eureka on the evening of December 6, staring at the yellow wall-papered innards of the studio apartment in Henderson Center he'd secured before leaving Provo. Lenora hadn't tried to stop him from going, and he wondered now why he hadn't done it sooner. All this time he'd thought she would go crazy if he left her. All this time he had lived a constrained life for no reason. *Estrangement.* A

231

new word for a new beginning. The next day he would call his old boss at Morland Memorial Services and talk about resuming work for the company. Do a little fence-mending. Apologize again for the shit that had gone down when he'd quit ten years before (the files he'd recklessly erased, the contracts he'd lost, the petty sabotage). Prepare to reenter Eureka society with his tail out from between his legs.

It was with pleasant thoughts like these that Shane sat on a lawn chair in the middle of his nearly empty apartment, a suitcase of Bud Light propped open by his side, enjoying a vigorous handjob, when his phone rang.

"Yeah," he said, flipping the phone open and staring with old curiosity at his swollen cock.

"Shane Larson?"

"Who's asking?"

"My name is Martin Nemec, and I write for the *Times-Standard*. I'd like to talk to you if you have a minute."

"About what?"

"Do you know a man named Leon Meed?"

As though by command, Shane's erection began to fall. "I remember the name."

"Were you aware that he was found dead recently?"

"No, but I'm sorry to hear it."

"Yes—"

"Have his funeral arrangements been made?"

"I—don't know. I wrote a story about his death in last week's paper, and since then I've become interested in what happened to him. Maybe you know that he was a burl sculptor."

"If you're not handling the burial, any idea who is? Widow? Kids?" Shane's cock reversed its course to upright. Stiffs made him stiff. He looked around for a pen and paper but of course there was nothing and wasn't it typical that business would fall into his lap when he wasn't prepared for it.

"I think his body is being interred at the morgue, and as far as I know he's not survived by anybody. But if you'll give me a second, I want to say that I've gained access to Leon's possessions, the things impounded by the police from his home, and I've read his journal, which is an interesting document. You're the last person mentioned in it."

Shane's dick again reversed direction, contracting with snail-like temerity.

"The journal suggests that Leon had a mental illness of some kind, and I'm wondering if you could tell me about your encounters with him."

"My encounters? I barely knew him. We didn't really have any what you'd call encounters."

"He wrote that you attacked him once and tried to take him to the police in order to collect a ten-thousand-dollar reward his mother had offered for his return."

Shane stood up, zipped his pants, and looked out his window, half expecting to see a stalker sitting on the curb across the street, staring up at him. All he saw was his own reflection. "What is this?"

"I'm not—"

"I just tried to do my civic duty by turning in a guy who'd gone missing, and I'll testify to that in court. You hear me?" Shane turned around and walked back and forth in his room, stepping over the beers and his half-unpacked bags.

"I'm not trying to threaten you. I would—"

"I don't give a fuck what you're trying to do. That journal doesn't prove a goddamned thing."

"I know. It only shows that Leon was mentally unstable. That's what I'm saying. For example, he wrote that he got away from you, specifically that he got out of your car one night, by disappearing into thin air. I have no intention of opening a case against you. On the contrary, I'm interested in how Leon's disease afflicted him."

Shane didn't say anything.

"Whatever it was, it made him think he was being miraculously transported all over Humboldt County. You're one of about ten people he names who saw that happen."

"Is that right?"

"I'm planning to write a human interest story about Leon, about a man whose wife and daughter drowned in a tragic boating accident, and who then gradually lost his capacity for reason until, on the tenth anniversary of their death, he lost his wits altogether and began to believe that he was literally disappearing. This could be a very big story for me; it could make my career. So what I'd like is for you to give me your impressions of Leon and tell me what actually happened when you were with him. You could describe what it was like to see a man unhinged by grief, someone who had fallen out of touch with reality."

Shane sat back down on his chair and cracked open a fresh beer. After a long, burning sip, he belched and said, "I hate to disappoint you, scoop, but I can't do that."

"Why not?"

"Because what actually happened was, Leon disappeared."

On December 7, CosmoCuisine Day was held at the Eureka Gazebo. Joon-sup Kim arrived at ten a.m. to set up the Joon-sup Experience, his Korean barbecue stall, in between a kebab stand and a bratwurst booth with weatherproof menus. He carried glass pans of marinating chicken and pork and beef, and although it was cold he'd begun sweating. He poured ice into a tub full of soft drinks and mineral waters. He said hi to the other food vendors and heard their speculations on the day's turnout and was upset to learn that the kebab guy got grade B beef from Teddy's Meats for twenty cents a pound less than he did—when Teddy had sworn in hushed tones that he was giving Joon-sup a deal!

Joon-sup had been operating this stall for eight years all over Humboldt County and believed he had built up enough name recognition to open a brick-and-mortar restaurant. The college kids from southern California told him they would flock to it. They were all recovering vegetarians and loved the unadulterated meatness of the

Joon-sup Experience. They told him that they would be regulars, as would their friends and their friends' friends.

Joon-sup was engaged to be married. His mother, who had been dying alone in Pusan for two years during which he visited her only once, had secured him a twenty-year-old bride late the previous autumn. The girl was homely and a poor student and difficult to raise for her parents, close acquaintances of his mother's, but what else could Joon-sup expect given his age (thirty-three) and his financial prospects (nearly none)? His mother demanded an answer from him in a weakened, illness-worn voice. He was lucky to get an ugly, stupid, antisocial girl.

But now that his mother had died Joon-sup was in the process of breaking off this engagement—he'd agreed to it just to please her, though the girl was so unlikable that his mother had cried and admitted that the only thing worse than Joon-sup's marrying her was his not marrying her—and had sent the girl a letter to that effect. He hadn't written that his affection for her was a sham from the start, or that he'd been living with a woman named Justine for six years, or that any Korean girl who didn't care what was happening to Seoul's air quality was a flibbertigibbet. Instead he'd lied that his interest in Zen Buddhism, until recently of little importance, had developed to the point where he planned to enter Shasta Abbey, a monastery three hours east of Eureka, and become a monk. He knew that the girl's feeling of rejection would be lessened by knowing that he'd renounced women as a whole rather than her specifically.

When Joon-sup's crisis of ten years ago—during which he'd fantasized the strange and unnerving Leon Meed—abated and he got his bearings again through the help of thrice-weekly therapy, he stopped thinking about the unpublicized environmental disaster that had tweaked his mind. Leon Meed was packed up and placed in mental storage along with other memories from his NorCal hippie period: of mushroom collecting at the beach, of ornamenting walking staffs, of forty-minute bongo jams that bruised your palms and fingertips. All side effects of getting too American too deeply, too indiscriminately.

The trick was to live in this country with its dangers and temptations without losing your head. To stay vigilant. That, despite Joon-sup's efforts, Leon had recently appeared in the paper was almost too horrible to believe.

Keeping his legs straight, he bent and touched his hands to the ground, because he valued his flexibility, and when he stood up a few isolated needle pricks of rain struck his arms and he saw Eve approaching.

"This is the worst day for an outdoor food festival," she said, tapping her short fingernails on the countertop of his Experience and glancing up at the sky.

"I didn't think you'd come."

"I called you back last night."

"Did you leave a message?"

"Yeah."

"Maybe Justine erased it by mistake. I'll ask her."

"I don't want to cause trouble between you two."

"We've been going to relationship counseling for a year. We already have causes."

Eve rolled up a paper menu and looked through it telescope-style at Joon-sup. Nothing was made larger or smaller. "If you don't want to have kids, you should tell her."

"I want kids."

"When?"

"I don't know."

"Justine's forty-two. She can't wait forever for you to make up your mind."

Joon-sup looked away. A few more needles fell. The kebab guy was perched on a high bar stool, playing a handheld video game. The day was dark. "How's your back doing?" he asked.

"Better, thanks," she said, standing up straight as though to prove it. "But are you okay? You look pale."

"I didn't sleep much last night."

"You look like you've lost weight."

"I weigh the same as always. You know, lean but powerful."

"Oh," she said skeptically.

Joon-sup folded his arms and in a low, confidential voice said, "The reason I wanted to talk to you is because a reporter from the *Times-Standard* called me."

"He called me, too."

"He did?" This was his worst fear realized, though being a realist he had expected it. The prelude to everyone who saw Leon's disappearances being rounded up by the government and themselves made to disappear. The fulfillment of an awful prophecy he'd never understood, only learned to ignore as a supposedly irrelevant past incident. Like the downwinders in Nevada who'd gotten cancer from nuclear testing, he and Eve couldn't hope to win against forces too big to oppose. "I denied it," he said, rotating strips of beef in a tray of marinade, "and so should you."

"Deny what?"

"That you saw Leon disappear. I went online and searched for Martin Nemec's name, and he's only been writing for the *Times-Standard* a month."

"So?"

"So he's probably a spy and this article is a ruse to make us to admit we're suffering from something we shouldn't be, so they can debrief us—or worse."

"Who would want to do that?"

"The government. Whoever was responsible for making us see Leon. You remember how I told you Soulbrother took his Geiger counter to the mouth of the Klamath River back then, and he found nine hundred picocuries of radioactive iodine per liter of water?"

"That's ridiculous. This guy is just writing a story for the paper. It's not a conspiracy. And anyway, my religious experience is private, so I told Martin I didn't want to talk about Leon."

"Good. You did the right thing." He was sorry that Eve's was such a major misinterpretation of Leon Meed, ignoring as it did the obvious geopolitical factors involved and instead dragging an irrelevant, nonexistent god into it, but he had been sorry about it from the beginning. Nothing new. For now he was glad she'd refused the newspaper imposter.

The needles of rain came down more steadily then, as though a giant sewing box were being slowly overturned in the sky, and Eve said, "Are you going to pack up if the rain gets worse?"

After a moment of contemplation, Joon-sup nodded and grabbed the rain slicker he'd stuffed under his booth. Eve, he noticed, was wearing a black cashmere sweater and had her hair down to her shoulders. It was a good look on her, brought out her blue eyes. He wasn't surprised so many men asked her out, approached her even when she and Joon-sup were eating together and might reasonably be thought to be a couple. What surprised him was how she always, without explaining, told them no. In all the time he'd known her, she hadn't dated anyone. He started to put away condiments and boxes of plastic utensils. "What happened with the banker who bought you a ticket to Hawaii?" he asked.

"Nothing."

"You said no?"

"Yeah."

"You weren't tempted? It was your chance to see Hawaii."

"I've read about it so much at Going Places I don't need to go."

Joon-sup felt a small surge of relief and unplugged the barbecue warmers and folded up a tray stand. Just before he'd met her, Eve had had a boyfriend. That he'd died was terrible, but it didn't justify her iron-clad solitude. Joon-sup stretched aluminum foil over the meat trays and Eve packed napkins and utensils in a big storage box. Fitted on lids, wiped off water beads. He looked at her and the expression for what he'd long felt but not formulated came to him: she lacked joy. Not that she had to float in a kind of spiritual exaltation, but for someone who'd made deep sacrifices for Christianity she seemed discontented, as though she'd once temporarily substituted endurance for happiness and then forgotten to switch back. This struck him as a great loss and he wanted to help her. Surely she could be doing better. Surely they all could.

He said, "How about we run the day after tomorrow at the river if it isn't raining?"

Eve, bouncing up and down on her toes to stay warm, said, "We don't have to if you're not up for it."

"I'm up for it."

"You haven't wanted to go the last few times."

"Remember last week it was Soulbrother's dance recital? And the week before I was doing something, I forget what."

"If you're sick you don't want to push it."

"I'm not sick."

Eve started to back away down the street as the rain came down with building, piercing force. "Okay! The day after tomorrow!"


An hour later Elaine entered the Shanty in Old Town Eureka and became the only woman there. This didn't excite much untoward behavior from the other patrons, two men with ecstatic white hair who were bent like wilted dandelions over their drinks at the bar, but still she couldn't understand why Sadie had chosen this place to meet rather than a good coffee shop. Elaine sat at a table and waited for ten minutes and was about to leave when her friend came trudging in, wiping rainwater from her face with a knotted handkerchief.

"Two Bloody Marys!" Sadie said to the bartender before crossing to embrace Elaine in a light hug.

"I'll have tea instead," Elaine said.

"This place is known for its Bloody Marys," Sadie said, catching her breath and peeling off her jacket. "You'll be amazed."

Elaine unbuttoned her purse and took out her phone. She called home and left a message for Steve and Trevor saying she'd be back in an hour or two.

"You didn't mention how smashed you're going to be by then," Sadie observed.

"I'm only having one drink."

"Is that what you think?"

"I can't go home drunk. There are those problems I mentioned."

"All the more reason to fortify yourself."

"It'd be the wrong kind of fortification."

Sadie turned her head when the bartender snapped his fingers to indicate that the drinks were ready. "Hold on." She went to collect two large red glasses and then returned to the table.

Elaine said, "Thanks for coming on such short notice."

"Of course. What's happening?"

"It's Steve. We had a bad dinner the other night. From the beginning of it he was sullen and cold, like he resented me for something, and when I tried to brighten the mood by telling him about a teacher award nomination I'd gotten, he got worse. Then out of the blue he told me he used to be a speed addict years ago, that before he and I got together he was doing crank all the time."

"You didn't know that?"

"Did you?"

"I must have told you about when I was set up on a blind date with that HSU professor Roger Nuñez, and my sister and Greg were there, and Steve showed up and got in a fight with Greg."

"Was he on something that night?"

Sadie leaned back in her chair, considering. "I would say many things."

"Okay, so that was a confession I could partly deal with. But then he said that a man named Leon Meed vanished in front of him once, as in actually disappeared. He swore it. And when I suggested that he'd had this—I don't know, paranormal experience—because of the drugs he was on at the time, he stormed out of the restaurant."

"Leon Meed?"

"Yes. But the story gets worse. Last night a reporter called from the *Times-Standard* and—"

"I know the rest." Sadie took a finishing gulp of her Bloody Mary.

"You do?"

Holding up her middle and forefinger, Sadie signaled for two more Bloody Marys and the bartender silently acquiesced. She got up, went to the bar, and within a minute was back, placing another glass beside Elaine's barely touched first one.

"Jesus," said Elaine, blinking at the twin drinks, "I told you I can't."

"As a licensed therapist I insist you take this medicine, and as advisor to myself I must take it also. Now let me tell you something." Sadie placed a plump, joint-wrinkled hand over the top of her drink as though to decline a refill. Her heavy-lidded eyes settled on Elaine and her frosted hair iced the outline of her face. She sat perfectly still and made no move to speak. Basketball scores blasted from the bar.

"What?" Elaine finally said.

"I had my own encounters with Leon back then, and he was an expert prankster and a magician. Not to be too respectful of him, because he was weird as anything, but he broke into my house a couple of times and then 'disappeared' with terrific skill. For a while I thought I myself was losing it until I learned that he was performing this trick all over the place for what reason God only knows. One time I caught him in my shower before he was able to escape and I beat on him—I mean I whacked him with a crowbar like he was a piñata—and then I called the police. And do you want to know something? I answered the door when they arrived, and by the time I got back to where I'd left him tied up, he'd escaped like some kind of greased pig."

Elaine took a healthy swallow of her drink. "According to this reporter—"

"Ignore him. A patient came in to see me back then, a Korean fellow I now see for other reasons, who begged me to write mental-ward commitment papers for him. He described symptoms of schizophrenia that revolved around seeing Leon Meed appear and disappear." She shook her head. "Leon caused major psychological damage in some people and then skipped town. It was a disgraceful episode. And now he's died and left this hoax diary behind and there's a sentimental reporter chasing a story. Don't encourage it. Don't tell him anything."

"Okay, but my major concern is Steve. I want to ask if you could see us—me and Steve as a couple—and I'd pay and it would be strictly professional. After that dinner we've basically stopped talking. We're at a standstill and I want it to end."

Sadie sucked dry her second Bloody Mary. She held a big breath and then exhaled. "I'm sorry. I wish I could help, but I can't."

Elaine frowned. "Why not?"

"I don't believe in couples therapy anymore."

"How can you not believe in it?"

"Too many couples get nothing out of therapy except the realization that they're not working out. I'm not saying this about you and Steve, but in my opinion couples that need therapy actually need to break up."

"That's the most cynical thing I've ever heard."

"Not all therapists think this. It's just my experience. I'd be happy to refer you to someone else."

"You honestly think counseling doesn't help?"

"I'll get the next round," Sadie said, pushing her chair out and standing unsteadily. Elaine didn't try to stop her.

When the two women said good-bye, Sadie drove home through early evening traffic and took a long shower. A year ago she would gladly have counseled Elaine and Steve; she would have advocated a talking cure for their problems, based on concessions and mutual acknowledgment of each other's feelings and beliefs. She would have said, "Wellness, in a body or relationship, takes time and commitment. There are no fast roads to recovery. There is no superhighway to health." But not now. Now she knew that all roads ended in cul-de-sacs, and that the longer you traveled down them, the longer it took to get back.


That evening Prentiss sat at home drinking ice water and taking antacids to relieve his heartburn. They were taking their time. He wandered the carpeted rooms of his apartment hoping that movement would dislodge the pain. Ferdinand trotted after him and Prentiss gave him a treat and he darted into his small pighouse beside the refrigerator. Prentiss saw in the bathroom mirror a youthful forty-two-year-old man. Nobody had responded to his personals ad. The mildew on his shower-tile grout was becoming an irreversible problem. He could be witty and charming, and if he just met the right woman under the right circumstances, if luck would favor him—if only because luck was tired of favoring everyone else and thought Prentiss had novelty value—then what he wouldn't do. What he wouldn't give.

He picked up his phone and listened to the day's messages. Pre-recorded telemarketers, a wrong number. No one calling to ask him to dinner. No chance for romantic connection. There was always the supermarket, sure, where he could accidentally ram his shopping cart into some attractive woman's, but that was so obvious he might as well sell tickets beforehand. Meeting people was supposedly easy and others did it all the time. He called Steve's house.

There was no answer because Steve was on his first antidepression drive in ten years. It had taken less than a week for depression to erase the time between its appearances in his life, so that Steve now felt as if he'd always been depressed. A decade's collapse and he returned to its most acute moment, when, sitting in his old living room ringing with Leon Meed, he'd been unopposed to suicide but too fixated on the messes of overdose, wrist slit, car crash, gunshot, and rope noose to act. An afternoon of thinking about Leon and obsessing about Anne until, almost more amazingly than the former's disappearance earlier, the latter called to say she was in Eureka for a few days and wondered if his offer of dinner from Christmas Eve was still good. Her voice was warm and friendly, and he said no, rescinded his invitation not out of spite or retribution but because he didn't want to see her again. As simple, as incomprehensibly complex as that. After months of wanting Anne back, the instant she expressed interest in seeing him he was freed from the torment of loving her. If only Leon could come again and make him see that he would live as easily without Elaine as he finally had without Anne.

Steve drove through the rural hinterland of Eureka, past pastures of moonlit cows, on a two-lane road going fifty-five miles an hour. The *Nutcracker Suite* danced out of his stereo. In the distance a car rounded a bend and came toward him with its high beams on. He flashed his own to alert the other driver, but the lights stayed high and became more excruciatingly bright with each second. Then it passed him. The driver of the other car was probably drunk or insane or both, and he imagined he'd be called in later that evening to stitch together whatever was left of him after the inevitable accident. It was all a big déjà vu.

When his cell phone rang he answered it.

"Steve," said Prentiss. "It's me. What're you doing?"

"Driving."

"Where to?"

"I'm on Elk River Road."

"To get down to it, I'm feeling a little on edge like it might be nice to get out of the house for a while and meet up with you someplace. Have a juice."

"I'm in the middle of introspective time right now."

"I hear you. All right, then. Good night."

"You're not wanting to drink, are you? Is this a reaching-out phone call?"

"No. It's just I'm in a lonely mood and I'd like to meet some-body—a woman—and it'd be better if I was at a bar with a friend, you know, so I didn't look desperate."

"You don't want that."

"No."

"Well, let me think. How about we meet at the Ritz?"

"I'd appreciate it."

Half an hour later Prentiss and Steve sat together at the Ritz. As part of the bar's new safari-themed décor, a pith helmet and imitation leopard skin hung on the wall above their table next to a battered Winchester and a picture of wildebeests migrating across the Serengeti. At one end of the bar counter two butterfly nets crisscrossed, and at the other was a giant plastic fern. The room was dark and humid. The thematic effort ended there, however, and in most ways the bar looked and felt like it always had, its exhausted velvet lining a testament to the glamorous effect it had once striven for.

The two friends drank guava juice, Prentiss because that's what he always drank and Steve because alcohol seemed then like an empty pleasure. The former wore a mahogany brushed-suede jacket and the latter a badly stained Humboldt State University sweatshirt. Prentiss's hair was shiny and well combed, Steve's was dull and wispy. Besides them, the bar was deserted.

"I'm sorry I didn't change my clothes," said Steve. "In this state I'm probably a liability to you with women."

Prentiss waved his hand and knocked his napkin to the floor. "There'd have to be women here for that to be the case. I'm seeing that the Ritz isn't the magnet it used to be, probably on account of this jungle environment."

"Eureka doesn't like kitsch."

"Maybe we should try someplace else. The bars along Second Street. Or the Carter Hotel. I can't feel good about keeping you from home if it's just to sit here like this."

"There's nothing for me to go home to."

"I seem to remember you having a wife."

A pair of women came into the bar. One had dirty blond hair and the other was a brunette. Beyond that, Prentiss couldn't make out anything specific because they moved quickly and at an inopportune angle to the counter, where they were blocked from view by the fern. Prentiss would have asked Steve, who was in a better position to see them, to relay his impression, but his friend said at that moment, "She's going to leave me."

Prentiss turned his attention from the hidden women. "Elaine? Why?"

"The main reason is that she's up for a teaching award that will require her to move to Sacramento for a year, starting in the fall."

"Wait a minute—this is a deep conversation all of a sudden. She's moving? Without you? When did this happen?"

"Last week."

"And you won't go with her?"

"She hasn't suggested it. She told me what the award means and that was pretty much the end of the conversation. We were out to dinner and as soon as she explained it she went on the attack and got argumentative. Like she had to start driving a wedge between us right away."

"I'm sorry. You were just saying a few weeks ago how good things were between you. It was a high moment."

"Yeah, but in the back of my mind I knew it couldn't last."

"Is she going soon?"

"I don't know. I feel like if I confront her about it that might speed it up; she could feel pressed to split us up before Sacramento. Part of me, though, thinks that since it's inevitable I should get it over with."

The women who'd come in got their drinks and walked to a table; again Prentiss couldn't see them clearly. They draped their coats over their chairs and sat down. The brunette adjusted the collar on her blouse, and the blonde crossed her legs and laid her hands flat on the table, as though about to hear her fortune read. A lion roared out of the bar's music speakers with the announcement of a two-for-one drink special that would last no more or less than two minutes.

One of the women, Eve, said to the other, Justine, "I'm glad you called me. I've been friends with Joon-sup forever, and I know you don't have a problem with that, but I've always wanted to meet you anyway. If I had a boyfriend I'd want to know his women friends at least by sight so that if we met on the street I could say hi."

Justine smiled and held her head still, in agreement, and said, "I meant to do it sooner, and now it has to be under these circumstances."

"Is something wrong? He didn't look well today."

Justine's smile faded. "You saw him today?"

"At the food fair. He wanted to talk about—"

"About what?"

Eve faltered, "Soulbrother's dance recital."

"Oh. Well, I wish I knew how to prepare you for what I have to say. Or myself, even. So I'm just going to say it. Joon-sup has heart disease."

"He does?"

"A month ago he saw a cardiologist for chest pains he's been having, and his test results came back positive two weeks ago. Apparently he has a genetic disorder. The good news is that it's at an early stage, and he could have years still."

Eve set down the drink she'd been holding. It seemed to slide across the table without reaching the edge. She felt cold. Joon-sup, thirty-three, had heart disease. The face across from her was devoid of pleasantry and pretense, an expression more common in holy men and lunatics than in people you'd meet in a bar. Eve shivered and had nothing to draw around her shoulders. A Tarzan yell went up in the bar along with a message announcing that rum drinks were for a limited time only five dollars. Eve said, "Two weeks ago that's when he stopped running with me."

"He wants to keep it a secret. He thinks people would feel sorry for him and treat him differently if they knew, so as long as possible he'd like them not to know."

"Of course." Tribal drums thumped along behind chants that were meaningless in any language. "This is so sudden. I don't know what to say it's so sudden."

Justine laid a hand on Eve's too cold to help. "Joon-sup especially doesn't want you to know, because your boyfriend died so young, but I'm telling you because I'd like you to watch out for him. You could stop him from doing anything that would get his blood pressure up or cause him too much excitement. The doctor said it'd be best if he stayed away from physically strenuous activities."

"Of course, I'll do what I can."

"Thanks. Joon-sup was right about you."

"I haven't even offered my condolences. This is so sudden. I remember losing Ryan; I know what you're going through. This is a terrible, sudden thing."

"Can I ask you for help in another way?"

Eve nodded dumbly.

"Joon-sup's best friend from South Korea, Hyun-bae, lives in San Diego, which is where I'm from. I think it might be good if we moved down there. The weather's better, and my family is there. I suggested it to him and he doesn't like the idea, but if he mentions it to you, would you say whatever good you can about southern California?"

Eve had known for a long time that what was given was taken away, that the greatest earthly folly lay in attachments to people, to places, to things. For these returned to dust. Only God could bear her absolute dependence. She knew this, but she also didn't know. Joon-sup was too young to die. Everyone, regardless of his or her age, was too young. You couldn't populate a world with creatures whose spiritual goal was to not need one another; it ran contrary to what Eve knew beyond scripture and enlightenment. Eve needed Joon-sup. She needed. And if she had to lose him—which she did, she'd been told—then she wouldn't bury her feelings under the weight of its inevitability. She wouldn't say that his absence was really evidence of his presence, because it wasn't.

When pygmy chimps screamed a prelude to another drink special, the bartender shut off the sound system. Prentiss glanced at him approvingly and said, "I'm thinking that all is not lost for you. If you come up with a strategy for how you'd make your lives work together in Sacramento, it seems to me Elaine would listen. You got to fight for this. Tell her how much your marriage means to you."

Steve shook his head. "Sacramento is just an excuse. She'd leave me for some other reason if not for this. Every woman I've ever been with has left me."

"You and Elaine love each other."

"My first wife, Anne, and I loved each other."

"So what was it made her leave?"

"I don't know."

Prentiss gave Steve a scolding look. "I think you do know."

"Anne left because I withdrew into myself when I felt the relationship going badly."

"What's that mean, you withdrew?"

"I figured that since I was going to be abandoned, I had to become strong on the inside and detach myself to make it hurt less."

"So you're saying she left you because you withdrew, but at the same time you withdrew because she was going to leave you. What came first?"

"I don't know."

"Let me know when you figure it out." They sat in silence for several minutes until Prentiss said, "You want to hear something funny?"

"Okay."

"I got a call yesterday from a newspaperman says he has Leon Meed's journal or some type of book, and my name's in it and it mentions how he disappeared in front of me and some other people."

Steve scraped the logo from a drink coaster. "That's funny."

"I haven't got to the funny part yet, and that's how you brought up Leon recently. A man deducing might think you're one of the other people the reporter was talking about."

Steve's expression was unreadable. "I don't like to talk about it."

Prentiss sipped his juice. "Why's that?"

"No sane person would believe it."

"I do."

"Maybe you should get your head checked."

Prentiss took another sip of his juice. "When you think on it, it's incredible that we been friends all this time and never knew." Another sip. "Day I met him, that afternoon I went on a binge where I flushed everything away, job and AA and friends and what have you. Me and Leon went to the Shanty and had some drinks and he told me what was going on about the disappearing, and before I could pin him down he was gone. Just gone. I used to think about him later when I was detoxing hard, and how he told me no one was worse off than him. Man looked at me and said he would have swapped places with me if he could. Only time anyone ever said that to me." After a moment of Steve studying him with concern, he said, "What're the ladies like who came in a while ago?"

"Fine. Good."

Prentiss tried to be subtle in turning his body from Steve. One of the women Prentiss recognized as a patient from the week before, and the other was—

"Justine," he said, almost in a whisper.

"What?" Steve said.

"We got to leave this place."

"Now?"

"Unless we can get out sooner."

"You don't think they're attractive?"

"I went on a date with one of them a while back and it didn't go too good."

Steve shrugged and they got up. Keeping his face to the wall, Prentiss walked quickly to the exit, followed by his friend. They proceeded to four more bars, each more normal and better patronized than the last, until they found themselves after midnight on a shoulder-to-shoulder dance floor with a group of three women accountants, one of whom suggested that Prentiss take her home. When Prentiss said no it was because he didn't want sex. This dawned on him while he was removing the woman's hands from his hips and thanking her for the dance and explaining the inexplicable. He wanted something else. Not ecstasy. Not the easy thing. Something else.

## 3

Eureka had been unknown to Martin Nemec, age twenty-eight, when
he accepted a full-time position at the *Times-Standard* after graduat-
ing from UC Berkeley's journalism school. But he looked at it on the
map and pictured the romance of its geography. The farthest west
point on the continental U.S., where you could walk along beaches
unmolested by tourists and smog and detritus. Where the redwoods
reached up like towers of Babel, supporting their animal inhabitants'
chirps and hoots and calls that added up to one language, incompre-
hensible to all, signifying life itself. He thought, hanging up the phone
with the editor who hired him, that he was lucky to get to work in so
enviable a location.

When he arrived on a shadowless day in November, the harsh gray
reality of Eureka hit him so hard he felt like he'd gone color-blind.
His apartment was a monochrome dump and his office turned out to
be a narrow desk in a small building on Seventh Street that smelled
of burnt garlic from the Chinese take-out restaurant next door. And
when, after three days of assignments, it was obvious that the inves-
tigative skills Martin had honed in graduate school wouldn't be called
for, he began to feel the glacial creep of despair. A demythologized
Eureka was one thing, was perhaps to be expected, but to have been
promised the chance to practice a wide variety of journalism and
then be given only accidents and violent crimes—anything, in short,

involving medical trauma—was to find yourself swindled and stuck. You had no choice then but to look, to hope, to pray for an escape.

On December 13, a complete photocopy of Leon Meed's journal, power-stapled together, sat beside Martin's home computer. After reading it three times and taking notes and nurturing the idea of writing a story about it, something extracurricular that his boss wouldn't know about until it was finished, he'd become discouraged over the last few days by the refusal of everyone named in it to talk to him—everyone, that is, but Shane Larson. He hadn't expected to be invited over for dinners and fireside chats, but he'd hoped for at least two or three forthcoming witnesses who would share their memories of Leon's psychosis. How else was he supposed to produce a feature complex and human and long enough to put him in the running for a journalism award that might someday land him a job at a bigger paper with an expanding circulation in a city for which the future wasn't too painful to discuss?

Martin put on his basketball shoes. Hunted around for his sweatpants and had to make do with an old pair of nylon track bottoms. Then, in the hallway just outside his apartment, he bumped into a husky man with a black crew cut. Martin apologized for their physical contact and moved to get around him, but a hand landed firmly on his shoulder.

"You Martin Nemec?" the man said.

Martin nodded.

"Shane Larson. I figured we should meet in person if we're going to work together. Put faces to names, right? So we could talk here at your place or I'm parked outside and we could go somewhere else. It's your call. I mean, you're writing this thing, you've got the artistic vision; I'm just an advisor and business partner."

Martin peeked around Shane's head and saw none of the neighbors who normally stood idly in front of their doors at all hours of the day, waiting for whatever they waited for. "Shane, it's nice to meet you, but like I told you on the phone, I'm dropping the Leon Meed story."

"Why would you do that?"

"Because no one will even confirm that they knew him. As far as I know the journal is just a short story he wrote and he didn't suffer a nervous breakdown."

Shane smiled and seemed to take up even more room in the hallway, making passage for Martin impossible. "You got the last part right. Leon didn't have a nervous breakdown."

"I know your theory, but—"

Shane shook his head. "For the sake of this story, he had magical powers. Now, let's talk about who's on your list and see if we can't get them to pony up some quotes. If you're going to write about a guy who could disappear, we'll need maximum corroboration. My wife's brother-in-law knows people at the *National Enquirer* and the *Weekly World News*—he's a newsman such as yourself—and even though he and I aren't exactly close as we speak, you get me the story written down with all the t's crossed and i's dotted and I'll make sure he gets it to the right insiders. This is why I'm here, Martin, to reassure you."

Martin saw no chance of getting past this man, who was either the dumbest or most intelligent person he'd met in Eureka. "I appreciate that," he said, and because it seemed wiser to humor Shane than not, he turned around and led him into his apartment. After pouring them each a glass of water, he pointed to the wobbly breakfast table in the kitchen and they sat down.

"The thing you got wrong a second ago," said Shane, pushing his water away, "was how nobody admits they knew Leon. For starters, there's me. I'll back up the disappearing thing till I die. The others will, too, if you give them time. You know what sheep people are; they just need to be persuaded that the shepherd knows what he's doing. Once I talk to them and set an example, you won't be able to shut them up."

"Oh?" said Martin. "Well, I wasn't going to approach the journal as a historical record of the facts. I was more interested in Leon as a mental illness victim. I like your initiative, though, and your desire to help is very generous, but—"

"You think that's going to sell for more money?"

"I'm sorry?"

"The mental illness thing. You think that'll command more dough?"

Shane smiled widely and had oppressively white teeth and gave Martin a look that barely passed for good humor. "Wrong again. If we played that angle, we'd pull in ten, fifteen cents a word, tops, because we'd be looking at the *Times-Standard* or the *Humboldt Beacon* to publish, maybe the *Chronicle* if we got lucky, the point being they all have limited readerships. The way I see it, we go with the disappearing story, sell it to one of the national papers for a dollar a word, or better yet one of the slicks for two or three bucks a word, and then get an agent and do a package book/film rights deal for a mill minimum."

"That's—wow. You've given this some thought." Martin stared helplessly at his water.

Shane drummed his fingers on the table. "Now I think we should take a second to discuss business. You haven't brought it up and I understand it's a delicate subject, but I'm thinking that since I'm your key witness—like you said, I'm the last person mentioned in the diary—and since I got in on the ground floor, what seems fair to me is a sixty/forty split, my favor."

"Shane—"

"Of course I respect your artistic vision—like I said, you're the writer—but I am going to do a hundred and ten percent of the selling here. You don't know how to finesse a sale. No offense, but it's true. You struck out trying to line up interviews, and they aren't even businesspeople. So sixty/forty seems like the right breakdown."

Martin sat up straight and cleared his throat and avoided Shane's gaze by looking instead at his chest. "I don't think we should keep discussing this. I'm not writing a sensationalistic piece about an old sorcerer and all the people he performed for. And this isn't a business deal and we're not partners and while I thank you for your thoughts, I have to tell you right now to leave it alone. There is no Leon Meed story. I'm not doing it."

Shane breathed in sharply through his nose and tilted his head to the right until his neck made three distinct popping noises. His smile was unchanging. Then, reaching across the table, he grabbed hold of

Martin's chin with his thumb and forefinger and said, "You don't go in for a lot of bullshit. I like that about you. So I'm willing to go fifty-five/forty-five on this, and in return you'll quit thinking about the mental health of Leon Meed and start concentrating on making it the most sensationalistic story about a sorcerer that's ever been. Understand?" He moved Martin's head up and down as though testing a light switch, stood up, and then went to the desk in the front room. "So is there a list of the other witnesses around here, or what?"

The next afternoon Lillith met her friend Tina for coffee at Ramone's. Tina was no longer a Wiccan, but they were still friends and she had agreed to join in a postmortem on Lillith's *Live from Somewhere* appearance. The two women sat down on wide rattan chairs beneath a hanging geranium that at long intervals rained down fingernail leaves of pale green and auburn. Photographs of children begging in São Paulo hung from wall hooks around the room and were so detailed and hyperhued that customers, in a conscience-salving move, assumed they were movie stills.

"I felt humiliated in front of the whole county," Lillith said.

"You shouldn't. Not that many people listen to the show," Tina said, getting up to wipe down their table with a rag she stole from a nearby bus tray. "Plus it's not like you started crying on the air. You kept your dignity."

"Thanks."

"A lot of guests have done worse with more important topics."

"What's that supposed to mean?"

"That the host is a prick. Remember what he did to Franklin, how he fucked him and then didn't call? Franklin's not a casual sex kind of guy; it was a big deal for him to go home with Barry, and then to be dropped like that was devastating."

Lillith opened a packet of sugar and poured a quarter of it into her coffee. "One-night stands aren't exactly freak accidents in the gay community. I'd forgive that."

"I'm saying that in the end he's only hurting himself and you shouldn't take it personally. You just made an especially easy target on his show by representing neopaganism, which is such an obvious joke to most people. Maybe you should call and let him know what's on your mind."

"He probably knows what an asshole he is."

"Men can never get enough reinforcement of that nature."

Lillith poured in a few more grains of sugar, trying to count them. "Can I talk to you about something related to this?"

"Sure."

"You know how that reporter wanted to interview me about Leon's diary and I said no because I figured he was in collusion with Barry?"

"Yeah."

"This morning someone called and said that if I don't do the inter-view I'll be in trouble."

"Who? The reporter?"

"He didn't say."

"You'll be in trouble how?"

"I don't know, but I got the sense that it was a physical threat."

"The guy sounded serious?"

"Yeah."

"Have you gone to the police?"

"No."

"You have to. He could be a psychopath."

"I know."

Tina flicked off a pair of leaves that had landed on her forearm. "This never would have happened if you'd forgotten about Wicca and moved on."

Lillith dropped the sugar pack. "Excuse me?"

"I'm on your side, don't get me wrong, but by broadcasting this stuff you attract all the überpervs out there. You're twenty-six; you can't go around talking about the Astral Plane forever and not expect something like this to happen."

"You're blaming me, the victim?"

"Go to the police and report the call, and then you need to consider giving up this pseudofeminist mysticism. It sounds foolish coming from an adult. I'm sorry; you don't want to hear this, but I've indulged you for too long and it's true."

"Mysticism? You were there!" Lillith was practically shouting. "You saw Leon disappear too!"

"It was dark and we were in your bed; he could have come in and gone out your bathroom window for all I know." Tina laughed a little and then went to get a coffee refill.

Lillith tried not to think about the indefinable pain of friends renouncing a shared understanding, especially one that had been forged at such a critical time in her life, when she'd gotten an abortion and had a reckoning with her mother about religion. Tina came back and talked about her job and the miserable sex she'd endured recently with two brothers, neither of whom knew about the other. Lillith blocked the renunciation from her mind and went along with the conversation and only in the smallest, quietest part of her brain did she hear the words repeated, again and again, that she was an adult and foolish.

If Barry had been superstitious, he might have thought that the flurry of Leon activity lately meant something for him personally. He might have added up a death, a newspaper article, an interview request, and a heavy breathing phone call telling him to talk about Leon or else, and found a message of which he ought to take heed. Instead he considered it only a reason to tell the police that someone with a sick sense of humor (or worse) was out there. After changing into pants and a sweater, he was prepared to leave his apartment when his phone rang.

It was his friend Donald inviting him to the annual Knavetivity Scene party on Christmas Eve, a deeply sacrilegious and sexually bottom-heavy event.

"I'm not sure I can make it this year," Barry said.

"Don't make me laugh," said Donald sternly.

"I haven't been feeling well lately. I might need to be alone."

"I just want to know if you're coming as a Joseph or a Mary."

"Better plan the party without me."

"If you're angling to be the Baby Jesus, there can be only one and I'm him."

"It's not that."

"All right, I'll let you be one of the wise men. You know I never let anyone come as one of those ridiculous sages."

"Seriously, don't count on me. But if I come, I'll be Mary."

"Just so you can ensnare more Catholic men?"

"Bye."

Barry locked his apartment and walked four blocks to the county courthouse, where he climbed to the fourth floor and entered the sheriff's office. A policewoman at the front desk asked his name and business.

"I'd like to file a report about a threatening phone call, please."

"From this morning?"

"That's right."

"What's your name?"

"Barry Klein."

"And the call pertained to an interview request made to you earlier this week by a Mr. Martin Nemec?"

Barry apparently didn't have to say anything to signal his assent, because the policewoman gestured behind her with a pen, consulted the computer screen in front of her, and said, "You're the seventh person to file a complaint. Mr. Nemec came in this afternoon to answer questions and give us a list of everyone he believes was called."

"Is he under arrest?" Barry looked in the direction to which she'd motioned, but behind her was only a tan wall with digital bulletins, a small dry erase board, and two closed doors.

"Mr. Nemec denies all foreknowledge of the calls and claims that someone else placed them, a Mr. Shane Larson. Unfortunately, the calls were made from a pay phone and we don't have enough evidence to book either man."

The name Shane Larson, like the voice on the phone, rang distant bells for Barry. "What should I do?"

"Our advice is to keep your doors locked and stay in public places."

"That's it?"

The policewoman nodded and looked flatly at Barry, who then left. Outside, he walked through Old Town and turned a corner onto E Street and saw Lillith step out of her car in a strapless red evening dress in front of Mazotti's Restaurant. This was fortune handing him the opportunity to apologize and clear his conscience. She seemed to be having a hard time getting her key in the car door. He saw what he had to do—confess to her that the worst temptations of his job had overcome him, that he'd been exactly the sort of talk show host he most disliked, and beg her forgiveness—but he felt a familiar paralysis from the past, from the time before he came out of the closet. Lillith dropped her keys, yet Barry stood rooted to the corner of Second and E, waiting for something to scare him into motion (where were the Leon Meeds of yesteryear?). Why was he so prone to knowing what to do and being unable to do it? With a groan of relief Lillith locked her door, turned around, didn't see Barry, and walked into Mazotti's. Barry went home to open a bottle of whatever.


Inside Mazotti's, Lillith was the first to arrive at the Coastal Orthopedic Medical Group holiday office party, an event that attracted people from all areas of the health-care community due to the famous hospitality of local orthopedists. Three waiters stood next to a food cart loaded with appetizers. Lillith turned on her cell phone to verify that she hadn't any messages and tried not to appear idle while walking around the room. At the food cart she removed a slender breadstick from its cloth-covered bundle and said hello to the waiters, who nodded but didn't take the conversation further. The breadstick was buttery and she mentally adjusted her breakfast the next morning to include a pear and to exclude the croissants she'd bought that day, her diet being a zero-sum game.

There were depressing things to think about while she waited. The possibility that Leon hadn't gone to the Astral Plane and she hadn't performed real magic. The police's inability to protect her from the threatening caller. The Wiccan retreat she'd organized which had been canceled that day because of storm damage to the bridge leading to Wolf Creek Park. The countless phone calls and leaflet printings and confirmations—she would have to reschedule and find a new venue, if she even had the heart to continue her neo-pagan activism.

Through the doorway one of her bosses, Dr. Steve Baker, entered with his wife, Elaine, followed by a radiologist whose name Lillith couldn't remember. They hung up their jackets and zip-up sweaters on the coat tree by the door and walked into the empty space the way couples did at an unexciting open house, looking to find the realtor and get it over with. The waiters broke out of their gossip circle and assumed the right attitude of servility.

Lillith met Steve and Elaine at the wine table. "Hi," she said, "happy holidays."

"Same to you," Steve answered. He picked up a glass of Chardonnay and held it close to his side.

Elaine shook her head no at the wine he offered and said, "Lillith, I heard you were on the radio recently."

"I was on *Live from Somewhere* to promote a Wiccan festival for the winter solstice, except that it got canceled." Lillith had met Elaine at the previous summer's July Fourth office barbecue at Sequoia Park and spent a long time with her searching for Dr. Shikoda's daughter, who'd wandered away and was, in the end, found hugging a tree stump for safety. Lillith liked her better than the other doctors' wives, who were generally condescending and rude, as though working as a young secretary at their husbands' office made her a vamp.

"The show got canceled?"

"No, the festival did."

Steve said, "If you'll excuse me," and left in search of the bathroom.

"Is he all right?" Lillith asked.

"I don't know," Elaine said, looking after him.

A number of people entered the restaurant at once, bringing with them the hum of small talk and shuffling feet and rustling jackets. Prentiss approached the table where they stood and raised a glass of apple juice in greeting. Elaine smiled at him and pulled a tissue from her bag because she was coming down with a cold and could feel her sinuses alternately blocking and clearing. Turned her head away to blow. With equal tact Prentiss and Lillith paid no mind. A thin waiter wearing a hint of purple mascara placed fresh antipasto on the table. Candles were lit in the room's corners as an Italian rendition of "Jingle Bell Rock" began to play.

"Prentiss," said Elaine, pocketing her tissue, "do you know Lillith?"

"I don't. How do you do?"

"Good, thanks," said Lillith.

"Lillith was just saying she was on *Live from Somewhere*. Have you ever heard that show?"

"On Wednesdays in the afternoon?"

"Yeah," Lillith said.

"I listen sometimes. What were you on for?"

"Let's not talk about it. It was a bad experience."

"Okay," Prentiss said, rolling up a cheese and salami slice. "We could talk about our New Year's resolutions instead. I'm giving up pork. As of January first, I'm going to make other important renunciations, but the pork is to begin with."

"That's good," said Lillith. "I'm going to stop watching television."

"All of it?"

"Yes."

"Even the occasional special news reports, such as if a president gets shot or a man lands on Mars or something?"

"I'm donating my TV to the Salvation Army."

Prentiss nodded. "You're right to do it. Aim as high as you can. The best way to move forward."

He seemed nice and was perhaps a little old but Lillith had some-times gone for the quote/unquote mature male, and the guys in her age range around Eureka were all married, engaged, sleazy, gay, or unavailable for more than unsatisfying single-shot sex slams, which, if books and movies and television shows were to be trusted, was true of men everywhere. Yet that was an oversimplification and she wasn't helping the world by repeating the clichés (*aim high, move forward*). She'd never dated a black man, not because of a dating policy but because she'd never known one in the right capacity. It was going to be hard for him to give up salami; he was on his sixth slice already. She attracted überpervs. She was foolish.

Steve returned then and shook hands with Prentiss. The music crept up a decibel, and with it rose the pitch of everyone's conversa-tions. Someone spotted a stick of mistletoe stapled above the entry-way and a collective "oooh!" arose. Two or three women pushed each other toward it with laughing resistance. A man taking off his jacket at the coat tree grinned obscenely.

"I know what you're thinking about me eating salami," said Pren-tiss to Steve, "considering I have a pet pig, which is why I was just say-ing I'm giving it up for the new year." There was a moment of silence as Steve seemed unwilling to comment. Prentiss continued, looking at Lillith and Elaine for support, "At any rate, there's supposed to be an anonymous gift exchange tonight."

Lillith said, "I didn't bring a gift."

"Me, neither."

"Not everyone does," said Elaine. "I haven't for the last couple of years, not since I got a broken shortwave radio once."

"Who'd do something so low as bring a defective gift?" Prentiss said.

"Actually, Steve did. He said it was an accident but of course he would say that."

"You going to defend yourself against this charge?" Prentiss asked Steve.

Steve shrugged gloomily.

"If you've got laryngitis," said Prentiss, "you can prescribe yourself something."

"Don't take it personally," Elaine said. "He's giving me the silent treatment and you're getting caught in the crossfire."

"Could I talk to you for a minute?" Steve said, taking Elaine's arm and walking to the end of the table and bowing his head toward her confidentially. Prentiss and Lillith subtly turned away from them.

"How do you know this crowd?" Prentiss asked.

"I'm a clerical assistant at the office," Lillith said. "What about you?"

"I'm an RN at the hospital. I probably wouldn't have come, but Steve and me are friends and he said it would be a good time."

From nearby they heard Steve's badly constrained voice, "I'm the one picking fights?"

Prentiss said, with enough force to tamp down the nearby indiscretion, "What's going on with the wooded area up next to your office parking lot? They thinning it or what, because the other day I drove by and it's not dense like it used to be."

"People from the park service are removing sick trees," Lillith said. "But you're right that it's really noticeable. Maybe they're taking out more than they're supposed to."

Prentiss was about to speculate when they heard Steve say, "I'm referring to Leon Meed. I told you about him and you dismissed me like I was crazy."

"Is that what this is about?" came Elaine's equally strident voice.

"It's not about anything."

Prentiss and Lillith uncomfortably sipped their beverages and neither found anything to say.

"Isn't it?" Elaine said. "Because I talked to Sadie, and she saw Leon back then, too, and you know what? She said he was a magician who pretended to disappear all over Humboldt County. It was a trick, an act. He tricked you. That night at dinner I was just pointing out that there was probably a reasonable explanation for what you saw, which I then found out there was."

"So you believe Sadie and not me."

"This isn't about belief."

"No, it's about trust and support and faith that you don't have."

"Faith in what?"

Almost against their will, Lillith and Prentiss turned to see Steve leaving the room, ignoring on the way boisterous back slaps and half-articulated invitations for him to stop and chat. When the door closed behind him they turned to resume talking—about anything—and Elaine approached them then with the color drained from her face.

She said, "Steve's not feeling well. He wanted me to say good night to you for him."

"Of course," Lillith and Prentiss overlapped.

Elaine appeared ready to cry. "So we were talking about New Year's resolutions, right? You both don't want to—I'm sorry, I think I should go, too. He might need help getting home." She touched Prentiss and Lillith briefly on the elbow before picking up her purse and following the path her husband had taken out.

When she was gone, Prentiss said, "I'm torn at this moment because I know something about their argument, and I could go after Elaine and offer my perspective."

"About the magician they mentioned?"

Prentiss nodded.

Lillith had too little time—the split second accorded to all responses between people who don't know each other well—to decide what to say. "I knew him, too."

"That right?" Prentiss said.

Don't be foolish. Don't go into the pseudofeminist mysticism of it. "We met ten years ago, just briefly." She was grateful that before Prentiss could say anything two of her secretary colleagues stopped to join them, and the conversation turned to their bosses' moodiness and the declining reputation of Eureka's public schools, and Prentiss, unable to contribute, broke away and annexed himself to a group of men discussing the proposed Highway 101 rerouting. Lillith and Prentiss stole glances at each other for the rest of the night, but never at the same time.

❀    ❀    ❀

In her kitchen the next morning, Sadie smoked seven cigarettes in a row, lighting each one after the first with the ember of its predecessor, the room seeming to grow smaller the longer she sat in it. The idea was occurring to her, as it had before, of moving to San Francisco to attend culinary school and become a chef. She'd always enjoyed cooking and, if her Swedish pancakes were any indication, had great reserves of natural ability. The change would be stimulating and perhaps she'd even find as well as know what to do with love. Sadie Jorgenson: late-blooming nomad, epicure, and romantic heroine. Why not? Because, she considered, passing the baton of life from one dwindling cigarette to another, her professional crisis extended beyond herself now. Elaine had asked for help and she had said no. They were friends. And no matter what she'd said and thought about therapy not working, some of her patients did improve. Some conquered addictions and overcame guilt and laid phobias to rest. Some stopped disliking themselves. Some saved their relationships.

And forget that Sadie was professionally equipped to facilitate Elaine and Steve's communication, she had a moral obligation to do so. If a corollary to the Hippocratic Oath existed, it was that you shall not withhold treatment when needed. There were duties. There were thou shalts and she knew them and scooted her chair back and took an elephantine drag on two cigarettes simultaneously, one a long thin finger and the other a bony stub, and spied her cornflower-blue telephone on the countertop made ghostly by sifted flour. She knew Elaine's number.

When her kitchen became too small to accommodate these thoughts, she got up to go for a walk. Slipped into a jogging suit that she used primarily for walking—and then only rarely—and a pair of unscuffed tennis shoes. Outside, she made it to the bottom step of her front porch before noticing a tall man approach her on the stone slab path from her gate.

"Sadie?" he said.

"Who're you?"

"Shane Larson. I was about to knock on your door." When he came near enough, she could tell that he wore an imitation wool suit and cologne that smelled like a child's bubble bath. With the ersatz smile and penetrating gaze of someone who decided others' personalities in an instant, he was either a salesman or a therapist. "We talked on the phone the other day about an interview request you turned down."

"What are you doing here?"

"I want to talk to you."

Sadie said, "You left a disturbing message on my phone."

Shane shrugged as though be-that-as-it-may. "I'm hoping you can help me understand why you lied to someone who's trying to write about local events for the *Times-Standard,* why you denied knowing Leon Meed."

"That's none of your business."

"I've taken the trouble to visit you and I'd like an explanation."

"As if I give a shit. Now, really, I'm busy so you'd better leave."

"I'm not going anywhere until we work this out. Maybe you were scared and didn't think it over and so that's why you went to the cops. I'd accept that as a reason, and I'd say that you have a chance to make things right by calling Martin today."

"I'm not calling anybody."

"Yes, you are."

"No, I'm not."

Shane took an intimate step forward, as though to give Sadie a kiss, and she saw his pockmarked skin and overlarge eyes. She thought of Little Red Riding Hood. He said, "You and me are going inside so you can make that call. I have the number with me, so there's no reason to put it off."

Sadie nodded, leaned back, and at the top of her voice yelled, "Fire! Fire! Fire!"

Shane, startled, slapped his hand over Sadie's mouth so fast and hard that blood began pouring from her split lip. "Shut up!" he hissed at her. "Shut the fuck up you crazy bitch!" Wide-eyed with pain, she kept up her muffled cries of "Fire" and tried to wiggle her head free while lamely swinging her arms at Shane's back and shoulders. Then she bit into the meat of his right palm and heard his half-stifled cry as he tore the hand away and they each looked at a glistening red cavity in his palm the size of a quarter. She spat out bits of flesh and resumed screaming until Shane's left hand loosely replaced his right over her mouth, after which he struck her several times in the stomach with his bloodied right fist, making savage grunts as he did so. Winded, she fell onto him and they both hit the ground hard, where Shane groaned and then climbed on top of her to wrap his slippery hands around her neck. She screamed "Fire" with decreasing force as he said, "Shut up, you crazy bitch! Shut up!" Grabbing a thorny branch from a rosebush beside the walkway, Sadie whipped Shane in the face with it and gained a moment's leverage while he rubbed his eyes and coughed. Before either could again assault the other, two police cars pulled up in front of Sadie's house, having been called by a luckless Jehovah's Witness from across the street going door-to-door with pamphlets.

"He tried to intimidate me on my own property," Sadie said to the ranking officer ten minutes later. The officer recommended she go to the hospital and she said she was fine, that the blood on her neck and face was mainly Shane's. Then he filled out a restraining order for Sadie and supervised while a scowling Shane was escorted to the back of a patrol car.

Once alone, Sadie went to the bathroom to daub her wounds with a cold washcloth and take four aspirin. The very place where ten years earlier the cause of this idiocy—the reporter's and Shane's and Steve's and hers and Joon-sup's and everybody's—Leon Meed, had appeared twice. Back then he'd been a nuisance, a gadfly buzzing around the county doing his performance art, unwanted everywhere. She hadn't been able to account for him and had subsequently become angry that he'd caused so much pain for others. There were online culinary school applications to fill out. And yet she had to acknowledge that when dismissing her bathroom experience ten years ago, as well as

Joon-sup's paranoid speculations, she had, somewhere behind the cellar door of her thoughts, understood that her Leon Meed incident, that communion with something beyond herself, had been left open-ended, unresolved. She would someday have to find closure. San Francisco rent was on another plane altogether from Eureka's, and how would she support herself as a student? Now, washing the last trace of red from her neck, she regretted that Leon was not coming back, that he was dead and unable to contribute to the *Times-Standard* story or tell her why. Why. And Sadie, an intelligent, irascible, bored, rational sensual atheist woman, felt this loss with the force of three a.m. nicotine, an unfortunate surge of energy when oblivion would have been sweeter.

At the Eel River that evening, Eve got out of her car wearing turquoise nylon shorts and a sports bra. She recognized Joon-sup's car two spaces over from hers at the parking area, and then Joon-sup himself as he stepped out to greet her in running clothes and a bright purple headband. She wasn't prepared to see him, having assumed he'd not show up and then later make an excuse unrelated to his health. Perhaps there would've been an emergency at the Better Bagel, or he would've been working on a new recipe and lost track of time. The sun was an amber hump beyond the surrounding mountain range. Joon-sup looked, if possible, thinner and more sallow-complexioned than he had the day before; the hair hanging over his headband was dry and lackluster.

"You're here," she said, trying to sound cheerful.

"Nothing gets past you," he answered. "What do you think of my new running shoes? They're going to give me the speed of the gods."

"I thought you weren't coming since we didn't talk on the phone to confirm," she said.

"I'm going to be better about our runs. No more skipping out. We don't see each other much otherwise." Joon-sup jogged in place and wiggled his arms and looked ready to collapse.

"Does Justine know you're here?"

"No."

"Where did you tell her you were going?"

"To a movie."

"Why?"

He looked away. "Just because."

Eve walked in a circle like she normally did, stretching her calves and hamstrings and raising her arms to loosen her shoulders and neck muscles. Of course Justine wouldn't want him running. Eve had promised to deter him from exactly this kind of activity. She ought to give an excuse about why she couldn't run now—she was feeling a creeping nausea or dizziness—and suggest they validate his lie by going to a movie instead. Make him do something sedentary and retiring. Make him ease slowly into death, as if it were cold water.

But before she could say anything he was running toward the riverbank path they always followed, shouting, "You'll never catch me!" and laughing like a child. There was something openly carefree about it, as though he'd forgotten his condition or at least deemphasized it in his mind—as though being with Eve, who he thought knew nothing about his heart disease, sent it into remission.

"Wait!" Eve called after him. "Come back!"

He kept going and was now seventy-five feet away, kicking up pebbles.

Eve had no choice but to run as fast as she could until she reached him. "Is this a race?" she panted. "I wasn't ready."

"That's the point."

"But your new shoes already give you an advantage."

"No, they don't. I was just saying that."

They ran in silence and Eve tried to think of ways to steer them back to their cars, but none came to mind. She couldn't feign feeling unwell now that they were already matching strides. An opportunity lost. She had to hope—and it wasn't an impossible hope—that the run would be uneventful, or even good for him. Who knew but that the happiness he derived from forgetting his illness might slow its progress?

"Did you get the threatening call about Leon?" asked Joon-sup.

"Yes."

"You think they'd do that if it were just an innocent news story?"

"It's not 'they,' " Eve said. "It's not even the reporter. It's somebody named Shane acting alone because he thinks there's money in it."

"That's one possibility."

Eve lacked the strength to go over it again. Government conspiracy or divine plan, environment or numen. She had nothing new to contribute to the argument, and just then she felt unable to uphold her end. Because what if she'd been wrong to suppose Leon's disappearances were acts of God? Leon had given her no message, pointed toward nothing explicitly higher than himself. There was a bite in the air, a pain accompanying deep breathing. Usually she lived with this ambiguity—with her doubt—as a crucial part of her Christian faith, but just now, seeing her friend huffing beside her, she wanted Leon to return, if only for an instant, to tell her she was right to interpret him as she had. She was right to accept death and solitude as God's will. After a moment, she said, "Have I ever told you how much I like Justine?"

"You've never met her."

"She's answered the phone a couple times when I've called. She seems warm and considerate."

"Those aren't the first words that come to my mind about her."

"I know you have problems, but all couples do. The core thing is that she loves you and you have a deep commitment to each other."

"Our fights are getting worse. And now she wants us to move to San Diego, as if I didn't hate that city more than anywhere besides Pusan. We'll be in the middle of a huge row and she'll launch a pro–San Diego campaign, like it's the answer to all our problems."

"San Diego is beautiful and has a world-class zoo."

"She thinks that I'm too attached to my friends, and that if we moved there I'd be more open to having kids. It isn't about my friends, though."

"You might like San Diego. It's changed a lot in the last fifteen years, gotten more liberal."

"I doubt it. But anyway that's just a fantasy. We'll probably break up tomorrow."

"You can't think that. That's not going to happen. She wouldn't let you guys get to that point."

Joon-sup looked at her. "Do you know something I don't?"

"I don't know anything."

"Then why are you saying how deep our commitment is to each other? I've never been less happy, and she's miserable. There's no reason for us to stay together except out of habit, which is a bad reason to go on."

They came to an abandoned four-wheel recreational vehicle parked on the river's edge covered with mud and clumps of grass, its rubber wheel flaps chewed up and perforated; next to it lay a dead Chinook salmon like a corroded metal instrument. A mile in the distance the riverbend where they would turn back began its arc. Eve listened for any change in Joon-sup's breathing to indicate stress or fatigue. The rocks below them grew indistinct in the twilight; some were pointy and painful to land on in her thin-soled shoes.

Eve said, "There are difficult times in every relationship, but you'll work through them."

"How would you know? You haven't been in a relationship in ten years."

"I haven't forgotten how hard they are." The bottom of her left foot began to ache and there was an unpleasant edge in Joon-sup's voice.

"That's what I don't understand," he said. "For everyone but you relationships are great. A million men would love to make you happy, but you won't give them a chance. It's like you might as well be a nun."

They ran slower and her ache was more pronounced. "Nun, that's extreme," she said. Her face was red and it could have been from the cold or the exercise or the effort of withstanding the pain. She'd never heard Joon-sup be so mean.

"You've isolated yourself in a dangerous way," he said. "You've kept people out for so long that they may not be able to get back in. You're going to end up all alone."

Eve knew that Joon-sup was talking out of anger—at himself, at his illness, at the world—and she forgave him. They ran slower still as she began to favor her right foot. Her sports bra was losing its firmness and she'd have to get a new one. When they neared the turn-around bend they were little better than walking; she explained about her foot and he said he understood. Maybe there was truth to his criticism, whether or not Leon was a fuse burning all the way to God. She had rejected every suitor since Ryan, had worn porcupine quills that maybe weren't as detachable as she'd thought they were. And now she wanted so much to stop Joon-sup and take his hand and tell him that she was there for him during this awful time, that she cared about him deeply, that *he* wouldn't end up alone. You didn't think you had all the time in the world with people, but you thought you had more than there ended up being.

At the bend's most acute point Eve asked to stop. She lifted up her left foot and it felt like it was still being pressed into the ground. Joon-sup said they could walk back slowly, and he offered his shoulder as a crutch on which to put her arm. As they pivoted around Eve thought how strange it was, in an almost auspicious way, that their roles of care-provider and care-recipient were reversed, if only for a little while.

But then what? When Joon-sup died and the number of her deceased friends someday overtook that of her living, when her chances for companionship had disappeared because she'd once seen a miracle? You only found God when you were ready for Him, yet finding Him didn't guarantee understanding or ever being sure of your discovery. She hopped along on Joon-sup's shoulder and there was no final adjustment.


That night St. Joseph's Hospital was busy, its halls like arteries pumping doctors and patients and nurses and gurneys throughout the building's central nervous system. In one of its outer extremities, the cafeteria, Steve and Prentiss sat down at a table with a snow globe at its center—seasonal flair—drinking coffee. They'd just done a total hip and were exhausted. Doctors and patients wandered in and out like wraiths among the visiting relatives and friends who, depending on the vagaries of fate and medical science, were either cheerful or despondent.

Prentiss said, "Allow me to ask how you're doing."

"I'm fine."

"You know what I mean."

Steve pulled a five-dollar bill from his open white coat and creased it down the middle. "I'm going to get a cream pie. You want one?"

"No thanks."

Steve wrapped the bill around his thumb and went to the dessert counter. Set on a bed of ice and decorative lettuce leaves, pieces of pie and cake were cellophaned and as glossy as wax figures. He pressed the top of a lemon meringue wedge and left a fingertip indentation. When he got back to the table, Prentiss said, "Of course I'm referring to Mazotti's. The way you didn't say nothing all night except argue with your wife and then leave her standing there."

"I'm sorry if it made you uncomfortable."

"I don't care about that. What's important is you think she's going to leave you, but I don't see it. She don't believe you about Leon Meed? So fucking what, man. You know? You said the other day how you never talk about it on account of no one'd believe you."

Steve took a bite of cream pie. "Let's not discuss it. Tell me about your love life. What's going on?"

"I'm worried about you."

"I appreciate it, but there's nothing more to say."

"This withdrawal thing you talked about at the Ritz. It's going to mess you up, and I don't want—"

Steve said sharply, "We're either going to move on to something else or we're going to shut up, okay?"

Prentiss leaned forward and said with an acquiescence uncannily like a warning, "If you want to lose your grip, don't think I'll force it."

"I don't mean to be like this. I'm not feeling well."

"I know." Prentiss sat back in his chair and laid his fingers on the edge of the table as if it were a piano. He looked warily at his friend. "I called a woman the other day."

Steve managed a smile. "That's great. Who?"

"Lillith Fielding."

"Lillith. She's attractive."

"She is that."

"How'd it go? The conversation."

"Didn't happen. I left her a message and she didn't call back."

"Maybe she's been busy."

"No, she's not interested. It's what I expected."

"Don't say that."

"I was being my most charming self on her voice mail, too. You're aware that no one responded to my *Times-Standard* personals ad. I'm putting myself out there and people aren't taking advantage."

"The *Times-Standard* is the wrong approach. It's not the place to look for love. You had the right idea going to the Ritz. Or try the Internet, or take dance lessons. I heard that ballroom dancing is the place to meet women."

Prentiss smoothed down his freshly created goatee and smiled at a cowlicked baby staring at him over its mother's hunched shoulder. "I was the one told you that, and that's on account of a friend of mine met his girlfriend there, but I went once and there was about ten men for every woman, which supposedly was unusual but I can only go by my own experience."

"Don't get discouraged. It's hard to find someone."

Prentiss finished his coffee and stared at a painting of the Virgin Mary on the cafeteria wall. She had a pitiful look, like she could dole out sympathy until Kingdom Come and still have more left over. "Lillith saw Leon back then."

"What?"

"After you left, we talked about it. She didn't say much, but I could tell she had an opinion and we would've got into it except some other people came up to us then. So I thought I'd call her and see where she's at, because I been thinking, turning this matter over in my mind, that maybe me and her had this happen to us for a reason. You, too. Maybe Leon's the thing in a mysterious way made us be friends. Like maybe we saw him disappear so later on we'd sit in this cafeteria here and I'd tell you how to save your marriage and you'd tell me to hold out for love. You know, like there's a purpose to it all."

Steve said, "It's just a coincidence."

"But then it wouldn't mean nothing."

"Why does it have to mean something?"

"It just does."

Steve looked at the cream pie and it was perfectly immobile. He and Anne had had cream pie on their first date, and on their second, and on their third, so that it became their flirting activity, and their celebration activity, and their why-not activity, which he'd never told Elaine, because he'd had cream pie with her also and didn't want her to think it had any old-romance connotations. Although it did. Everything had old-romance connotations. Making love, going shopping, making plans, going over your day, making up, going away, making dinner, going for a walk. He'd done it all with Anne, and although he thought he'd successfully wiped away the associations so that what he and Elaine had, at least in the beginning of their relationship, felt new and unloaded with meaning—so that he'd cleared off the palimpsest—those old associations had simply gone into remission. A cream pie could never be just a cream pie and Elaine would move to Sacramento.

# 4

Elaine talked about the potential highway rerouting to her class on the final day of school before winter vacation. She couldn't remember the last night she'd slept fully and was now going into a level of detail about Eureka's economics that mystified her fourth-grade students. They stared at her like she was speaking in tongues. The hyperactive boys who'd been separated at the beginning of the year stopped carving comic-book epics into the undersides of their desks, and squinted at her. Girls quit writing notes about the cuteness of this or that boy or television actor or purse set, and tried to decide if they could be tested on this information later. On the chalkboard Elaine drew three likely routes the bypass would follow and calculated the exponential harm done to local businesses based on their distance from it. The final bell rang at noon and the kids got up and filed out.

Elaine leaned against the American history calendar tacked up beside the American flag. To belong to a country so big. To see your little corner of it go through upheavals. Elaine had not had sex with her husband in three weeks, which in some marriages was unmentionably brief. In some marriages once-a-month sex was a goal to be worked toward with instructional videos and frank bedside confessionals. Not in hers, though, at least not before now. Elaine didn't care that much—you could live without sex, millions did, and other pleasures became correspondingly sweeter, as blindness enhanced one's hearing and sense of smell—and she would have quietly accepted it if it weren't symptomatic of the rupture taking place between her and Steve. She was supposed to have graded and handed back her students' math and English tests. She was supposed to have finished teaching a unit on North Coast agriculture. Christmas was almost there, and Steve now slept in Abraham's room. Trevor was going skiing during vacation with his friend Toby, a dangerously scatterbrained kid whose mother had called her twice to say that he'd been arrested for shoplifting and to ask if she could help her prevent him from doing it again.

She was unsure if she could prevent anything from happening.

The room's radiator droned irritably as she packed her bag for break. Humming a melody that began as something jazzy and ended up a commercial jingle without her noticing the transition, she unplugged the globe and the computers, abandoned her desk plant, turned off the lights, and walked out to the faculty parking lot, where hers was the last car. The day was wet and thick with ashy fog. On her way home the brakes of her car screamed at stoplights and the mistakes of other drivers made her panic. Pulling up in front of her house, she saw Steve's car in the driveway, where it shouldn't have been at one seventeen on a Wednesday. She had a brief, stoptime flashback of the day she'd caught Greg with another woman. Her stomach turned at the idea of going inside. She could drive away and come back later.

Elaine turned off the car's ignition and got out and walked to the window, where overgrown bougainvillea hid her presence. The living room was empty and there was something different about it: a blank space on the wall above the couch where there used to be an Egon Schiele print. Suitcases sat by the coffee table. Steve walked in carrying his dress clothes in protective wrapping, with plastic coat-hanger rings poking out of the top like question marks. His model tools sat in a box next to the suitcases.

Elaine went inside. "What's going on?"

Steve set down his clothes and looked at her and said, "Aren't you supposed to be in school?"

"It's a half day. Shouldn't you be at the office?"

He seemed confused by the question, then said, "I'm leaving."

"Were you going to tell me, or was I supposed to piece it together on my own?"

"We're not talking."

"And whose fault is that?"

"Nobody has to take the blame."

"So this is like an earthquake? An act of God?" Elaine wasn't crying. A steel band was wrapped around her head and heart. She felt nothing.

"I see where we're headed. I know what's happening."

"Then maybe you could tell me, because I don't see anything and I have no idea what's happening. If this is really about me not believing that you saw a man disappear ten years ago, then fine, I'll believe. I'll believe anything you tell me. If this trip into your head and out of this house is really about Leon Meed, then let's forget it and move on because otherwise we're not half the couple I thought we were. Otherwise I've been a fool for laboring under the misconception that we love each other, and I'll have to take it all back."

"I love you, and that's the problem."

Elaine placed her hands on the headrest of a sofa-chair. "Don't say that; that doesn't make sense. We don't need to be completely rational, but we have to be honest about how we feel."

"I am being honest."

"If you love me, why are you going? Please answer that question."

"It's not permanent. It's just a test, to see how it works."

Elaine waited a minute and said, "Is this all you'll give me?"

"What?"

"This cryptic bullshit about love being the problem and testing our separation. Is this all you have to say?"

Steve went into the bedroom.

"Okay!" Elaine called after him. "You're moving out because of a dinner spat weeks ago and you've done an incredible job of helping me to understand what it means. So have a fabulous life."

Elaine left the house. Her car was hollow tin. She got in and closed the door and started the engine and pulled her seat belt tight across her and only then heard the sound of the door closing. Men left. It's what they did. She would live the next two years alone with Trevor, and after that simply alone until she died. These days your children drifted away (it's what they did) and your house became a museum of which you were the sole custodian, and occasionally your kids and their kids visited—the museum was free to them—to see the exhibit you'd kept in working order. Humans weren't such exceptional animals after all. They did not mate for life and their claims otherwise and their impermanence were pitiable and typical and yet—

Teresa Harrison was walking someone else's dogs. A newspaper boy was flicking rubber bands at a crying girl. Eureka had no ice-cream vans. And yet didn't everyone succumb to defeat sometimes and convince themselves of dark underpinnings, and say good-bye cruel world and sit with the fool on the hill and have sympathy for the devil? Everyone did. Everyone composed funereal elegies for themselves. And then everyone felt differently. Then they thought they'd been wrong to be so cynical—that what they'd built, the intimacy they'd worked so hard and so joyfully and so painfully to establish, shouldn't crumble to nothing. That they shouldn't let it. That they should work through emotional wind and sleet and snow to protect it so long as they had the strength.

When Elaine got home that night she made dinner and watched an old comedy, all misplaced leopards and myopic zoologists, and ignored the draftiness of her house's newly emptied spaces.


A less original man than Shane—one more susceptible to cliché, more stupidly optimistic—might have sought comfort in an adage like "When you have nothing, you have nothing to lose." Having botched an attempt to partner and make money with that invertebrate dickhead Martin Nemec, and then been sucker-kicked by a fat bitch in a tracksuit, and then spent a sexually erroneous night in the county jail, he might have said to himself, "If life hands you lemons, make lemonade." But Shane wasn't a Pollyanna fool. He was too angry for bullshit self-help mantras or mental Heimlich maneuvers that head shrinks on TV tried to sell you. The only maxim he liked was maximum revenge. So as he made one unsuccessful call after another to old friends asking them to post his bail—hearing so many variations on the theme of "Shane Larson? When did you get back? And you're in jail that's too bad. I'd love to help but I've got X payments coming up and money's tight right now"—and as he was then forced to go with a bondsman named Hector, an upstream swimmer from the barrio whom Shane would have enjoyed bashing-thrashing as a youth, being as the guy was a dirty spic and likely to have moved into a Eureka neighborhood that, once spoiled, would attract further racial impurities until it became as muddy as Los Angeles, Shane composed a list of things he could do to those responsible for his current woes.

The acts he considered were, in no particular order: burning down their houses, mugging them, hurting their families, raping them, stealing their cars, kidnapping them, breaking their bones, planting drugs or weapons or child pornography in their homes and then alerting the police, injecting them with AIDS, or something worse, the specifics of which he hadn't yet worked out.

After the bail came through from Hector and the release papers were signed, Shane left the county jail and dropped the sheaf of restraining orders filed against him into a trash can and went home to his apartment. He was tired and ass sore, but at least he had a mission. Kicked off his shoes and sucked dry three Bud Lights. Then, flipping through his mail on the fire escape outside his kitchen window, he opened a letter from Mort Rasmussen, one of Eureka's top estate lawyers, whose father had bought a beautiful platinum-coated coffin from Shane ten years earlier, informing him that he'd been named a beneficiary in Leon Meed's will. He was to call Mr. Rasmussen at his earliest convenience to arrange a time to pick up the inheritance, though when he tried the number a prerecorded message listed the law office's hours of operation as nine to five. His watch said six thirty p.m.

What could Leon have left him, and why? The why didn't matter. The important question was *what*. Shane's wife was divorcing him, Morland Memorial Services hadn't hired him back, and he was riding a hefty balance on his credit card. He needed an infusion of cash and would have asked no questions of a crippled child delivering blood-soaked bills in a paper bag. Perhaps, he thought as he sat down on his lawn chair, Leon had left him the ten-thousand-dollar reward money that was rightfully Shane's from years ago. Choking on his deathbed, Leon may have felt some of the remorse that should have been his constant companion ever since sneaking out of the car when Shane wasn't looking and then condescending to forgive him a few days later at a bar when they ran into each other, when Shane had been temporarily dispirited.

This unexpected windfall almost overrode Shane's anger before falling back to become a healthy but second tier consideration. There was nothing to do about it until the next day, whereas his plans for retribution required immediate planning. With so much fresh and substantiated evidence against him lodged with the police, he'd have to be subtle in dealing with his malefactors. He'd have to have airtight alibis and ghostlike stealth to pull off robberies or maimings or arson and get away with it.

Unless—and here's where *nothing to lose* actually became useful—he was to avenge his honor and then leave Eureka. Considering what he didn't have—a wife, a job, property—and what he did—a police record, soured professional prospects, sudden wanderlust—he could punish everyone and then go far away, disappear.

Late the next morning, Joon-sup saw Eve's phone call as a sort of deliverance. From the moment Justine had woken up and told him her dream—of a family reunion at which her table was surrounded by adults and empty chairs, a scene utterly without children—they'd argued about who wasted more food, who sacrificed more for the other's happiness, whose hang-ups were getting in the way of their shared goals. They'd trotted out the old examples, made the old protestations, used the old rhetorical strategies. Which had left Joonsup desperate. He didn't want kids and although he'd never admitted this even to himself, he might have built up the courage to say it out loud if the phone hadn't rung when it did. He turned away from Justine to take the call and then hung up and refused Justine's demand to see his phone's display to verify that it was, as he claimed, Soulbrother rather than Eve who needed help because of car trouble. During his subsequent drive to Sequoia Park he was full of gratitude and something more to Eve, who, when he pulled up beside her three-wheeled car, was sitting on the sidewalk, hugging her knees to her chest.

He rolled down the passenger side window and pointed to a long, body-sized object wrapped in a white bedsheet jutting halfway out of her hatchback trunk. "What's that?"

"My statue from Leon Meed."

"What statue?"

"The one he did of me. Yours is still there."

Joon-sup raised his voice: "Mine?"

"Didn't you get the letter from Mr. Rasmussen? Leon left you a statue in his will. It's being held in the estate holdings room of Rasmussen & Somebody law offices. That's where I was coming from when my tire blew."

He got out of his car and walked to Eve's trunk to examine what looked like a rigid white ghost. "We both inherited statues from Leon?"

"Yes," said Eve, standing up and rolling a spare tire to his car. "Do you mind lifting this into your backseat? I torqued my back a little when I jacked up my car and took the tire off. Actually, maybe it's too heavy for you. We could lift it together."

"I can do it." Joon-sup wedged the small tire into his backseat crowded with boxes and kiosk materials.

"It probably doesn't matter what garage we go to. They all charge the same."

"You going to leave the trunk open like that?"

"There's nothing worth stealing but the statue, and that's too big. It'll be okay."

They got in Joon-sup's car, and Eve looked elegant and why would the government give them statues instead of kidnap them? He turned his key in the ignition and looked behind him to see if any cars were coming before pulling onto the road. Beside him Eve buckled her seat belt and his heart beat faster seeing her right hand fumble with the strap. The surface story—that Leon had died and left them gifts, and that a young reporter wanted to write a newspaper article about the event—was, surprisingly, turning out to be true. Eve looked worried and melancholy.

"I hope I didn't interrupt anything serious at home," she said. "You sounded edgy."

"Don't worry about it. Justine and I were arguing."

"About what?"

Joon-sup downshifted into third gear for no reason. "You name it."

Eve stared straight ahead and rubbed her nose violently. Her fingers were red and swollen, probably from unscrewing lug nuts. She shifted in her seat but didn't seem able to find a comfortable position, so Joon-sup looked in the backseat to see if he had any clothing she could ball up and use as support for her lower back. She said, "Just remember that you guys will move past this."

Finding nothing, he faced forward—really the best thing for their safety—and said, "Justine stopped taking birth control. She's been trying to get pregnant without telling me."

"She has?"

"I noticed her birth control packet was empty last week, and when I checked yesterday she hadn't replaced it."

"Maybe she's on her period."

"Nope."

Eve hyperextended her back and twisted to the left and right and then curled forward slightly. "You shouldn't blame her."

"Who else would I blame if she got pregnant?"

"She knows that if she's ever going to have a baby, it has to be now."

Joon-sup said, "Then she should go to a sperm bank or find some-one who wants to be a father. She betrayed me."

"But she did it out of love for you."

"Why are you defending her?"

"I told you. I like her and she's good for you, especially now."

"Why do you act like now is an important time for me, like I'm vulnerable and without her my life will be over? She hates you and attacks you every chance she gets; you shouldn't take her side. Maybe you're turning the other cheek, but I'm telling you that's unnecessary."

"Justine hates me?"

Joon-sup pretended to concentrate on the stoplight in front of them, muttering about how long it was stuck on red, and a minute later said, "Is Wonder Brothers over there okay?" He pointed to an open three-car garage across the street and signaled left.

"It's fine. Why does she hate me?"

He shrugged and avoided her eyes and said, "She's crazy. What exactly are we doing here?"

"I'm going to have the spare fixed so I can put it on my car and then drive back to have the real tire fixed."

"Why didn't you bring the real one directly and cut out the mid-dleman?"

"I didn't think of that," Eve said. "Do you talk bad about me to Justine?"

"No. Just the opposite." Joon-sup cut off the engine and might have made connections then had not a tall, willowy man in his early sixties with oil-stained rags stuffed into his two torn breast pockets, and with a chrome-gray handlebar mustache, approached the car and asked how he could help them.

After the spare was fixed and Eve paid for it, they headed back to the park. Along the way Joon-sup said, "I'm sorry for calling you a nun the other day."

"That's okay."

"I don't think that about you."

"I know."

Joon-sup's heartbeat began racing again and he had a hard time controlling his voice when he said, "Ryan's death was a tragedy."

"Yes."

"But I think—I think it doesn't mean you shouldn't fall in love again."

"Thank you; I appreciate the concern. You've always been the dearest friend to me and I know I get controlling sometimes. I'm the one who should apologize."

Joon-sup couldn't say anything.

"You're going through a lot right now with—" said Eve, hesitating, "with Justine, and I want you to think of me as purely supportive. Even if she doesn't like me I know the two of you are good for each other, and I'll do what I can to help you stay together."

Joon-sup felt an almost physical repulsion at Eve's offer and didn't talk until they arrived at her car, when he asked if she needed help attaching the spare. She said she'd be fine. He insisted it would be no trouble and she more forcefully insisted that she had it under control. To end the argument she took his hand, thanked him for the ride, kissed his cheek, and hoisted herself out of the car with a grimace. Good-bye, they both said, she loudly and he softly. Good-bye.


Steve stood outside the Rasmussen & Wei Legal Services building on Fourth Street at three that afternoon, shivering in a long-sleeved dress shirt and blue jeans faded white at the knees. He no more wanted to go inside than he wanted to leave, but as the temperature was too low for much deliberation, he opened the door and entered a blue-carpeted reception area. A young man seated at a long, skinny desk with nothing on it but a clipboard and stack of business cards, took his name, and ten seconds later, Mort Rasmussen, slightly shorter than Steve but in a tailored pinstriped suit that made him appear taller, came in to shake his hand.

"You got our letter about Leon Meed's estate."

"Yes," Steve said.

"He signed his release forms already?" Mort asked the man behind the desk.

"Not yet," the man replied. "I haven't put them together."

"Do it while I take him to holdings." Mort turned and touched Steve on the shoulder. "You play racquetball at CalCourts, don't you?"

Steve nodded.

"I've seen you play Bill Peterson. Your serve is dynamite, but then you don't fall back quickly enough. You lose a lot of advantage on the court by hesitating. Come on and I'll show you your inheritance." Mort led him through a maze of cubicles, a door, a courtyard furnished like an arboretum, and finally down a wide hallway ending at a door marked Estate Holdings. "How well did you know Leon?"

"Not very well. I saw him for a knee injury a few times."

"I myself only met him once, to write up his will, but he seemed like a decent guy." Mort removed a large bundle of keys from his pocket and flipped through them. "I've never seen your name on the Boys in the Wood racquetball tournament roster at CalCourts. You should enter next year's competition, once your postserve positioning improves." When he got the door open, they walked into a twelve-hundred-square-foot room with green plastic cafeteria-issue tables, on each of which were boxes wrapped in identification labels. "There you are," said Mort, pointing to a group of wooden figures lined up along one wall. "That's yours."

"All those statues?"

"Just the one of you."

Steve walked slowly, his armpits itchy with sweat despite his still being cold, and soon confronted a tawny chiseled version of himself in slacks and an unbuttoned sports coat. The left arm of his statue was raised in salute like a preperestroika Lenin monument, and his varnished hands were as cold and smooth as polished marble. The real Steve ran his fingers over his double's arms and neck, the smooth contours of his cheeks and forehead and hair, the eyes so intense they seemed to be shrinking. Examining the statue was like halting time; in contrast to looking at a mirror, where no matter how controlled your expression minor alterations were inevitable, this was him perfectly still and himself, superior to a photograph in its size and depth and tangibility. But what could it mean? What purpose could Leon have had in sculpting it and leaving it to him? Steve felt a twinge of the depression from his drive along Elk River Road the week before, when he'd almost prayed for Leon to come back and, as had happened with Anne, facilitate his belief that he would be okay despite Elaine's leaving him. Except that now the depression abated almost as soon as he felt it, in the way that pain from an old injury will subside, once the awkward movement that triggered it is abandoned.

"Do you have a truck or an SUV?" Mort asked. "That'd make it easier to transport home." His cell phone rang. "If you'll excuse me." He pivoted away to answer and spoke in loud monosyllables. "Someone else is here to collect his statue," he said to Steve after hanging up. "My assistant's bringing him over."

Steve again touched the raised left hand of his statue. The gesture looked less like a salute than it had before. Perhaps it was a farewell. But to whom was he waving? To himself? His ex-wife? Leon? Maybe the outstretched hand meant "Stop," or "Slow down," or "Go away." Steve stared at the statue until the door opened and a familiar-looking Korean American entered, accompanied by the man from the front desk.

"June Soup Kim," Mort said, beckoning the newcomer to them as the assistant withdrew. "It's good to meet you. I'm Mort Rasmussen and this is Steve Baker."

"How do you do?" said Joon-sup, looking at each in turn and vaguely recognizing Steve. He had just come from dropping off Eve and felt fear mixed with desire to see what Leon had left him.

"As you might have guessed," said Mort, pointing to one of the statues, "that's yours."

Joon-sup took a few steps closer to a burl depiction of him with dreadlocks, wearing a skein of necklaces, a flowery sweatshirt, overlarge drawstring trousers, and sturdy hiking boots. His statue's eyebrows were knit together to suggest scorn or disapprobation or confusion, and Joon-sup's first thought was to wonder if this was how Leon had always pictured him.

"I know how you feel," Mort said. "My wife brought out one of our high school yearbooks recently. Made me wonder not just about myself, but about my friends who let me look like that."

This was Joon-sup's complete Americanization. A man so determined not to appear or sound Korean that he'd immersed himself in an obscure California subculture and mimicked the accent of television actors. There were wooden peace bracelets around his wooden wrists like planetary rings, the diamond-shaped stud in his nose suggesting a birthmark. He, the flesh-and-blood Joon-sup, had long since removed the nose ring and cut his hair and worn inconspicuous clothes. He'd changed. But the truth was that he didn't appear any less American now; he merely appeared grown up. More responsible. More conventional. At that moment he felt a hot flash and overall discomfort, as if the room, despite its airiness, had closed in around him. Ten years ago he'd been free to go to tree-sits and on monthlong road trips. Ten years ago he'd had untamed hair and guiltless access to a variety of beautiful women. There'd been no home responsibilities. There'd been no threat of children. Ten years ago he hadn't yet met Eve or Justine.

"I was just asking Steve," Mort said, "if he had a vehicle that could carry his statue home, and I should ask you the same question."

"I don't," said Joon-sup, "but I could maybe borrow one."

"Excellent," Mort said, looking with satisfaction at the two quiet men beside him, both staring with uneasy fascination at their wooden doppelgangers, drifting slightly out of earshot. "Excellent."


The statue of Barry stood in the corner of his apartment. There was no note, no instructions, no explanation. Just the statue. An exact replica of Barry as he'd been at age twenty-four, improbably beautiful, with fine, symmetrical features. Barry walked around it, seeing himself from every angle, and then looked in the mirror and saw one hundred and twenty months of decay. 3,650 days. That's forgetting leap years. Perfect statue, imperfect flesh. As though *The Picture of Dorian Gray* were just a fantasy and in the real world you couldn't disguise your sins or transfer their effects onto attic-bound works of art.

Barry sat on a velour couch in his living room and turned on a KHSU rebroadcast of his *Live from Somewhere* show from two weeks earlier, when his guest had been Charles Giaccone, the Eureka City superintendent of schools. Giaccone was saying that K–3 education in the city faced a serious threat in the budget negotiations going on in Sacramento, because legislators' commitment to education depended on their reelection prospects and their districts' receptivity to the necessary tax increases, so that they called schools inefficient and bloated one day, and their primary concern the next. Giaccone said he understood the political tightrope that had to be walked by state lawmakers, but he couldn't condone further cuts in a budget already chopped off at the knees; children's needs shouldn't, he said, be sacrificed in order to safeguard politicians' approval ratings.

"Yes," Barry heard himself say, "but how do you answer charges coming to light that you've sexually harassed area teachers and administrators during your time as an educator in Humboldt?" In what had been a serious discussion of how schools are underserved and scapegoated, Barry had gone for the jugular.

He shut off the radio and kicked his cat's alarmingly lifelike toy mouse into a corner. It was five thirty and he wasn't gay. He was sad. There were such major flaws in his character. Rilke had once written, "You must change your life." Brooding accomplished nothing. Barry stood at a five-foot remove from his statue, which in another time and place might have sparked in him a vain nostalgia, but which now called for but couldn't produce hot tears for a lost innocence. You must change your life. The phone rang and he crossed the room to answer it.

"I want you to know," a woman said, "that you are your own worst punishment."

"Is this Lillith Fielding?"

"People like you think others enjoy being used so you can sound smart, as if we were dumb masochists, but—"

"I don't think that."

"You're not a public service; you're just an ego looking for applause. Everything you say is calculated to show that you're wiser than everyone else, but you're just one of those people who can't create anything yourself."

"That's a little unfair."

"Your behavior is unfair."

"People like to hear conflict. It's what hooks listeners; I'm just doing my job and I have no intention of—"

"Your job is to be an asshole?"

"I try to put on an entertaining program."

"Exactly like all the other talk show terrorists."

"I'm not a terrorist."

"Yes, you are. You didn't let me mention the festival—that was the whole reason for me going on your show."

"You're the one who went off about fairies and harpies and then stormed out of the studio early. If talking about the festival was important, you should have done it. Don't blame me just because you were too dumb to follow your agenda."

Barry stopped chastising what had become a dial tone. His cat was acting standoffish and a pair of wooden eyes coldly examined him, their censure resolute. They were redwood and ancient and right.


At seven p.m., Prentiss heard a knock on his door and rose from his bath, dried off, and walked lightly down the hallway so as not to disturb a weak floorboard that he feared would split apart if stepped on carelessly. Steve must have left without his key that morning. Barechested and towel-waisted, with vein-stained eyes from a penetrating new shampoo, Prentiss pulled open the door and saw his houseguest's wife standing in the yellow haze of his porch light.

"Prentiss," said Elaine. "You were in the shower—I'm sorry. I would've called first but I was in the neighborhood."

He inched left to hide behind the door. "It's all right. I was starting to get wrinkly anyway."

"Is Steve here?"

"He's out somewhere, maybe at work, but come in and wait if you like." He closed the door behind her and led the way to the living room and removed a stack of pet catalogues from the fauteuil. "Give me a minute and I'll put on something less comfortable." Prentiss went to his bedroom and then emerged in slacks and a Fortuna rodeo T-shirt, penny loafers, the glasses he wore at night. Elaine stood at his red oak bookcase examining pictures of Ferdinand and of Prentiss's mother, and there was a deliberateness to her expression, a focus so total he hesitated to break it.

"That's my mother," he said.

"She's beautiful."

"She's passed on now, but that one was taken out in Cutten, where she lived up to the end."

"Did you take it?"

Prentiss nodded. "I had some photography courses in college. You want something to drink? Water? Guava juice?"

"I'm fine, thanks."

They turned back to the picture of a ninety-one-year-old black woman with thin white hair, almost translucent, combed out three inches. She was seated in a broad-backed rocking chair, with a book in one hand and a wide-meshed black shawl wrapped around her shoulders. Her smile, if it was one, seemed to be just beginning, as if, had the picture been taken a few seconds later, it would've exposed a dazzling set of white teeth, both plastic and real.

"How you holding up?" Prentiss asked, turning to Elaine.

"All right."

From a certain angle this was a difficult situation. Prentiss sensed that the enormity of her marital problem, their lack of prior confidences, the possibility of Steve coming back, their instinctive mutual regard, and a postprandial slowness would prevent them from openly discussing why she'd come. Could he even hope to comfort someone facing the end of her marriage, preparing to pack up and leave her romantic home? Would it help to say, I've been out on the street forever; you'll get used to it? No, because that was a lie. Prentiss had never stopped looking for love, for someplace to live; he'd never gotten used to it.

"Did your mother pass away at home?" Elaine asked.

"In her sleep. She had all kinds of things wrong with her, but the doctor said it was old age got her at the end. A weak heart. It was her time."

"The same thing happened to my father. He had a brain tumor, but he died because his heart just stopped beating one morning, and—Prentiss!"

He was startled by the change in her tone of voice and turned to look where she was pointing. "Yeah?"

Beside a shedding ficus tree and Ferdinand's bed, a life-sized statue of him, Prentiss, faced them, a mute witness to their conversation. "What's that?"

"It's supposed to be me," Prentiss said, as Ferdinand came in and ran a lap around the room. "It looks bad me having it out in the open like some kind of royalty who keeps an oil portrait of himself on display, so I'm going to move it. I haven't decided where, maybe the garage."

"Oh."

"You'll see from the good posture how it's supposed to be a younger me. I slouch now pretty bad and it draws an unfavorable comparison."

"You don't slouch."

Elaine either hadn't looked closely or was being nice, because it was obvious that over time Prentiss had lost some of his stature. Had shrunk literally if not figuratively. The statue was a gift and he didn't resent it—really he was grateful to Leon for remembering him—but Prentiss saw enough of himself in the five minutes it took to shave in the morning. He didn't need an in-house wooden twin, especially one that called attention to his worsening posture. What he considered, though—what seemed a distinct possibility given his brief meeting with its sculptor—was that although he may have declined physically in the last ten years, and although there was much to lament about his future diminution, he had improved in a number of ways. He had weaned himself off of alcohol, for instance. Whereas the statue-era Prentiss was obsessed and compromised by his addiction, the current Prentiss standing with Elaine could comfortably never drink again. He owed the passage of time, the lateral moves he'd made since that night at the Shanty, his life. And wasn't that, despite the emphasis it then placed on his loneliness, a reason to be grateful?

Elaine squinted at the statue and said, "Did you commission it?"

"No. The artist left it to me in his will."

"Who was the artist?"

"Leon Meed."

She took a step in the statue's direction. "Were you two friends?"

"Not technically friends, I wouldn't say that. We spent some time together once during the infamous disappearances. I was going to tell you that the other night at Mazotti's, let you know that someone else had a peculiar experience with Leon. I should've done it; I apologize."

"Thanks, but my trouble with Steve goes deeper than what happened between him and Leon."

"I figured as much."

Elaine looked at him and folded her hands. The base of her nostrils was wet. "I don't suppose you could repeat what he's told you about us."

"Well, on a certain level he's thinking that you're about to move to Sacramento and leave him."

"He doesn't believe that." Elaine wiped her nose subtly and crossed her arms.

"I won't say I get the whole picture with him, because I think he doesn't even know himself. Maybe that makes it worse for you, but to me it doesn't seem he's doing it out of spite."

Elaine nodded and looked again at the statue for a moment. "It's late. I should let you have some privacy."

"You don't have to go. You could sit and read till he gets back. Watch television."

"Thanks, but he might be on call or in surgery."

"Want me to give him a message?"

She moved toward the door. "No thanks. I'll call him tomorrow." With her hand on the doorknob she said, "I appreciate what you told me."

The door closed and Ferdinand came to sit by Prentiss's feet.

When Sadie heard the phone ring too early in the morning, she thought it might be Elaine returning her call from the night before. Pushing up her eye mask and running her tongue over her teeth, she clicked on her phone and heard a still, small voice say, "Dr. Jorgenson? It's me, Joon-sup. I need to talk to you."

"What time is it?"

"This is an emergency."

"Seven? Is it seven yet?"

"Can I come over?"

"Now?" Sadie stared at the pixilated darkness of her room.

"Please," said Joon-sup.

She reluctantly agreed and then went hungrily to the kitchen, where she poured herself a cup of cold coffee and sat dazedly in front of the previous day's newspaper until her doorbell rang.

Five minutes later she and Joon-sup faced each other from two reclining chairs in the living room as sunlight striped in through the blinds. She'd offered him a cup of the same cold coffee she was drinking, assuring him of its continued potency and flavor, but he'd refused. Said that he was too jittery as it was. Said he couldn't eat or drink under the circumstances, and she'd understand once he told her what happened. She erected an internal dam to hold back her boredom, hoping that however high her indifference rose she'd prevent its spilling over with her cement-reinforced professionalism.

"Have you left Justine?" Sadie asked.

"No, I'm here about Leon Meed."

She moved a pillow from under her leg. "Because of the newspaper reporter and the threats?"

He shook his head. "My friend Eve got a statue from him and it's ruining her life."

In spite of herself she felt a prickling of curiosity; the dam thickened. "Is that right?"

"Yes. He left me a statue, too."

"So that's what the letter from Rasmussen & Wei is about."

"You got one?"

Sadie hadn't yet done anything with the missive that had come the day before and now lay facedown on her desk. She'd not bothered to guess what she was to receive. "How do you feel about your statue?"

"My feelings aren't important. I'm worried about Eve."

"What's happened?"

Joon-sup squeezed his fingers together. "She's decided to become a nun."

Sadie didn't owe it to a patient to discuss his friends, especially the religious extremists among them. She fought back a strong desire to pursue the subject of Leon's leaving various people statues.

"Is Eve unhappy about her decision?" she asked.

"No."

"Then why are you worried?"

"Because she doesn't see the danger. She thinks she's being freed from worldly attachments, and that she has to cut off ties to people and to Eureka and take vows. I called her last night because she's seemed unhappy lately—in fact, I think she's been a little unhappy the whole time I've known her—and she said that when we saw Leon ten years ago, she was wrong to take it as a sign from God to just become a Christian. Now she thinks it was really God telling her to go further, to become a nun. She says the statue makes this clear."

"How does it do that?"

"In it, she has her hands clasped and her eyes closed."

Sadie didn't listen to the voice saying that this was Leon's way of telling her why. Why. "So you're worried about losing her as a friend."

"That's part of it."

"What's the other part?" She noticed that Joon-sup hadn't blinked while telling the Eve story. He seemed full of indignation and concern. As though his anxiety were the missing ingredient for a cure to what had afflicted her for months, Sadie suddenly felt infused with energy.

"I don't want her to make a mistake."

"But if she doesn't view it as a mistake?"

Joon-sup blinked uncontrollably for ten seconds and ran a finger down the center crease of his pants.

Sadie said, "Didn't you once tell me her boyfriend died of a drug overdose?"

"Yes."

Reformulating a truth she'd gone over a dozen times, and which required no thought, and which she should have resented repeating but now enjoyed going over, she said, "Losing a romantic partner is different from losing a parent. You carried on well after your mother's death, but people who lose loved ones often feel a void that has to be filled. If religion works for Eve, you should be grateful to Leon Meed." She felt uncommonly good.

"But she could fill the void in other ways."

"Maybe she doesn't recognize them."

"Men ask her out all the time."

"Maybe they can't provide the love she needs."

"Yes I can—"

Sadie finished her cup of coffee. Joon-sup looked like he'd run over a dog. There weren't any clouds in the yellowing sky outside. Behind her dam the boredom level had completely evaporated. "Joon-sup, I've known you for ten years, and during that entire time you've been telling me about your plans to open your own restaurant."

"So?"

"So I want you to do it. Now."

"What?"

"If in two weeks you haven't taken steps in that direction, I will refuse to see you anymore as my patient."

He coughed and said, "Where is this coming from?"

"Go home. You still have time before work to get some sleep. There's something I've got to do."

Lillith was quartering a small semithawed onion bagel in the staff lounge of the Coastal Orthopedic Medical Group office when Steve walked in holding a personalized mug. She'd just poured all but the last few drops of coffee into her own cup and now glanced with embarrassment at the nearly empty carafe.

"Hi," Steve said. His short gray hair lay in limp shiny swirls on his head, as though it hadn't been washed or combed or even acknowledged that morning. Jowly and haggard, he scared her a little in his knee-length white surgical gown over tweed slacks and a dark purple dress shirt, the whole clashing ensemble uniformly wrinkled. The coffeemaker sizzled at him when he removed the carafe and held it up to see how little was left.

"I was about to make more," said Lillith, rising from the table.

"Don't on my account." Steve sat down on the seat across from her bagel while she went to measure coffee grounds and pour water. Wipe up spilled imitation sweetener. Wonder how long she'd have to stay in the room before leaving wouldn't appear rude. Steve said, "We haven't spent much time together."

Lillith hoped he was talking to himself and so continued cleaning up around the beverage area. Straightening cups. Arranging stir straws.

"I'd be afraid," Steve continued, "to know what you think of me after that argument with my wife at the holiday party."

Apparently he was addressing her, so she returned to her bagel. Picked up a quarter. Took a small bite. "When my parents were married," she said, "they fought worse than you guys did."

Steve appeared grateful for the information. "Are you seeing any-one romantically right now?"

She kept on chewing. Workmanlike. If only she'd risked minor inconsiderateness by leaving the room as soon as he came in! Surely he wasn't about to ask her out. Surely. "Like you said, we haven't spent much time together, and I don't—"

"Because Prentiss Johnson is a good man. He didn't ask me to talk to you, so don't think of me as a messenger on his behalf. I respect his privacy and yours, and I'm sorry if it's out of line for me to bring it up now. You must have your reasons."

"Reasons for what?"

"Not calling him back."

Lillith relaxed her shoulders and felt an incipient tension headache begin to recede. "I don't know what you mean; he never called me."

"You don't have to make excuses. All I'm saying is that he's extremely nice. Yet not boring. Not one of those bland guys who says all the predictable things. And he's funny. You can ignore this if you want, but Prentiss is a wonderful guy."

Before going to work that morning Lillith had stopped at the law office where her statue from Leon was being kept and asked that it be given away or destroyed. She didn't want it. The lawyer asked her to at least look at it before ordering its destruction, and after refus-ing for a minute she relented. The statue was her at age sixteen, without embellishment or flourish or suggestion that she'd rescued its creator. It was plainly, simply Lillith. An ordinary girl. Unexcep-tional. Powerless. She felt the bitterness and contempt for Leon and her decade-old delusion that had been building since her radio show appearance. There was no Astral Plane. Wicca was a sham and Barry had been right to burn her at the stake of public ridicule. Almost out of spite she accepted the statue and, with the strained help of two short paralegals, tied it onto the ski rack attached to the roof of her car.

"Honestly," she said, "I never got a call from him."

"Then here's his number." Steve wrote it down on a Coastal Orthopedic Medical Group prescription pad, tore off the top sheet, and placed it in front of Lillith.

She folded up the paper and stuck it in her shirt pocket. "Thanks," she said.

Steve nodded and left the room.

# 5

Martin had worked at the *Times-Standard* for so brief a period that omitting it from his CV wouldn't make future employers suspicious. If asked, he'd say he took time off after graduate school to visit friends in Louisville before entering the job market. It would be as if he'd never come to Eureka or explored the Leon Meed story or gotten fired by an apoplectic editor in chief for creating what was referred to as a "public relations nightmare," a ridiculous claim given that the people involved—Sadie Jorgenson, Steve Baker, Lillith Fielding, Prentiss Johnson, Eve Sieber, Barry Klein, Joon-sup Kim, and Elaine Perry—hadn't pressed charges against the paper or drawn media attention to the matter.

This didn't excuse his gluing himself to a Shanty barstool on the morning of December 24 and ordering successive gin and tonics so that by five in the afternoon Martin felt made of rubber and wire, but it was enough to quiet his conscience. Sitting next to him were a couple of old men with Walt Whitman beards and Will Rogers wisdom. The television above the bar played *It's a Wonderful Life* and the wonderfulness—the life—hit vertiginous heights. At some point during the movie, he slid his credit card to the bartender. Food became a distant and important goal. His seat neighbors agreed that the *Times-Standard* wasn't worth dick, so he placed their drinks on his tab and would brook no argument against his generosity. The men obliged.

Then it all went wrong. A hand landed familiarly on Martin's shoulder followed by the nasal pinch of Shane's voice. "Martin," it said.

Martin turned around and his companions, imagining a friendly reunion in progress, lifted their drinks in Shane's honor. "I have a restraining order against you," Martin said, too drunk to panic. "This is illegal contact."

"Always the Boy Scout, huh?" Shane squeezed onto a seat beside him, ignoring the confused displacement of Will and Walt. "I wasn't even looking for you. Can you believe that? It must be fate."

"You know I live across the street. I could call the police right now."

"Go ahead."

Martin shouted out for the phone, which the bartender placed on the counter's only dry spot. Shane grabbed and pocketed it while Martin was still trying to ascertain its exact location. "Let me have that," Martin said, staring thickly where it had been.

Shane said, "Relax."

"You are pure evil. Do you even know that?"

"Only God knows what we are."

"You got me fired."

"And you turned down my business offer. And had me thrown in jail. And have been rude and disrespectful to me since we met. If we were keeping score, I'd have beaten you a long time ago."

Martin looked around for someone to share his incomprehension. "What do you want?"

"I want you to come with me."

"No way." Martin had barely spoken the words when his left arm was twisted behind his back and he found himself walking on buckling legs out the Shanty's front door into an overbright, cold, misty, friendless day. This can't be happening, he thought as he and Shane crossed the street in a tight embrace, Shane's hand dug into his jacket pockets, and his key was fitted into the door leading to his apartment.

*   *   *

An hour later the Shanty's atmosphere turned festive when six of the Eureka Free Clinic's volunteer psychiatric staff came in and ordered pitchers of Bloody Marys. Sadie and her friend Bob were part of the group that pushed together two tables in the smokeless half-light of a corner by the video poker machines and began a conversation that was at first a polite garden in which only odorless stories about local and national news cropped up, although as the pitchers were emptied, shoots of inappropriate confessions and sexual innuendo sprouted. Someone described her patient's recent sex change. Someone followed with the tale of a friend's penile fracture. Bob, cultivating a rocky patch of self-deprecation, admitted that this was his first social night out in a year, and that it was lucky his patients didn't know about his lonely life, or they'd want to counsel *him* and he'd never regain the upper hand.

As the conversation rose in earthiness and then partitioned into smaller units, Sadie, who'd had two mescal shots since her first Bloody Mary, placed an arm around Bob and thanked him for what he'd told her at Amigas Burritos a few weeks earlier. She squeezed and rubbed his shoulder. Despite being an impotent pariah, he was a wise man and had helped to restore her sense of herself as a therapist.

"That's nice of you to say," Bob answered. "Half nice, at least. A backhanded compliment is what it is."

"I mean it in a good way, Bob."

"Are you still filling out applications to culinary schools?"

"I threw them away."

"You did?"

That morning Sadie had placed a statue of herself that was thinner and younger looking than she was now in her kitchen. Interestingly, there was a crowbar in its right hand, which instead of being gripped in the air like a weapon was pointing down and touching the ground like a walking stick. The statue's guard was lowered. She put her arms around it, danced in place with it, kissed it, draped a fuzzy blanket around its shoulders. "Leon," she said aloud, "you can come back now and say what's the point of this and I won't get mad. I'll listen. Don't be one of those people who only shows up when he's not invited." She stared and didn't expect a Pygmalion-style awakening or the ghost of Leon to appear to provide a short dissertation on his aims and strategies. Her statue was indeed her, and the world hadn't grown dull in ten years. Her job hadn't become less interesting, marriage less tenable, or Eureka less hospitable. People who were bored were themselves boring. Sadie, she realized in a wave of self-recognition that completed the change in her attitude begun with Joon-sup the day before, had simply forgotten the basics.

Bob said, "Do you really think that you and I are such a bad idea? Because I could switch my prescription. Say the word and I'll be a man again."

"I couldn't ask you to do that for me."

"Sure you could."

Sadie took the temperature then of her drunkenness and told herself not to have anything more; she was meeting Elaine for dinner later and had to be sober enough not to yell in the restaurant. Her phone rang and it was Elaine, coincidentally, saying she had to cancel because Steve wanted to talk that night. They hung up. Sadie stared at her phone and she could— she *would*—lead Elaine and Steve to reconciliation. She had the power and means. This very night. Bob poured her another Bloody Mary and ordered her another shot, and she was too excited to say no.

At six o'clock, Eve was waiting for the Sacred Heart Church to begin its Christmas Eve mass. She wore a black skirt and white blouse with pearl earrings. Children scuffled with each other not far from her on the pew, which vibrated against and provided relief to her lower back. Time passed with ceremonial grace. She chewed a piece of gum secretly, moving her mouth with a ventriloquist's skill, as the priest came out of the vestry carrying a single book.

Eve had attended Sacred Heart for ten years. In the beginning it provided her with a sense of sanctioned community, where there were no drug-addicted young men or despairing rock songs. Appetites once integral to her sense of self and future identity had been buried with Ryan, and she grew older and relieved to be done with them. She now prayed for Joon-sup. She prayed that his slide away from the world of the living wouldn't be so fast that he knew, in the end, only the sensation of freefall. The children in her pew were reprimanded by their parents, so they quit fighting and played with their shirt cuffs and listened to stories in their heads, on an unending quest to amuse themselves.

The priest, a bowlegged man with thin gray hair and ears that stuck out at the tips, took his place at the podium and gave a sermon about Christ not being an idol. This was the last mass Eve would attend as a layperson. She agreed that celebrating Christ's birth was not idolatry and was instead an opportunity to study His Beatitudes. The priest led them in prayer and Eve kept her eyes open throughout. The children beside her were ambivalent toward the service and God was not the most important element in their lives. They'd sooner give Him up than their families or best friends, and this prioritization of people over God was man's primal instinct. Placing Him above all others was a learned exaltation. During communion she ate bread and drank wine that in transubstantiation was the body and blood of her Savior.

Eve accepted a votive candle. For years she'd struggled against dependence on others as though life were a test to be taken alone. No cheating. Dozens of men had asked her out, and some had been warm and attractive, and it had required a certain coldness to dismiss them. Now she was going to leave those considerations forever. She was going to a place beyond the reach of loss. Closer to eternity. Nearer to God. And if it turned out to be no different a solution for emotional pain than numbness was for physical pain? If she were merely covering up her heart rather than healing it?

Ferdinand the pig had been in the kitchen all day, lying beneath the water cooler and sniffing at the bowl used to collect drips from its leaking spout. Prentiss, hunting for his car keys under a mound of magazines and newspapers, keeping the left half of his attention on the clock, worried that his pet was sick.

"I'd stay with you," Prentiss said, turning from the bad news, "but as you know I got a date. Proof of miracles."

In the bathroom, Prentiss flossed and brushed his teeth, ran a pick through his hair, and leaned close enough to the mirror to look down and see the reflection of most of his outfit. He was presentable, perhaps even attractive, and he felt a twinge of optimism before realizing that these were the same slacks and sweater he'd worn at the holiday party where he'd met Lillith. He went to his bedroom and changed into different clothes, thankful to have avoided an accident.

Driving along H Street, Joon-sup carried in his lap a completed thirty-four-page small business loan application for the Joon-sup Experience. With his right hand he worried a corner of its cover sheet and then, to stop himself, stuffed the whole thing in his suit jacket's inside left pocket. The sidewalk around the church was lined with cars—among them Eve's hatchback—forcing him to park five blocks away. He then spent fifteen minutes removing lint from his coat with shaking hands, doing breathing exercises, telling himself it was going to be okay. If his statue clarified anything, it was that as an adult he shouldn't wish to be otherwise. His conservative, middle-aged clothes weren't a reason to be upset. Borrowing fifty thousand dollars required collateral. You had to have little or no debt and a clean police record, whereas Joon-sup had three thousand dollars riding on credit cards and two arrests from his environmental activism days. He was a bad loan prospect. He was aging and would continue to do so. He'd operated his stall for eight years and been crime-free for almost as long. He had a solid local reputation among other restaurateurs and was a Better Bagel manager in good standing. Who knew how his application would fare when reviewed closely?

❖    ❖    ❖

Not far from where Joon-sup idled in his car, at a house on I Street, Barry arrived at the Knavetivity Scene party and was greeted with the usual cries of "Lock up your sons, ladies, it's Baseline Barry," and "Barry, you slut, don't sit down unless you're ready to discuss your exploits *now*!" To which he rolled his eyes and said, "Waste my drama on you Puritans?"

The party was unevenly divided between Josephs and Marys, with the majority of attendees dressed as the latter. This made seven Josephs and thirty-two Marys. Only the host was Baby Jesus, which, given his predilection for being swaddled and nursed, was no surprise. One of the Josephs whom Barry didn't recognize smiled at him from beneath a voluminous fiery red beard. Algerian disco music thumped and cried—you could almost feel the hot night air on your back and the cool sand on your knees—from the sound system installed in a crib at the center of the room. Barry (Mary) sat on a couch between Robert Mary and Derrick Mary, and the three of them in their matching headdresses and sandy robes looked like Nazarene sisters.

Soon would be the Yuletide blow jobs. Soon a stranger or a friend or someone you barely knew would grab your crotch—or you would grab theirs—and there would be preliminary stroking—not much, because everyday life provided enough delayed gratification—and, if mutually approving, the two of you would find a room or a closet or simply some floor space in the living room on the night before Christmas. The red-bearded Joseph eyed Barry hungrily and was aflame, and Barry showed not an iota of life.

"That beard is raping you with his eyes and you aren't even playing the coquette," Derrick Mary said to Barry Mary. "What's the matter?"

"This."

"What?"

"This whole thing."

"Uh-oh," sang Robert Mary gaily, "sounds like someone's disgruntled. You are such a one for brooding."

Barry Mary looked at Derrick Mary, at the laboriously crafted effect of a twenty-first-century American man trying to look like a sixteenth-century Italian painter's conception of the first-century Madonna. Barry Mary stood up and deflected the advance of the hirsute red Joseph by going to the kitchen, having a glass of wine, and returning to the manger (living room) to press the hands of those present with a *I know it's early but I have to go.*

It had been a while since Shane last brought the pain to a guy who was in essence a pussy. Doing so was beneath him, because men who couldn't fight were no different from women, and Shane drew the line at the fairer sex. He wouldn't beat up a woman any more than he'd put the hurt on a small child or an old geezer—not that he hadn't wanted to smack the pensioners who'd haggled with him in the past about casket prices and then gone over to the competition—and when the pain recipient was as drunk as Martin had been something shameful marked the proceeding. Shane, while driving away from Martin's apartment, rubbing the blood from his knuckles, searching the radio for some decent power chords—in a big city he'd have more options—made a short, flexible promise not to demean himself like that in the future. He'd chosen to destroy his enemies' property rather than their bodies in order to maintain the honor that walloping on a weak drunk like Martin tarnished.

In this case it couldn't be helped. Martin hadn't been given a statue and was therefore unable to lose one. Shane had had no choice but to beat him up before drugging him for the night and taking his car (Martin couldn't go to the police or secure an alibi). No choice at all. Plus, after Shane's disappointment at Rasmussen's office, when he'd been told—without an accompanying apology—that his inheritance was nothing but a useless statue, that there was no money component, he'd needed a workout to steady his nerves. Turning right on Buhne Street, he already felt better. An intoxicating kerosene smell came from the three red metal gas cans sloshing around in his backseat. He felt the bulge of matches in his front pants pocket. The night was still and holy.

❊   ❊   ❊

Elaine had brought up divorce with Steve on the phone that morning. If two people were so distant from each other. If confidence were so completely eroded. She'd stood in the kitchen and talked in endgame terms as their chances for reconciliation slipped away.

When Steve came over at seven that evening, they sat at the dining-room table—how strange and familiar the scene was—and discussed the logistics of a divorce, and she joked about how much better they would be at it this time than they'd been before. Practice makes perfect. They laughed, and she wondered at how things had deteriorated so quickly, not expecting a response. He said he didn't want to be left behind. She said she hadn't planned to leave him and his believing otherwise was crazy. He said he knew the signs of abandonment; he knew what Sacramento meant. Elaine said, without meaning to insult him, that that was the dumbest thing she'd ever heard. Hadn't all of her entreaties for him to open up to her proven that she wanted to save, not end, their marriage? She'd only suggested divorce today because his withdrawal into himself had been so ominous and complete. She would do anything to restore their marriage, but she couldn't do it alone. He had to help. While he stared at his soft surgeon's hands on the table, she repeated: he had to help.


Something unexpected happened while Lillith was cleaning her apartment in preparation for her date with Prentiss. Her statue, which she pulled out of the broom closet to get to the vacuum cleaner, made her happy. She looked at it in the living room's seventy-five-watt light and realized she'd been missing the point. True, she was ordinary and unexceptional and powerless in most respects, a generic specimen of humankind. She could be considered foolish or gullible or romantic. But it was for these reasons she'd become a Wiccan; they were the key to her religion's success. That Leon chose to sculpt her naturally, unadorned, didn't invalidate her beliefs; instead it reminded her of what she gained from them. Strength. Self-confidence. Courage to withstand the very shame that had recently infected her. She would own her faith and be proud of it and refuse to let others' incredulity sway her. We were all made differently. We were all made the same. She looked at her statue and felt a suffusion of compassion for it, for herself, like a mother for her first child, and at that moment a car engine fell silent outside. She put away her broom, dustpan, and bucket of cleaning sprays and liquids. She said "The Lady's Prayer" and would not live in fear of attracting überpervs. She heard someone ascending the stairs leading to her apartment door. She straightened the magazines on her coffee table and had time to sit down before a knock came at her door.


When the mass ended, Eve gathered her coat and purse and stood up, a relief to her lower back, which had worsened over the past hour. The children in her pew filed out with their parents' hands on their shoulders. The organist played solemn Bach. Eve looked for the priest to thank him, but he was gone.

Outside she stood at the doorway and watched everyone recede from the church like a human tide. Then, as she followed them down the steps, she came face-to-face with Joon-sup next to the church welcome sign. He wore a suit and his hair was parted at the side in salary-man style.

"What are you doing here?" she said, happily surprised, squeezing his left arm.

"I have to talk to you."

"Now?"

He nodded. "Can we go someplace?"

They walked toward Seventh Street, he ahead of her by a half-step, and stopped at the number 9 bus stop. Eve looked at Joon-sup preparing to tell her his news and felt as though they were in a play they'd rehearsed a thousand times, one she could perform without thinking. She knew by heart the coming dialogue and facial expressions.

She saw in advance every studied gesture, every crafted emotion. Joon-sup cleared his throat and rubbed the coins together in his pockets.

"I should keep this to myself," he began, "but your decision to join a convent has forced me to say it."

There was no room for improvisation, no chance for the unexpected. In plays, in the now according to God, the end was preordained. She saw a man meekly following a script to an abhorrent conclusion.

"Should we sit down?" she asked, indicating the bench under the bus stop awning and internally noting, with dreamy, sad detachment, her intonation and blocking.

"I'd rather stand."

"Okay."

"Go ahead and stop me at any time." He paused.

"Okay," she said.

He pulled a packet of papers from his coat pocket and held it up for her to see. "I'm meeting with someone from Humboldt Bank in a few weeks to discuss my loan application."

This was expected and heartbreaking. For him to do what he'd postponed forever, merely for thematic closure and to have one fewer regret when death stopped for him. Eve stared at his careful lettering in the application's information boxes, the conscientious words describing his biographical and economic coordinates. The hopeful figure in the amount-requested space. "That's great," she said, her voice catching in spite of knowing everything in advance.

"Don't cry. I won't say it. We can forget this happened."

She wasn't aware she'd been crying but when her fingers touched her cheek it was wet. "I know it already, but I should hear it from you."

"No you shouldn't. If it's upsetting—"

"Of course it is, but I can't keep hiding from the fact. That's not fair to you or me."

"I'm sorry." He gestured with his hands that he didn't know what more to say.

"It's not like you have any choice in the matter. No one does. It's a cruel accident."

He breathed out—too dramatically, perhaps—and stood so that the streetlamp light accentuated his cheekbones. There was fear in his eyes; his performance was in most ways irreproachable; the set was elaborate and every attention had been paid to detail.

Eve said, "Justine told me a couple of weeks ago."

Joon-sup frowned searchingly, as though waiting for a line prompt. "Why didn't you say anything?"

"I promised not to."

"Did she threaten you?"

"No. She invited me out one night to talk because she thought I had a right to know. I don't think she's told anyone else."

"I'll bet she's told everybody."

"It's a mistake to keep it a secret. It's a tragedy. Your friends can help you if you let them."

"My other friends have nothing to do with it. You're calling it a tragedy. That's it. End of discussion."

"I'm just saying you don't have to go through it alone. If you need daily help when your condition gets worse, I can spend mornings and nights at your place and reduce my hours at Going Places."

"What?"

She put her arms around Joon-sup and held him for a dark, desperate moment. Pulling back, she said, "I hope I didn't crumple your application."


Martin tried but couldn't get up. The scratch groove of his record player warped and woofed through the small speakers in his apartment. He didn't remember putting on a record. Or passing out. Or waking up. His only clear memory was of Shane repeatedly hitting him and calling him a fool, saying he'd had the chance to get rich on the Leon Meed story and chosen not to. He was a sick man, Shane said.

Martin felt beyond the powers of alcohol. His head was thick with illegible data and he couldn't see properly. Why would he or Shane have put on a record? Martin called out for help and his voice was barely a whisper. His stomach roiled and lurched in every direction.

"Help!" he wheezed.

Warp warp woof.

"Help!"

Even though he'd been beaten, he felt no pain, just an undulant nausea and gross distortion of his visual and auditory senses. A thought drifted through his head with cloudlike serenity: Shane had drugged him and taken some of his things. Martin had the drive and agility of a rag doll. Shane had said, with television sarcasm, "You're an antisocial fuck, you know that? Burning down people's houses just because they don't want to be interviewed. I hope they lock you up and forget about you. I really do." Martin remembered this sinister sound bite and passed back into slumber.


Looking up from his hands (that had repaired so many bodies—opened them up, sewn them together), Steve said that it wasn't going to work between him and Elaine. They sat at the kitchen table they'd bought on their honeymoon in Mexico—maintained beautifully, it was without stain or blemish—and after a moment's hesitation she began crying. He wanted to comfort her but couldn't. She stared unseeingly into space and quieted down for a few breaths before breaking again into sobs, staggering her absorption of their end with ten-second intervals of calm.

Although unsure of when he'd begun to think seriously about Prentiss's question at the Ritz—how could his withdrawals be a response to women leaving him, when the reason they left him was his withdrawals?—Steve had learned the answer that afternoon, sitting in front of his statue from Leon Meed, studying its fixed eyes. They didn't hide or turn away from his inquiry. He could tell Prentiss and Elaine and Abraham and anyone who'd listen that he was the innocent one in relationships, more sinned against than sinning, but that was untrue, a thick subterfuge he'd deployed without knowing it. The truth was that a dark corner of his unconscious engineered his withdrawals in order to drive away his partners, just as some criminals wanted to get caught and so left incriminating evidence behind. All he could hope upon learning this was that perhaps, like them, his self-betrayals would lead to a greater good.

Just then he watched his wife cry and wondered if and when he would join her.


The waiter at Mazotti's was doing too much to imply that Prentiss and Lillith were already romantically involved. He'd recommended they share an order of manicotti, placed a bunch of daisies on their table, suggested how they spend Christmas morning together (the other restaurant where he worked had a superb brunch), and offered them complimentary champagne normally reserved for couples getting engaged.

After he delivered their entrées with an ingratiating bow and walked away, Lillith said, "If he slips us a hotel room key with the check, he'll have crossed the line."

"I reckon it's the holiday cheer's got him excited."

They looked at their steaming plates and basket of breadsticks. The candle in between them flickered when a busboy speed-walked past. There was a heavy aroma in the air of cheese and olive oil and cheap disinfectant.

Prentiss said, "This place hasn't put up any new decorations since the holiday party."

"That's true," Lillith said, surveying the restaurant's interior. "There's still mistletoe over the door. Do you do anything at home to celebrate Christmas?"

"You mean do I roast chestnuts and put up a tree?"

"Not necessarily a tree; that's actually a pagan symbol."

"Is that right?"

Lillith cut a piece of eggplant parmesan into diamond-shaped bites. "In the Old Testament, the prophet Jeremiah said: 'Learn not the way of the heathen, and be not dismayed at the signs of heaven; for the heathen are dismayed at them. For the customs of the people are vain: for one cutteth a tree out of the forest, the work of the hands of the workman, with the axe. They deck it with silver and with gold.' Christians stole the tree tradition from pagans."

Prentiss said, swallowing a bite of calzone, "You know all the Bible by heart?"

"No, just the stuff that helps explain Wicca."

"What's Wicca?"

"My religion. It's a type of neopaganism."

Prentiss's gaze panned slowly to his right as though following an object crossing in front of him. "Is Wicca the religion where you worship the Earth Mother and there's a store in Old Town sells charms and crystals for it, the Dangling Druid?"

"The Dancing Druid. That's a good shop, but I go to the Terra Connection in Arcata or order online."

Prentiss unbuttoned the top button of his suit; his calzone was spiced with hot flakes of hard red pepper. "Is there a Wicca church around here you go to?"

"Not officially; for worshipping we alternate between different people's houses or meet at Sequoia Park."

Lillith sipped the champagne Prentiss had turned down in favor of grape juice. The waiter came by twice to ask if they were enjoying everything. They smiled without encouraging him.

"Look," said Prentiss, whose top three buttons were now undone, "the other night at the office party, you said how you knew Leon Meed ten years ago. I been meaning to ask you something. Don't get upset if it sounds unusual."

Lillith held a forkful of eggplant over her plate. "Okay."

Prentiss pushed back his shoulders to sit up as straight as he could. "Did you see him disappear ten years ago?"

She set down her fork. "You mean truly disappear?"

He nodded.

"That's what Dr. Baker and his wife were arguing about, wasn't it?"

"In a way, yeah."

She said, after a moment, "Yes, I did."

Prentiss rolled up his shirtsleeves and placed his elbows on the table and said, in a low, serious voice, "I saw him, too, and it's my idea that everyone who did is linked somehow. Like Leon's a connecting tissue between us. I mean, there you are working at Steve's office, and you and me now are sitting here. I'm thinking there might be a purpose behind it."

Lillith looked at Prentiss. Her breathing quickened and she said, as though confessing to a dream that would expose her but couldn't be passed over in silence, "Do you want to know the truth about what happened to Leon?"

"I think I know, see, because—"

"He was kidnapped by a god named the Horned Consort and trapped in a hidden world called the Astral Plane until me and some friends cast a spell that saved him."

Prentiss's shoulders relaxed and fell forward; he looked down at the plate in front of him and said, "You making fun of me?"

"No, of course not."

"Then what's this about a plane when I'm talking about interconnectedness?"

She frowned and said, "Well—what's this about interconnectedness when I'm talking about a plane?"

The waiter, without either one noticing, had returned to stand a half-foot away from their table, as though hoping to be given an order. Prentiss looked up from his plate at Lillith and in an instant his disappointment faded and he broke into a wide smile. In a mirror action, she smiled back, and neither then knew who started laughing first, but soon they were both leaning back in their chairs, grinning at the absurdity of themselves and of each other and of a conversation that couldn't be had. The waiter left and returned with two desserts that, although unordered, he knew they'd appreciate.

*    *    *

Shane had never operated on such a large scale or so ambitiously. Like a Vulcan Santa Claus, he would begin with Steve Baker and Elaine Perry's home—its two-for-one aspect pleased him—and carry the torch to each person's house on his list, ending with Eve Sieber's. Follow the alphabet. Shane parked Martin's mini sedan equidistant between two streetlamps on Madrone Avenue, put on his ski mask, and reached behind him for a gas canister and screw-on hose pump. There was nothing sociopathic about seeking justice against those who had wronged you. It was the American way.

He had a headache from the kerosene fumes and wished he was feeling better for his Eureka swan song. This was the biggest night of his life, and he wanted to experience the magnitude of it on every level. The effigies made by Leon Meed would burn up with the houses around them, by which light Shane would teach everyone a lesson.

He got out of the car and walked the dead suburban street to the address he'd written down in his daily planner. There was a great mass of bougainvillea in front of the house; to get to the building he had to wend his way through stabbing brambles. Motion detector lights went on and Shane ducked down, grateful now for the foliage, waiting for Steve or Elaine to come out. When after a minute they didn't, he began walking the perimeter of the house, spraying its baseboards with kerosene. Before he'd gotten halfway around, though, a car pulled up to a stop in the street—a taxi—from which a large woman emerged, Sadie Jorgenson. Shane tiptoed to the back of the house while Sadie weaved up to the front door and banged loudly on it.

Crouching by a cord of firewood, he removed a matchstick and held its sulfurous head to the rough striking patch of the matchbook. With a flick of his wrist he would redress the injuries done to him—wash them all clean—in a baptism of fire.

*    *    *

For two hours Barry trolled the warehouse district of Eureka, where he was twice mistaken for a theme prostitute—even after removing his headdress—and once threatened with castration by a carload of zombie boys who spat mouthfuls of beer at him. He couldn't go home and face his statue. The night air, spiked with invisible fog, was forty-eight degrees according to a neon bank sign broadcasting the time in digitized minutes. He regretted having shaved his legs that afternoon and toyed with the idea of returning to the warmth of the party.

If his statue was such a problem he could get rid of it: borrow Derrick's truck the next day and haul it to the city dump. Or have a woodcutter convert it into firewood. Or interest a local burl vendor in selling it for him. There was a line in the Bible about cutting off the part of your body that caused you to sin. Hand, eye, what Beckett dubbed his so-called virile member, etc. Smite the unclean body. And it would be a fine analogy except that the statue was not at fault; Barry was.

He came to the spot in Old Town where he'd seen Lillith try to lock her car door the week before, where he'd not gone forward to apologize. He stood there until he tired of ruminating on his disagreeable qualities, thinking he and Lillith and everyone would be dead soon enough and freed from worrying about their trespasses against one another—at that moment of resignation, of Barry ready to pack it in for the night, Lillith stepped out of Mazotti's. A large black man came after her. They pulled their coat collars together and walked toward him.

When they were near enough to be addressed in a normal voice, Barry said, repositioning the headdress under his arm, "Merry Christmas."

"Who're you?" Lillith said.

"Barry Klein." Turning to Prentiss, he held out his hand and said, "How do you do?"

"We met before," said Prentiss. "At the Ritz a long time ago. You knew my old AA sponsor. I'm Prentiss."

The two men shook hands and Barry said to Lillith, "I want to say I'm sorry. About the show. You were right that I'd told you it would be a chance to talk about your winter event, and then I got aggressive and went into an attack mode. It was inappropriate and uncalled for, and I hope you can forgive me."

"You do the same thing to everyone."

Barry said, "I'm going to try to change."

"This a New Year's resolution?" Prentiss asked.

"Something like that."

"Good luck, then."

"Thanks."

Lillith looked at Barry for a few seconds and her expression softened, she relaxed the squint of her eyes. She said, "I'll think about it."

"Okay," Barry said.

When they walked away, he waved good-bye to their receding backs and then dug his hands into his headdress. He went home a few minutes later and wrapped the accessory around his statue's head and took a bath in scalding hot water. There, imagining his future course of action, he was able to forget he'd ever been cold.


Sadie leaned against a banister with a hand on her forehead, and when Steve finally opened the door of 1353 Madrone Avenue she clapped and embraced him. There was still time, despite her having stayed at the Shanty longer than necessary, fending off Bob's meaningless advances, enjoying the holiday cheer, to salvage her friends' marriage.

"Hello, Steve," she said, trying for a clear, professional tenor.

"Are you drunk?"

"That's not important."

"I hope you didn't drive."

"There was a cab." Sadie frowned. "Why's your coat on? Are you leaving?"

"Yes."

"But I just got here!"

"I'm staying with a friend."

From inside the house Elaine called out, "Who is it?"

Sadie shouted her name and Steve gently rubbed his left ear. Elaine came to the door and hugged her friend and her eyes were red and Sadie said, turning to Steve, "You can't go yet. There's work to be done."

"Sadie," said Elaine, taking hold of her friend's elbow, "come in. It's okay."

"But I want to talk to you!"

"Is one of the gas pipes broken?" Steve asked.

"Both of you!"

"Do you smell gas?"

"Don't you?"

"I thought it was Sadie."

"It smells like kerosene."

"Let's all go inside and we'll sit down together. Elaine, is there coffee?"

"This is alarming."

"What should we do? The gas company's not going to send someone out to fix it on Christmas Eve."

"What are you two talking about anyway?"

With a loud crepitation suddenly audible from the south side of the house, Steve and Elaine turned in time to see a five-foot flame burst full-grown along the ground. They grabbed Sadie and stumbled down the steps and onto the brick pathway as the fire ribboned around the base of the house and sent up yellow phantasms of heat and light. A dark figure ran unnoticed down the sidewalk. Stupefied, Elaine, Sadie, and Steve stared at the instant blaze for ten seconds and cast lengthening shadows before neighbors from across the street threw open their doors and barked out exclamations and came over, still digesting puddings and pies. Steve pulled out his phone and called 911 and a car tore out onto the road, its engine growling over and then under the angry percussion of a burning house. People hovered behind Elaine and Steve, asking if anyone was still inside, consoling, subtly charging them with negligence, hoping their own houses wouldn't be touched, marveling at the speed with which the fire was growing. Sadie blocked the hot wind from her face with the palms of her hands, took pained steps backward into awestruck children. Elaine and Steve didn't answer their neighbors and instead watched the blaze's progress and from time to time looked over to see how the other was responding. Nothing could be done to slow the wood's consumption, and they were quiet, almost respectful of the raging metaphor before them.

As the flames reached the house's second story, nineteen blocks away a two-door mini sedan ran head-on into a recreation vehicle. The fire trucks called by a witness of the crash would have come straightaway if they weren't already en route to the fire at the Perry/Baker residence. The delay, said doctors later, made all the difference in killing one driver and badly burning the other.

Martin opened his eyes and felt he wasn't alone. Perhaps Shane had come back to finish him off. Perhaps the police or paramedics had intuited his need of them and arrived with a waiting ambulance outside. Shifting his gaze upward with reptilian slowness, he dully regarded the window facing Second Street, a bulletin board with a constellation of pushpins, and his desk, on which lay the offending copy of Leon Meed's journal. A portrait of the artist as a grief-stricken madman. All the time his record player warped and woofed.

This was unlike any inebriation Martin had ever experienced. This strange partial lucidity and inability to move. He was dying of a lethal dosage of some drug that Shane and his future coroner alone would know. How awful to be aware of his impending death. He tried to assemble words to say to those he'd leave behind—some end-of-life summary poignant enough to justify his short existence—but before he could someone else spoke.

"You're not going to die," the person said.

"What?" Martin said, staring forward, not expecting to be heard.

Leon Meed, with a shaved head and dressed in the same blue gown he'd worn in the Kimbote Psychiatric Hospital pictures Martin had seen, took a seat at the desk. He had an open smile that revealed two rows of small off-white teeth. "I was once in your position," he said, picking up his journal to read: "*I'll be dead soon and I want to leave a record of my last days.* I lived for ten more years after writing that."

"That's because you were taken to a hospital."

The desk chair squeaked as Leon leaned back and flipped through the journal, staring at Martin. "Yes."

"I need to go to one."

"You'll be fine in the morning. Harmless barbiturates."

Martin was relieved to hear this and might have closed his eyes again to sleep if a thought hadn't struck him: "But if you're here I must already be dead."

"I could read the passage from my notebook where I thought I was dead. Lies are never so persuasive as when we tell them to ourselves "

This was what Martin had found annoying about Leon's journal, this tendency toward aphorism. "I don't trust you," he said. "Your doctor at the sanatorium told me you never stopped believing you'd disappeared, and that you only said you did in order to get released."

Leon nodded. "The staff at Kimbote were generous people. They saw through my admission but let me go anyway. Part of them understood and sympathized with my need to visit the grave of my wife and daughter one last time."

Martin said, feeling his distrust vindicated, "Your wife and daughter drowned in the ocean and their bodies were never found."

"By grave I mean the plot of ground where I buried their statue."

"Which statue?"

Leon said, very quietly, as though raising his voice would alter the words' meaning, "The one I made of them dead. I buried it outside my cabin."

Martin tried drawing in his arms to push himself up, thinking it would be good to raise himself to a more civilized height for this conversation, but the gulf between his thoughts and abilities was still too wide. "Why did you do that?"

"In order to be cured of my condition."

Martin said, clarifying the slur of thoughts in his brain, "Your condition was called a brief psychotic episode that at its worst made you black out and roam the streets of Eureka unaware of where you were and what you were doing. You had moments of consciousness when you'd tell whoever was around that you were disappearing, because you couldn't think of any other way to explain what was happening to you."

Leon smiled sadly.

Martin was a formless being. "Dr. Holbrook explained it to me. Your illness was triggered by the tenth anniversary of your wife and daughter's death, on which you tried to commit suicide by drowning at the South Jetty. When you couldn't do it, you entered a trance that lasted six weeks. Then you stabilized enough to go home. The authorities found you there and committed you to Kimbote."

Leon set down his journal and stood up. He wasn't a tall man, but from Martin's vantage point on the floor he looked gigantic, an overgrown blue-robed monk. He placed his hands behind his back and looked down pityingly, though it wasn't clear whether the pity was for himself or for Martin. "That is a concise and faithful account of the doctors' report, but I ought to tell you that it isn't true. I did disappear and it wasn't because of grief—though I know that feeling well—but rather because I refused to accept the death of my wife and daughter. The truth is that for years I lived at so great a distance from reality that it lost control of me."

Martin was too tired to fully absorb this at once. "I see."

Leon, perhaps sensing Martin's desire for them to be on a more equal level, sat down Indian-style on the ground. "I came to realize about my disappearances that they were contained within a maze of those places in Humboldt County that had once been dangerous for my wife or daughter. A club in Old Town where my daughter had gone when she didn't want to come home at night. The house where my wife had grown up with an abusive father. The truck I'd made my wife sell when I read a report about that model's bad brakes. The apartment we had lived in when she'd had several miscarriages.

Something in me needed to return to those places. Maybe to appreciate what had been survived instead of only regret what took them in the end. I'm not sure. Finally at home it occurred to me that I was in a denial from which only I could rescue myself, and that I had to make a statue of my wife and daughter as they were, not as I wanted them to be. I had to recognize their death."

Martin felt like a student falling behind with his lecture notes; it seemed impossible to catch up. To stall for time, he said, "And that ended your disappearances?"

Leon said, "Yes."

Martin felt himself fading. There were questions he felt he should ask. He was forgetting them. "And you really don't think I'm dying?"

"No."

"That's good."

Leon stood up again and said, "And don't be discouraged by what happened to you at the newspaper. You'll find another job."

Martin blinked for longer and longer stretches of time. "It's a hard business to break into."

"You could always do something else."

Martin closed his eyes and tried to open them but they were sealed shut. He didn't see his apartment again until a phone call woke him up the next day, long after noon.

# 6

After an extended stay in Eureka, you might have decided it was time to continue your trip north. You might have thought again about Portland or Seattle or Canada, about everywhere that awaited you, and so stopped on your way out at Going Places for maps and travel guides. There, more likely than not, Eve Sieber would have been restocking supplies and greeting customers and ringing up purchases, the gray dyed out of her hair and makeup covering the last vestiges of her adolescence. She hadn't become a nun or joined a convent. The final throb of communication from Leon hadn't, at last, demanded that she enter a cloister or even renew her fidelity to God. Its message was subtler, to be pondered while grocery shopping or paying bills. She even half believed its significance was nullified by Christmas Eve, when after the awful surreality of their bus stop talk Joon-sup had arrived at her house in the middle of the night and confessed his love for her and been astounded by her conviction that he was dying of heart disease. Nothing had been less true. He'd said, she recalled sometimes, that he wanted to help her, that she didn't have to be alone, but she hadn't heard real love beneath the midnight proclamation, and she'd said they were friends, would always be so, but could not be lovers.

If you'd come in at the right time, you might have heard her talking on the phone to her boyfriend, Prentiss Johnson, who after

Christmas Eve had gone to dinner with Lillith once more before deciding that he didn't want to compete for attention with her neo-pagan activism. He'd rather be alone and wait for a woman who wanted what he did. Then one day in January as he wheelchaired Eve out of ER following her third lower-back spasm in twelve months, being a quiet, disinterested helper, she asked if something was wrong. "Not that I know of," he said. "When I was here last month," she said, "you seemed to be in a better mood." He pushed a large silver handicap button on the wall and waited while two doors slowly opened outward. "My pet pig died yesterday of pneumonia and it's affecting me. I don't mean to be gloomy." Eve turned as far as her back pain allowed to look up at Prentiss. "I know what it's like to lose somebody you care about." His fingers rested on the wheelchair han-dles and he looked at her for what seemed like several minutes, though it could have been only so many seconds. Then, when she faced forward again, he pushed her through the doorway and down a long corridor with pastel paintings on the walls and green-clad medics and inscrutable beeping machines, walking slowly past the obstacles until she said abruptly, "Would you like to go on a date with me sometime?" After a deliberate pause, during which they kept moving forward together, some people acknowledging them with a smile, others intent on their work, he said, "That would be nice." And then one date turned into many dates, and what he figured was, your posture got worse and your chances for romance decreased, but they never actually hit zero. Love moved in mysterious ways.

The first person to congratulate Prentiss on his good fortune was Steve Baker, who shook his friend's hand and hoped the new couple would let him treat them to dinner soon. They sat in the doctors' lounge, postsurgery, and in answer to Prentiss's question Steve said that he and Elaine were in marriage counseling, which although not yet a reconciliation was at least an improvement over their cold war preceding Christmas. He said that after discovering his culpability in relationships—a self-recognition that he marveled could have come so late in life—he had thought his romantic life finished until Sadie

Jorgenson helped him understand that knowing his real motivations could liberate him as easily as confirm his sense of destiny, that he was not predetermined, that he had a choice. Prentiss said this was the best thing he'd heard from his friend in months.

Activity at Steve's office, the Coastal Orthopedic Medical Group, was no greater or lesser than usual, so its secretaries, specifically Lillith, could still steal occasional hours to work on their own projects. For Lillith this meant converting the scrapped winter retreat plans into a summer solstice celebration to be held on June 21, a minor Sabbat. With a carryover budget and new contributions already pouring in from all over northern California, she'd booked a high-rent location at the crescent bend of the Eel River near Garberville, as well as quality PA equipment for the music and spell recitals and announcements. For the program, she had confirmed a good roots band and two baroque/fx disc jockeys and a highly placed witch from a southern Washington coven. A Wiccan caterer had volunteered to work for cost. Through all of this Lillith felt free of the disappointment that had afflicted her in December; putting a foot forward she didn't doubt the solidity of the ground beneath her.

To promote the solstice celebration, Lillith would appear on *Live from Somewhere* with Barry Klein, who over the past two months had become one of her closest friends. The day after his Christmas Eve encounter with Lillith, Barry had gone to her house and apologized again, and what should have been a short visit, the first of a series he was making to former guests on his show, turned into a three-hour tête-à-tête. When he left they agreed to have lunch together the following day, and so began a relationship that in later years would make Lillith think that Prentiss might have been right about the interconnectedness. For his part, Barry didn't so much think he'd improved as a human being—lost his cattiness or love of cruel humor—as recognize and respect the factors contributing to others' beliefs and customs that were alien to his. It was as though his mental aperture had widened overnight. It was as though he'd changed his life.

Leaving Eureka, with or without the radio on, you might have passed the street corner of Seventh and H, where a three-foot-high white banner announced the grand opening of the Joon-sup Experience in four months. Joon-sup was there every day, working with an architect, city code inspector, chief contractor, and crew of three carpenters to convert what had once been a stationery shop into a fifteen-table restaurant. At night he went home to his girlfriend, Justine, whose news two months before that she was pregnant had not, as he would have bet his life before then, upset him. Instead his whole body had started trembling and he'd had a foreglimpse of parenthood, of incredible future joy and heartbreak, which made insignificant every objection he'd had to it. Now when he got home he experimented with recipes and debated boy and girl names and practiced the harmonica and found as many ways to help Justine as she did to help him. Once a week he and Eve went running, and he wondered, when not too overwhelmed with embarrassment, what had caused him to declare his love for her. He never looked at his statue. His child would be wholly American, and he was neither proud nor ashamed of the fact. It was only a starting point, after all.

With the possible exception of Joon-sup, no one was prouder of the Joon-sup Experience than Sadie. She missed him as a patient—their meetings had stopped the day he mentioned his turnaround about fatherhood—but the prospect of seeing him at his restaurant while eating one of his barbecue entrées made up for it. She began power walking two miles on Mondays, Wednesdays, and Fridays, the same days she had lunch with Bob. They flirted and she no longer discussed her patients other than to vaguely allude to this or that success: this lasting detox, that quell in the panic disorder. Instead, for conversation they turned to the Highway 101 rerouting vote then approaching, and to the fall's mayoral candidates. Sometimes, to spice up the afternoon, Sadie recounted the latest goings-on in the state's prosecution of Shane Larson. Having testified that Shane was, as far as she knew, the only person to have terrorized her, she was given regular updates by the district attorney.

Shane's condition lent the case a touch of pathos, for in his Christmas

Eve car crash he had been severely burned, and lost sensation in over sixty percent of his permanently scarred body. If convicted of both charges against him—involuntary manslaughter (the victim, Shannon Koslowski, was a semiretired trucker) and arson—he would spend a maximum of twelve years in the Pelican Bay State Prison an hour north of Eureka, near Crescent City. He was resigned to whatever happened. He admitted his guilt and expressed remorse, for there seemed little point in anything but contrition now. He lay in a prison hospital bed at night, forever unaroused, and saw the futility of his former schemes and rages. He hadn't been meant for wealth, and now the varieties of his suffering were all one, although perhaps, he thought in the darkness after lights-out, someday the miracle of modern science would restore his capacity to feel.

One of the key witnesses in the trial, Martin Nemec, had gone back to work for the *Times-Standard* shortly after Christmas, when the combination of his innocence and the arson story's appeal to local readers prompted his editor to invite him back gruffly and with a small raise. Martin saw it as a temporary return and began networking right away with his graduate school friends for openings at other papers around the country. At the same time, he also received calls, one by one, from the people mentioned in Leon's journal. He declined their offers for reminiscences and Leon stories, because although this was the West, when the legend became fact he would not print the legend.


On a cold morning in March, the only person not to have volunteered her account of Leon to Martin, Elaine, lost a contact lens at the front of her classroom while explaining the checks and balances of the U.S. government's three branches. "Oh, shit," she said unconsciously, eliciting a ripple of laughter from the boys and girls in their extravagant clothes and accessories—the cherry-flavored lip gloss and ankh earrings and leather-tasseled friendship bracelets—who took the opportunity of her bending down to talk and hit one another. "Everyone quiet down!" she said, on her knees and frustrated at not finding the lens. The kids obeyed for ten seconds and then the noise built again to crescendo. Elaine stood up carefully holding the dirty lens like a drop of holy water. Grabbing her purse, she appointed Roderick in charge while she went to the bathroom. There were no checks and balances here, but a strict hierarchy of command.

Elaine fixed her vision and was back in the hallway when she heard a muted scuffle coming from her classroom. She neared the door just as a loud thump sounded against it. "What's going on?" she demanded, walking in on a scene of Usman and Darrel standing over a floor-sprawled Roderick like ten-year-old mercenaries. "I leave you alone for two minutes." The boys were silent and the class looked as though this were a television nature show whose outcome they could not affect, as though these rules of the jungle could only be observed and were no more malleable than those of their government. "Would anyone like to tell me happened?" No. "Are we going to have to go to Principal Altman's office?" Yes. "Do you understand how much worse it will be for you there than here?" No answer. "All right, let's go."

Elaine led the boys down the hallway and to the left past the trophy display case—Muir dominated the seventh- and eighth-grade basketball world and had always done so—and the wall-hung flags of California's bear and America's stars. A vast collection of gold-tinged holiday pictures drawn by kindergarten Klimts. The door to Principal Altman's secretary's office was open, beyond which the secretary sat in front of a computer clutching reading glasses and a translucent tissue.

"Is she in?" asked Elaine.

"Talking on the phone," said the secretary. "She wants to see you, though, so it's good you're here."

"I need to deposit these children with her. They've been naughty."

"She won't be much longer."

"I'll just leave them, if you don't mind. Tell her I'll come back during my class's PE period."

Usman and Darrel looked at each other; Roderick was not part of their confidence and appeared worried. They whispered something to him. He took a step back. Elaine pointed to the chairs they were to sit in.

"It looks like she's off now." The secretary rose and opened the door and spoke into the room.

"You called her already?" shouted Gale the principal. "Elaine, come in!"

Elaine closed the door behind her and—impatient to get back to her classroom—briefly recounted the disorderly but tight-lipped scene she'd found in her classroom, and how she had to leave young Usman, Darrel, and Roderick in Gale's hands. "Roderick is clearly the victim," she said, "but you know the code of ethics boys have. He can't say anything or they'll beat him more. Maybe you could pretend to punish him in front of Usman and Darrel, and release him later."

"Good idea." Gale sat up straight in her chair and folded her hands on a stack of manila folders. A computer nodded off to sleep in front of her. "Have a seat and prepare yourself. I have news."

"What is it?"

She broke into a grin. "You won the Humboldt County Teacher of the Year Award."

Elaine stopped fidgeting.

"I was just talking to some of the state superintendent's representatives, and they think this assures us a higher ranking and designation as a California Distinguished School, which means more money, more resources, more everything. When I talked to the nominating committee they said that your reputation, as well as your student success statistics and the fact that no one from Humboldt has ever won, give you a better than fighting chance of winning the state award."

"That's—I don't know what to say."

"Then just sit there and smile."

"You're sure there hasn't been a mistake?"

"Positive."

"I should probably tell you that I couldn't accept the state prize if I won."

Gale frowned and knitted her fingers tightly together. "Why not?"

"I don't want to leave Eureka."

"Don't worry about that now. You should be in heavy celebration mode. Take Steve out for dinner tonight."

Elaine's feeling returned that this was wasting valuable teaching time. "Steve and I are separated."

"Oh, Elaine." Gale's eyebrows rose and her fingers relaxed. "Now I'm the one who doesn't know what to say. I'm sorry."

"Thank you."

"How long has it been?"

"A couple of months."

"Is one of you filing papers?"

"I'm hoping it won't come to that. We're seeing a good therapist."

Elaine got up and shook Gale's hand, which was warm and held hers tightly for a moment, and then walked out. She heard Gale downshift into a stentorian voice to summon Usman, Darrel, and Roderick. Back in her classroom, she picked up where she'd left off, explaining pitch-perfectly the beauty of legislative, executive, and judicial power sharing. It could be abused, she said, as could everything, though in the end fairness would prevail. In the end it had to.

When it was time for physical education with another teacher, Elaine's students were up and out the door, every day the same amount of energy, the same boy/girl intrigues and breathless resumption of yesterday's softball or basketball games, with kids pairing up or forming groups of three and four. Some were blessed with beauty and physical coordination and a certain playground wit that made them, for a time, life's victors—just as there were their counterparts, the kids who looked wrong and couldn't catch a fly ball and said extraordinary things, and then the children in the middle who felt neither anointed nor damned because sometimes they were in one camp and sometimes in the other but mostly in between, unremarkable, a position they strived for once they learned they were not the prettiest or most graceful or cleverest. Let us simply exist, they said at a certain point. Although, and Elaine was unwrapping her cucumber and avocado sandwich now, they would never get their wish. At its simplest, existence was complicated beyond description, so why ever tell herself that she was working toward a state of tranquility when tranquility was a chimera that, if ever attained, would undo her?

Her sandwich was bland. Reaching into her purse for one of the salt packets she stole from fast-food restaurants, she felt and took out the letter she'd gotten from Leon Meed. Written on recycled brown paper in a light, steady hand, it had come in early December, been misplaced without being read, and then been found a month later when she was sifting through the remains of her house. Although she'd almost memorized its contents, she read it again.

Dear Elaine,

You may not remember me, but we met ten years ago, once at Muir Elementary School and once outside your home. I want to apologize to you for those unwarranted and strange interruptions into your life, but also to tell you they were accidental.

Two weeks ago I was released from Kimbote Psychiatric Hospital, where I received treatment for many years for what was called a "brief psychotic episode." I have moved into the cabin on Neeland Hill where I lived before I was institutionalized and plan to return to sculpting burl art soon if my health allows it. This brings me to the second reason for this letter. The people I troubled ten years ago will someday receive statues I made of them while at Kimbote. But you won't—I'm not able to sculpt you. Although I tried to sketch your face as I remember it, and then to translate your two-dimensional image into three dimensions, I had to stop when it became clear that I was in fact sketching and preparing to sculpt my dead wife. You don't physically resemble her—your nose is thicker and shorter than hers, your brown hair more hazelnut than her chocolate, your eyes wider apart and your lips paler—but I couldn't help conflating the two of you in my attempt to carve you out of wood.

This letter, therefore, besides an apology, is all I have for you. There is no sculpture, and although a letter is inadequate, I think for you it might be enough. At both of our meetings you demonstrated a resolve—in protecting your students and carrying on in the face of what I presumed was a bad divorce— that reminded me of my late wife. She always went directly through her losses, confronting them, instead of going around them.

I know what the truth is—that we lose everything we're given. Even our own lives. But some of us can act beyond that inevitability—like my wife, like you. So you see, I can't carve you, because there's no need for you to be carved.

Sincerely,
Leon Meed

Elaine looked at the clock and had four minutes before her class returned. She removed the instructor's edition math book from her bag and checked her makeup and saw a minor disturbance, as a momentary breeze would alter a sand portrait, which she repaired with a tissue and eyeliner. Better. She heard children in the halls, parading as quietly as their chaperone could make them. The sky visible through the room's windows, cut into boxes by the panes' dividers, turned partially overcast.

The door to her classroom creaked open. Her students spidered in to their desks and there were carryover smiles and looks and assess-

ments. When they faced forward Elaine knew: children led dangerous, thrill-seeking lives because they needed practice for what came
later. And as she walked to the front of the chalkboard with its clean
erasers resting along the bottom sill, she said, holding open her book,
with a confidence bolstered by all she'd lost and might yet recover,
"Let's begin."

# Epilogue

According to the Coast Guard information service, it was an abnormally calm day on the ocean when Rachel and Adeline Meed decided to go whale watching. That's what Rachel told her husband in the morning when he asked: "Abnormally calm." The three of them sat around the breakfast table, and when they finished eating Leon stood up and said, "Have fun out there." He blew kisses at them from the door.

When he was gone, Rachel and Adeline watched the morning news. A celebrity had moved past the drugs and faux religion that almost killed her. A growing territorial dispute between Russia and Japan inspired a thousand diplomatic speeches. Storms chastened the East Coast. A baby who'd learned to talk at nine months was now, at age two, an accomplished singer/songwriter.

Rachel shut off the TV and pushed away her dirty plate. To postpone cleaning up, she and her daughter read junk mail and catalogues, sharing factoids with each other, before packing a lunch and driving to the Eureka marina. They signed in with the harbormaster and heard that contrary to the Coast Guard's earlier report, there was now a small-craft advisory in effect. At the dock for their fifteen-foot sloop, they boarded, put on life jackets, and, relying on motor power to start them off, steered out toward the middle of Humboldt Bay. Three crabbing vessels and a salmon trawler passed them coming in.

This was their fourth attempt in two months to photograph the gray whales then migrating south from Alaska to breed off the coast of Baja California. They'd failed to see any on the last three voyages—had spent long, futile hours waiting—but this time, made hopeful by friends who'd spotted dozens of whale backs over the past week, they expected success.

As they came to the mouth of the bay, the ocean spread out before them as a vast expanse of green topped by strings of kelp and curled whitecaps. Rachel asked Adeline which direction she wanted to go. South. The sky was brighter there and would provide better lighting. They shifted the rigging and caught a ten-knot southerly wind. The beaches along Samoa, an old logging company district that Eureka had more or less abandoned, moved steadily past.

"Anything?" asked Rachel.

Adeline, slowly pivoting in her seat with a pair of binoculars for eyes, said, "No."

"And yesterday there was supposedly an armada out here."

When they came to the South Jetty, they drew in the sail in order not to go so far that returning would take all afternoon. Adeline hummed a pop song; Rachel massaged a pulled muscle in her left calf. They ate peanut butter and jelly sandwiches and scanned the water and made themselves comfortable. It became late morning.

"This is boring," said Adeline.

"Mmm."

"What if we missed them already?"

"Then we missed them."

"I hate it when you do that."

"Do what?"

"Act like something bad is okay."

"You'd rather have me get angry?"

"Maybe."

They sat in silence until Rachel said, nodding toward shore, "We should motor away from the breakers." The boat had begun to rock more pronouncedly as it inched within two hundred yards of the building swells.

"We're pretty far away."

"Just to be safe why don't you start the engine?"

Adeline turned to do it, but before she could pull the starter cord she sat back on her haunches, as though knocked off balance, and pointed up. "Look," she said.

"What is it?" Rachel craned around, thinking Adeline had spotted a blowhole, and with disappointment saw nothing in the water. In the air, however, a flock of birds, stretched across the horizon, flew toward them in numbers so great they seemed to be refracted through a prism. There were thousands, perhaps tens of thousands, a pulsating sheet of black being pulled across the sky. "Pacific black brants," Rachel said, dropping the rope she'd been tying.

"That's the type of bird they are? There's so many."

"Hand me the thirty-five millimeter, please. Hurry."

Adeline passed the camera to her mother, who took a dozen pictures sitting up and then, as the birds flew overhead at an altitude of forty feet, lay flat on her back, resting her head on the prow, to shoot more. "This has the black-and-white?"

Adeline said, "Yeah."

"Do you want to take color with the eighty?"

"Okay."

Adeline removed the lens cap from the eighty-millimeter camera, adjusted the development speed, and scooted into a horizontal position beside her mother. From above they looked stitched together, like two swatches of color framed by a white boat on an emerald background. The clicks from their cameras came at a staccato rhythm and sometimes overlapped; the only other sounds were of water sloshing against the boat, waves crashing nearer and nearer, and their own infrequent exclamations at what they were witnessing. The stream of birds flew lower—thirty feet, twenty feet, fifteen—until they were just ten feet above the ocean, and Rachel and Adeline could see details of the birds' white bellies and long, tapered wings, their retracted legs and narrow black heads. When the women set down the cameras at the end of their first rolls of film, and wind pressed against them from so many beating wings, Adeline asked if they should use the rest of the film or save it for the whales. Rachel said, looking up at the assembly of brants filling the carved-out sky—at the current passing over them without caution or break— that this was what they had come for, that they should not save anything.

# Acknowledgments

For their invaluable support and wisdom, I'd like to thank Susan Golomb, Katie Ford, Matthew McIntosh, Bret Johnston, Dan Pope, Amira Pierce, and Rich Green. I am also very grateful to the James Michener–Copernicus Society of America for its generosity. Everyone at Scribner, particularly Nan Graham, Samantha Martin, Erin Cox, and Susan Moldow—and most especially particularly Sarah McGrath—deserves a thousand graces.

## About the Author

Raised in northern California, JOSH EMMONS currently lives in New Orleans, Louisiana. He is the recipient of a James Michener–Copernicus Society Award.